Anne ... eneral
Hospital but after he ... ive first in Libya
and ... in Nige ... tive
Birkenhead where she worked as a Health Visitor for over
ten years before taking up writing. She now lives with her
husband in Merseyside. Anne Baker's other Merseyside sagas
are all available from Headline and have been highly praised:

'A wartime Merseyside saga so full of Scouse wit and warmth
that it is bound to melt the hardest heart' *Northern Echo*

'Baker's understanding and compassion for very human
dilemmas makes her one of romantic fiction's most popular
authors' *Lancashire Evening Post*

'A gentle tale with all the right ingredients for a heartwarm-
ing novel' *Huddersfield Daily Examiner*

'A well-written enjoyable book that legions of saga fans will
love' *Historical Novels Review*

'A warm and evocative Merseyside saga' *Bookseller*

CAROUSEL OF SECRETS

Anne Baker

headline

First published in 2006
by HEADLINE PUBLISHING GROUP

First published in paperback in 2007
by HEADLINE PUBLISHING GROUP

7

ISBN 978 0 7553 2468 2

Typeset in Baskerville by Avon DataSet Ltd,
Bidford on Avon, Warwickshire

Printed and bound in Great Britain by
CPI Antony Rowe, Chippenham, Wiltshire

Headline's policy is to use papers that are natural, renewable and
recyclable products and made from wood grown in sustainable
forests. The logging and manufacturing processes are expected to
conform to the environmental regulations of the country of origin.

HEADLINE PUBLISHING GROUP
A division of Hachette Livre UK Ltd
338 Euston Road
London NW1 3BH

www.headline.co.uk
www.hodderheadline.com

CAROUSEL OF SECRETS

CHAPTER ONE

13 January 1931

USUALLY, GRETA Arrowsmith was cheered by the chatter of the other girls working in the laundry, but for most of today she'd been sunk in her own thoughts.

'Wake up,' her friend Phyllis Wood called. 'Switch the cold water on.'

Greta did so, and brought her mind back to the job. She could hardly see across the room for the steam. Phyllis had opened the tap on a great cauldron where the whites had been simmering; the boiling water had gushed out and the cauldron was now filling with cold so they could handle the contents. Their job was to check each article to make sure it was thoroughly clean. Woe betide them if the supervisor saw a stain on a sheet once it reached the ironing room.

The Peregrine Laundry took in washing from a nearby nursing home and the sheets were often badly stained. They needed a lot of bleaching.

'At least you persuaded the boss to give us rubber gloves.' Phyllis pulled hers on. 'I used to have hands wrinkled like an old woman's.'

1

'Stops them smelling of bleach too,' Greta agreed.

'We need goggles as well,' Phyllis said, wiping her face with the back of her glove. They all hated bleach; the fumes stung their eyes. 'Be a sport and ask for them, Greta. You could charm blood out of stone.'

'But not out of Miss Green.' She was their supervisor. 'I've already asked her and the answer was no.' She sighed. 'She said we'd get used to the fumes.'

'I never have.' Phyllis was indignant.

Greta agreed, but she consoled her friend, saying, 'Come on, by the time we finish this it'll be time to go home.'

At the first clang of the bell the girls abandoned their work and stampeded towards the cloakroom. Within seconds, the narrow room was a tight crush of laughing chattering girls stripping off their green overalls and putting on outdoor clothes. Greta, who was smaller and slighter than most, had trouble pushing through to her coat peg. In the mirror, she caught a glimpse of herself: tired green eyes, and fair skin now flushed and moist from the heat.

Someone said, 'It's a horrible night, raining cats and dogs outside.'

'I'm keeping my turban on,' Phyllis sang out. 'It'll keep my hair dry.'

'Me too,' Greta tucked in the few strands of her blonde hair that had escaped from the regulation green triangle of cloth. It was a rule at the Peregrine Laundry that they must cover their heads tightly to prevent any hair getting on to customers' clean washing, but they were all keen to cover their hair anyway because the steam would ruin any hairstyle.

Greta had slightly wavy hair and it made hers frizz up. Phyllis, who put curlers in her straight brown hair every night, found the steam made the curl drop out and left it lank.

They were both swept out in the stream of workers rushing to catch buses and trains. Though it was only five o'clock, it was already dark. They lived in the same direction and walked to work. Phyllis fastened the top button of her coat and shivered. Greta linked arms with her and they hurried along a mean street of high shabby buildings while an icy wind blew off the Mersey and blasted rain full in their faces.

Liverpool's vast and prosperous port, with its miles of docks and warehouses, had created the wealth to build magnificent buildings stretching from the river to Rodney Street and beyond. It had also attracted the poor from all over the world. They came flocking to seek work. This part of the city had developed a rash of factories, railway sidings and overcrowded rooming houses.

Phyllis suggested, 'Why don't you ask the boss if he'll give your boyfriend a job?'

'Rex isn't really my boyfriend, but I've already asked about a job for him,' Greta told her. 'He said business was slack and he couldn't take on anyone else at the moment.'

'It's a rotten place to work anyway. Rex wouldn't like it. None of us do.'

'It's a job,' Greta said. 'It's better than nothing.'

At the busy corner of St James Street, Phyllis left her. Greta lived further away, but she always walked to and from work to save the bus fares.

Her father had been killed in the Great War and Mam had found it a real struggle to bring up Kenneth, her younger brother, and herself. They were poor, even though they now had Greta's wages to rely on. Usually she found the walk home pleasant after being cooped up for long hours in the laundry, but not tonight. She was tired and had been unable to get Rex Bradshaw's troubles out of her mind.

She'd known him all her life. As children, they'd been thrown together and ended up being firm friends. He and his family lived in the same street, almost opposite; his mother, Esther, was Mam's friend. They were both poverty-stricken widows and had helped each other out with child-minding and shopping for years. Greta had been going with Rex to the children's matinée at the local cinema on Saturday afternoons since she was seven – whenever they could raise the twopenny entrance money.

She was now eighteen. Rex was four years older and since he'd left school at fourteen, he'd had problems finding work. He'd wanted an apprenticeship to train as an engineer but that had proved impossible.

He'd found work off and on in various workshops, and for the past year he'd been working in a garage, helping to service cars and motorbikes. But business had fallen off in the present depression and the owner was having trouble covering the wages bill and making a profit. Rex had been given a week's notice and from next week he'd be on the dole. Greta knew what that would mean to the Bradshaws. Rex was upset and they'd spent the previous two evenings arguing.

On this cold wet night, Greta was glad to turn the corner

into Henshaw Street, where she lived. On both sides were terraces of tiny flat-fronted houses with two rooms upstairs and two rooms down. In the glow of a streetlight, she saw a bedraggled dog coming slowly towards her, the picture of misery and exhaustion. He must have heard her step because he lifted his head to look at her. They both stopped; the dog backed away, his eyes sparking fear. Greta felt sorry for him.

'It's all right,' she said, trying to sound soothing. 'I won't hurt you. What's the matter?' She put out her hand and stepped forward to stroke his wet fur. The dog retreated a few steps.

'Are you lost?' She felt drawn towards this creature so obviously in trouble. She could see him shivering; he was sodden and rain was dripping off his coat. His eyes seemed to plead, and he looked hungry and frightened. She remembered then that she had food in her bag.

A good hot dinner was provided in the canteen laundry for eightpence a day. Today it had been stew, cabbage and potatoes, followed by a thick slice of Manchester tart, which was jam tart covered with Bird's custard made thick enough to set solid. Mam had told her she must eat there. The meal was subsidised and therefore good value for the money, but today Greta's worries had deadened her appetite. Occasionally, when she wasn't hungry, she brought the pudding home as a treat for her brother and kept a small tin box in her bag for that purpose.

On the spur of the moment she tipped the tart out on the pavement, offering it to the dog, though Kenny would have loved it and Mam would call this wanton waste.

The dog sniffed but kept his anxious gaze on her. Then, taking two tentative steps closer and ready to shy off at the first sign of danger, he stretched out until his jaws snapped round the tart. Three rapid gulps and it was gone. He licked a blob of custard from the pavement and looked up hopefully for more. She smiled before knocking out the last crumbs from the tin, and his tongue was instantly on them.

'Sorry, that's all I have,' Greta told him, putting the tin back in her bag. She extended a hand and he let her stroke his head. The dog seemed to be lost; she felt a rush of sympathy for his plight. The rain was pelting down more heavily than ever. Putting up the collar of her coat, she said, 'Goodbye,' and hurried on.

As she turned into the back entry, she realised the dog was padding after her, a dozen paces behind.

'You can't come home with me,' she told him. They couldn't possibly cope with another mouth to feed. 'Go on, on your way.'

He dropped back another pace or two but still followed. Greta steeled her heart and was about to shut the yard door in his face, when she heard her thirteen-year-old brother shout, 'Hang on, Greta,' as he came hurtling down the entry behind her.

'Where did you find this dog?' he asked excitedly. 'Isn't he great? Let him come in – I want to see him.'

'No,' she said, but they were all in the yard and Kenny had the back gate shut before she could stop him. The light streaming from the scullery window sparkled on his mop of red curls and eager freckled face. Greta got a good look at the dog for the first time. He was a long-haired black and white collie, timid and frightened.

'Poor thing, he's wet and cold.' Kenny put his arms round the dog. 'Let's get him inside.'

'No,' Greta said, 'Mam'll have a fit.'

But the back door was opening. Mam had seen them. 'I'm not having that dog in here,' she said firmly. 'Don't even ask. He'll make a terrible mess.'

'In the wash house then.' Kenny already had the door open and the dog by the collar. It was warm and steamy inside. Greta lit the hanging oil lamp they kept there.

'Don't let him dirty the washing.' Their mother had jumped the few paces across the wet yard in her slippers. 'Let me peg those sheets higher so he can't reach them.'

Greta lifted a basket of ironing and balanced it on top of the mangle. Her mother took in other people's washing to help make ends meet.

'What d'you bring that animal home for? You know we can't keep it. He's filthy – just look at him.'

'I think he's lost.' Greta wasn't going to mention she'd already fed him. She took off her wet cotton turban and her golden hair cascaded to her shoulders.

She was about to peg the turban on the line to dry, but her mother pulled it from her. 'It might as well be washed, Greta.'

'Poor dog,' Kenny said. 'Gosh! He's got lovely blue eyes. I thought all dogs had brown eyes.'

'Yes, especially if their coat is mostly black,' Mam said. 'It'll make it easier for its owner to recognise him.' He had a white patch on his forehead and matching white front paws.

'He's quite handsome. Or he would be if he was clean.'

'He's wet and tired and hungry.' Kenny's voice was full of pity. 'You'll let him spend the night here, won't you, Mam? You won't turn him out in this downpour? He'll feel better if he has something to eat and a good night's sleep.' He had found a dry rag and was rubbing the dog down.

'He's wearing a collar.' Greta turned it round, looking for a name and address, but there wasn't one. 'An expensive collar, almost new. Where've you come from, laddie?'

'Can I make him a bed here in the corner?' Kenny asked.

'For heaven's sake, a bed? We'll never get rid of him if you make him too comfortable.' Mam sounded shocked.

'That old laundry basket that's breaking up –' Kenny suggested, pointing – 'you said it would do for starting fires, but we can use it for that after. Go on, you've already got a new one. He needs some old coats or something in it, just to get him off this concrete floor.'

'Newspapers,' his mother said. 'Screw them up. Newspapers will be good enough for him.'

They rarely bought newspapers, but the fish-and-chip shop on the corner of the street paid Kenny in kind for collecting old newspapers from their neighbours and he left the tattier ones here for lighting fires.

Kenny filled the old basket with crumpled newspaper and patted it. The dog was pressing himself back against the far wall and looked as though he wanted nothing to do with the bed.

'Let's leave him,' Greta said, propping open the wash-house door. 'He's scared stiff. He might lie in it when we've gone.'

'But what about—' Kenny began.

Greta took his arm and walked him towards the back door. 'He can't get out of the yard, can he? He'll be better left on his own to calm down. Come on, he'll still be here in the morning.'

They were all blinking in the scullery gaslight. Her mother was just thirty-nine, but there were dark circles under her eyes. She looked haggard and worn out. She'd had a hard life. It was no secret that Mam had often gone to bed hungry in order that her children could have what food there was. Mam had had an inadequate diet for years.

She said, 'We can't keep that dog. It's another mouth to feed and we can't afford it.'

'I'd love to,' Kenny breathed. 'Please, Mam, I've always wanted a dog. Greta likes it; she wants to keep it too.'

'It must go to the police station tomorrow,' Mam said firmly. 'They have a pound for strays.'

Greta understood just how hard it was for her mother to make ends meet. She'd neglected her own clothes, preferring to buy strong shoes and warm coats for her children. Mam's hair was greying, but it was fair and didn't show very much. She was honey blonde rather than golden like Greta, and once her face must have been pretty. Now her figure was gaunt and stringy and her back was beginning to look hunched from bending over the wash tub. Her hands were often chapped and wrinkled from being in water too long.

Things had been easier since Greta had started work and would be easier still once Kenny was old enough to earn his keep, provided he could get a job. For women and boys, who weren't paid so much as men, that was hard with the depression, but still possible.

Greta recognised the double tap on the front door and knew it was Rex Bradshaw before she opened it. He was tall and slim, with sharply chiselled features and dark straight hair that had been cut by his mother. All the girls at the laundry thought he was handsome.

'Hello, Greta. I've brought back the cup of sugar Mam borrowed yesterday.' He put it in her hand. 'I'm sorry I've been a bit touchy the last few days.'

Greta could understand that.

'Let's go to the pictures tonight. One last fling, yes?'

She hesitated; they couldn't afford money for the pictures any more than they could for a dog.

'It's Laurel and Hardy, with Jean Harlow. We could do with a good laugh, couldn't we?' he smiled. She knew it was meant as an olive branch, no more arguments. Rex had a lovely wide smile with strong even teeth. It lit up his face.

'Yes, let's,' she agreed. 'We've got to have a bit of fun.'

'Good. I'll call for you after tea.'

Greta went back to the table where Mam was setting out plates of food. When she went out with Rex, she always paid for herself. She always had, even when she'd had to raise the money by running errands for the neighbours or by taking eyes out of potatoes at the chip shop on the corner.

Rex was responsible and thoughtful; mature for his twenty-two years. As a friend and companion, he was great, and she was fond of him. But recently she had sensed he was getting serious about her. She just couldn't feel romantic towards someone she had known since he'd had scabby knees.

CAROUSEL OF SECRETS

For the last few weeks, Rex had been half expecting to lose his job. He'd seen the signs and had worried about it. Lots of their friends and neighbours were being laid off. It hadn't come as a surprise to either of them.

What had come as a shock to Greta was Rex's frustration and the intensity with which he'd said, 'That's the death knell to my plans. I wanted us to be married and settle down in a little house of our own.' He'd shaken his head in agonised disappointment. 'But I've got to have a job, haven't I?'

That had taken Greta's breath away. 'You've never said anything about getting married.' She'd thought they'd shared all their hopes and fears.

His dark eyes had looked into hers. 'We've always been together, haven't we?'

'Well, yes, but . . .'

'I love you.'

'You've never said that before either.'

'I thought you knew. You let me kiss you the other night.'

'But I couldn't stop you.'

Greta didn't know whether she loved Rex enough to marry him. She was indignant; he'd sprung this on her. 'I don't want to marry anyone.'

She'd hardly thought of marriage, except as a sort of Hollywood romance that would lift her right away from the life they all lived in Henshaw Street.

Marrying Rex, even if he found another job, would guarantee more of the down-to-earth hardship she faced every day. Anyway, feeling as she did, it wouldn't be fair to him.

*

11

Ruth Walsh felt exhausted, but it gave her satisfaction to dish up generous portions of the hotpot she'd made from scrag end of mutton and to watch Kenny and Greta tuck into it. To have a hot meal every evening and a bright fire in the grate made all the difference in mid-winter. The gaslight was brightening Greta's golden head and Kenny's ginger one, she felt full of love for them both.

Her life had been a disaster and she felt she couldn't do much to improve her own lot. For her the die was cast, but she was determined her children would have better lives. It had always been her aim to do her best for them. To see them now, growing up strong and healthy, made her feel she was achieving this, but she wanted them to be happy and enjoy themselves too. It had not been easy to tell Kenny he couldn't keep this dog. She could see how much he wanted to, but she could buy only so much food, and a dog licence cost seven shillings and sixpence.

If only . . . But it was no good thinking of what might have been, if only the Great War hadn't happened.

Ruth had married John Arrowsmith when she was nineteen and their daughter, Marguerite Mary, had been born in 1913 when Ruth was twenty-one. She'd thought it a pretty name but it seemed too formal for a small child and she'd shortened it to Greta. She'd thought she had everything she wanted in life, but a year later, John had been killed in the trenches and she'd been a widow.

Ruth had left the rooms she and John had rented and gone home to live with her mother, thinking her chance of having a normal happy life had gone. She'd worked in a munitions factory to earn a living for herself and her daughter, while her mother had cared for Greta. It had taken her two dreadful years to recover from John's death.

She had started to find her feet again when she'd met Peter Walsh. He was home from the front, recovering from a gunshot wound to his shoulder. It had been a prolonged home leave. He'd had an infection in the wound but Peter said he couldn't see that as ill luck. He'd swept Ruth off her feet. She'd fallen head over heels in love with him and couldn't believe her good fortune when he said he felt the same way about her. She'd thought of Peter as her second chance of happiness, and when he'd asked her to marry him two months later, she'd been thrilled.

Greta had taken to him too. He'd planned to adopt her officially, but he'd been sent back to the front in November 1917 and by March the following year she'd been widowed again. Kenneth had been born the previous Christmas.

This time there'd been no getting over it. Ruth had spent years grieving, not only for Peter, but for her mother too. She'd died in the influenza pandemic that swept the country when the war was over. Ruth had thought being a widowed mother hard the first time, but with a new baby to look after as well and no mother to help, the following years had been a nightmare. It had been her neighbour, Esther Bradshaw, another war widow with a young son, who'd helped her pull through.

For some time now, Ruth had spent three mornings a week cleaning for a hairdresser and a further two cleaning for the wife of the chemist. Both shops were handy, being a short walk away in Balfour Road.

There were hidden benefits to be had from both. The chemist had advised her on dosing the childhood ailments from which Greta and Kenneth had suffered, and had even given her the medicine. The hairdresser did not take payment for cutting either her hair or that of the children, though last Christmas Greta had paid a discounted price for her mother to have a perm. Ruth thought of these things as her bonus.

She noticed Kenny was not finishing all his hotpot this evening. 'Eat that up, Kenny.'

'I'm saving a bit for the dog.'

'No, you eat it all. You're a growing lad; you need it. There's plenty of bones the dog can have.'

'Ma-am, please, just this bit of potato and gravy. I've had enough, honest.'

'Eat it, Kenny. There's a bit of stale bread the dog can have.'

The children always cleared away and did the washing-up together. 'It's your turn to sit down,' they told her.

Greta was lively and seemed to exude energy. She had the sort of looks that drew the eye, with her golden blonde hair, eyes of jade green, flawless features and fair translucent skin. She looked innocent and childlike, was dainty and light on her feet, but underneath all the sweetness and charm, Ruth knew she had an iron determination. Greta had proved a support to her over the last few years and she was proud of her daughter.

When Kenny went out to give the dog the bits of food he'd collected for its supper, Ruth went to stand at the scullery door to watch. It took the dog no time at all to crunch up the

14

bones, and he was licking the bowl clean in moments.

She retreated to the fire. It was a tiny house. The stairs went up from the scullery into the first bedroom where there was just enough room to put a single bed for Kenny. She and Greta shared a double bed in the larger front bedroom. The place was big enough for her little family, but it would be nice not to have to go out to the yard to the lavatory.

Nice, too, if she had a hot-water cistern, though the wash house gave her plenty of space for her laundry work. She had to light a fire under the copper to get hot water, but it did for their baths too. The large zinc bath that hung on the wall was used for both. Ruth looked up to see Kenny half dragging an unwilling dog to the fire.

'Kenny!'

'He's dried off, Mam. He won't dirty anything. Have we got a brush I could use on him? All this dried mud would brush off now. I could make him look nice.'

'There's an old scrubbing brush outside. You could use that if you wash it again afterwards.'

'Thanks, Mam.'

'But do it out in the yard.' The rain had ceased by now.

'All right. Come on, dog.'

The back door opened again and another cold blast took the temperature down. Ruth was about to throw more coal on her fire but stopped herself. They couldn't afford it. She closed her eyes and lay back in the rocking chair.

It seemed no time before Kenny was back with the dog.

'He looks much better,' she agreed.

'He's a handsome dog, isn't he? Poor thing, we can't leave him alone out there all the time.'

She sighed. 'You mean you want him to stay with us by the fire?'

'Can I, please? Just for an hour or so. I want to play with him.'

Ruth hadn't the heart to say no. There were few treats she could allow. She said, 'I don't think he wants to be in here, though.'

'He does, Mam. Look, he's licking my hand. He likes me. I wonder what his name is.'

'It's not on his collar so there's no way of knowing.'

'What shall we call him? I'm trying to think of a name. D'you think Bill would suit him?'

Ruth saw her mistake: Kenny was bonding with this dog. 'We needn't call him anything; he'll be going to the dog pound tomorrow.' She should have taken him straight there.

'Mam, please, please, I'd love to keep him. Greta would too. Please let him stay.'

'We can't, Kenny, I'm sorry. He doesn't belong to us, anyway. He must have an owner somewhere who'll be fretting for him. You must take him to the police station in the morning before you go to school.'

School for Kenny didn't start until nine o'clock. She and Greta had to start work by eight. Ruth made sure they all began the day with stomachs full of porridge and tea. Kenny was up and playing with the dog when she left. A small portion of porridge had been saved for his breakfast this morning, and Kenny was still wheedling to be allowed to keep him.

'No, Kenny, we can't, and that's that. Take him to the police station now.'

Ruth hurried home at midday to light her fire. During the winter months, she made a big pan of soup, which, with a slice of bread, did her and Kenny for lunch all week. She spent threepence on bones and threw in all her vegetable scraps and leftovers to spin it out.

While the soup pan was heating up, she went to the wash house to bring in the ironing she needed to do that afternoon, and was shocked to see the bundle of black fur still curled up on its newspaper bed. She felt a rush of anger too. Kenny usually did as he was told.

He came running up the yard moments later.

'I just couldn't, Mam,' he choked. 'I tied a piece of string to his collar but he didn't want to go. His eyes were pleading, he looked so pathetic, and he isn't a stray, anyway.'

Ruth said, 'He's got to go. I'll take him myself when I've done the ironing.'

'No Mam, please. Let me. I'll do it after school.'

At the table Kenny broke his bread in half. 'For the dog,' he said. 'Can he have just a drop of soup over it? There's plenty here.'

Ruth was exasperated. 'One meal a day is enough for a dog. He doesn't need three.'

The dog licked his bowl clean in moments. 'He is hungry,' Kenny said. 'That proves it.'

'He's eating more than we are. He's not thin so perhaps he's greedy?'

'Mam! Before Greta found him, he'd had nothing to eat for days. He was starving, you know he was. After today, one meal a day will be enough.'

Ruth sighed. 'You can give him that big bone from the

soup. It's been boiled for hours, we'll get no more nourishment from it.'

'Thanks, Mam.' Kenny had a wide smile on his face. 'He'll love that. I'll take him for a walk first. Dogs have to have walks. He can gnaw at the bone all afternoon.'

CHAPTER TWO

WITH THE house to herself again, Ruth put her flat irons in the fire and set about the ironing. Every time she went into the wash house those bright blue eyes seemed to plead with her to be allowed to stay. The dog was worming his way into her affections too, but she wasn't going to change her mind.

Later in the afternoon Ruth crossed the street to see Esther Bradshaw, and met her coming out of her front door.

'I'm just popping down to Riley's the Newsagent to get the local paper. Rex wants to see if there are any jobs advertised.'

Esther was only three years older than Ruth, but looked to be in late middle age. She too had had a hard struggle to bring up a son on her own. Her brown hair had faded to a softer dun colour and was now sprinkled with grey; she wore it pulled back into a tight bun in the nape of her neck. Her fair skin was crazed with tiny wrinkles and her tawny eyes looked defeated.

'I'll walk with you,' Ruth said, 'then you can come home

with me and I'll make a cuppa.' Esther had not been herself since Rex had been given a week's notice. Ruth told her about the dog in her wash house.

When her friend went into the shop, Ruth read the notices pinned on postcards down the side of the window. Her eyes were drawn to one headed 'Lost Dog', but it was a brown terrier that was missing.

Esther was opening the paper to study the Situations Vacant columns as soon as Ruth got her into her living room. She said, 'Not many jobs here today.'

Ruth lowered the kettle on to the hot coals. 'It's this depression.'

Esther turned the page with a sigh. 'There's nothing much Rex could apply for. He's desperate to find work. D'you know what he said?'

'What?'

' "I'll have to join the army, Mam. Then I wouldn't be an extra mouth for you to feed." '

Ruth was aghast. 'Don't let him.'

'I told him no, absolutely not. I couldn't stand the thought of him going in the army. It killed his father.'

'I should think not! Both my husbands were in the army and look what happened to them.' Her eyes went up to the photographs on her mantelpiece. On one side she was John Arrowsmith's bride, and on the other, Peter Walsh's. She looked so young and radiantly happy, yet all her hopes had come to naught.

'He says it's peacetime and nobody's getting killed now, but if there was another war . . . Anyway, I want him here with me. I can't cope without him. He's all I've got.'

'I know,' Ruth sighed. 'Here's Kenny home from school.'

From the scullery window, she watched him come up the yard and go straight to the wash house. The dog met him at the door, his tail wagging a vigorous welcome.

'Mam, did you see that?' Kenny and the dog came into the scullery. 'He was smiling at me, showing his teeth. Isn't he great?'

'Dogs don't smile,' Esther told him.

'This one does. Look, he's still shivering with excitement. Mam, can I have a slice of bread and jam?'

'I told you you'd be hungry. You'd no business to give that dog some of your dinner.' Ruth got up to cut him a round of bread. 'You take him straight round to the police now, d'you hear?'

'Ah, Mam, please.'

Esther said suddenly from the table, 'Just look here. Somebody's put a notice in the paper about a lost dog. "Two-year-old black and white border collie bitch," ' she read, ' "with blue eyes. Answers to the name of Jess." '

'A bitch?' Ruth wanted to laugh. 'Is it?'

'Of course it's a bitch,' Esther giggled. 'What were you thinking of?'

Kenny came to read the notice for himself. The dog was curled up on the floor already half asleep.

'Jess,' he said in a loud voice. Her head came up immediately and she turned to look at him.

'That's her,' Ruth said. 'There's a phone number here. I'm going straight down to the phone box to let them know we've got her.'

'I wanted to keep her.' Kenny's lip quivered.

'There'll be a reward, it says,' she consoled.

When she walked down to the phone box outside Riley's paper shop, Kenny and the dog trailed behind her.

Ruth said, 'This is the right thing to do. He'll be better off back with his rightful owner than in the police pound.'

'It's a she, Mam. I didn't think she was a girl, did you?'

'No.' Ruth felt that was the least of her worries. She asked the operator to connect her with the number and a woman's voice answered.

'It's about the notice you put in the paper,' Ruth said. 'A black and white collie followed my daughter home last night. It's got bright blue eyes.'

'That sounds like Jess. Whereabouts are you?'

Ruth dictated her name and address and the woman wrote it down with painstaking slowness.

'I'm sorry, Mr Masters hasn't come home yet. He went to Prestatyn. I'll let him know Jess has been found.'

'Your husband will collect Jess then?'

'Oh, Mr Masters isn't my husband. I'm the maid.' The woman kept her talking. 'I don't think he'll come tonight unless he just sends the car for her. What day is it tomorrow? . . . Yes, he often has business in Liverpool on Thursday afternoons. It'll probably be more convenient if he calls tomorrow evening, say between six and seven, before he comes home. Though what if it's not the right dog?'

Ruth was afraid the money would run out and she didn't want to spend more on this.

'Does she have a red collar?' the maid asked.

'Yes.'

'It sounds like Jess. If he can't collect her until tomorrow you'll keep her safe?'

As Ruth agreed, the money dropped and she was cut off.

Kenny had propped the door of the booth open, so he could listen to what was said. 'We're to keep her till tomorrow? That's marvellous.'

'A maid and a car,' Ruth marvelled.

Kenny sighed. 'Jess's owner must be rich. I expect she'll want to go home.'

The following night, as soon as they'd finished their tea, Ruth got the children to tidy up more quickly and thoroughly than usual. She was never comfortable with strangers in her home; she'd come down in the world and was ashamed of its shabbiness. She banked up the fire in the range and swept the hearth again. The dog had gone to sleep under the table. She'd given Kenny a generous amount of food to feed her now it looked as though it would be her last meal here.

She made Kenny wash his face and comb his unruly red hair. She didn't want him to look as though nobody cared for him.

'Greta, why don't you change out of your working clothes? You must have something smarter than that old jumper and skirt.'

'Why?' Kenny wanted to know.

'I like us to look our best for visitors.'

'Especially rich visitors,' Greta told him.

Kenny had parted the curtains at the front window and was watching the dark street. Ruth ran upstairs to take off her pinafore and comb her hair. At least her children had taken after their fathers instead of inheriting her pale washed-out looks.

She heard Kenny call, 'I think there's a car coming. It's lighting up the street. Yes, it's stopping here. It's a big posh car.' His voice became a squeal. 'He's even got a driver.'

Their front door opened straight from the living room to the pavement. By the time Ruth had run downstairs, Kenny had pulled back the curtain they kept drawn to shut out the draughts and had opened the door. A large man was offering his hand to Greta.

'Mungo Masters,' he said. 'I believe you've found my dog? You are Ruth Walsh?'

'No, I'm Greta. Do come in.'

He took off his bowler hat and had to bend to get inside. Ruth thought he seemed larger than life. He was a striking figure, wearing a sharp grey suit and a bright waistcoat, with several heavy gold watch chains crossing it. He had dark hair and rather swarthy skin, a gold tooth too, which showed when he smiled.

'I'm Ruth Walsh, Greta's mother. I telephoned about the dog.'

When he took her hand in a hearty grasp, his rings hurt her fingers. Self-confidence shone out of him like a beacon. This was a man who knew what he wanted and how to get it. His dark eyes lingered on her face; he was handsome in a rather exotic way, but flashy. He wore too much jewellery and Ruth thought him altogether too showy.

*

Mungo Masters stepped into the tiny room and was surprised to find it so clean and comfortable. He couldn't tear his eyes from the girl. Greta, she'd said her name was. She was slim and slight, and he'd never seen a more perfect face. 'Dainty' was the word that came to his mind. Wide-set green eyes smiled up at him; he had to stop himself putting out his hand to touch her long golden hair.

'This is the dog,' she said. Her voice was soft and had none of the rough accent he'd expected to find in this neighbourhood.

For the first time he saw Jess. She was under the table, her back rigid, her nose pointing and on full alert. He took a step closer and stopped. The damn dog was backing away in terror.

'That's my Jess, all right. I'm very grateful to you for looking after her, and for ringing up about her. Very kind of you.' He moved towards a rocking chair by the fire.

'Won't you sit down for a minute?' the older woman invited.

'Thank you.' He lowered himself on to it. It was easy to see the mother had been brought up in better circumstances; she was polite, with a gracious manner.

'This is my little brother, Kenneth,' the girl said. 'He's looked after Jess.' They were not alike in any way, though he was a nice enough-looking lad.

'I love your dog,' he said. 'I wish I could keep her.'

'Kenneth!' his mother said. 'You know that's impossible.'

Kenny said, 'How did you come to lose her here? She was frightened.' His face was screwing up with concern.

Mungo smiled at Greta. He'd thought they might ask this.

'My driver had an accident, not a bad one. He rammed another car at the traffic lights out on the main road. I got out to see how much damage he'd caused, forgetting about Jess. I didn't close the car door behind me and she took off like a rocket. I expect the bump scared her.'

'Poor old thing.' Kenny was stroking her head. 'When was that?'

'Let me see, that would be Friday afternoon. I came over to check on my business in Southport and then came into Liverpool to discuss a new contract with a factory near here. I live over on the Wirral side.'

'It was Tuesday evening,' Greta said, 'when she followed me home.'

'She was starving and wet through,' the lad added.

'May we ask what sort of a business you have?' The mother turned her eyes on him.

'Funfairs.'

'In the plural?' She was smiling and he realised she had a faded beauty. She looked drawn, old before her time, perhaps not in the best of health.

'Three.' He couldn't keep the pride out of his voice. He'd vowed to get on when he was a lad and he had. 'Covered arcades. It means I get the trade even on wet days. In fact, that's when business is best for me – when everything else is rained off.'

His eyes drifted to the girl again. She was like a magnet, pulling at his senses. How old would she be? Twenty? He realised he was staring and switched his gaze to the lad. With his red curls and freckles, he didn't look much like either of the women. Mungo had meant to reward them with a pound for looking after Jess, but now he had a better idea.

'Do you like funfairs?' he asked Kenny.

'You bet I do. Not that Mam lets us go much.'

'We can't afford to spend on things that aren't essential,' Ruth choked with embarrassment. She didn't want him to think she disapproved of such places.

'My biggest one is in New Brighton. Why don't you both come over and have a day out?'

'Both?' The word lingered on the girl's tongue.

'All of you, I mean,' he said hurriedly. Mustn't upset the old girl. 'I promised a reward for getting Jess back. You can try out all the rides, everything free, of course. You won't have to go to school on Saturday – what about coming then?'

Kenny was almost jumping up and down in anticipation. 'Have you got chairoplanes?'

'Yes, and Dodgem cars.'

'Mam and I have to go to work on Saturday mornings,' Greta told him regretfully.

'Afternoon then? I could send my car for you? What time?'

The mother asked, 'Wouldn't it be just as quick if we walked to Pier Head and took the ferry across?'

He smiled. 'You're right. It's quite a performance going across on the luggage boat, and even worse having to drive up to the transporter bridge at Widnes. I do wish they'd get on with building this tunnel they're talking about. It would make life much easier.

'Yes, come over on the ferry and I'll get my driver to pick

27

you up at New Brighton pier. What time shall we say? Two o'clock?'

He stood up, satisfied now he knew he would see Greta again.

'Thank you, Mr Masters,' she said. 'You're very kind.'

'Mungo, please.'

The mother was frowning. 'You're not from these parts? Your name . . . ?'

'Well, yes, I am. It's a family name. I believe some of my forebears came from Glasgow, where it's not uncommon. Some came from Ireland too. I'm a real mixture.'

He hadn't been christened Mungo – the mother had been quick to pick up on that. As a child he'd been called Micky, but Micky Masters made him sound like the sort of Irishman who was always ready to put his fists up. That wasn't the impression he wanted to give. Mungo had the right ring about it for using in his business.

He looked round. 'I'd better go; take Jess home.'

Kenny asked, 'Will I be able to see her on Saturday?'

'Yes, if you want to.'

The lad persuaded her out from under the table. She came without fuss. 'Come on, Jess.' He led her out to the car, fondling her ears.

'Just fancy,' Ruth said, when they went back to the fire after saying goodbye. 'He kept his driver sitting out there in the cold and the dark all that time.'

'But he's very kind,' Kenny said, his brown eyes sparkling. 'It's a lovely reward, isn't it? We'll have a fine time on Saturday.'

Greta said, 'Yes, but Rex was expecting me to go out with him.'

'You can do that any time,' Kenny said easily. 'An afternoon at the fair is different.' After a moment he added, 'But I'd rather have kept Jess.'

'I'd never have guessed his forebears came from Glasgow,' Ruth said slowly. 'I'd have said some Mediterranean region. He was flashily dressed, not in the best taste.'

'He's handsome,' Greta said. 'Rather flamboyant, I thought.'

'Wears too much jewellery.' Ruth thought for a moment. 'Did you see his rings? About four on each hand.'

Three,' Greta corrected. 'There's something romantic about him, isn't there? He reminds me of Rudolph Valentino.'

Ruth hadn't liked the way he'd stared at Greta. She hoped she was doing the right thing in agreeing to visit his funfair. Mungo Masters was nearer her age than Greta's. He'd paid altogether too much attention to so young a girl. It would have been more appropriate if he'd taken more interest in her.

Ruth sighed. She had to accept that she'd reached the age when men no longer looked at her. Something told her he was doing this to see more of Greta, but at least he'd done the right thing and invited the whole family.

By Saturday, Ruth had even more misgivings about Mungo Masters and had even thought of telephoning with some excuse not to go, but Kenny was so thrilled at the prospect of the funfair and of being able to see Jess again. They set out wearing their best. Greta had made a big effort and was looking lovely. It was a grey wintry afternoon.

The arrangements Mr Masters had made went like clockwork. His driver, wearing a pale grey uniform with lots of silver braid and buttons, was waiting for them on the pier as they came off the ferry. As he led them to the car, he told them his name was George Higginbottom, but that Mr Masters had started calling him Georgio and now everybody did. Ruth could appreciate just how large and expensive a car it was now she saw it in daylight.

Georgio was older than Mungo and heavily built. He had the broken nose and slightly swollen face of a boxer and his hands seemed to be the size of spades when they were spread out on the steering wheel of the Bentley.

Kenny could hardly speak for excitement. It was his first ever car ride, but they'd only gone a few hundred yards before she could see an immense wooden structure with the words 'Mungo's Pleasure Arcade' picked out in neon lights that were flashing on and off even now in mid-afternoon.

The car rolled to a halt in front of huge double glass doors that were propped open. Hurdy-gurdy music was blaring out. It made Ruth want to dance. She hadn't been keen to come but now she could feel her spirits lifting. The driver rushed to open the back door to let them out.

'Doesn't this make you feel important?' Greta whispered.

Georgio ushered them inside. Here the noise was even louder: the buzz of machinery, screams of excitement, raucous laughter and crashes from the Dodgems were added to the music. The driver led them up some stairs to an office.

Ruth had a glimpse of Mungo Masters poring over ledgers on his desk before he leaped to his feet to greet them. His eyes went straight to Greta but he gave them all a warm welcome, offering glasses of lemonade or pop.

Kenny shook his head. He was jumping up and down with excitement. 'No, thank you. I can't wait to see your funfair.' He was already in front of one of the two large windows looking down on the fair below.

Ruth agreed, feeling the first prickle of anticipation.

Greta was smiling at Mungo, her cheeks rosy and her green eyes sparkling. 'Let's go straight down to the fair. This music is getting me in the mood.'

Mungo Masters took three gold-coloured cards from his desk drawer and wrote the date on them.

'Show these when you're asked for tickets. The men will know I want you to have free rides.'

'As many rides as we want?' Kenny asked breathlessly.

'As many as you can stand,' he told him, but his gaze was on Greta. 'Come on, I'll show you round.'

Kenny had to have a ride on the chairoplanes as soon as he saw them.

'I hope he won't get lost,' Ruth worried.

Mr Masters said, 'I'll ask Georgio to keep an eye on him, make sure he doesn't.'

Ruth could see there was an understanding between him and Georgio. He was not only his driver but his general factotum. Georgio seemed to run his errands and look after him generally.

'Thank you,' she said, wondering if she'd misjudged Mungo. He was very thoughtful.

He stood between her and Greta, holding on to an arm of each, a commanding presence. It was easy to see he was the boss by the way he spoke to the men running the round-abouts and side shows and his staff were deferential. Mungo's funfair was well patronised. The clientele was all young, mostly youths or children. They all seemed to be enjoying themselves.

'As you can see, it's a mixture of side shows and roundabouts,' he told them. 'Do feel free to try anything you fancy.'

Greta stopped at a cocount shy. She hit a coconut with one ball, and it wobbled but stayed put.

'You've got to put more weight behind it.' Mungo picked up her last ball and hurled it with all his might. The coconut was pitched out. He led Greta forward to choose a prize from those displayed on shelves behind. She chose a china ornament to hold rings on her dressing table.

He led her then to the rifle range, and they were joined by Kenny, who wanted to learn to shoot. Ruth found herself by a stall where pennies were being rolled down in the hope they'd land on squares that were designated prize winners. One glimpse of her gold card and the stall holder gave her ten metal tallies. She ended up winning fourpence.

Mungo had won a stuffed toy dog for his shooting, before he was recalled to his office. He gave it to Greta but it was Georgio who carried their prizes round. They tried the ghost train, the swing boats, and the merry-go-round with horses that pranced up and down. Ruth watched while Greta and Kenny enjoyed the helter-skelter and other more vigorous rides. The music whirled and the crowd shouted and screamed. Ruth won a vase at the hoopla stall. She couldn't believe how quickly the afternoon was going, or how much she was enjoying it. She felt exhilarated.

Georgio told them Mr Masters had asked him to take them back to his office at six o'clock. The office was built out on pillars above the refreshment bar. Ruth could see Mungo watching them from one of the windows. He raised his hand to wave to her.

When they went up, he said to her, 'I'd like to take you all back to my home to see Jess and have a bite of supper. Is that all right? Georgio will bring the car round to the front.'

'That's very kind,' said Ruth.

He put Kenny in the front with the driver. Ruth couldn't help noticing that he ushered her into the back seat first so that he could sit next to Greta.

Mungo pointed out the fish-and-chip shop next door to his funfair. 'I own that too,' he told them. 'Did you notice the refreshment bar in the fair itself? I believe in providing everything the customers are likely to want.'

'Kenny had an ice cream at the fair. Georgio said it would be all right.'

'Of course,' Mungo said.

Ruth decided his manner was somewhat bossy. He was instantly in control of every situation, but he was a good businessman. She told him that and asked where his other funfairs were.

'I have one at Southport and one in Prestatyn, in North Wales.'

'Quite a business empire,' Greta said. 'How long has it taken you to build it up?'

He smiled disarmingly. 'All my life. I worked in a fair as a boy. It was my ambition to be the boss.'

'But what about the war?' Ruth asked. 'Surely you were called up to fight?'

'Yes,' he said. 'Weren't we all? A terrible time . . . I try to forget it. I was twenty-nine when it ended and I was discharged from the army. I decided then I'd had enough working for other people.'

Ruth was trying to work out how old he'd be now. Forty-one? Just about her own age.

'I knew it was high time to get on with it if I was ever going to achieve anything.'

'You've achieved a great deal,' Greta told him.

He sighed. 'If it weren't for this slump, I'd be doing better. I'd get more customers.'

Ruth said, 'I was surprised to see how many people you drew in this afternoon.'

'There'll be more tonight – there always are in the evenings. I provide a warm place on cold grey days. A place where there's light and fun to be had. It takes people out of themselves for an hour or so; makes them feel better about everything.'

'You draw in the young, then they spend money they can't afford,' Ruth said before she could stop herself.

'More than likely,' he smiled. 'But I don't force them to spend anything, I just show them what's on offer. If they don't spend in my fair, their money would go on cinema tickets or beer. I aim to have a share of the money people spend on entertainment.'

'I take my hat off to you for doing that,' Ruth said. 'It

must be hard when so many are being thrown out of work. I have a friend living across the road – her son has just been laid off through no fault of his own.'

Greta said, 'Rex provided most of the income going into that house, but he hasn't much chance of finding another job.'

'The queues outside the labour exchange are frighteningly long,' Ruth added. 'They're both feeling desperate. He'll be on the dole next week.'

'Is he young?'

'Too young to be thrown on the scrap heap. He's twenty-two.'

Mungo smiled at her. 'Old enough to be responsible. I can always use another pair of hands. Ask him to come and see me on Monday. If he seems a reasonable chap, willing and keen, I'll give him a try.'

'Will you?' Ruth was amazed. 'He'll be very grateful and so will his mother. Me too. You're very kind.'

Greta laughed out loud. 'Thank you. I'm thrilled. Rex has been so worried. We're all very grateful to you.' Ruth thought this was a wonderful outcome of their day out.

She noticed then they were leaving the town. 'You don't live in New Brighton, then?' she asked.

'Just outside, really, in the country. Officially the address is Meols.'

The car turned right into a drive. A sign on the gatepost read 'The Chase'.

Greta was craning to look. 'Your house looks straight out to the Irish Sea? What a lovely position.'

'On fine days,' Mungo smiled. 'In the winter it gets the full force of every gale. Fortunately, it's a quarter of a mile back from the coast.'

Ruth was craning her neck too. The car came to a halt in front of a large modern stucco building. She could hardly get her breath. He lived in a magnificent house.

He took them into the hall. It was vast, and furnished with a lot of mirrors that made it seem bigger still. The drawing room had two french windows leading on to a terrace and overlooked a well-kept garden enclosed in high hedges.

'Where's Jess?' Kenny asked, pulling on Mungo's sleeve.

'She has a kennel outside; she stays there when I'm not home. I'll have her brought in.' He pressed a bell push and a maid, wearing a black dress with a white muslin apron, appeared as if by magic. She was a gaunt, grey-haired woman in late middle age, who wore her starched and frilly cap pulled well down on her forehead.

'This is Norah,' Mungo told his guests. 'Bring Jess in here, please.'

Norah reappeared a few moments later, dragging a reluctant dog on a lead.

Kenny stepped forward. 'Hello, Jess.' She changed instantly, the tail almost wagging the dog as she shot towards him. She was smiling and snorting and looked absolutely delighted to see him again.

Kenny sat down on the carpet with his arms round her. She was licking his chin.

Greta got up to fondle her ears. 'She's lovely, isn't she, Mam?'

Norah was asked to bring sherry for the adults and a soft

drink for Kenny. Ruth sipped hers. 'Is there no Mrs Masters?' she asked, hoping she didn't sound nosy.

'There was once.' Mungo tore his brown eyes from Greta to look at her. 'I'm divorced.'

'Oh! I'm sorry.'

The very word made Ruth feel uneasy. It was rare. She didn't know anybody else who'd been divorced. There was something not quite nice about it. She'd thought divorced men unprincipled, without morals and not to be trusted, perhaps a little shifty. They had, after all, broken their solemn promise. It made her wonder what had become of his wife. What had she done to deserve to be divorced?

But having seen how kind and thoughtful Mungo could be, Ruth decided perhaps she shouldn't condemn him out of hand. All the same, she didn't like to see him paying this sort of attention to her young daughter.

There was something stigmatising about divorce. She certainly wouldn't welcome a divorced man as a suitor for Greta.

He'd mentioned a bite to eat – it turned out to be a full dinner served in style in the formal dining room. Soup, followed by roast beef and all the trimmings, and a chocolate sponge pudding to finish off. It was all delicious and Ruth had developed a good appetite. Mungo told them he had a cook.

She marvelled that he employed two people to look after his own domestic needs. Her gaze wandered round the room and she was very impressed by all she saw. To Ruth, who was used to the wash house in Henshaw Street, this represented unimaginable wealth and comfort. She found it almost impossible to take in.

He asked a little about her own circumstances. She told him about being widowed at the age of twenty-two and again at twenty-six by the Great War, and also about the hard life she'd had since. She made a point of telling him Greta was eighteen now. She wanted him to know how very young she was.

Without being asked, Kenny was prattling on about his school and Greta told him about her job in the laundry.

When it was time to leave, he escorted them out to his car, which was going to drive them back to New Brighton pier to catch the boat. He even went to the trouble of looking up the times of the ferry in a timetable. All their prizes were already in the car, together with another box.

'A few sweets for Kenny,' he explained.

Ruth thanked him for his kindness and said she'd had a lovely day. Greta and Kenny said a lot more in the same vein.

'It was a lovely reward for looking after Jess,' Kenny said.

'You must come and do it again.' Mungo was looking at Greta.

'Can we?' Kenny's eyes were wide with hope. 'I'd love to.'

'Come next Saturday, if you want to,' he said easily. 'All of you.'

He didn't look at Ruth. She knew it was only good manners that made him include her, and she politely declined, though she was afraid what he really wanted was Greta on her own.

'You know where to find us now.'

'Yes, it's only a few steps from the pier – we won't need the car.' Kenny was full of enthusiasm.

Ruth couldn't help but notice Mungo was addressing Greta again. 'Come up to my office and say hello as soon as you arrive.'

'All right,' Kenny called. 'Goodbye, and thank you very much.' As the car drew away, he said, 'You will come with me next week, won't you, Greta?'

'You bet,' she said. 'Try and stop me. We've had a great day, haven't we?'

CHAPTER THREE

GRETA WAS tired as they walked up Henshaw Street. At the Bradshaws' house, the glow of gaslight was showing through the front curtains.

'They're in,' Mam said. 'We'd better call and say we might have found a job for Rex and that he must go to see Mungo on Monday.'

It was Greta who knocked and Esther who came to the door.

'Rex has gone to talk to the lads next door,' she said. 'I made him go, thinking it would cheer him up.'

'We've got news that might cheer him more,' Ruth smiled.

'Good. Come on in and I'll put the kettle on.'

Greta hesitated. 'You go, Mam – you fixed it up, anyway. Kenny needs to go to bed. I'll go home too.'

When Greta unlocked their own front door and let herself into the living room it felt cold. No fire had been lit in the range all day, and it was too late to think of lighting it now. She didn't even light the gas but found candles for herself and Kenny, and followed him upstairs, deciding she'd have an early night. She undressed and got into the double bed she shared with her mother, closed her eyes and turned to the wall, wanting to savour the events of the day.

She was exhilarated and miles from sleep; she could feel blood coursing through her veins whenever she thought of Mungo. She'd had a fantastic afternoon and evening, and had been very conscious of his eyes playing with hers. She thought Mungo had really wanted to give her more attention, though he'd made an effort to talk to Mam. At times their conversation had sounded quite stilted. She relived the moment when his fingers had brushed her wrist and she'd shivered with pleasure.

Greta was dazzled that a man of Mam's age might be interested in her. She was almost sure he was, and that he wanted to kiss her. That was why he'd invited her and Kenny again next Saturday. He probably would kiss her next week. The thought excited her.

She marvelled that while poor Mam looked old and drawn before her time, Mungo was very attractive. She found his manner seductive; he had an aura of masculine vitality.

All Greta knew of the facts of life she'd picked up from the girls she worked with. They talked of their boyfriends all the time as they sorted and soaped the soiled linen in the laundry. Vera Humbert, in particular, could come out with some lewd details, which sometimes caused the others to burst into coarse laughter.

Nevertheless, all the girls wanted to be married and the sooner the better. Mam had been married twice but, she said, she was surprised she'd been able to manage it, that when she was growing up before the Great War there had already been more girls of marriageable age in England, but by 1918, when the war ended, almost a generation of young men had been wiped out, making the imbalance much worse. It was then no longer possible for all the young women to find themselves husbands. Now, in the early thirties, the position had improved slightly for young girls.

All the same, every girl at the laundry dreaded being left humiliatingly without a partner and in time becoming an 'old maid'. It would mean working all their lives in the laundry and ending up like Miss Green, their supervisor, whose only pleasure in life was bossing them about.

Greta had grown up with all sorts of beliefs about it. It was said that whoever accepted the last slice of bread or the last cake on a plate would end up an old maid, so however much Greta wanted it she'd press it on Kenny or Mam instead.

Mam never spoke of her married life. According to the girls at work, all mothers had been born in Queen Victoria's reign and the secrets of the marriage bed had to be kept. Poor Mam had had little enough of married life, both her husbands having been sent off to fight in the trenches. Despite saying little, Mam had managed to impart the fact that girls who let men touch them before they were married were absolutely finished. No decent man would want to marry them after that. They had ruined their chances in life.

Greta heard her mother arrive home and come straight up with her candle. She undressed quickly and slid in beside her.

'Mam, your feet are freezing!' She turned over and moved

closer, curving her own body round her mother's and putting an arm round her waist.

'Esther's over the moon,' Mam whispered. 'Full of gratitude that we've got Rex this chance.'

Greta hugged the thought to her. She was pleased for Rex, but perhaps this was her big chance too. Poor Mam, her chances had been ruined but it hadn't been her fault. She could type and do Pitman's shorthand and had earned a good salary, but she'd worked in the council offices before she was married and the Council didn't employ married women. She'd had to resign from that. It had been Mam's ambition that Greta should learn to type too, but they'd never been able to save enough money for the lessons.

Greta had worked in a grocer's shop for a year when she'd first left school. That had been a job she'd enjoyed, once she'd got used to being on her feet all day, but when the depression tightened its hold, the grocer had told Greta he'd have to cut down on staff. The only job she'd been able to get after that was in the Peregrine Laundry.

On Sunday afternoon, Rex came knocking at the door to ask Greta to go for a walk with him. She wasn't keen – the temperature hadn't risen much above freezing all day – but he said they needed to talk and it was the only way they could be on their own.

Rex hardly seemed to notice the cold. Swaddled in scarf and gloves she tramped round the city with him. They visited the site where the new cathedral was being built. Freezing fog hung over the trees and not much progress appeared to have been made since their last visit. From there, they headed towards the Pier Head.

Rex was elated that he might be able to get another job quickly. 'I'll be forever grateful to you,' he told her.

'It was Mam who put it to Mungo, not me.'

'Yes, but you found the dog. If it works out and I get a job, we'll be able to think of our future again.'

Greta bit her lip. She wasn't ready to say she wanted to spend the future with him. That's what they'd been arguing about last week. She felt he was pressing her for a commitment and refusing to believe she was in no hurry. She had to make her feelings clearer.

'It's the past we've shared, Rex,' she said as gently as she could. 'We were thrown together and we've been good friends but you talked of us getting married . . .'

He pulled her closer. 'I love you, Greta.'

'I hadn't realised.'

'You don't love me? Is that what you're trying to say?'

'I'm very fond of you. You're my best friend.' She could see that wasn't enough for Rex.

'We've always gone about together. I thought I was showing you I loved you. You always seemed happy with that.'

Greta hesitated. Had she been leading him on? She hadn't meant to. 'I don't want to think of getting married and settling down. I'm not ready.'

His hand tightened on her arm. 'I think of that as the next step.'

'Perhaps, but not yet. I don't want to be tied down. Anyway, we can't, it's impossible, even if you get this job. We don't earn enough, not to set up home on our own.'

'I'm sorry.' Without thinking, he moved further away from her. 'I should remember you're much younger than I am.'

'Yes, I want a bit of fun first. Perhaps see a bit more of life.'

'Right . . .' He was hurrying her along now. 'I suppose it's all pie in the sky anyhow.'

'My mam will need my wages at least until Kenny's earning. Your mam needs yours and always will.'

'You could come and live with us.'

'No,' she said firmly. 'No.'

She knew just how hard it would be to make ends meet, particularly if they had a family. Penny-pinching had been with her all her life. She didn't want to starve herself so she could put children to bed with full stomachs. By looking along Henshaw Street, she could see women who had damaged their health and made themselves old before their time by doing that; and all in the name of love.

'I do care about you, Rex,' she told him. 'I'll be thrilled if Mungo gives you a job in his fair. But it isn't going to bring you riches.'

At Pier Head, visibility was down to a few yards, and the wind off the river was cutting through their coats. They hurried home for some hot tea.

Greta had an arrangement with Phyllis that they'd wait on the corner of St James Street in the mornings so they could walk in together, but only until twenty to eight. They had to clock in and would lose pay if they were late. Mam had given Greta a Timex watch last Christmas. Now she checked the time as she hovered, but within seconds she could see Phyllis, her dark tight curls bouncing on her shoulders as she ran down to meet her.

'How did you get on on Saturday?'

Greta had already told her friend about Mungo Masters' reward for looking after his dog.

'He gave us a marvellous time. Even Mam enjoyed it. He made such a fuss of us all and his funfair was great. He's invited us again next Saturday. Just me and Kenny are going this time.'

'You jammy thing! He must have taken a fancy to you.'

Greta described Mungo Masters' dark curly hair and exotic good looks over again. 'Mam says he's old enough to be my father, but I think he's lovely.'

'He'd have to be older than you to have built up three funfairs, wouldn't he?'

'You should see his house. It amazed me. It's fabulous – beyond anything I've ever seen. It's a different world, a million miles from Henshaw Street and the Peregrine Laundry.'

Phyllis's dark eyes were wide with wonder. 'He's a millionaire?'

'I think he must be. Money's no object. He gave us lovely food.' All the more wonder that he seemed interested in her. She'd been hugging that thought to her, but now she had to tell Phyllis.

'I think he likes me.' Greta remembered how Mungo's eyes had played with hers. 'I'm almost sure he does.' She gave a little laugh. 'Would you believe it?'

Phyllis was serious. 'With your looks, of course I would. Greta, this is your big chance to get out of this dump. You've got to go for it.'

None of the girls liked working in the laundry, handling other people's dirty washing. It was heavy and monotonous work in an atmosphere of choking steam.

'Yours is a real-life fairy story. Just like that film we saw at the Electric Picture Palace last week.'

At least once a week Greta went with Phyllis to the pictures straight from work. They bought a pennyworth of chips from Broughton's chip shop at the end of the road so they wouldn't be hungry, and went to the first house and sat in the fourpenny seats at the front. Sometimes Mary Geraghty and Lily Bates went with them.

'Greta, don't let this Mungo slip through your fingers. Go all out to marry him.'

One thing the girls at work were unanimous about was that the only way out of poverty was to marry money. The big lament was that they didn't know any men who had it. The miracle for Greta was that she now just might have a real opportunity.

'I don't know.' She was undecided. 'There's no guarantee Mungo will ever offer marriage and anyway, Mam doesn't approve of him.'

'Why not?'

'I hardly know him and he's so much older . . .'

Phyllis said, 'You've never known your real father, so it's only natural you'd be attracted to an older man.'

'He seems to know everything,' Greta said slowly. 'He's done so much and I've done nothing. Would we have enough in common?'

'See him as a father figure,' Phyllis advised. 'If there's anything you want to know, just ask him.'

Greta knew that would be a sensible thing to do.

'If I were you, I'd grab him,' Phyllis said. 'With both hands.'

Greta smiled. 'Perhaps . . .'

While she sorted the dirty laundry, she relived the memory of how Mungo's eyes had followed her on Saturday. She couldn't help comparing him with Rex, though it made her feel disloyal. Mungo was having an exciting life running his businesses and enjoying every comfort in his home. He could indulge himself and others. He'd be able to change her life.

When she got home that evening, Greta expected her mother to know how Rex had got on.

'Esther says he set off at half-nine this morning and hasn't come home yet.'

'That's good news, isn't it? Mungo must have taken him on.'

'I do hope so. It'll make a world of difference to them.'

They'd eaten their tea and washed up. Kenny had gone to play with a school friend who lived a few doors away.

'I wonder if Rex came home without us seeing him,' Mam was saying. 'Pop across and find out, Greta, will you?'

She did so. It was a cold, dark night. Mrs Bradshaw opened her door within seconds.

Greta said eagerly, 'We were wondering if Rex was back.'

'No. I wish he'd come so I'd know one way or the other. It's lonely waiting for him on my own. Why don't you and your mam come in for a cup of tea?'

Greta felt at a loose end too. Knowing how Rex had got

on with Mungo suddenly seemed very important. She smiled. 'Why not?'

Mam had opened the living-room curtains so she could see her. Greta waved, indicating she should come over. No sooner were they all sitting round Esther's fire with their cups of tea than they heard Rex opening the back door. Anticipation made Greta leap to her feet.

'How did you get on?' they chorused in unison. They could see by his wide smile that he was pleased.

'Wonderfully well,' he chortled, throwing his arms round Greta and waltzing her about the room.

'I'm going to be all right, Mam,' he said, kissing her cheek too.

'Come on, tell us what happened.'

Rex's eyes were shining with satisfaction. 'Mr Masters was pleased I'd had some experience in a garage. I'm to help maintain and repair the fair's machinery – the roundabouts and Dodgem cars. He has an engineer called Charlie, but he's already old enough to retire. Mr Masters says he needs someone to help him and that Charlie will show me what's needed. He wants me to learn but also to help out on the roundabouts. I couldn't have found a job I want more.'

'How much is he going to pay you?' his mother asked.

'I'm to start on the same as I got at the garage. Isn't that marvellous?'

'You've been working today?'

'Yes, I'm to start at two o'clock and work till the fair closes, the same hours as Charlie. Closing time depends how many there are in. It closed early tonight, at eight o'clock. In the summer it can be midnight.'

'I'm so pleased for you,' Greta told him.

'Oh, he actually said he'd give me a month's trial to see how we got on together. If we don't get on, he said we'd part with no ill feelings. I had to agree.'

'That's fair enough,' Esther said. 'You've got to pull your weight in his business.'

'That's what he said, but I'm sure I can do what he wants. It'll be fun.'

Greta was sufficiently at ease in Rex's home to pour him a cup of tea.

'I made a stew tonight,' his mother said. 'I must warm your share up. Have you had anything to eat today?'

'Yes. Mr Masters owns a chip shop next door. He gave me a gold card and said I'd better have a free lunch otherwise I wouldn't have the stamina to work for the rest of the day.'

'That was kind,' his mother said.

'There's a couple of tables in the shop to sit down at. I had fish, chips and mushy peas with bread and butter and a cup of tea. They treated me like royalty.'

'Mungo is very thoughtful for others,' Ruth said slowly.

'That he is,' Rex agreed. 'I think he'll be a good boss.'

Greta stood up. 'Now we know you've fallen on your feet we'll leave you to eat your supper.'

Esther got up too, to see them out.

'Ruth, I'm so grateful for what you did. You've given Rex the chance he needs, now he'll be able to get on.' She slid an arm round Greta's shoulders and gave her a hug of joy. 'And you and he will be able to settle down. I'm so pleased.'

Greta jolted to a halt and opened her mouth to protest.

She didn't want to spoil their pleasure in tonight's events but she couldn't help herself.

'I won't be settling down just yet,' she said, and shot out into the street to gulp cold air. The Bradshaw family seemed convinced that she couldn't wait to marry Rex. It made her feel she was letting him down, though she'd never said anything to give Esther that idea. The first she'd heard of it was from Rex last week when he thought he'd have to go on the dole.

She felt he was being pushed at her. He was more like a brother to her than a lover, though she couldn't tell him that. The fact was, since she'd met Mungo Masters she'd never stopped thinking about him.

Her mother took her arm and hurried her across to their front door. 'You know,' she said, 'I didn't actually ask Mungo to give Rex a job. I was just talking about him.'

When she got into bed, Ruth couldn't get to sleep. Her mind wouldn't stop whirling. She was glad Esther's worries were over. Ruth understood only too well what she must have gone through, but it had upset her to see Greta was displeased when Esther had talked of her settling down with Rex.

Ruth blamed herself for that. When she'd been alone with Esther, they'd surmised that it could happen. They both hoped it would. Ruth had seen Rex grow up and knew he was dependable and would make a good husband and father, though he might never have much money. She knew just how hard it was for those trapped in dead-end jobs to break out. Would Mungo Masters help Rex to do that?

Ruth turned over slowly, afraid she'd wake her daughter.

The day Mungo had come to collect the dog, he'd seemed to overfill her small living room, and he'd disturbed her.

Having seen him again, she had to admit Greta might find him attractive. He'd been a thoughtful and charming host, and generous not only to them, but to Rex. Personally, she didn't care for his heavy gold jewellery and showy style – a gentleman would be more discreet about his wealth – but she was afraid her daughter's head had been turned by it. Greta was certainly looking forward to next Saturday when she'd see him again. Did she find him seductive too?

Ruth thought of him as being in her own age group, but she was in no doubt it was Greta he was interested in, and not her. How could she trust him when he was a divorced man of middle age, twenty-four years older? Greta was so innocent and knew nothing of life. Ruth couldn't see how they could possibly be happy together. As a mother, she'd prefer to see her settle down with Rex. He was more their sort.

Ruth knew it would have been wiser not to allow her family to accept his 'reward'. If she could have the time when he'd come to collect his dog over again, she'd put her foot down and say no thank you.

Now she thought about it, Mungo hadn't seemed that interested in the dog on Saturday, and neither did the dog seem overfond of him.

That night Mungo Masters sank into the sumptuous leather cushions in the back of his Bentley as he was being driven home from the fair. He'd had a bad day and hadn't been able to keep his mind focused on his work, which was very unusual. To make a success of his business was his prime interest in life and always had been. Its affairs normally engrossed him, not only when he was at the fair but when he was at home too.

Today his mind had been on Greta Arrowsmith. She was haunting him. Her big green eyes had bewitched him from the moment he saw them. He could see her smiling up at him as she had last Saturday. On a whim, he'd lied to her mother by saying he was divorced. He'd been afraid that if Ruth knew he was still very much married, she'd have taken steps to keep her daughter away from him and he very much wanted Greta in his life. That surprised him too. Greta was too young for him. He'd always gone for women who were older, who could teach him something, but Greta was different. He wanted her; she had made him ache with longing.

Perhaps it was because for the first time in many years, he didn't have a woman in his life. He'd been shocked and upset when Evelyn, his long-term mistress, had been caught up in a traffic accident. The bus on which she was travelling had collided with a loaded pantechnicon on its way to the docks. She'd been badly hurt and had lingered in hospital for several months, before dying. He felt barely over it now.

Mungo prided himself on the discretion with which he'd managed both wife and mistress. He'd rented a little house and set Evelyn up in it. Fanny, his wife, had never known of her existence.

He was careful and disciplined with women, as with everything else, and he was able to trust Georgio not to talk about the places to which he drove him.

Mungo's car proceeded majestically up the drive of The Chase and drew up at the front door. His home was exactly as he wanted it to be, except that he would like to install Greta here.

Mungo blamed Fanny for his problems. Ten months ago, in March 1930, he'd come home for his lunch to find she'd left him after a marriage of over twenty years.

It was a shock, but she'd left him twice before and come back. Their son, Louis, had been a child then and she'd taken him with her. Mungo had been furious with her for doing that, but Louis was grown up now, and Mungo relied on him to run his fair at Southport. He visited it almost weekly, because he didn't entirely trust Louis to do the right thing.

This time Fanny had taken the dog with her and this didn't please him either. Mungo didn't know where she'd gone, but he knew where to find Louis. He'd set off to Southport the next morning and demanded to know where she was. Louis had said he didn't know but Mungo found that hard to believe. Fanny and Louis had always been close enough to make him feel excluded.

Louis had been living in lodgings in Southport for several years, but he'd come home on Sunday evenings in time for dinner and spent Monday, which was his day off, with his mother. Mungo had been sure she wouldn't move out of his house permanently and turn her back on the wealth and comfort he was providing. He was also sure Louis knew where she was. Mungo had waited for some weeks, expecting Fanny to return, but time had gone on and he heard nothing.

He blamed Louis. He must have encouraged his mother

to leave and stood by her through it all. Mungo found it very hurtful that his wife had upped and left him, and those he'd nurtured had turned their backs on him.

Even now, he couldn't think of what Fanny had done to him without gnashing his teeth. She must have been planning to leave him for months. She'd packed all her belongings and taken them with her, as well as stripping out small things of value from the house that were not hers at all.

Fanny had even taken the jewellery he'd bought for her year after year – diamonds and rubies and necklets of gold – and some shares he'd bought in her name. When he realised that, it really had made him see red. He'd pitched one of her empty scent bottles at her mirror and broken both. It was out-and-out rejection of him, and it cut him like a knife.

Up till now, Fanny had always done what he wanted and he'd believed she always would. He'd grown used to having her both in his bed and taking care of his home. After twenty-three years, she understood what he wanted.

He thought of Evelyn with much more affection. Her little house had been a haven for him when Fanny was being awkward. It was very unfortunate that she'd died. He'd grieved for her and been unable to seek out anyone else. Until Greta Arrowsmith caught his eye.

CHAPTER FOUR

Eight months earlier

FANNY MASTERS knew that leaving her husband had taken a toll on her health, and even though she'd shut the door on that house for the last time nearly two months ago, she was still a nervous wreck. Now she was having breakfast in bed at her lodgings. Her son, Louis, was eating his breakfast with her to keep her company, balancing his tray on the side of her double bed.

She sighed, putting down her knife and fork. 'I can't eat any more.'

'It's lovely bacon,' Louis said. 'Go on, I'm sure you could manage that last slice.'

'It'll do for Jess.'

At the sound of her name the dog lifted her head from the bedside rug where she'd been dozing.

Louis speared the bacon onto his own plate. 'She'll get fat if you give her everything you don't eat. Anyway, it's too good for a dog.'

'You're very kind to me.' Fanny was blinking hard. She'd told him many times how grateful she was for his help.

Everybody was bending over backwards to help her. She had to snap out of this depression.

Louis said, 'I'll take Jess out for a little run before I go to work. I'm going to get ready.'

Fanny watched her son carry both trays out to the landing so Mrs Robbins, the landlady, could collect them without disturbing her. She thought him handsome. Louis was now twenty-three and, to look at, he was the spitting image of his father at the same age. He had tanned cheeks with dark eyes and dark wavy hair, his colouring more Italian than English.

It seemed such a short time since Louis had been a child and dependent on her, and now she was relying on him to stand between her and Mungo; in fact, to stand between her and the world. She was proud of him.

When he left the room, the dog got up and padded after him.

'OK, Jess,' she heard him say from the landing. 'Come and watch me clean my teeth first.' He raised his voice. 'I'll bring her back in five or ten minutes, Mam. I'm a bit late this morning.'

Fanny lay back on her pillows and listened to the noises of the boarding house. Ten minutes later, when Louis let Jess back into her room, she came to put her head on the counterpane. Fanny stroked her soft silky coat. Jess was barely out of puppyhood, but she was a companion and a comfort to her.

She ought to get up and take the dog for a walk herself. It was a beautiful May morning. Perhaps she would later on. Now she closed her eyes. She hadn't slept well and it would do her good to have another ten minutes.

Fanny didn't know how long she'd been studying her bedroom ceiling. Time just swept over her. It was broad daylight. She leaned over and pulled her watch off her bedside table.

'Heavens!' It was almost eleven o'clock. She fastened it to her wrist. Jess, who had been stretched out on her bedside rug, heard her move and got up, her claws clicking on the lino. Fanny told herself she was being lazy. She had to find the energy to do more, make more effort and get fit again.

The past six weeks hadn't been easy, and she'd had to come to terms with many changes in her life. The trouble was, with nothing settled between her and Mungo, she felt stuck in limbo.

She scrambled out of bed and caught sight of herself in her dressing-table mirror. She was forty-seven and looked ten years older. Once her hair had been a rich nut brown; now it was faded and heavily sprinkled with grey. Her jaw hadn't been set properly when Mungo had broken it twelve years ago. One side of her face was numb where he'd damaged the nerves on another occasion, and now her face had an odd lopsided look.

Slowly she began to dress. 'I'm all right,' she told herself, though to see her reflection made her feel deflated.

But even worse than the physical hurt was the sheer terror that Mungo could instil in her. She'd lived in a permanent state of dread, of anxiety so acute that she could think of nothing else but how to avoid his fists. She'd hidden from him, sought the protection of Norah and Mabel in the kitchen because she knew he wouldn't lash out at her if there were others watching him.

But inevitably the time came when they went to bed and were alone. One night they'd had a particularly violent row. He'd punched her and made her nose bleed, and she'd shrieked, 'I can't live with you any longer. I want a divorce.'

'You'll never get one, Fanny. I won't let you go. I want you here. I love you.'

He'd said 'love you' with all the feeling he might put into saying he loved potatoes.

'I beg of you, Mungo, let me divorce you. I can't live like this.' Terror of his black moods and the tension and drama he brought to everything was slowly driving her over the edge.

That she'd asked for a divorce infuriated him more and he'd attacked her again. He'd broken her arm that night. She'd found she couldn't move it and any attempt brought pain like the stabbing of red-hot needles.

When he'd calmed down she'd asked him to take her to hospital, but he'd said she didn't need it and she was making a fuss about nothing. The next morning, he'd got up and gone to work, leaving her in bed. She'd got herself dressed somehow and got Norah to phone for a taxi.

She was admitted to a hospital ward that day, but it wasn't the fracture that had kept her there. Black depression had descended on her mind, clouding out everything else, and she'd been transferred to a hospital near Chester and treated for a nervous breakdown.

Being in hospital had given her six weeks away from Mungo's dominance. She remembered them as weeks of rest and peace. He'd come to visit, bringing her flowers and chocolates and seeming to others to be the supportive husband. It had scared her to see him coming through the door. She knew he was just putting on an act.

Louis had visited her more often and the nurses had said how like his father he was; that he was a real chip off the old block. He'd inherited his father's looks but Fanny was very thankful that in personality he was more like her.

Some of her friends visited her too: Florrie from the refreshment stall, and Ned Parry, who'd started out working for her father. Fanny felt much better by the time she was ready to be discharged, but she knew then that if she was to survive she had to get away from Mungo permanently and make a different life for herself.

Mungo had taken her home and been on his best behaviour, but just as she'd known it would be, it was only a matter of weeks before he was back to his old ways. Fanny had done her best not to irritate him but his mood was often sultry, reminding her of the heavy atmosphere before a thunderstorm. A sudden flash and Mungo would light up with fury. His abuse wasn't only physical, it was mental too. He was soon finding fault with the way she looked and everything she did.

Louis was working in the Southport fair and had lodgings there, so for much of the time she was alone with Mungo. She'd confided in Louis because she had to talk to somebody.

'He never takes me out and he says he doesn't want me to go out by myself. He won't even let Georgio take me shopping.'

'If you want to, Mam, why don't you just go? He's often out himself.'

'And I'm more than thankful he is.' Louis must know it

was fear that stopped her crossing the threshold if Mungo forbade it.

'There's no question of my having a life outside his house. He wants to know exactly what I'm doing every minute of the day. I go to bed earlier and earlier to get away from him,' she said. 'I'd like to stop sharing a bedroom with him but he won't allow that.'

Fanny had felt isolated at The Chase. There were no other houses near. Of course, Norah and Mabel were there, but Mungo had Norah firmly on his side and both servants understood that if they showed too much sympathy for her they were risking the sack. The master was like that.

Louis was sympathetic. 'You've got to get away from him, Mam,' he'd told her. 'Don't change your mind this time.'

She began stealthily packing her clothes and gathering together the things she wanted to take.

'I can find lodgings for you,' he'd told her. 'I think my landlady will have a vacancy soon. Shall I tell her you'd like it?'

Fanny had said yes, but the thought of Mungo finding out had given her nightmares.

'You'll be all right,' Louis had assured her. 'I'll look after you.' Over the following weeks, Fanny had given him boxes of her belongings to take back with him.

'You've got to come, Mam,' he'd said. 'You can't stay here. It's bad for your nerves.'

It was. Fanny had changed her mind a dozen times. How was she going to manage? Mungo had seen to everything for years. She felt engulfed, suffocated and crushed, but, at the same time, unable to cope on her own. It was years since she'd had to. Even worse, she felt it was her own fault she was in this state.

Then early one Tuesday morning, when Louis was going back to work at the Southport fair, she'd put Jess in the back of his Austin Seven and finally gone with him. She'd found that traumatic. For days, she'd sat in her lodgings stroking Jess and trying to still her shaking hands.

Louis told her firmly she mustn't dwell on what Mungo had done; that would only upset her again. 'You'll be all right now you've got away from him.'

'I'm all right,' she kept saying to herself now. 'I'm all right now.' It was a mantra of reassurance.

Fanny knew she wasn't doing enough. It would do her good to get out and see people, but she couldn't summon the nerve to do it. She told herself she hadn't the energy but it wasn't really that.

She sat down on the chair at the window. Jess came and put her head on her knee again. She'd stay here till Louis came home. He'd take her out to the shops later.

It hadn't taken Louis long to realise his mother wasn't nearly as well as she'd been when she first came out of hospital. She'd found the move to his lodgings very wearing and it had affected her nerves badly. He'd hoped that with Mrs Robbins to look after her she'd improve, but after nearly two months, if anything she seemed worse.

Louis knew his mother was afraid Pa would come looking for her while he was at work and insist on her going back. Pa had found these lodgings for him some seven years ago when he'd first come to work at the Southport fair. He'd tried to explain that Pa had had no contact with Mrs Robbins since, that he'd probably forgotten the address.

Georgio drove Mungo over regularly to the fair to check the books and assure himself that all was well. As he always came unannounced, Mam wouldn't come near the fair, not even with Louis there.

Mrs Robbins, 'Bobbins', as he'd come to call her, was kind and motherly and was concerned about his mother.

She said, 'All she does all day is sit up in her bedroom with her dog.'

Louis knew she felt her bedroom to be the safest place. She kept saying things like, 'Mungo will surely guess where I am,' and, 'Every time someone comes to the door, I go all fluttery, expecting it to be him.'

Louis had felt responsible for his mother since he was fifteen. Now, because he'd encouraged her to leave Pa and join him here, he felt doubly so. He had to do his best for her.

'Mam, we need a house of our own,' he said one evening in late May. 'A place Pa doesn't know about. We'll have to rent but that needn't be a problem. It's what most people do.'

He took her round the estate agents because he thought it was good for her to go out, and he wanted her to choose a house she'd be happy to live in. They saw several that Louis thought would suit them, but Mam was in no fit state to make decisions. In order to speed up the move, he chose a red brick Victorian terrace house in the quiet backwater of Delaney Street, partly because she'd be close to other people and partly because the woman next door had seemed friendly.

They were in by mid-June and Mam said she felt much

safer. They both liked the house because the rooms were small and could be made cosy without the need for a lot of furniture. Mam was worried about money. She'd been saving for years, but only what she could take without Pa noticing. She hadn't been well enough to work in the fair for almost a year, which cut down the amount she could save and meant now they had a finite amount of capital. If Pa refused to pay maintenance for her, they'd have to survive on what he, Louis, was earning.

Mam, of course, was worried about everything. Louis blamed Pa for driving her into this state and was determined that his father would never have that effect on him.

Once they moved to the new house Mam seemed to pick up. Louis thought it was good for her to have more to do. She had to keep the place clean, go out shopping and cook their meals. Ena Gunn, who lived next door, was always about and ready to stop for a chat. She was a widow in late middle age and invited Mam into her house for cups of tea. Fanny took to her. She thought her lonely and that they had a need for each other. Bobbins, their previous landlady, called round to see her and the new house. She invited Fanny to call back to the lodgings for a cup of tea when she felt like it. Louis hoped all would be well and Mam would recover.

He thought she was settling down. She had more energy and was cheerful again. He began to talk to her about getting a legal separation from Pa. He thought she'd feel better still when she had that.

'A divorce is what I really need,' she told him. 'Then I'll get on top of all this.

*

Louis had been thrilled to receive an Austin Seven car from Pa for his twenty-first birthday. His father had been in a good mood that day. 'To make it easier for you to come home and see us,' he'd said, but Louis wondered if he was trying to buy his goodwill. He kept his car in a lock-up garage a short walk from the fair. By the time he'd walked to it from Delaney Street, it was hardly worth getting the car out to drive to work. He'd got into the habit of walking both ways.

Today, as he strode out, his thoughts were in the distant past. He'd grown up with Pa and seen him escalate from calm into a wild temper countless times. He couldn't believe, now, how long it had taken him to realise it wasn't normal behaviour. He'd thought of Pa as strict and that in order to run his fair he had to boss people about.

It was the permanently tense atmosphere at home that had driven home to him that all was not well. Mam had tried to hide her injuries from him. She dismissed a black eye as nothing and protected him from his father when she could.

Louis hadn't seen much of anybody else's family life. Pa had never liked him going home with other boys from school and he was not allowed to take his friends home. Since he was ten years old, most of his leisure time had been spent in one or other of the fairs. This was partly because Louis had wanted it – the fairs had drawn him and he'd seen them as places of fun – and partly because Pa wanted him to grow up with a working knowledge of how to run the family business.

It was at Mam's suggestion that he'd been sent to work in the Southport fair when he was sixteen. To widen his experience Pa told him, but Louis knew now that Mam wanted to get him away. He found it provided greater freedom. Frank

Irwin was a kind and conscientious boss who explained things clearly and gave him more and more responsibility.

His landlady got him up for breakfast in time to start work at ten o'clock. She had an evening meal ready for him and scolded him if he was late going to bed. She was motherly, but if he went out in the evenings she insisted on knowing where he was going and who with. Unlike The Chase, his lodgings were an easy stroll to the cinemas, theatres, pier shows and everything else in town. Louis felt he was living it up and enjoyed it all.

When Louis reached the fair that summer morning in 1930, two men who worked for him were already waiting for him to open up. He let them in and went to the next-door building. Pa had taken out a lease on that two years ago; Louis's office was upstairs with a view over the promenade to the sea. The rooms downstairs had been made into a teashop, where his lunches were provided free. Mrs Jordan, the manager there, thought he needed feeding up. He found the arrangement very handy because he could always get something to eat, but it had the disadvantage of making him feel at a distance from the fair.

Louis spent a lot of time walking round the attractions. Too much time, his father said; it would be better spent doing something useful, like keeping the paperwork up to date.

Shortly after being sent to Southport, Louis had discovered girls. Ivy, the teashop assistant, had introduced him to her sister, Iris. That affair had lasted two years before Iris grew bored with him and attached herself to someone new. Louis was not heartbroken; he too had been looking for someone else who would be more fun.

He took out girls who were on holiday and staying in the same boarding house. Others he picked up at the fair. Of necessity these affairs were short-lived. He wrote to one or two after they'd returned home, but the relationships always fizzled out.

Doreen lasted longer than most. She was a good-looking redhead, but Louis felt she liked him more for his long-term financial prospects than for anything else. She wanted to see all the latest shows and asked for the best seats. She would stop in front of expensive shop windows in Lord Street and point out things she'd love to have. Louis decided eventually she was too mercenary and went on seeking the perfect partner. Every now and again he went out on a pub crawl with the lads at the fair.

While his mother had been in hospital, he'd visited her on Sunday afternoons. Pa expected him to go home on Sunday evenings for his dinner as before. Louis would have preferred not to, but Mam pleaded with him to go so as not to upset Pa.

Mostly they talked about the business. Louis felt there wasn't much else he could talk to his father about. Once Pa went to work on Monday morning, Louis returned to Southport. He now felt more at home there with his friends.

Two months after she'd moved into her new home, Fanny Masters sat down at the table in her front room and set about writing a letter to Mungo with the grim determination she gave to everything concerning her marriage. She unscrewed the top from the expensive fountain pen Mungo had given her years ago, but she hardly knew where to start.

She really did feel much better now she had a home of her own that Mungo knew nothing about. She was enjoying the peace it brought her and felt she was well on the way to recovery. The house was nothing grand, not like The Chase, but it was hers and she could see to the housekeeping herself. It had been such a weight off her mind to get it. She'd never go back to Mungo, whatever happened. She couldn't live like that.

Louis had said she must consult a solicitor. He'd made an appointment for her with a Mr Danvers and taken her to the door of his office, half afraid she'd lose confidence and change her mind before going in.

Mr Danvers had turned out to be a small, slight man nearing retirement age, who did his best to put Fanny at ease. He wore a winged collar and spats, and looked at her over steel-rimmed spectacles.

He'd explained that the only grounds on which a wife could obtain a divorce was for her spouse to be guilty of adultery.

Fanny swallowed hard. That was a blow to her hopes. Mungo was not the sort to chase women; she didn't think he'd ever committed that sin.

'But he's been cruel and violent to me for the last twenty years,' she said. 'It's damaged my health. I can't live with him.'

Mr Danvers looked sympathetic. 'In the eyes of the law that allows you to seek a judicial separation but is not considered sufficient grounds for divorce. By deserting your husband, sadly, you've made yourself the guilty party.'

He had gone on to explain that a judicial separation

might mean Mungo need not maintain her. The law might not require him to pay her anything. It would depend whether she could prove him guilty of persistent cruelty. Also, Mungo could divorce her on the grounds of her desertion, and in that case he would also not have to pay her any maintenance.

Fanny saw that as a major problem. It was grossly unfair. As she had no income of her own, she would either have to earn her own living or rely on Louis, but how could she expect Louis to support her for the rest of her life? He was still young; he'd want to marry sooner or later, and it was only right he should use his income for his own needs.

Louis had been put in charge of the fair at Southport, mainly because Mungo had had a disagreement with the man who'd been running it for the previous eight years. If Mungo knew how much help Louis was giving her, Fanny was afraid he wouldn't allow Louis to continue. It might be that he'd have to look for a different job, but Louis kept saying she mustn't worry about money, he'd take care of her.

Fanny had been saving what she thought of as escape money for years, but it wouldn't last her for ever.

'I want a divorce,' she had insisted. 'There must be some way I can get it?'

Mr Danvers said, 'You must write to your husband and put it to him. Ask him.'

Fanny had sighed. 'He's told me that he'd never agree to it.'

'He might be prepared to provide a small income for you on compassionate grounds.'

Fanny had shaken her head. Mungo had no compassion for anyone.

'Anyway,' Mr Danvers said, 'it would be sensible to make sure he hasn't changed his mind.'

So now Fanny picked up her pen and wrote,

Dear Mungo,

This is a formal letter to let you know what is in my mind. After a separation of five months, I would like to make it permanent. I expect you are of the same mind by now.

Will you please provide me with the grounds I need to divorce you?

She sucked her pen. Fanny had read in the newspapers many times of men doing the gentlemanly thing for their wives. In order to provide what the divorce courts thought of as proof that adultery had taken place, they took a woman to a hotel and allowed a chambermaid to see them together in a bedroom, so that later she could testify to that fact in court.

Even as Fanny penned the words, she knew Mungo would refuse, but she had to try. Apart from everything else, such a divorce would make him the guilty partner and would mean he'd have to maintain her. He wouldn't like that; not an unending charge against his earnings.

I'd be very grateful if you would, but in any case, please let me know your intentions as soon as possible so we can proceed.

She'd rather Mungo divorced her for desertion than that she

went back to live with him. It was going to be either that or a legal separation. Either way she would have to think about how she could earn a living.

Fanny shivered. Hate for Mungo rose as bitter as bile in her throat. He'd duped her into marriage all those years ago. It had been her father's money he wanted, not her. He'd said he loved her and perhaps he had for a while, but his blinding obsession was for getting on in the world. That had always been far stronger than his love for her. He'd changed her from being an innocent young girl to the bitter old woman she was.

Mungo thought of the funfairs as being entirely his property. He'd long forgotten where the money had come from to set them up. But she had not.

The rasp of a key turning in the lock made Fanny jump, but it was only Louis letting himself in.

'I'm all right,' she told herself. 'I'm all right now.'

It gave her some satisfaction to know she'd taken Mungo's son away from him, though she didn't think he loved him as a normal father would.

A few days later, Mungo was at his chrome and glass desk in his study when the post came and Norah brought the letter in to him. He recognised Fanny's handwriting immediately and wondered what she wanted from him after all this time.

He laughed aloud when he read it. Give her grounds to divorce him? The stupid bitch! She should be put back in that mental hospital if she thought she had any hope of that. He had no intention of keeping her in idle comfort for the rest of her life.

Mungo had expected Fanny to come crawling back. He had never wanted a divorce. He pushed her letter back into its envelope and into his pocket. He mustn't leave it lying around where Norah might read it.

Later, lolling back in the Bentley as he was being driven to the fair, Mungo took out Fanny's letter again. She'd written that he should send his reply to the solicitor she'd consulted.

The nerve of her! That really had made him angry. That she'd gone to a solicitor at all surprised him. He hadn't thought she'd have enough drive to do it. Well, she could whistle for a reply.

In the following days, Louis knew his mother was watching for the postman, expecting Mr Danvers to send on Mungo's reply by every post. But the days and then the weeks began to pass and no reply came. Slowly, Mam began to accept that he wasn't going to give her a divorce. Louis persuaded her to see her solicitor again and talk about a judicial separation. He thought any permanent break with Pa would make her feel better. He never had had much hope that Pa would do the honourable thing.

There was no love between him and his father. Louis was determined to stand up to him and not get upset and depressed by him as his mother had been. Mam was not only frightened of him but full of hate and spite for him as well. He didn't blame her: she'd suffered a lot, but to feel such resentment and a burning need for revenge had made her ill and unhappy. Louis didn't want to get like that.

He put on a front of affability to Pa that he didn't feel, remembering all too clearly the way Pa used to beat him as a child. He recalled Mam screaming at him to stop and even sometimes trying to come between them. That had had the effect of switching Pa's fury on to her. With an upbringing like that, there was no doubt where Louis's sympathies lay.

Pa hadn't tried to cane or punch him since he was fourteen.

'Not since you grew strong enough to punch him back,' Mam had said.

Not that Pa had stopped his endless sniping or trying to put him down. He grumbled, complained and found fault with most of what he did. Louis had never had a word of praise from him, though the Southport fair ran smoothly and earned a reasonable profit.

He'd gone home to The Chase only because his mother needed him. She'd kept him effectively shackled to Pa and his business.

Now he'd got Mam away from The Chase, Louis would have liked to get himself another job and cut all ties with his father. Mam wanted that too, but was worried because, as manager of the fair, he was paid a little more than he'd be likely to get elsewhere and it might be all they'd have to live on.

Louis had started job hunting without saying a word to either parent. He'd applied for dozens of jobs: clerking in the Liverpool shipping industry and in local government, working in the Blackpool fairs, but he'd not been offered another job that would suit him. There were very few vacancies in the present depression and there were dozens of men chasing each one.

Mam had always been a worrier, but as she began to see

the future more clearly and feel more secure in their new home, her health improved. Louis was able to persuade her to come to the fair and work a few hours daily. It was the only sort of work she'd ever known and if she was to earn a living for herself, which seemed increasingly likely, they both thought it better that she should start as soon as possible. He put her on the payroll as Daisy Parker.

His mother could do any job in the fair and was very useful to him. Being in the thick of it again made her more confident and much more her normal self.

But his mother's worries about money persisted. She suggested to Louis that she bleed a little out of the daily takings.

'It wouldn't be hard for us to take a few pounds out. We're going to need it and your father would never notice. It's what I did for years at the refreshment counter.'

Louis didn't want her to. 'You don't have to face him with the figures, Mam. If he suspects anything like that, he'd give me the sack.'

Mam kept impressing on him that he must remain on good terms with Pa in order to keep his job. If he were fired, she would see that as a major disaster. Louis felt precariously balanced between the two of them.

When Pa came to the Southport office these days, he always asked where Mam was. Louis told him he didn't know but Pa knew well enough it was a lie. Lately it had become, 'Found out where your mother's holed up yet?'

Pa kept pressing him, determined to find out where she was, and Louis was equally determined he would never know. To escape this, Louis got into the habit of going into the fair, leaving Pa in the office on his own. It also gave him a chance to warn Mam, if she was in the fair, and get her out of sight.

The months were passing, Christmas came and they cooked a festive dinner and invited their next-door neighbour, Ena, and Bobbins to share it. Louis thought Mam enjoyed it.

When the New Year came, she said, 'I feel better, I'm coping and over the worst.'

Louis said, 'Let's hope Pa can be persuaded to settle things in the New Year. Then you'll be fine.'

CHAPTER FIVE

9 January 1931

THE WINTER began to bite. A gale blew off the Irish Sea and brought driving rain with it. It had become routine for Mam to clear up the breakfast dishes and then go down to the shops to buy something for their supper, taking Jess with her for the walk. Then she'd come on to the fair.

Louis was beginning to rely on her to do certain jobs. They both knew Pa might walk in on them without warning, but it was a risk Fanny said she was prepared to take. He had been in the habit of visiting every week or ten days, but he wasn't coming nearly so often now.

Louis had talked to Mam about what she should do if he turned up unexpectedly. He always came to the office before going round the fair, so that was where he'd be most likely to catch her. Mam was spending quite a lot of time working at a small desk in the far corner.

If they had sufficient warning – and they might because Louis's desk was in the window recess, giving him a good view not only of the sea but of the road outside – Mam would run down to the café and sit at one of the tables like a customer. Pa usually called a greeting to the staff there on his way up. Even if his voice was their first warning of his approach, Mam had only to cross the landing to the store-room and close the door. Once Pa was in the office, Louis would close that door and Mam could creep quietly down-stairs and be away without coming face to face with him.

Mam had been working in the fair long enough for both of them to feel it should be possible to prevent Mungo knowing she was there.

One particularly cold Friday morning Louis opened up the office, and about an hour later Mam and Jess arrived. Mam looked frozen but settled down to work on the ledgers. Louis went down to the café to get them both a cup of tea. He was drinking his, watching the north wind whip up white horses on the angry sea, when he glimpsed a large grey car pull in to the kerb outside on the windswept Marine Drive. His heart began to thump and he spilled some of his tea on to his blotter even as he craned his neck to see if it really was Pa.

'Mam!' He could see Georgio getting out to open the back door for Pa. He kept his voice low. 'Mam, Pa's coming.' He was doing his best to stay calm because he knew she'd get agitated. 'Go down to the café.' He took her green felt hat from the peg and flopped it on her head, held out her coat for her to put her arms in, then heaved it on her shoulders. 'There's plenty of time.' He wasn't sure that was true but he had to say it. 'You'll be fine.'

'Louis, what if . . .'

He hooked her shopping bag over her arm; picked up her half-full tea cup from her desk.

'. . . he sees me? I'm scared.'

'No, you'll be all right.' She was hesitating so he took her arm and led her down to the café door, pushed her in and yanked out a chair. 'Sit here with your back to the door.' He put her tea cup in front of her. 'Drink that and then go home.' The colour had drained from her face; he could see her hands trembling. 'You'll be all right.'

Pa's voice boomed, 'Good morning, Mrs Jordan. Are you well?'

'Don't turn round,' Louis hissed at his mother, and shot into the hallway. Pa was already halfway up the stairs. Louis's knees had turned to jelly and he could hardly get his breath.

'Hello, Pa.'

'Hello. What are you doing down here? Not enough work to do?'

Louis couldn't think of anything to say to that. He just had to ignore it. As soon as he was back in the office he noticed with a jolt that Mam had left the ledgers open on her desk – surely that must tell Pa something? He helped him off with his overcoat and hung it up. Pa went straight to the desk in the window and sat down, treating it as though it was still his.

'How's business been, Louis?'

'Not bad.'

Keeping his eyes on his father, Louis backed off to close those telltale ledgers, thankful that Pa now had his back towards him. The gentle click of claws on lino brought the blood rushing to his face. Louis turned to see Jess's black nose coming out of the recess in Mam's desk. He had to swallow back his cry of shock and put out his hand to stop her, her nose was cold and wet. Heavens, they'd forgotten about the dog! She often dozed in there, seeming to think it some sort of a kennel.

Louis felt desperate. One glimpse of Jess and Pa would have his proof that Mam was near. Pa's view of the desk was sideways on, it was against the wall and the drawers came to within three inches of the floor. It would hide Jess, if only . . . How did one indicate silently to a dog that she was to shrink back and stay out of sight? He edged a waste-paper basket up a foot in an attempt to keep her hidden.

'What were the takings yesterday?'

Louis struggled to bring to mind the amount he'd locked in the safe. He could no longer think straight.

Mungo looked with distaste at the tea cup still half full and with the saucer awash. He moved it to the edge of the desk and clucked with impatience at the stained blotter.

'Where are they?' he asked.

Louis looked confused. 'Where are what?'

'The ledgers, of course. Don't I always check through them when I come?'

'Yes, Pa.' He shot to fetch them from the desk on the other side of the room. Mungo studied his son as he opened them. His forehead was wet with sweat.

'Has something happened?' he asked.

'No, why?'

'You're all on edge. At sixes and sevens.'

Louis gulped. 'I need to go over to the fair.'

'Is everything all right over there?'

'Yes. We've sold a lot of potato crisps this week. I had to

order more. They should have delivered them by now. I'd better go over and check.'

'Go on, then.'

As the door clicked shut, Mungo pulled the cash-book closer and looked at the figures. The silence was broken by a soft sound he couldn't place, which made him turn round. To his amazement a dog was padding over to the door. Her nose stretched up to the handle, giving every indication that she wanted to follow Louis and was waiting for him to open it.

Mungo began to chuckle. 'Well, if it isn't Jess!' So that was why Louis had ants in his pants. 'I knew Fanny wasn't far away.' Had he disturbed them? He laughed out loud. 'Come here, Jess. I wish you could talk. You'd tell me where she was, wouldn't you?'

The dog eyed him warily and didn't move from the door.

'Fanny will be very put out to lose you.' To have Jess gave him the upper hand. Fanny would come running to collect her. Mungo closed the ledgers. This morning he had better things to do than check Louis's figures.

He wondered where the dog had been when he'd arrived, and went over to the small desk. Possibly she'd been asleep in the recess; it was the only possible place. Somebody had been using this desk recently. It made him wonder if Fanny was coming here to help. It looked a bit like it.

Mungo felt a wave of anger wash over him. Louis had no right bringing her into the business. He didn't want Fanny poking around in the ledgers, finding out exactly what the Southport fair earned. But it enraged him more to know Louis was colluding with her, while she was doing her best to wring money out of him.

'Come on, Jess, you're coming home with me.' He looked round for her lead but couldn't see it. The dog cowered back, which annoyed Mungo further. On the spur of the moment he scribbled a note to Louis, then he put on his coat and grabbed for Jess's collar, pulling her to the door and then downstairs. He wasn't going to hang about. Louis would be sure to keep on saying he had no idea where his mother was.

Georgio saw him half dragging the dog along the pavement and got out to open the back door of the Bentley for him. Mungo pushed her to the door and shoved his shoe toe behind her tail to encourage her to get in. Then he heaved himself on to the seat.

'Back to New Brighton?' Georgio asked.

'I want to call in at Dransfield's bottling plant. It's just off St James Street in Liverpool. Do you know the place?'

'Yes, haven't we been before? Near the docks?'

'That's it.'

Mungo was looking for a new firm to supply his soft drinks and he particularly liked Dransfield's dandelion and burdock and also their cream soda. The firm he'd used for the last decade had gone into receivership. It was happening to a lot of small companies in the present recession. At least he was in no danger of that.

It began to rain. The dog had curled up in a ball in the far footwell, as far away from him as possible. Her eyes were agitated and followed every movement he made.

'Nothing to worry about, Jess,' Mungo assured her. 'You're going home to the kennel, you know.'

The bottling plant was in a grim five-storey building in a

canyon-like street in the industrial area near the docks. When the car drew up outside it, the rain was coming down in sheets.

'Nearer the front door,' Mungo ordered.

A car was just moving out of the prime space and Georgio moved up to edge the much larger Bentley into the space. It took some manoeuvring to get it in.

'Do we have an umbrella?' Mungo asked as he waited for Georgio to open the door for him. The boot was opened and one was found. Georgio had it up before he swung the car door open.

As Mungo got out, he glimpsed a bundle of black and white fur hurtle past him and go racing down the street.

'Hell!' he swore, turning to Georgio. 'Why didn't you remember the damn dog? Go after her, make sure you get her.'

He was early for the appointment he'd made with Dransfield's but they'd no doubt welcome him with open arms. Regular orders such as he was about to bestow were few and far between these days. He went inside and drove a very hard bargain on prices.

When he came out an hour later it was still raining and the Bentley was locked up. Mungo could see Georgio coming slowly up the street towards him, looking wet through and very tired.

'Sorry,' he said. 'The dog just disappeared. I've walked in circles, must have covered miles. There's no sign of her.'

Mungo was infuriated. Georgio's uniform was sagging with moisture – the next thing, he'd need a new one. Jess had outwitted them both.

'She can't have gone far. Drive round slowly; perhaps I'll spot her.'

But he soon got bored with looking at the wet pavements in this forbidding part of the city. 'How am I ever going to get the dog back now?' he thundered.

He'd been so sure Jess would draw Fanny back. Then he'd teach her a lesson for running away from him.

'We could try a lost dog notice in the *Echo*,' Georgio suggested, as the car gathered speed.

'See to it,' Mungo snapped. It was a long shot, but it wasn't as though Jess was a thoroughbred and worth anything much. He'd bought her in a pet shop in New Brighton at a price that seemed enough to pay for a dog that was to be a present for Fanny.

Louis felt wrung out. He was watching his father's car from the safety of the refreshment bar window, the glass cold against his forehead. Mam would see it as a disaster if he took her dog away, and he surely would if he saw her.

Perhaps he should have opened the office door and whistled to Jess to come. She'd have run to him, and he might have got her away. The trouble was he hadn't thought of that in time. He couldn't think properly when Pa was around. He couldn't argue with him either. That was why he'd had to leave him.

But he could go back, and if Jess had stayed out of sight, he could give her a whistle and run off with her now. Louis was trying to summon up strength to do that when he saw Pa come out, dragging Jess by the collar. He'd left it too late.

He stayed there until the Bentley drove off and then with a heavy heart went slowly back to his office.

Mrs Jordan stopped him as he was passing the café door. 'What's going on? I've just seen Mungo dragging Fanny's dog away.'

'I hope she bites him,' Louis said, but he knew she wouldn't. Jess had no more fight in her than he had.

On the desk in the window was a note in his father's scrawl, propped up against the inkwell.

I've found Jess and I'm taking her home. Tell your mother I'll find her too. I know she's with you. Tell her to come and get her dog. I want to speak to her. I hope you aren't employing her in my business. I strictly forbid that.

Louis tore it to tiny pieces and dropped them in the waste-paper basket. Mam was going to be upset. She knew Mungo was asking for her whereabouts but it wouldn't help to see his intentions spelled out.

He went home to look for her and when she came to the door he could tell from her eyes she'd been crying. 'I forgot about Jess. How could I do such a thing?'

'He's taken her,' Louis said. 'I panicked, didn't think. I'm sorry.'

'*You* panicked? I fell apart at the seams. He has proof now that I'm close. What am I going to do?'

Louis knew he'd have to persuade her to carry on. 'You're happier when you work, Mam. You know the people there. You feel better.'

It kept her feet on the ground in the normal world. He

couldn't leave her at home by herself as he was afraid she'd get depressed again.

'We'll have something to eat and then go back to the fair and carry on as we were.'

'Go back?' He saw her shudder. 'I couldn't . . .'

'Pa didn't see you, did he? It worked out all right. It won't be such a shock when he comes again because we'll know what to do. And he certainly won't come back this afternoon. We've got to carry on, Mam.'

'Are you sure?'

'Yes, it'll be perfectly safe.'

'But my dog – I do wish he hadn't taken her.'

CHAPTER SIX

19 January 1931

A T WORK, Greta was given the job of sorting the incoming dirty washing into piles. Some things needed delicate handling and some a boil-wash. There were articles that needed soaking first; others needed a light bleach. The girls were moved round regularly so as to take turns at ironing, which was popular.

Greta got through the long hours of work by thinking of Mungo Masters. He looked so healthy compared with the men working in the laundry or those who lived on Henshaw Street. He had lovely sun-tanned skin and glossy curly hair. She was really looking forward to seeing him on Saturday.

At home, Kenny couldn't stop talking about going to the funfair again. Greta thought Mam seemed to be disappointed not to be coming with them, though last week, she'd told Mungo she would not, that she had too much work to do.

When Saturday finally came even the boat ride over to New Brighton was thrilling. With Mam, they'd sat in the saloon downstairs, but the sky was brighter today, and Greta and Kenny went up on the top deck, and hung over the rail, watching the muddy river water cream up into sparkling foam.

They walked to the fair and went straight up to Mungo's office. He seemed as pleased to see them as they were to see him.

'I brought Jess with me this morning, so you could take her for a walk,' he said, but Kenny had seen the dog the moment they went in. She was under a table in the corner and fastened to it by a lead attached to her collar. Jess came out, snorting a welcome and showing all her teeth in a smile. Kenny hooted with delight and wrapped his arms round her in a hug.

'I've never seen a dog do that before.' Greta couldn't stop giggling at the sight. They were all laughing, which broke the ice.

'She's a very unusual dog,' Mungo said. 'She only smiles to greet people, though. She doesn't seem to have a sense of humour.'

That set them off giggling again, and Kenny was torn between taking Jess out and running straight down to the fair. One office window looked out across the promenade to the Irish Sea. Greta saw a wintry sun shining on the waves.

'How about a walk?' she said to Kenny. 'I'll come with you.'

'We'll all go.' Mungo unfastened Jess's lead from the table leg and handed it to Kenny. He reached for his coat and then their footsteps crashed on the wooden stairs.

On the way out they met Rex Bradshaw.

'Hello, Rex,' Kenny sang out as he raced past. 'This is the dog we found – isn't she lovely?'

'Hello,' he said, and nodded at Greta. 'Mr Masters, I've fixed the hobbyhorse roundabout. It's working smoothly, no trouble now.'

'Good lad,' Mungo said, and walked on.

It was the first time Greta had seen Rex and Mungo side by side. Mungo's sun-tanned skin and glossy hair exuded health; his stance showed confidence. He was a man at the height of his powers and made Rex look a mere boy struggling to find his feet in a new job. Rex was pale and stressed.

Once outside, Mungo said to Greta, 'I'm glad I took on that neighbour of yours. A background in car mechanics is a great help to me. Look, the tide's out, we'll be able to walk along the sand.' It was firm and clean and golden as the tide receded.

'Kenny, we can let Jess off here to have a run.' Mungo did it for him and Jess bounded away with Kenny in her wake. Then Mungo took Greta's arm; his touch made her shiver with excitement.

'It's lovely here,' she said. The seagulls swooped and called overhead. The wind was blustery and smelled of ozone. 'It seems a million miles from the laundry where I work.'

'Aren't you happy working there?'

'Well . . . it's not that I'm unhappy now I've got used to it, and I like the girls I work with, but to spend hours and hours sorting through soiled bed linen isn't much fun.'

'I can always find a job for you,' Mungo said, and his dark eyes smiled into hers.

Greta felt a moment of pure joy. She gave a little hop, a skip and a jump. 'What doing? I mean, I don't want to be a burden to you. You've been very good, fitting Rex in.'

'You could sell tickets for the rides, but you might find it lonely because you'd be shut in a little booth by yourself.'

Greta wanted to jump at it. Phyllis would say she was a fool not to – a better job and the chance to see Mungo every day. But she knew Mam would advise caution.

'Think about it,' he said, and Greta was heartened because he seemed to be striking a note of caution too. 'I'd be glad to have you working for me.' Greta could see he really meant it. He went on, 'My wife used to sell the tickets at one time. It has to be someone I can trust with money.'

Mungo rarely mentioned his wife. Greta had wondered what she was like many times and was bursting with questions she wanted to ask but she was afraid it might spoil this special moment if she did. She felt on top of the world as they stepped out together.

He smiled down at her. 'I sometimes come out here to stretch my legs. It keeps me going for the rest of the day.'

She felt invigorated when they returned. Mungo took them straight up to his office, and when Jess had been tethered again, he gave Kenny a gold card to use on the attractions. 'You'll be all right on your own?'

'Course I will. Mum still treats me like a baby, but I'd rather be on my own.'

Greta listened to Kenny's footsteps receding down the stairs and quivered with longing. She was alone with Mungo for the first time.

She stole a glance at him. His dark eyes were burning down at her.

'Greta, you're so beautiful. I can't take my eyes away from you.'

Her heart was pounding and she could hardly breathe.

'You bowled me over the moment I saw you. I want to kiss you – may I?'

Greta took a step nearer and raised her lips to his. An instant later his arms were around her and he was raining kisses on her face.

'I can't stop thinking about you,' he whispered.

'I feel just the same about you,' she told him.

She could feel his body pressing against hers and was almost overcome with desire for him. This was heavenly, utter bliss.

As the days passed, Mungo decided to make it routine for Greta and Kenny to visit his fair on Saturday afternoons so he took the dog to work on that day. For Kenny, Jess was a big attraction and he was more than happy to take her out, leaving Mungo alone with Greta.

The second such Saturday, Mungo thought the fair was drawing Kenny back much too soon. When he heard him on the stairs, he was quick to draw apart from Greta. He didn't want the lad to go home and tell his mother he'd caught them necking. Greta backed herself on to an office chair and spun herself round, seemingly in a state of exultation. He was pleased and wanted to laugh.

As it seemed Kenny was going to have a couple of rides in the fair and then rush back to play with Jess, Mungo settled himself in his chair, put his feet up on his desk and asked Greta about Rex and his family.

Unfortunately, an hour alone in his office with Greta was no longer enough. To hold her in his arms and kiss her increased his need and was making him frustrated.

He said, 'What about coming to work for me? You said you were going to think about it.'

'I've thought of little else,' she said shyly.

That cheered him up. It meant he'd have her here every day and without her little brother as chaperone. He'd be able to make some progress then. 'I'd like to see more of you.'

She smiled at that, and the smile lit up her face. She had the sort of beauty he wanted to feast his eyes on.

'Come and see the booth where you'll sit and I'll show you how the ticket machine works.'

He'd set up the system so the men running the roundabouts would find it more difficult to cheat him, as he had cheated his employer in his early days at Fhundi's Funfair, where he'd first started work.

'You need to keep the door locked so no one can snatch the takings. I know I can rely on you to be honest.' Lack of honesty in his staff was his biggest bugbear.

'Of course,' she said. 'But doesn't the ticket machine ensure that for you?' It surprised him to find her pick up on that so quickly. The machine was meant to prevent theft.

'Yes.' He knew most systems could be beaten with a little enterprise, but better if she believed otherwise.

'I'd want you to be here from the time we open at ten until two o'clock.'

'I thought your busy time was in the afternoons and evenings?' Her green eyes were wide and innocent.

'It is, especially the evenings. You'll start when it isn't busy to get your hand in. You'll be on your own, you see.'

'Right, I think I could work the machine.'

Mungo smiled. 'How soon can you start?'

'Just like that? I get the job?'

'Why not?'

'I'll have to give a week's notice at the laundry.'

'Let's say, a week on Monday then?'

'Ye-es . . .' She seemed to draw back. 'Really I should talk it over with Mam first.'

'You haven't yet?'

'No.'

Mungo thought he knew why. Ruth would see it as the means by which he'd increase his influence over her daughter. She didn't entirely trust his motives.

'A permanent job, I promise. I'll pay you what you earn at the laundry, plus your ferry fares for six days. That's fair to start?' He didn't want to seem mean, but he couldn't be overgenerous or Ruth would read more into that.

'Very fair.' Her smile was radiant. 'What will I be doing in the afternoons? Ten till two is only half a day, isn't it?'

Mungo had very definite ideas about how they'd spend the afternoons, but this was not the time to tell her. 'You'll need a break for lunch, then perhaps work on the refreshments stall. Dorothy comes in to sell the tickets from two till ten, but it's useful for you to overlap and fill in if she doesn't turn up.'

'I'll do it,' Greta said. 'I want to. I don't think Mam will be all that keen but I'll talk her round. She takes in washing at home so she knows laundry work isn't very pleasant.'

Mungo sighed with satisfaction. 'You won't regret it, I promise.' He kissed her and moments later he was damping down desire that was shafting through him with the force of an explosion. Not yet, he told himself. Not yet. Catching a woman was a bit like catching a fish: you had to play them a bit before they could be properly landed.

Ruth was concerned about what Mungo Masters might get up to with her daughter. The Saturday afternoon visits to his fair were becoming too regular for her peace of mind. She didn't trust him. She wondered how he'd come through the war unscathed while her two husbands, as well as Esther Bradshaw's, had died. Kenny always came home from the visits chattering about the dog and the rides he'd had, but Greta said little.

Tonight, when Greta started washing up their supper dishes, Ruth sent Kenny up to bed and picked up a tea towel to dry up herself.

She made herself ask, 'Does Mungo Masters treat you properly?'

'Yes, he goes out of his way to be kind. Kenny says—'

'That's not what I meant, Greta,' Ruth interrupted. 'Does he respect you?'

Greta wouldn't look at her. She was scrubbing hard at the pan in which they'd cooked scrambled eggs. 'Yes, he's very gentlemanly.'

That was the last word Ruth would have used to describe him. 'Mungo Masters is not a gentleman, Greta. Not like your father. I'm sure he'd feel he wasn't a suitable . . .'

'Mam, don't keep on about class. The war ended all that.'

Ruth didn't think it had; it couldn't. She didn't see Mungo as an upright and honest gentleman, and she was afraid he had no morals.

Greta drew herself up. 'He's very kind, he's offered me a job selling tickets for the rides. I want to take him up on it.'

Ruth felt a jolt of alarm. She was drying the same plate over and over. 'Are you sure that's wise?'

'It sounds a pleasant job and it'll get me out of the laundry.'

'To be honest, Greta, Rex says he's seen the way Mungo Masters looks at you. He reckons he's enamoured with you. I'm a little worried because, well, to put it frankly, he's old enough to be your father.'

Greta's voice was little above a whisper. 'He doesn't seem that old.'

'Perhaps not, but he's more experienced in the ways of the world than you are. I wouldn't want him to take advantage. You're very pretty. I noticed straight away that he was attracted to you. I don't want you hurt.'

'Mungo wouldn't hurt me,' Greta said hotly. 'I know he wouldn't.'

Ruth felt she was getting into difficulties. 'I don't altogether trust him, I suppose. Men have needs . . .'

It stuck out a mile to Ruth that there could be only one reason why Mungo Masters sought the company of her daughter: it had to be for sex. But how could she possibly say that to such an innocent as Greta? She was hardly more than a child.

'I really think it would be wiser if you didn't work for him, love. It would give him so much more opportunity.'

'Mam, I've already told him I want the job and that I'll give my notice in this Monday. I want to start with him the following week.'

Ruth was staggered. 'What?'

Greta would never be able to say no to him. She was bound to be in awe of him; Mungo had a lot of power and he was a rich man. Ruth felt a little in awe of him herself.

'My mind's made up, Mam.' Greta's eyes were defiant. 'It's what I want.'

'It's just that I can see the danger, love.'

'I knew you wouldn't like it, but it's up to me, isn't it? My decision?' Greta's voice shook with anguish. She'd turned her back to the sink and was supporting herself against it. 'Does it not occur to you that I might be a little enamoured of him too? This is for me to decide, Mam.'

Ruth swallowed hard. That possibility had occurred to her but that made Greta's acceptance of the job doubly dangerous. 'I'm sorry. Yes, of course it's your decision. Just be careful you don't get into trouble.'

Greta went up to bed early and turned her face to the wall. She was going against Mam's wishes and it was upsetting them both.

She felt very much in love and poised on the brink of big changes in her life but it was hard to talk about things like that to Mam, who was suspicious of everything and everybody.

Fancy her asking, 'Does he treat you properly?' Greta knew what she really meant was, 'Is he taking liberties?'

She'd had to admit she loved Mungo, though she'd used Mam's old-fashioned term 'enamoured', which didn't go far enough to express her feelings. What Greta could never have admitted was the depth of her feelings. She fantasised about what it would be like to be his wife; to sleep in his bed with him every night; to have real love from him. To see him across the breakfast table and the dinner table every day. He was so handsome. The problem was, she didn't know whether Mungo's feelings were as deep as her own, nor what his intentions were. It seemed almost impossible that he'd want to marry her.

Greta felt she was really in love for the first time, and she knew very little about men. She'd gone out once or twice with a boy she'd known at school but otherwise Rex Bradshaw was the only boyfriend she'd ever had. Yes, she liked Rex a lot, but he seemed almost part of her family, and a callow lad compared with Mungo.

She couldn't not work for him when he so clearly wanted her there. It was her chance to get to know him better.

On Monday morning she gave in her notice and told her friends at the laundry all about Mungo. They were wildly envious.

She and Kenny went over as usual on Saturday afternoon, and Mungo's face lit up with delight when she told him she was ready to start working for him.

'Marvellous,' he said. 'I'll look forward to seeing you at ten o'clock on Monday morning.'

Mungo felt a quickening of excitement on Monday, just to know Greta was working downstairs in the ticket booth, and he would be able to spend much more time in her company.

It was a quiet morning. At two o'clock, when Dorothy came to take over, he took Greta home in his car. He'd already told Mabel, his cook, to have a light lunch ready for them. The first thing Greta wanted to do was to see Jess. Mungo took her out to the kennel and watched her make a fuss of the dog.

It was a bright afternoon of winter sunshine. He felt full of desire. He wanted her here with him for ever, but she was young; he mustn't rush her. He mustn't touch her yet. Before they went back to work, he took her upstairs and showed her one of the bathrooms and one of the guest bedrooms he'd prepared for her use. He'd equipped the bathroom with fancy soaps and bath essences and the fluffiest of bath towels, and laid out brushes and combs, together with perfume and powder bowls, on the dressing table in the bedroom. He hoped she'd feel free to use them.

She seemed shy, and hung back. He said, 'You can leave some of your things here, if you like. You'll need to freshen up before the afternoon session.'

'Thank you, you're very thoughtful.'

He watched her pull a comb quickly through her hair before going to the bathroom and locking herself in. He went downstairs to wait for her. Greta was to sell ice cream and lemonade in the afternoon.

Within a day or two she seemed to be settling in and was more at ease, both at the fair and with Mungo. She told him she was enjoying her new job.

By Friday he could stand it no longer. He had made it a routine for him to spend twenty minutes kissing and petting Greta before they went back to work. Today, he went upstairs with her to the bedroom she was using, and on the threshold, he took her in his arms and kissed her. He wanted more; Greta was a dear sweet child. That she raised her lips so readily to his quickened his desire. He fondled her and the words were spilling out before he could stop them.

'Would you let me take you to my room and make love to you?' That was what he'd wanted to do since he'd first seen her.

Greta's lips brushed his cheek in a series of feathery kisses. 'We're making love here, aren't we?'

That brought him up short. He had to say, 'I mean really make love. In bed.'

Greta broke out of his arms. Her eyes were shocked when they came up to meet his. 'I couldn't do that!'

His mouth was suddenly dry. He'd faced up to Fanny's rejection but he hadn't anticipated another. 'Why not?'

He was afraid he hadn't handled it right. She was so very young and he didn't doubt a virgin. He and Fanny had been young together and Evelyn had been married when he'd met her. She'd known what he expected of her but Greta didn't. That he'd have to teach her both thrilled him and made him anxious.

Greta looked scared. 'I wouldn't dare. I just wouldn't be able to. Not unless we were married.'

'Oh!' Was she scheming, or even more innocent than he'd supposed?

'I mean, Mam would be horrified if I did, and I'd be worried stiff about having a baby. I don't know anything about things like that.'

'I do,' Mungo said, trying to seem at ease. 'I can take care of all that.' But he knew it would be safer for them both if he put off gratification for a bit longer. Greta was responsive.

He'd thought it would be easy to bend her to his will but really, at this moment, he should bow to hers.

He kept telling himself he must be patient and not try to hurry her. He needed to wait until she felt secure and confident with him. Ideally, her family should feel that way too. Marriage was what he wanted but it couldn't happen, not the way things were. Even if it did, it would still be years off. He wanted Greta now.

She looked upset. He put his arms round her again in a hug of comfort, backing her against the bed. They fell on it together.

He was on fire. He tore at the buttons on her blouse. He just had to—

Her hand covered his. 'Mungo, you wouldn't?'

That stopped him. He could see she was scared. He leaped up and walked round the room.

'No,' he said soothingly, though he wanted to scream with fury. 'No, not unless you agree. Trust me, I won't ever. I wouldn't want to, unless you agree.'

'Thank you.'

She stood up and kissed him again and he felt her relax. He said, 'I'm falling in love with you.'

She gave a chuckle of delight. 'Are you? Mungo, that makes me so happy. I think I love you.'

'Only think?' He was able to tease, more in control now.

She sighed, 'I wish I knew more about you. About your family and how you come to own three funfairs.'

Mungo didn't want to say too much about how he'd come to own his business – she might not approve.

'Why don't you tell me?'

'It's a long story and not all that exciting. I built it up slowly with hard work.'

'And your family?'

With pending problems between him and Fanny, that wasn't too easy either.

'My wife deserted me ages ago. I found the situation very hurtful and it upsets me to talk about it.'

'You have a son, haven't you?'

'Yes.' He'd never mentioned having a son to Greta. He couldn't stop himself adding sharply, 'Who told you that?'

'Agnes Watts, on the refreshment counter.'

Mungo felt the heat rush into his cheeks. He'd have to watch Agnes in future.

'They're bound to talk about you,' Greta said softly. 'You're the boss. You'll never be able to stop that.'

Mungo found her words soothing and he knew he must not get huffy. He said, 'My son's called Louis. He's grown up and runs my Southport fair.'

He wished he could find someone else to do it. Louis was too close to Fanny. As his son, he'd trained him to manage a funfair from boyhood. That was his birthright, not that he'd shown much aptitude for it.

'How old is Louis?

'Twenty-three.'

'Older than I am,' Greta giggled.

Mungo felt galled. 'Don't rub it in,' he said as lightly as he could. 'You'll meet him sooner or later. He usually comes over on Sunday evenings for a meal.'

'I'd like to. It must be a great help to have a son working in your business.'

Mungo stifled a sigh. Not when Louis sided with his mother and he knew she was seeking maintenance. He shook his head.

'I'm not sure he's happy working for me, but I don't have anyone else.' He wondered if he could go on trusting Louis to handle the money now. As a child, he was always drawing and painting. He'd wanted to be an artist.

She smiled. 'Like me, you don't have many relatives?'

'I was an orphan, brought up in an orphanage.'

'I didn't know that! What was it like?' Her jade eyes burned up at him, full of interest.

'I hated it. We were made to work for our keep and beaten black and blue if our efforts didn't please.'

'Mungo! Tell me about it.'

He never had been one to talk about his roots and, anyway, he wasn't in the mood.

'Some other time,' he said. 'We must get back to the fair. We've had a longer lunch than usual.'

CHAPTER SEVEN

IN THE days that followed, Mungo continued to take Greta to his home in the lunch break. When they'd eaten, he always took her upstairs for a cuddle on the bed, but she kept asking about his early life. He realised she wouldn't stop until he'd satisfied her curiosity.

'What d'you want to know?' he asked eventually, turning on his back and staring up at the ceiling.

'Everything about you. Start at the beginning.'

Mungo knew he couldn't possibly tell her everything. He'd have to give her an edited version. He said, 'I was born in 1889 and put in an orphanage at the age of two weeks.'

'Good gracious!'

His parents had given him the fine-sounding name of Michael Lawrence Murphy Masters but nothing else.

'It was a cold comfortless place. There were countless rules, and heaven help those caught disobeying them. We were told discipline had to be strict to keep us boys under control.

'I was caned hard and frequently, sometimes until my

back and legs were raw and bleeding. I always seemed to be the first one to be picked on and got more than my fair share of punishments. Once, when I was twelve, I was accused of throwing a paper dart in class when I hadn't, but the teacher wouldn't believe I was innocent.'

'He caned you?'

Mungo nodded.

'That wasn't fair,' Greta said.

'Nothing there was ever fair. I told him he'd been unjust.' This was one occasion Mungo had never forgotten. He'd been so furious, he'd snatched the cane from the teacher's hand and turned on him. It had given Mungo real satisfaction to see the man cringe away as he'd whacked at him, but the other boys in class had been shocked. One had run to fetch the superintendent of the orphanage.

'I was accused of insubordination and told my behaviour was out of control. My punishment was a week in solitary confinement on a diet of bread and water.'

'Could they do that?' Greta was horrified.

'They could do anything they liked. I spent the time staring out of the window, vowing that when I grew up nobody would have that sort of power over me.

'Fortunately my friends felt sorry for me and one of the dormitory windows happened to be directly over my prison. After dark every night, they lowered odds and ends of food to me. The food was never good and, as there was never enough of it to be had in the dining room, we were all often hungry. My friends gave me what they couldn't eat themselves, but even cold cabbage and bits of fatty meat are better than dry bread. I was ravenous and welcomed it.

'As I was growing up, like most of the other boys, I became curious about my parents; about why I'd been put in the orphanage at all. That Christmas, when the super-intendent seemed in a better mood, I asked him about my parents. He said he knew nothing.'

Greta was spellbound. 'Go on,' she said.

'We all had to help with the running of the home and when I was sent to work in the kitchen, one of the women working there was kind and used to give me titbits: sweets and cake, that sort of thing. Her name was Martha. She whispered that my mother had been a friend of hers and years ago had worked in a hospital kitchen with her. Of course, I wanted to know all about my mother. She told me her name was Alma, and that her husband had been a sailor on a cargo vessel trading in the China seas and only returning to a British port every two years or so.'

' "Deep sea" is what they call that,' Greta said. 'There's some in Henshaw Street who are always away.'

'Well, it seems Alma fell in love with someone else, and had had to rid herself of the result before her husband returned.'

'Rid herself of the result? That was you?'

Mungo couldn't mistake Greta's hug of sympathy. He nodded. 'Yes.'

'And she didn't even tell you your father's name?'

'Yes, it was Mungo.'

'Oh, you were named after him?'

He hadn't been. Mungo had decided to assume the name. 'I demanded to know my mother's address but the woman pointed out that she'd be unlikely to welcome a visit from me.

I asked about my father, but all she could tell me was that he came from Glasgow and had been an itinerant worker in a travelling funfair.'

'Isn't that strange? That your father worked in a funfair?'

Mungo sighed. 'Every year we saw a travelling funfair come to some waste ground near the orphanage. It was called Fhundi's Funfair. We were all interested, of course, but never allowed to go. Once I knew my father had worked in a fair I became obsessed with the idea of contacting him. I climbed over the wall after lights out one night and went to see if I could find him.

'I asked several men running the stalls and merry-go-rounds if they knew of him, but nobody did. But I loved the whole atmosphere of the fair. It had everything life at the orphanage lacked: stirring music to lift the mood and cheer me along; bright lights and jostling, pleasure-seeking crowds. I felt starved of pleasure. I made up my mind there and then to run away from the orphanage, leave for good and join the fair.'

'Mungo! How old were you?'

'Thirteen.'

'That's Kenny's age. Mam would be horrified if he were to run away.'

'He's nothing to run away from.'

'You were very daring,' Greta said. She looked enthralled. 'Wouldn't the orphanage have helped you to find a job when you were old enough? I read somewhere that they do find work for their boys.'

'Yes, but the orphanage didn't find any of us good jobs; they disciplined us to know our place in life – on the bottom rung of society.'

Mungo lay back and thought of his life there. 'Many of the boys were sent to spend their last year on the *Indefatigable*. It was an old ship moored in the Mersey that trained orphans to climb the masts of cargo ships and unfurl the sails. These days they train lads to be stokers and deck hands.

'Or we could choose to be boy soldiers. I knew one lad with an elder brother who joined the army. He wrote back saying he was given tasks like filling sandbags, or digging latrines for other soldiers.'

'But you said you'd joined the army,' Greta reminded him. That pulled Mungo up.

'Yes, but that was much later, when the war started,' he hastened to tell her. He must keep his wits about him. 'We weren't expected to get decent jobs. We were conditioned to expect nothing. I had a friend at the orphanage called Philip, who had a real talent for music. He could pick out a tune on the school piano and begged to have lessons. He was half promised them, but they never did materialise and later, he was forbidden to touch the piano in case he damaged it.

'Philip was so ambitious, and wanted a musical instrument so badly, that when one of the teachers removed his jacket on a hot day and left it over the back of a chair, he stole some money from the pocket and bought a mouth organ with it. He taught himself to play it too.

'He was brilliant and could play almost anything. If the teachers wanted to punish him they'd confiscate his mouth organ because they knew that would upset him more than anything else.

'He wanted to join a band. I lost touch, but I'd love to

know what happened to him. He was so driven, I'm sure he'd have succeeded.'

'But to steal?' Greta faltered. 'That was wrong of him.'

'You have to be like that if you want to succeed,' Mungo said firmly. 'I was determined not to be turned into an obedient workhorse for other people.'

'But you didn't steal?'

'Oh, no, of course not,' he said hurriedly.

He couldn't confide in Greta, because he was afraid her principles were higher than his; she'd be easily shocked and he didn't want to lose her love. He'd always had to hide his true motives; it had become second nature. He'd been exactly like his friend Philip, prepared to go to any lengths to get what he wanted. As a boy he'd been equally obsessed to get on in life and had been determined not to remain an underdog. He'd wanted a funfair and had been prepared to use any method of getting it, honest or dishonest. And to fight anybody who stood in his way.

Greta was studying him. 'So you decided to run away from the orphanage when you were thirteen – that was risky, wasn't it? What happened then?'

Mungo shrugged. 'I bided my time, collected my few belongings together and went over the wall to the fair again twice that week. On the day I knew the fair would move to another town, I walked out of lessons, collected the bundle of clothes I'd hidden in a hedge, and went down to Fhundi's Funfair. I started helping the fairground workers collapse the roundabouts and load them on to carts and wagons. When the fair moved out, I attached myself to it. I told everybody I was fourteen and asked for a job.'

'They gave you one?'

'No, not for months. I found the fair wasn't owned by one person and there was no Mr Fhundi – he'd retired a decade or so before. There were several men, each owning a few roundabouts and stalls, who had banded together to make a fair of decent size. I hung around and helped where I could, setting up rides and stalls, looking after the horses. Sometimes, the women took pity on me and gave me food, sometimes the men gave me a few coppers. They let me sleep in the open wagons they used to move the fair around. When they had plenty of hay to feed the horses it was quite comfy.'

'But when it rained?'

'On wet nights, I moved my bed underneath. I made myself a palliasse from the hay.'

Mungo felt carried back to those times. When the fair was busy, he'd been asked to help. Soon, he was being allowed to run a roundabout and he'd been able to fiddle money from the fares customers paid. If he wanted to eat regularly he'd had to. He was living on his wits and soon learned all the angles. It was then he began to think he might have gypsy blood in his veins.

'I collected, bit by bit, the things I needed to make life more comfortable – a cushion here and a blanket there, some waterproofs and Wellington boots. Eventually, I was accepted by the group and one of the owners, Ludovic Pascoe, took me under his wing and found me a berth in a caravan belonging of one of the larger families.

'I stayed with Fhundi's Funfair for years and learned all there was to know about running such a business.'

'But this was a travelling fair?'

'Yes, and the drawbacks were only too obvious to me. They could only go where there was suitable common land on which the fair could be set up, or where they could afford to pay what town councils demanded for the use of empty ground. They had to move on to keep the customers coming. I thought long and hard about the best place to set up a fair. I wanted a heavily populated district where customers would keep coming to me. A seaside town is best, where people come for holidays and days out. I wanted to draw in youngsters who had saved up their wages and wanted a good time.'

'Did you like travelling round?' Greta asked.

'No, I hated that too. I wanted to be rid of all the work erecting roundabouts and stalls, only to collapse them again and have to load them on to wagons. I wanted to be rid of the horses too, the expense and the work of feeding and watering them.'

'And you wanted a house?'

'I longed for one – a big one instead of the cramped quarters of a caravan. Then there was the weather. We were totally at the mercy of that. A heavy bout of rain or a thunderstorm would send the customers racing for home and make it impossible for any of us to earn anything. I wanted an indoor funfair and, most of all, I wanted to run it myself.'

The last thing he'd needed was a group of owners arguing whether this should be done or that. Mungo knew he could run a fair more efficiently on his own.

'I knew that if I were in control and the fair under cover, people could come all winter. Holiday-makers would throng in when it rained to cheer themselves up.'

'And they have,' Greta told him. 'You've realised your ambition. Success like you've had must make you feel on top of the world.'

'Yes,' he agreed. But things were not going as well as they could for him. There were two things he hadn't foreseen: Fanny leaving him and the slowing down of the world economy.

Liverpool seemed in terminal decline. The mean streets had a grim and hopeless air, with unemployed men standing about on the corners. In New Brighton, the air of gaiety was slipping a little, but Mungo was still making a reasonable profit. Other businesses were not so lucky. It was hard to see what the future might bring.

Mungo took Greta back to the fair, half afraid he'd said too much. He stood at his office window, watching his business function below him. He couldn't see Greta, whether she was in the refreshment bar or the ticket booth, but perhaps he'd waste too much time watching her if he could. From his vantage point he could assess how much energy most of his employees put into their work. He could pick out those who gossiped too much and those who liked to stop for a quiet cigarette. Rex Bradshaw was keen. Mungo was pleased to have someone being trained up to take Charlie's place.

Mungo threw himself on his chair. It was a long time since he'd thought so much about his youth, but now he couldn't stop. There were things he must never tell Greta. He put his head back, closed his eyes and mused on them.

By the time he was sixteen, not only had he become

interested in girls, but he'd scraped together enough money by fair means or foul to climb on the first rung of the ladder. He'd bought, fourth-hand, a slow roundabout to provide rides for toddlers. That had made him part of the group at Fhundi's, but gave him little power amongst the other roundabout owners. They went more or less round the same circuit every year. Every man among them knew how much he'd made in each little town or village, not only last year but for many previous years.

As he grew older, Mungo realised it would be impossible for him to save enough money to get a fair of his own. He had to think of some other way to do it. He put his mind to the problem and within a few days had come up with the answer.

Frances Pascoe, known as Fanny, was a pretty girl working in the fair, who had already caught his eye. Mungo had been interested in her for some time, but she was five years older than he and he felt she rather looked down on him, treating him as a youth who still had a lot to learn.

Her father, Ludovic Pascoe, was a driving force in Fhundi's Funfair, owning the shooting gallery and three roundabouts. He was a widower but Fanny helped him.

Mungo was seventeen when Ludovic first became ill and began to find his work heavy. In order to gain favour with him, Mungo offered to oversee his shooting gallery and he helped Fanny where he could.

Now he could eat his fill, he was growing taller and broader. He had powerful shoulders and thought he looked older than he really was. He smiled to himself, remembering how he'd told Fanny that he'd lied about his age when he'd first come to the fair, wanting to seem younger so they'd feel sorry for him and allow him to stay.

He certainly had lied: he'd added a year to his age because he'd wanted to seem old enough to do a man's work. Now he wanted to make himself more attractive to Fanny by making her think he was nearer her age. He told her he was twenty and set out to woo not only her but her father, who was reputed to have some money put by.

Ludovic's illness made him rely increasingly on the help Mungo offered and gradually some of the power the Pascoe family had had devolved on to him. It gave Mungo confidence and he worked harder to get what he wanted.

He really did find Fanny Pascoe's flashing brown eyes and dark curling tresses attractive, and without him he didn't think she would be able to run the amusements she and her father owned. Mungo was in love with her, but she resisted his advances for months. She wasn't sure about him and told him he was bossy; she was strong-willed and wanted things done her way.

Mungo persisted; he wasn't one to give up and by then he really did hunger for Fanny. In the first weeks of 1907 she became his lover. He was just eighteen and felt a man. When she told him she loved him, he knew he was going to get his way. When she became pregnant with Louis she agreed they must be married. He gave his age as twenty-one for the marriage certificate, though he was only eighteen. There was no point in giving Fanny and her father a reason to be less than satisfied with their part of the bargain.

By that time, Mungo had a very clear idea about the sort of fair he wanted. The Fhundi fair was moving round the suburbs of Merseyside when he saw a large building for sale that would suit his purpose. It had been a roller-skating rink at one time, and was on the front in New Brighton, a seaside resort, but one that relied heavily on day-trippers from Liverpool. Although there was a big permanent funfair in the nearby grounds of the tower, which rivalled that in Blackpool, Mungo knew that in bad weather the crowds would flock to his because he planned to have all his amusements under cover.

Ludovic Pascoe's health was failing and he found it painful to have his caravan jolted over cobbled streets as it was hauled by a horse. It was now clear to Fanny that his was a terminal illness. Mungo suggested they rent a small house so that he might have more comfort and Fanny might have peace to give birth. With investment from Ludovic he turned the old roller-skating rink into a funfair and their roundabouts and the shooting gallery were given permanent places.

Mungo counted that a most successful year. From the beginning it was his funfair, he was in full control. Fanny had her work cut out looking after her father and her baby son, who was born that September. The winter had traditionally been a quiet time for them, but that year Mungo worked hard to extend the arcade and fill it with as wide a variety of amusements and roundabouts as he could assemble.

Ludovic Pascoe willingly paid for most of them and lingered long enough to make one brief visit to see it open and working. He was loud in his praise for his son-in-law. Mungo felt he'd succeeded in what he'd set out to do: build a good business that would bring him in the money he'd longed for. But he was never satisfied with what he had. He'd gone on adding to his empire and increasing his income in every way he could.

Now he was a wealthy man and wanted the world to know it. He went everywhere in a chauffeur-driven Bentley, and liked to wear heavy gold jewellery. There was no reason not to flaunt his success; he was proud of what he'd achieved. He'd come up from the bottom, and as the founder and owner of Mungo's Pleasure Arcades he had good reason to revel in his wealth.

Mungo allowed all his staff a short break in the early evening to have a rest and get a bite to eat. They took it in turns between five and six, when the fair was usually slack.

Mungo took Greta out. They walked up the promenade to the Sea Shells Café, for tea and cakes.

'I love these iced cakes,' Greta smiled at him. 'You're very generous.'

Mungo bit into his second cake, knowing he was downright selfish. Any generosity on his part was to further his own ends.

'Tell me how you spent the war,' Greta said. 'Were you sent to fight in the trenches like my father?'

Mungo knew he was entering a minefield and would have to be careful.

'Eventually, yes, but I'd been trained to use a rifle by then.'

Many of the fairground lads had volunteered in the first few months of the war and a lot of them had been underage too. The only guns Mungo had ever handled were the air rifles at the fair. He'd decided that joining up would not further his ambition and he'd been very glad he hadn't when he understood what the lads had let themselves in for.

Mungo didn't intend to explain to Greta why conscription had never come for him. When the Government brought it in, it had made him nervous. He'd been twenty-five at the beginning of the war, the right age for the army, but by then he had his fair, was married to Frances and they had a child.

Had he still been living in a caravan with no fixed address and no paid employment, he'd have felt a lot safer, but they were in the cottage Ludovic had rented. Fortunately the rent book was in Ludovic's name. Fortunate, too, that the last thing Fanny had wanted was for her husband to leave her to run the fair on her own.

They stayed on in the small cottage while Mungo longed to own a large and comfortable house. He searched for one but failed to find what he wanted, deciding, eventually, that he'd have to have it built. He found the ideal building site, but in wartime it was almost impossible to find building materials or a builder.

Fanny still owned the caravan they used to live in, and Mungo parked it in the acre and a half that would one day be his garden. He made up his mind that should he receive his call-up papers, he'd toss them behind the fire and give up the tenancy of the cottage. They could live in the caravan and, should he be tracked to there, they could return to a semi-nomadic life, moving frequently but never far from New Brighton.

By the summer of 1917 he was beginning to feel confident that he would evade conscription. He knew he still needed to keep a low profile and not attract attention, but he'd now earned enough to think of expanding his business and it was becoming an obsession to do so.

He took his family to Southport for a few days' holiday and saw what he thought would be a prime site for a fair. It tore him in two. Another fixed address could increase his danger of being called up. He was tempted to buy the lease in Fanny's name, but that stuck in his gullet too. To hide his identity he didn't use his real name, but bought the lease in the name of Mungo Masters. He gave his address as that of his New Brighton fair.

Six months later, he came across a site he liked in Prestatyn and bought the lease for that too, but he did little about developing either site, other than make his plans and save the money they would need. He did buy one or two second-hand roundabouts and other attractions when he saw them for sale, but he kept the doors locked and barred.

When the war ended, he was all ready to open his two new funfairs. It was a while before he could buy new attractions and fill his sites, but he got going before most in the army were demobbed, and before there was much competition.

'I feel very lucky to have survived the war,' he told Greta. Survival had been his first aim; too many of his employees had been killed.

'Were you ever near Arras?' she asked. 'My father was killed there.'

'No, but I fought on the Somme.'

'Did you? Kenny's dad was killed there when the war was almost over.'

Mungo hastened to say, 'I was there during the 1917

117

offensive. My regiment was back on support duty later in the war.'

'Was it awful in the trenches? I've never asked anyone who survived.'

'Total hell.' Mungo had read enough war books and soldier's reminiscences to tell her about the bully beef, and the rats, the lice and the fleas.

'The war was terrible for everybody,' Greta said sadly. 'It ended so many lives and ruined so many more.'

Mungo reflected that, for him, it had had its advantages. It had removed his competitors and so helped him on his way up.

Later that month the post brought Mungo a second letter from Fanny. It shocked him to find she was about to petition the Court for a judicial separation on the grounds of persistent cruelty. He thought she'd give up; she'd never seemed to have much drive.

Mungo was not pleased. It would do him no good to have Fanny turn their marriage into a public scandal. He wished now he hadn't let this drag on so long, but having done so, he'd have preferred Fanny to let things lie for another year or so.

Mungo knew nothing about legal separations or the divorce laws or how they worked. He realised he'd need a solicitor too. A Mr Bishop of Headingly and Bishop had handled his business affairs for some years. He felt Mr Bishop admired his financial acumen and he didn't want to confess the sordid details of his failed marriage to him.

A stranger would save him that embarrassment. Mungo

liked to keep his personal affairs separate and private from his business matters. He consulted the telephone directory and made an appointment with a different solicitor, a Mr Fredric Fox. Instead of going to the fair that morning, he went straight to his office and told him he'd been deserted by his wife. He pushed the letter from Fanny's solicitor across the desk to him.

After reading it, Mr Fox asked, 'You're happy to have a separation or do you want a divorce?'

Mungo no longer knew. He hadn't wanted a divorce at first but, of course, everything had changed now he'd fallen in love with Greta Arrowsmith.

However, all the aggression he felt for Fanny surfaced at that moment. He wanted to hurt her. She had initially asked for a divorce, so he felt the most important thing was not to allow her to have it. He said something about not wanting to pay money to Fanny to keep her in idleness for the rest of her life.

Mr Fox advised him to start by writing a letter to her in conciliatory terms, asking her to return. 'Because then, if she does not, it will amount to legal desertion and will make her the guilty partner. In that event, she might lose all rights to alimony.'

'I would not have to support her?'

'The law might not require you to, and your letter would provide evidence we could use in court.'

That seemed excellent advice. Clearly now, Fanny had no intention of returning. The important thing was to get evidence that she was the guilty partner and stop her fleecing him of every penny she could.

'However, she's claiming persistent cruelty . . . Have you ever been convicted of assaulting her?'

'Certainly not.'

Mr Fox stroked his moustache as he explained that a judicial separation would end the marriage but neither party would be allowed to remarry.

Wary of his relationship with Greta, Mungo made himself ask, 'What would happen if Fanny should add adultery to her petition?'

The solicitor's eyebrows rose. 'It would alter everything. I have to warn you that if she did, and the Court granted her petition, it would make you the guilty partner. She could divorce you and you would have to maintain her.'

That was bad news and it bothered Mungo. It meant that playing with Greta was like playing with fire. He thought it would be safer to get the court hearing over before letting his affair with Greta go any further and hinted at that.

Mr Fox went on to explain that getting the case over would not protect him. Fanny could bring another case against him at a later date, if and when she thought adultery had been committed. Mungo decided he'd have to risk it. Fanny had never found out about Evelyn in all the years he'd known her, and he didn't think she'd be likely to find out about Greta either.

As it now seemed Fanny had every intention of going through with it, Mungo wished he had not told Ruth and Greta he was already divorced. He was bothered about the outcome when they found it was not the case.

From the solicitor's office, Georgio drove Mungo to the fair, where he went straight up to his office and wrote: 'Please come home, Fanny. I'm ready to forgive and forget. Let's make a fresh start. I love you and I'm missing you.'

But he didn't know where she was and that made him cross. A man ought to know where his wife was living, even if they weren't on the best of terms. He ignored her request to reply to the office of Mr Danvers, her solicitor. Fanny would feel he was closer at hand and more difficult to escape from if he delivered the letter himself.

Mungo thought things over carefully. He would welcome a divorce even more than Fanny would. To marry Greta, he'd have to have one, but not at any price. To have to pay maintenance to Fanny for ever after was anathema to him.

It wasn't essential for him to marry Greta. He was confident she could be persuaded to come and live with him without that. He'd persuaded Fanny to do it, after all, until getting her father to set him up in a fair became more important. Marrying Fanny had been the price he'd had to pay for that.

His wealth would win Greta over. He'd heard it said that money was the finest aphrodisiac of all, and Greta and her family were poor. He'd recognised all the signs of poverty when he'd collected the dog.

He hadn't felt so excited about a woman in decades. He wanted Greta, she was turning the years back for him, giving him all the impatience and the desires of youth.

CHAPTER EIGHT

LOUIS MASTERS was sitting at his office desk one February morning, sipping a cup of tea and thinking about the staff position in the fair. Mam was doing much more now – she was a real help – but this morning she'd not felt well.

'A tummy upset,' she'd said. 'I was up a couple of times in the night.'

'Stay in bed this morning,' Louis had advised. 'We won't be that busy.'

It was a cold damp morning but it would soon be spring. The weather would improve and the holiday-makers would make the town busier. He'd need to take on an extra man before Easter as well as two or three boys as general help when the schools broke up. Easter was in early April this year.

Usually they took on two extra hands but with Mam working, one would be enough to cover for the staff holidays when they came later on, in the summer.

Louis could hear footsteps coming upstairs from the

teashop below. Could it be Pa? He hadn't been in for a long time. No, he didn't think it was. He listened, there was a tap on the door and a head came round.

'Hello, can I come in?'

It was the voice Louis recognised. He was shocked at the change in Frank Irwin, his boss when he'd first started working at the funfair. He remembered him as a young man of thirty, standing upright with his shoulders back, wearing a suit with a collar and tie, as befitted the manager here. He'd been calm, unhurried but firm; the men in the fair had respected him. Now, he was a shadow of his former self.

'Of course, Frank. Come and have a seat. How are you doing?' Louis knew he shouldn't have asked the moment the words were out of his mouth.

'Not well. I can't get another job. Well, not long term. I've had temporary work, manual labour, that sort of thing, but even that's impossible to get now.' He looked haggard and drawn. Frank had never been a heavy man, but the weight had dropped off him. He looked downright ill. 'In fact, I feel desperate.'

Louis could feel pity tightening his throat. 'How about a cup of tea and a cake?'

'Thanks, I'd love that.' Louis saw him relax with relief. Had Frank been afraid he'd turn him away without even as much as a chat?

'Right, just going down to the café. Won't be a minute.' He drained the last drops from his own cup and took it with him.

He'd never felt more sorry for anybody. Frank had had to come crawling back to ask for work. He'd been the manager here for over seven years and taught Louis most of what he knew. Already he had the downcast, hopeless look of the long-term unemployed, and there were millions like him all over Britain.

The café supervisor was taking a customer's order into the kitchen. 'Two teas and two fancy cakes please, Mrs Jordan,' he said.

He could see Ivy, her young assistant, through the open doorway, making the cheese and tomato toast his father was so fond of.

'Was that Frank Irwin I saw come in?' she asked.

'Yes, they're for him. Give me a couple of those toasts too.'

Pa had told him that his lunches were to be provided free, but he must not treat his friends to free meals. 'Be punctilious about paying for everything else you take from the café, because if you are not, you'll be a bad example to the rest of the staff.'

Louis always had. He rang up the till and, looking round, saw that both women had turned their backs for the moment. He removed three pound notes from the clip in which they kept them and slid them into his pocket. Never before had he ever taken money, but he reckoned Pa owed Frank more than that by any reckoning.

He put the food on a tray and went back upstairs, taking one cup of tea for himself and sliding the tray in front of his visitor.

'I say, is all this for me?'

'You look as though you need it, Frank.'

'Thank you. It's hard to find enough food for the kids and Jean. She has to eat for two now.'

Louis sighed, poor Frank. In the old days he used to take him home for the occasional meal. He knew his wife and his older children. 'When's the new baby due?'

'Only two more weeks now.'

'How long is it since . . . ? Over two years . . . ?'

Pa had sacked Frank and made Louis the manager.

'Two and a half. I've come to ask a favour . . .'

'I know.' Louis tried to save him the embarrassment of asking.

But Frank went on: 'I know the fair usually takes on extra hands just before Easter. I know it's a bit early yet, but I thought if I got in first . . .'

Louis smiled. 'I was just thinking about that when you came in.'

'I wondered whether you'd be good enough to ask your father to let me have a job?'

Louis rocked back his chair in indecision. 'He'll say no, Frank. You know he will.'

He saw the man's face fall and went on hurriedly, 'But if I don't tell him, he needn't know.'

Frank gave him a quavering smile.

'I'll put your wages through under a different name. Why don't you start tomorrow?'

'You'll do that for me? What if he sees me working here?'

'Then you'll be thrown out and I'll be for it. You know the score: Pa always comes to the office first. His Bentley won't be far away. Georgio usually goes into the fair for a chat; better if he doesn't see you either. You'll have to get one of the lads to do the job you're on and disappear for a while.'

'What if your pa found out? You'd risk that for me?'

Louis thought his eyes seemed suspiciously bright.

'Frank, you trained me up to manage this fair. You must have realised you were training me to take over your job?'

'I hoped he'd want you to manage a different site. He was always going on about how difficult it was to get managers who were reliable and honest.' He gulped at his tea. 'I didn't steal anything. I knew how much importance he attached to honesty.'

'I know,' Louis said. 'I checked. You made an error in your adding up. I pointed it out to Pa, but he wouldn't have it.'

He saw Frank really smile for the first time. 'That's what happened?'

'Yes, he used you. He wanted to be rid of you once he thought I could do the job.'

Frank was tucking into the toasted cheese hungrily. 'You're not like your father, I have to say that.'

'I hope I'm not in that respect. I'd rather treat people fairly, the way I'd want them to treat me if our positions were reversed.'

He put the three pound notes on the tray near the empty plates. 'I reckon Pa owes you this too. It'll tide you over till pay day. The teashop won't have a good day today.'

'I don't know how to thank you,' Frank stammered as he wiped a tear from his cheek. 'You don't know how it goes through me to put the lads to bed with empty bellies.'

'I can imagine. Look, keep on job hunting. If you're lucky enough to find something don't worry about how I'll manage. There's plenty of men who'd jump into your place.'

Frank nodded. 'Thank you for giving me this chance. I'm very grateful.'

'You always treated me kindly when you were my boss,' Louis smiled. 'You let me down gently when I made mistakes.'

'You were Mr Masters' son.'

'All the more reason to give me a hard time,' Louis grinned at him. 'But you never did.'

'I had to screw myself up to come and see you, but now I feel . . . all isn't lost yet, is it?'

'Course it isn't. But you know the job's only for the summer season, unless someone drops out? And I'm afraid it doesn't seem likely.'

'I know.' Frank got up and offered his hand. 'Thanks for putting your neck on the line for me and also for my lunch.' He patted his pocket. 'This too. I'll see you tomorrow then.'

Louis saw Frank down as far as the café, taking the dirty dishes with him. 'Ten o'clock tomorrow then. Make sure Pa never sees you working here.'

He returned to his desk to muse about how impossible it would have been to turn Frank away without doing what he could for him, when for years the older man had treated him so generously. He'd got to know Frank well, shared this office with him, counted him a friend.

Frank had worked hard and honestly for Pa, yet he'd sacked him without a second thought. At the time, Louis had tried to persuade him not to, but had been met with a torrent of rage. After that, Pa had stormed round the fair, finding fault with everything and everybody. Louis was continually surprised that the men didn't turn on him *en masse* and beat him up. He didn't know how anybody could love or respect Pa. Most people were afraid of him; Louis was a little scared himself but knew that now he was grown up he must never let Pa see it. It would make Pa feel he could do what he liked with him. That had been Mam's mistake. But whatever his feelings, Louis knew he had to stay on amicable terms with his father. His job depended on it.

Frank had been gone barely ten minutes when Louis heard more footsteps on the stairs, and Pa came bursting into the office.

'Hello,' he said. 'Everything going well?'

'Yes, Pa.'

Louis felt shocked at the close shave they'd had but now was a good time for him to come. Neither Frank nor Mam were here now, and it meant Pa wouldn't come again for a while. It would give Frank time to get used to things again. Also, the money he'd taken from the teashop till wouldn't show up in the books until he cashed up tonight. Louis was sure his father would find nothing much to complain about.

'Come on then. I've come to look at the books – let's have them.'

Louis got out his ledgers and opened them on his desk, then relinquished his chair to his father. Pa expected that.

He hovered uneasily at the window, unable to relax while this was going on. He was having second thoughts about taking money from the till for Frank, and decided he'd put one pound back in tonight. He'd try to borrow the rest from Mam. The takings had to balance with the bills Mrs Jordan gave to her customers, or Pa would accuse her of taking the money.

His father looked up and said, 'It's time you were thinking of taking on an extra hand for the holiday season.'

Louis almost told him that Frank had asked for the job. If Pa agreed to him working in the fair again, they could both relax.

'Forgotten, had you?'

'No, I've found someone. He's going to start tomorrow.'

'A bit too keen off the mark, son,' his father growled. 'No need to pay extra wages for another few weeks. We won't need him until Easter. You've got to learn to keep the expenses down.'

'I thought he could do a bit of painting first. The teashop front needs it.'

'Oh! Is it that bad? I hadn't noticed.'

Louis knew he was right to keep his mouth shut about Frank. Pa knew he'd treated him badly and he wouldn't want to be reminded.

'How's your mother?'

'I don't know,' Louis said.

'You do. She's with you.'

'She isn't, she's gone off on her own.'

'Don't tell bloody lies. She'd never be able to. You can't fool me. I'll find out sooner or later, so you might as well tell me.'

Louis said, 'Leave Mam alone, Pa. You're making her ill.'

'She's taken my silver alarm clock and the Crown Derby figures, and I want them back. They were not hers to take. That's thieving.'

'She says she took nothing but the presents you gave her.'

'Nonsense. I didn't give her that silver clock. I used it

every morning to get myself to work on time. I wound it up at night and switched it off in the mornings. It was always on my bedside table, not hers. I overslept the morning after she left me and had to send Georgio out to buy another clock, but it's ugly and unreliable. She can have that in exchange.'

Louis sat still and brooding in the chair Frank had vacated. He knew his father was winding up to a row.

'I suppose you've found rooms for her?'

'Pa, I don't want to tell you where she is. She doesn't want to see you, she wants a divorce. Why don't you—'

'Never,' he swore. 'Never, I wouldn't give her the satisfaction.'

Louis summoned up his courage. 'Pa, please send her some money. How can she live if you don't?'

'She won't get a penny out of me. You can tell her that. Not a penny.'

'Pa, she's worried stiff about money and she isn't well. A small allowance would make all the difference to her. It needn't be much – a couple of pounds a week would take away her worry.'

'She can starve in the gutter for all I care.'

'Please . . .'

'According to the law I don't have to pay her anything, because she left me. I've written to her.' He took an envelope from his pocket and propped it against the inkwell. 'I've told her I'll have her back and all will be forgiven.'

'It's gone too far this time, Pa.'

'You're a fool to take her side, but you always were a fool. What good will it do you? Or do her, for that matter? Write her off, Louis. She writes herself off.'

Louis leaped to his feet. Pa was going beyond sense.

'I can't stay and listen to this. I shall say too much and then I'll be starving in the gutter with her.'

'I'll leave this letter here for you to give to her,' Mungo called after him.

Louis rushed into the fair. For once the hurdy-gurdy music and the noise didn't lift his spirits. He was afraid he *had* said too much to Pa and now he felt overwhelmed by his parents' problems.

He walked round the amusements with intent in his step but it was all assumed. He talked to the men, trying to find some work to involve himself in, but business was slack, the talk just chitchat. Louis felt it was just as well: a session with Pa put his mind in turmoil so he couldn't concentrate.

He allowed an hour to pass before returning to his office. It cheered him to look along Marine Drive and see no sign of the Bentley parked there. He took the stairs two at a time.

Pa had left a dirty plate and a tea cup on his desk. It was only when he was piling them back on the tray that he thought of the letter Pa had told him to give to his mother. There was no sign of it, yet he'd seen Pa with a letter in his hand.

He returned the crockery to the teashop, thinking about it. He hadn't wanted to give Mam anything from his father as it would only upset her, but why had Pa changed his mind?

Mungo listened to Louis's footsteps crashing down the stairs, before turning back to the ledgers. He checked Louis's arithmetic carefully and whether the takings were up or down against previous year's figures. They were slightly up and he couldn't fault Louis's work.

He kept keys to Louis's desk and the safe on his own key ring, so he might assure himself that nothing was being hidden from him. He opened the desk drawers one by one, looking for something that might have Louis's present address on it. The contents were all to do with the business, insurance policies, wage registers and so on, and all were kept neat and tidy.

On his way here this morning, he'd called round at the boarding house where Louis used to lodge but found he had moved out. The woman said she didn't know where he'd gone, but Mungo felt sure Fanny was with him.

Mungo looked round the office. He'd set this up for his own use and made it as comfortable as possible. Once these rooms had been living quarters and there was a view over the Marine Drive to the sea. He stood looking down at the people below but it was a rough old day and there weren't many about. The original bathroom was across the passage and the other rooms were now used as storerooms.

He'd equipped the office with a filing cabinet and it now held a personal file for each of his employees, showing their addresses. He looked through them but found nothing for Louis. There was a cupboard in the alcove near the fireplace into which Mungo had had a safe fitted to put the takings in at night. It left him enough space to hang his overcoat beside it. Today, Louis's mackintosh and umbrella were there. They were still damp, so he hadn't used his car to come to work. He must be living nearby.

Mungo opened the safe. Louis knew he kept a spare key to it, but it was as well to check up on what he was keeping there. He hadn't yet been to the bank today. That made

Mungo wonder what he'd done this morning, but the amount tallied with his records for yesterday.

Mungo shivered. It was a chilly day for the time of the year. In his time, he'd had a real fire here, but Louis had had an electric fire fitted into the grate. It didn't give out much heat. He switched it off; he'd done all he needed to and might as well go.

On the spur of the moment he felt in the pockets of Louis's raincoat. He knew as soon as his fingers closed on a thick envelope that he'd struck lucky. It surprised him to find there was no address on it. He opened it and drew out a rent book in Louis's name for a house at 16 Delaney Street, Southport. The rent was fifteen shillings and sixpence a week, and a ten-shilling note and some coins were enclosed with it. It seemed Louis planned to pay his rent on the way home.

Mungo straightened up, smiling in triumph. He was carefully putting the envelope back where he'd found it when he came across Louis's key ring. It was easy to see which were his house keys and which were for his car. Mungo had always found it useful to have copies of other people's keys. He took them downstairs and asked Georgio to get a copy made of Louis's front-door key.

On the way back, he popped into the tearoom to enquire from the local woman he hired to run it the whereabouts of Delaney Street. To fill the time until Georgio came back, he ordered a pot of tea and some toast with tomato and melting cheese on top to be brought up to the office.

Mungo was pleased with his morning's work. He'd beaten them. Fanny would be with Louis, he was sure. He'd get his own back on her. The nerve, asking to be allowed to divorce him! He couldn't get over it, or that she'd switched so quickly to petitioning for a separation.

Before leaving, he picked up the letter he'd written to her. He'd deliver it in person now, and he'd get his silver clock back while he was about it. It gave him great pleasure to know he still had the upper hand with Fanny. She wasn't going to make a fool of him and get away with it. It would do both her and Louis good to know they couldn't keep anything from him.

Fanny had gone out for a little walk along the esplanade and the fresh air had made her feel better after her tummy upset. Before going home she'd gone to the shops and bought some lamb chops as a treat.

Today, Louis had said he'd come home at lunch time to see how she was, and she was peeling potatoes to make a hot dinner when the rasp of a key turning in the front-door lock surprised her, making her jump.

It could only be Louis letting himself in. 'You're early,' she called. 'I haven't started to cook yet.'

'Don't bother, I've not come for my dinner,' Mungo's voice answered.

She spun round and let out a little scream. The shock was so horribly unexpected that for a moment she was stunned.

'What d'you mean, bursting in here like this?' She was trying desperately to stand her ground. 'What d'you want?'

'To answer your letter, Fanny.' He was leering at her as he flung it on the draining board. 'I don't want to write to you via your solicitor. We haven't come to that yet, have we?'

Fanny could hardly get the words out. 'How . . . how did you find me? Surely Louis didn't . . . ?'

'Oh, he wouldn't tell me but you're fools, both of you, if you think I can't find out for myself. It just puts me to more trouble. Anyway, you asked for a quick reply and here it is. I don't know why you bother writing at all. I keep telling you, I don't want a divorce. Haven't I made it clear enough?'

'Get out,' she said. 'This is my house. I don't want you here.'

'I want the things you stole from me.'

Fanny was indignant. 'I haven't stolen anything.'

'I want my silver alarm clock.'

'You gave me that as a present years ago.'

'I certainly did not. I'm not leaving without it. I suppose it's up in your bedroom?' He made for the stairs.

'No, Mungo, you've no right.' She clawed at his jacket to keep him from going up.

'Every right.' His fist lashed out at her, she felt it cut into her cheek. 'Want some more?'

Fanny screamed and collapsed against the newel post at the bottom of the stairs. Tears were scalding her eyes. She thought she'd escaped from all this. Mungo could make her feel like a dancing doll, with him pulling all the strings. She hated to feel he controlled her, that he could do with her whatever he wanted. She listened to him going from room to room above her, taking away things that were rightfully hers. She'd reached the stage when she didn't care what he took, she just wanted him to go away without hitting her again.

She knew he was pleased with himself when he came scurrying down again.

'Just the silver clock and the Crown Derby ornaments that belong to me. That's all I've taken.'

Fanny knew she was powerless to stop him. He'd never allowed her to say no to anything.

'I don't care about your stupid clock. If it means that much to you, take it. Just get out of my house and leave me alone.'

'Come with me, Fanny,' he said, forgetting Greta briefly in his longing to have Fanny back under his control. She belonged to him and he did not like to lose his possessions. 'You'll be far more comfortable in my house than in this hovel. You're my wife, after all. I want you to stay with me. I'll help you put your things together, shall I?' He made a grab for her arm.

'No, no, Mungo,' she screamed as she grappled with him. One of the Crown Derby ornaments slipped out from his other hand to crash to smithereens on the lino.

'Now look what you've done,' he grated. 'I suppose you know how much that was worth?' She could see his anger pulsating below the surface and knew at any moment it would erupt.

'Please, just leave me alone,' she implored.

For a moment Mungo looked in two minds whether to hit her again as she cowered before him.

'Silly bitch,' he said, and the door slammed behind him.

CHAPTER NINE

LOUIS COULDN'T get Pa out of his mind. He'd waved a letter at him and asked him to deliver it to Mam. It niggled that it was no longer on his desk. One explanation was that Pa had decided to deliver it himself. Louis dismissed it as impossible, but he felt uneasy and couldn't settle to his work. It was still half an hour before his usual lunch break, but Louis decided to leave early to pay yesterday's takings into the bank and also stop at the estate agent's office to pay his rent.

As he walked up Delaney Street he took his keys from his pocket, but was surprised to see a key had been left in the front door lock. His heart began to pound with dread. Was it his mother's? No, it couldn't be. Both the keys he'd been given originally were of a silver-coloured metal, and well used. Louis felt suddenly sick. This one was brassy, new and shiny.

He turned it in the lock and found his mother in a terrible state.

'Mam!' His heart sank, he knew immediately Pa had been here. He should have come straight home when he'd first thought of it.

She was sitting on the bottom stair, trying to tell him what had happened but she couldn't get the words out and was hardly coherent. He tried to put his arms round her in a hug of reassurance but she pushed him away. Her face looked more lopsided than usual. She had a bad cut on it and what looked liked the beginnings of a black eye.

'Let me bathe that cut,' he said. Blood was dripping down from it to the collar of her dress. He went to take her hand to help her to her feet.

'Don't come near me, Mungo,' she screamed, snatching her hand away.

That scared him. 'Mam! It's me, Louis. Pa's gone. You're safe now. Safe with me.'

He helped her stand but she was unsteady on her feet. He got her as far as the kitchen where he sponged her face. He had nothing to put on her cut but iodine, and was afraid it would sting and she'd think he was hurting her. He gave her a clean tea towel to hold against her face, and took her to sit in the armchair in front of the living-room fire. It was the best he could do.

He could see she'd been preparing dinner when Pa had come. He started to cook it, thinking she might feel better if she had something to eat. Louis was furious with his father. Mam had been doing more, enjoying life again, and now Pa had tipped her back into this awful state.

He kept talking to her about the fair, about anything but Pa. He didn't want to mention him. Mam lay back and closed her eyes. Perhaps she'd be better after a little rest, after she'd had something to eat.

But when he dished up the dinner and got her to sit at the

table she stared at her plate, making no move to eat. He forked up a little, persuaded her to open her mouth but she chewed and chewed on the meat and didn't swallow. She looked unsafe on the dining chair, as though she might slide off it. Perhaps she'd be better lying on her bed for a while? A good rest would do her good. Louis was afraid he wouldn't be able to get her upstairs without help. He ran next door to fetch Ena. She too was shocked at the change in his mother. Together they got her upstairs and laid her on her bed.

'Somebody called to see her,' Ena reported. 'In a very posh car. Grey it was, and chauffeur-driven.'

'My father,' he told her, tight-lipped.

'You'll feel better after a little rest, Fanny,' Ena comforted. 'More your usual self. I'll sit here with you for a little while, shall I?'

Louis found the letter his father had brought round torn to shreds at the bottom of the stairs, together with shattered shards of china that had once been a Crown Derby figurine.

It was not difficult to guess how Pa had found their address. Louis felt devastated that he'd let this happen and knew he should have been more careful. He should have kept the rent book on him, not left it in his mackintosh pocket. He knew well enough what Pa was like.

Louis went back to the fair to make sure all was well and tell the men where he was should he be needed. When he returned home, Ena told him his mother could not be soothed, that she had alternate spasms of weeping and raving at Mungo.

'Had I better ask the doctor to call and see her?' Louis worried.

'Yes,' she said. 'He'll be able to give her something to help her settle.'

Louis ran to the telephone box in the next road and asked her doctor to visit. He came, and later on that evening an ambulance arrived to take her back to hospital.

Pa had deliberately sought Mam out, given her another hiding and frightened her so much, black depression had descended on her mind again. It was thought a further spell of rest in hospital would provide the best means of recovery.

Louis was left alone in the empty house, seething with rage every time he thought about what Pa had done to his mother. For eleven months, she'd been struggling to regain her health. Louis had been so pleased with her progress. Now he felt Pa had wiped out all that effort with one short visit, and he was livid.

Pa was petty to take her silver clock and break one of the Derby figurines so neither of them could have it. Last month he'd taken Jess from the funfair office too.

He pondered on what had made Pa come here now and do this. Of course, he was furious because Mam had walked out on him and he didn't know where she'd gone. It had robbed him of the power he'd always had over her. That much was clear enough. Pa wanted to show her he was still boss and that she couldn't escape from his clutches; he could find her wherever she went. It was his way of getting revenge.

For as long as he could remember, Louis had been telling himself he must distance himself from his father, otherwise he'd end up like him. He'd helped his mother because he'd hated to see her in such a state, but he hadn't wanted to get involved in their fighting. He'd meant to stay aloof and away from all that, but this had changed his mind.

He ached to make Pa pay for this. It was inhuman. Pa was evil; there was no fate too horrible for him.

Fear had always had a stranglehold on his family – Louis felt it like a rope round his neck. Mam had never admitted to him that she was afraid of Pa but he knew she was. Family ties were supposed to be of love, not fear.

The men in the fair were afraid of Pa too. None of them had ever admitted it either, but Louis could feel their fear when Pa came near. Nobody ever said a word against him but there were dark hints, slyly whispered asides and innuendoes. Louis had known from childhood that Pa could be violent and that he had a temper of volcanic proportions.

Louis hadn't made up the fire and it had gone out. Without Mam and Jess, the house seemed to echo with emptiness. Over the following days, he missed Mam at work too, and the men were always asking after her. He told them nothing of what Pa had done but they seemed to understand he'd caused her illness.

Louis wanted to stand up to Pa. Somebody ought to. But that would enrage Pa and he needed to stay on good terms in order to keep his job.

The days seemed to pass slowly at first. When Louis first went to visit his mother in hospital he could see she was worse than she had been last time. He was angry with Pa for doing this to her and he could think of nothing else. His anger was like a fever going round in his head all the time.

He wanted his own revenge. The need for it was building

up slowly but he couldn't make up his mind how he could achieve it. He wanted to fight Mam's battles for her, but he wasn't a fighter and Pa was.

He didn't know what to do for the best. Bobbins asked if he'd like to return to lodge with her. His own room had been taken but she had another that was vacant. Louis would have liked to as he felt lonely in the house by himself, and cooking and cleaning took time and energy.

He had no idea how long his mother would have to stay in hospital but he understood it would be months. When she was discharged, he'd have to have somewhere for her to live. He decided it would be better to keep on the house in Delaney Street.

To start with, Mam was agitated when he went in to see her.

'Mungo found me. He forced himself into our house and he had no business to do that.' Her faded brown eyes fixed on Louis's. 'I can't go back to live in that house.'

'Mam!' This problem had been at the back of Louis's mind, but he'd dismissed it. 'We've only just got the house as we want it.'

'I know, but he'll come again. I'll never feel safe there. Mungo knows where to find me. He's even got a key.'

'No, he hasn't, Mam. He left it in the front door. He took my key from my mac pocket and had it copied, but I have it now.'

'He knows where to find me. How d'you know he won't come back?'

Louis could see the terror in her face. 'He doesn't intend to, or he'd have kept the key.'

'All the same, I couldn't rest if I was there.'

Louis sighed. 'It's in such a good place, handy for the fair and the town, and you've made friends with Ena next door.' The thought of having to find somewhere else and move before Mam came out of hospital seemed a Herculean task.

His mother's eyes were filling up. 'I shake whenever I think of Mungo walking straight in.'

Louis knew the best thing was to start looking for another house right away. It would do Mam no good to take her to a house where she didn't feel safe.

When he returned to Delaney Street, Ena was watching for him at her front window. She rushed to open her front door.

'How is your mother? Come in, Louis, and have a cup of tea. I've just made a fresh pot.'

He told her Mam wanted to move house, that his father had spoiled number 16 for them.

Her face fell. 'I am sorry. Your poor mam worked hard to make next door nice.'

'We both did,' Louis said. 'I'll be sorry to move; I was just beginning to feel settled. It suited us.'

'There's an empty house at the other end of the street,' Ena said. 'That's up for rent too.'

'Is there?' Louis felt a shaft of hope.

'Would it be too near? It's only fifty yards or so away.'

'Pa wouldn't know where we'd gone, would he? I don't want to go far. I don't suppose she does, not now she knows you and the other neighbours. Who's the agent for it?'

'Same as for these houses. Same landlord too.'

Louis went to the front window and looked down the

street. 'The houses are all the same, aren't they? Is it exactly like this one?' He was thinking of the curtains Mam had made.

'I think so,' Ena said. 'Looks it from the outside.'

'I'll take a look now before I go home.' Louis was cheered. 'I could pop in to the agent tomorrow. If I only have to move up the street it won't be too bad.'

He found the house had been built as an exact copy, but Louis had had number 16 repainted and papered inside, and number 34 was badly in need of it. The rent was exactly the same.

When he told the estate agent why he needed to move, he suggested he change immediately.

'I could let you have both keys for a week at no extra rent because you've cleaned up number 16 well and it will be easier for us to rent,' he said.

Louis bought several tins of distemper, both cream and white, and sent two lads from the fair to paint the house. When it had dried, he got them to carry the furniture and fittings down from number 16. Ena took down the curtains in one house and put them up in the other.

'Thank you,' Louis said to her. 'I'm very grateful. It's been easier than I thought.'

'Tell your mam I'm not far away,' Ena smiled.

Louis was delighted to have their furniture arranged in the new house. It didn't seem quite so homely but at least he could tell Mam that Pa wouldn't know where to find her. In future, he decided, he'd keep his keys firmly on his person. He blamed himself for being careless with them, but even more he blamed Pa.

Pa used his power to get what he wanted, regardless of the harm he did to others. Anger and frustration made Louis dream up dozens of ways to hurt him, but they were all impossible. It seemed all he could do was dream about revenge.

Greta knew she was going within an inch of married love. Though Mum would be very shocked if she knew, Greta was growing more curious about what it actually entailed. For the last few weeks, Mungo had been taking her home and always after lunch he'd taken her upstairs to the bedroom he'd told her she could use.

'We won't be disturbed here, while we have a little rest,' he'd say as he locked the door.

Greta had got used to kicking off her shoes and lying down on the bed fully clothed. Sometimes, with their arms round each other, they did close their eyes and doze, but mostly he spent the hour making thrills rage through her body. This was how she'd imagined it would be when she'd fantasised about him. It no longer seemed enough – she was hungering for the whole experience. She knew Mungo wanted more too, but he always stopped as he'd promised he would.

One day their lunch-time 'rest' went on longer than usual. Mungo moved away from her and sat up. He left Greta aching with longing.

Without thinking about it, she asked, 'Couldn't we get married?'

He was smiling down at her. 'Is that what you want?'

'Yes, what about you? I do love you.'

'It's a lovely idea, but . . .' He was biting his lip.

Greta felt her confidence flow away. 'You're not sure? You don't love me enough?'

'Of course I want to, and I love you very much.' He kissed her lightly on the forehead. 'It's not that. I'm afraid I told you a fib when I said I was divorced. That's not quite the case.'

Greta could feel her stomach churning. She found it hard to believe he'd lie about that. She scrambled off the bed.

'My wife is petitioning . . .' He didn't know how much she knew about divorce and separation. 'But our case hasn't yet come before the Court, so legally that makes me still married to Fanny.'

'Married? You're still married?' Greta was alarmed. She shouldn't be doing this with a man who couldn't marry her. He'd misled her. What was her mother going to say? She was swallowing back raw disappointment.

'We can't get married then?'

'Not yet, but we will one day, I promise.'

'When? In a month or two?'

'No, it'll take longer than that. A year perhaps.'

'A year!' That seemed an age to Greta. Horror was crawling up her back.

His dark eyes were playing with hers. 'But we could get engaged.'

'But if you're already married . . .'

'I won't always be. An engagement would mean I've promised to marry you.'

'But you're married to someone else!'

'All that means is that we can't start making arrangements for the wedding just yet.'

148

'You're sure?'

'Of course I'm sure. I want to marry you, Greta. I wish I could do it straight away, but I give you my solemn promise it will happen as soon as it can.'

Greta still wasn't entirely sure but knew she'd have to be satisfied with that. 'Then let's do it.'

'Right, we'll consider ourselves engaged. We won't go back to work just yet. I'm going to take you out and buy you a ring. Then we can make it official.'

But now he'd suggested an engagement, Mungo wasn't sure it was the right thing to do. Would it make any difference to the difficulties with Fanny? Yes, it could. If Fanny thought there was any hint of adultery, she could cause him more trouble. She was showing a vicious streak he hadn't known she had. She'd turned on him and was out to squeeze as much out of him as she could.

'It might be better if we keep it quiet,' he said cautiously, and saw Greta's face fall.

'You've changed your mind?'

'No, no, of course not, but better if we don't tell everybody.'

'Not at work?'

'No, and there must be no annoucement in the press, no party, nothing like that.' Mungo was frowning as he explained why.

He was forgetting about the servants downstairs. They probably thought adultery was already taking place. What if Fanny sent Louis over to talk to them while he was out?

Greta said, 'I'll have to tell Mam. About us being engaged and you not yet divorced.'

'Yes.'

She was frowning too. 'She isn't going to like it.'

'I'll come with you,' he said. 'We'll tell her together.'

She looked agonised. 'I don't know . . .'

'Perhaps I should ask her permission to marry you?' He didn't think Ruth would have the nerve to refuse. Perhaps she'd be pleased that it would have to be put off for a time.

'Oh, Mungo, I'm not looking forward to telling her one bit.'

'The only thing to do, when you feel like that, is to get it over and done with. Come on, we'll go and choose the ring now and then go straight over to see your mother.'

Once they were sitting close together on the back seat of the Bentley, he said, 'If we're going to see your mother, we might as well go to Liverpool to get the ring. There'll be more choice there.

'Liverpool,' he said to Georgio, 'Dale Street.'

Greta was clinging to his arm. Nerves had clearly overcome her earlier excitement and she was relying on him to smooth things over with her mother. He liked that. He liked people to depend on him.

'What sort of a ring would you like?'

Greta looked half dazed. 'I haven't thought much about it. I haven't had time. Perhaps a diamond?'

'We'll see what they've got. You can try a few on.'

When he had her inside the shop and seated at the counter, she was shy and seemed almost overcome at the rings he'd asked the assistant to show her. They were sparking myriad shafts of light from the black velvet cloth laid on the counter.

'I want you to have a ring you can be proud of,' he told her, wanting it to proclaim his wealth and generosity. He'd ordered the price tags to be left on so Greta could appreciate that too.

Mungo picked out the biggest solitaire and slid it on Greta's finger.

'It's enormous,' she gasped.

The assistant was in full spiel about the importance of cut and colour as well as the carat size. He said, 'You have a dainty hand, perhaps several smaller stones would suit it better? Three in a row?'

'No,' Mungo said when it was in place, 'I don't care for that.'

He asked for sapphires to be brought. He rather fancied a sapphire. Definitely not an emerald; Fanny had had an emerald. Greta was certainly not out to get all she could. She was showing an interest in the smaller stones, but he couldn't let her have anything but the best.

'I like this one,' he said, picking up the large solitaire that had caught his eye in the first place and putting it back on her finger.

She was awed by its magnificence. 'It is lovely, but very expensive.'

It was. 'You'll be wearing it for a long time,' he told her. It had always been Mungo's way to flaunt his wealth.

Back in the car and on the way to the south side of the city where she lived, he laid her hand on his knee so they could both gaze at the ring. It really was a knuckle-duster.

'Lucky it fitted and we can show it to Mam,' she said.

The worst slums of Liverpool were said to be in the

Scotland Road area, but the meanness of Henshaw Street caught in Mungo's throat. Greta had a key to the front door but it wouldn't open.

'The bolts must be on,' she said, banging on the knocker. 'We often use the back way.'

It took time for Ruth to open it. She peered round the door with a turban covering her head and wearing a soiled pinafore. 'Oh!' She was clearly shocked to see them both.

Greta had to ask, 'Can we come in, Mam?'

'Yes, of course, sorry.' She was snatching off her working clothes and was clearly embarrassed that Mungo had caught her like this.

Ruth felt shaken to find Mungo and her daughter on her doorstep in the middle of the afternoon. Why had they come now when they were supposed to be working? Greta knew well enough she'd catch her on the hop at this time of day. They were both carrying packages, almost as though it was Christmas again.

Greta was taking off her coat and hat and divesting Mungo of his. She took them into the scullery to get them out of the way. Ruth tossed her turban and pinafore after them and closed the door. The turban always flattened her hair, she ran her fingers through it to lift it.

'Do sit down,' she said. She hadn't yet lit the living-room fire. She'd been out in the wash house and had to light the fire under the boiler there. She didn't feel the cold while she was cleaning through. Fortunately, she'd almost finished.

'Shall I light the fire?' Greta had already found the matches and was doing it. It was another cold afternoon.

'Come and sit down,' Mungo urged, taking charge of the situation. 'Both of you.'

They did so, and Ruth asked, 'What brings you here at this time?'

Mungo started. 'I've come to ask your permission to—'

Ruth noticed Greta's ring for the first time. 'Oh! My goodness! You're engaged?'

'Yes, we came to tell you,' Greta said. 'Do you like my ring?' She was holding her hand out for Ruth to inspect it.

'It's very grand,' Ruth choked. She'd never seen anyone wear such a magnificent ring before. It was the sort of ring film stars would have. It didn't seem right for her daughter to wear a diamond that must have cost a small fortune when there were so many children in the street who didn't have enough to eat. She could hear some of them playing outside now, probably without shoes on their feet.

The speed at which this engagement had happened shocked her: just a few short weeks. But she'd feared Mungo would seduce her daughter and so she should be glad he'd been honourable and offered marriage. She pulled herself together.

'It's a lovely ring, Greta.'

She couldn't say congratulations to him, she just couldn't. She was sure the whole thing must be a mistake. It had to be wrong when he was so much older. Why couldn't they both see that?

Ruth felt a wave of resentment that she'd lost two husbands in the Great War while Mungo had come through unscathed to claim a girl less than half his age. He'd said he'd been in the army – she would have liked to ask which regiment he'd been in and where he'd been sent but didn't like to.

Ruth was afraid it would seem more suitable to the neighbours if Mungo was attracted to her. He was a handsome man. She could feel herself flushing at the thought and had to ask herself if she was jealous. Perhaps she was. She asked, 'When will you be married?'

She was afraid he was going to say next week. The whole thing was moving like one of his roller coasters.

Mungo said, 'Not for some time.'

Ruth noticed then that he appeared uncomfortable.

'I'm afraid I told you a bit of a fib when we first met.' Then he was trying to tell her complicated details about divorce.

Ruth found it difficult to take it in. His divorce wasn't yet through? She was appalled. 'You're still married to someone else?' She could hardly get the words out. 'But if you are, you can't marry Greta.'

'I can't marry her yet,' Mungo said smoothly. 'But it's what I want and we'll do it just as soon as it's possible.'

Ruth was shocked. If she'd known Mungo was a married man she'd never have allowed him near Greta. She'd had her doubts about him all along. She should have been more careful. She wasn't sorry they'd have to wait. It would give Greta time to think it over. Mungo wasn't the man she'd have chosen for her. He was a real Flash Harry. Greta's father wouldn't have approved of him either. He'd ruined her reputation already . . . But there was no good making a song and dance about it now and getting his back up. With his money, he could give Greta a better life than she would otherwise have.

Last Sunday, Ruth had had a long discussion with Esther about this. For years, they'd both worked hard and struggled to earn enough for their families to live on. They agreed they'd been unable to do more than survive. Well, this would provide a way out for her daughter.

'I've brought a bottle of champagne,' Mungo was unwrapping one of the packages they'd brought. 'We have so much to celebrate.'

Ruth felt light-headed. She'd never ever tasted champagne in her life. Luckily, he'd thought to bring three glasses too or they'd have been drinking it from tumblers.

CHAPTER TEN

G RETA FELT more relaxed now Mam had agreed they could be engaged. She hadn't fussed or said anything to upset Mungo. Kenny came home from school with drizzle glistening on his red curls. She told him the news.

'Wow, that's terrific. Can I have a slice of bread and jam, Mam?'

'Yes, and put the kettle on. I'd like a cup of tea.'

Mungo stood up. 'Why don't I take you all out for afternoon tea? We could go to Fuller's Tearooms in Bold Street.'

'Ooo, yes, please,' Kenny beamed at him.

Even Mam jumped at the chance. Greta couldn't remember her ever having afternoon tea in a café. Fuller's was advertised as 'the Dainty Tearooms' and was just the sort of place to appeal to Mam.

'I feel I'm over the first hurdle,' Mungo whispered when Mam and Kenny went upstairs to change into their best clothes.

Georgio drove them there in the Bentley. Kenny was so

excited he could hardly sit still. He stared round at the other tables where well-dressed middle-aged women were speaking softly and sipping tea delicately, until Mam nudged him to remind him of his manners. Once the plates of tiny sandwiches came to the table, together with a three-tier cake stand groaning with scones, fruit cake, seed cake, cream cakes and French pastries, he gave his full attention to those.

Greta could see Mam was enjoying the treat too, though a little anxious that Kenny might eat more than was considered polite. Mungo kept pressing them all to have another cake.

'Do you think,' Kenny asked, 'I could come and work for you when I leave school?'

Mungo smiled. 'I don't see why not.'

'Can I really?' Kenny's eyes shone with pleasure. 'That would be marvellous. I'd love it.'

'When will that be?'

'At Christmas,' Ruth told him. Greta could see she was pleased too. Mam had worried about Kenny finding a job, though it was a little easier for school-leavers than it was for grown men.

'Christmas is not my busiest time, but I'll make a job for you.'

'Thank you.'

'Working in the fair is not the same as visiting it,' Mungo warned him.

'It would still be fun.' Kenny helped himself to a slice of Victoria sponge cake. 'More fun than any other job.'

'I'm glad to see you're keen.' Mungo was serious now. 'I'll

expect good time-keeping and also loyalty and honesty from you. The utmost honesty.'

'Yes,' Kenny breathed.

'If you shape up and you've got it in you, I'd want you to learn how the fair runs.'

'Oh, yes, that would be wonderful.'

'I'd move you round every six months or so. So you'd get the experience. When you can do all the different jobs, I'd have you in the office with me to learn how to keep the books, do the ordering and pay the wages. Then perhaps one day . . .'

Kenny's eyes were out on sticks. He couldn't believe his luck.

'I can't thank you enough,' Mam was saying. 'Such a weight off my mind. A real career for you, Kenny.'

'Thank you, thank you.' Kenny struggled to get beyond that. 'I'm thrilled, delighted, made up.'

Greta was too. Mungo was making all her family happy.

'What about a temporary job in your summer holidays?' he suggested. 'You could come over with Rex.'

'Could I?' Kenny had run out of words to express his pleasure. 'Could I really?'

'We're always busy in mid-summer. We need all the help we can get. Come over to get your hand in. We'll see how you shape up.'

'I will, thank you, thank you.'

Mungo smiled round the table. 'What about an ice cream to finish off?'

Kenny was the only one who accepted that. Greta could see him sighing with satisfaction.

Later, when the car drew up outside their house, Mungo suggested taking her to the early evening performance at the Empire Theatre. Never having been to a theatre before, Greta was thrilled. It was a vaudeville show and she enjoyed every minute of it.

As she undressed for bed that night, Mam said, 'It was as though he couldn't bear to tear himself away from you.'

Greta felt head over heels in love. Even going to work each morning seemed a treat because she'd see Mungo again. He continued to take her home with him for something to eat at two o'clock and then for a little rest on his bed afterwards. His lovemaking was becoming more forward and she grew more daring and let him take some of her clothes off.

It seemed to Greta that it couldn't be too wrong, not if they were engaged and, as Mungo said, they'd be arranging their wedding now, if only it was possible.

'I wish I had the courage to do what I really want,' she told him as they were getting ready to return to the fair one afternoon. She was beginning to feel she wanted the whole experience more than anything else.

'I wish you had the courage too,' he told her with a smile. 'But I've promised it won't happen until you're willing.'

'I'm worried I might have a baby,' she said.

'Don't be,' he assured her. 'I know how to avoid that. You'll be quite safe with me. I won't let that happen.'

It seemed to Greta that he must be right. He was a man of the world who would know these things.

He said, looking serious, 'I shouldn't let you do this.'

'Not go all the way?'

'You'll be compromised.'

160

'Not if we're going to get married.'

'I don't think you'll be able to put it off much longer,' he murmured, stroking her yellow hair off her forehead. 'I can sense that you ache for it as much as I do. Shall we let it happen?'

Greta said nothing but was very tempted. She didn't refuse him when a day or two later, he asked if he might. He was very gentle but her first experience rather surprised her and she didn't like it all that much. She didn't tell him, afraid he'd be disappointed in her. He seemed to thoroughly enjoy it and he told her over and over how wonderful she was and how much he loved her.

By May, Louis could see his mother was much better. She'd improved rapidly once she knew he'd moved their things into a new house. She said she was looking forward to coming home and began speaking of her own plans again.

'I've written to Mr Danvers and told him I want to go ahead with my separation from Mungo. I'll feel better when I'm no longer legally bound to him. Does he ever mention our separation?'

'I haven't seen him. He hasn't been near, not since it happened.'

'In all this time? It's been weeks . . .'

'Nearly three months,' Louis said.

'Don't you go over to have your dinner with him on Sundays?'

'Not any more. I don't want to see him. Not after what he did to you.'

Louis couldn't remember a time when Pa hadn't visited

the Southport fair every week or ten days. He was glad to be left alone. He didn't want to see him and it meant Pa wouldn't find out he'd employed Frank Irwin again. If he came, Louis would have to hide his real feelings about him.

He said, 'I wonder if Pa's ashamed of what he did?'

His mother was biting her lip. 'He's never ashamed of anything he does. But what about your job, Louis? You need to keep that.'

'I'm trying to get another. I've been applying for jobs for weeks now.'

'Any luck?' He could see from his mother's face that she'd be thrilled if he could get away from Pa.

He shook his head. 'No, there aren't many employers looking for new staff. I was interviewed by a soft drinks manufacturer but that was a fortnight ago and no job offer has come. It's difficult right now.'

'You mustn't upset your father. You have been careful?'

'Like I said, I haven't seen him, but I've been running the fair just as always.'

Louis knew he had to work for Pa in order to live and to help Mam with her expenses, but he was scared of Pa, always anticipating trouble.

By the end of May, Louis thought his mother seemed almost her old self. She even had a little colour in her cheeks and the sister on the ward spoke of sending her to a convalescent home, so she'd be really well when she finally came home.

'I'll have to get a job then,' Mam said. 'No way I can avoid that now.'

Louis nodded his agreement. Mam was having to use

some of her savings to pay her hospital bills. 'You can come back to your job in the fair. It'll get you used to working again. Employing you under a different name hid it from Pa last time. He never did find out.'

'I'll do that to start with but I don't want to work for Mungo.'

'Neither do I,' Louis said.

'I'm going to try and find something else. I hate him.'

Louis shook his head. 'That's difficult, Mam.'

'I'm going to try,' his mother sighed. 'And I've decided I'm going to try and get Jess back. I've been thinking about her a lot since I came here. Why would he want her? He never liked her much.'

During her last weeks in hospital, Fanny had been able to think clearly about Mungo and see him for what he was. The money he'd used to set up the fair at New Brighton had come from her father. Mungo had cheated them both to get it. He'd abused her for years and now he was refusing to pay her even a small allowance to live on. He was a man who always wanted his own way, who wanted to dominate everybody and bend them to his will.

The men who worked his roundabouts were strong and brawny, often rough-spoken and were given to swearing. Mungo was not a popular boss; he controlled these tough men by making them fear both his anger and the possibility that he might give them the sack.

An employee of his had only to step out of line, show too much aggression or resentment, and Mungo would dismiss him on the spot. Any sign of general anarchy and Mungo would sack the ring leader, bringing the dissent to a halt. In the present economic depression they hung on to their jobs.

Fanny knew she had their sympathy but they couldn't let Mungo see that. Everyone feared his whiplash tongue. Anger was a weapon he used against everyone. Like Fanny, many were wary of him, always on the alert for anything in his manner that might signal the approach of another bout of temper. Like her, they were only too ready to back down and be coerced into doing what Mungo wanted.

Fanny realised now that the more often she gave in to Mungo, the more she tried to keep the peace, the more outrageous he became. It made him feel powerful and showed him he could control her.

Greta was happy with her new job, though she found it unsettling to have Rex working in the fair too. He often came to speak to her in slack moments. She looked up and saw him coming towards the ticket booth, his finely chiselled features set and serious.

'What's this I hear about you being engaged to Mungo?' he said. 'I thought you didn't want to marry anyone.'

'I've changed my mind,' she told him. 'It's a free country.'

He didn't look happy. 'Is it because he can afford to buy you a diamond the size of a brick?'

Greta felt the heat run up her cheeks and slid her left hand down where he couldn't see it. She felt guilty for the next hour because she'd hurt Rex's feelings and she wondered if there was some truth in what he'd said.

But apart from that, she found the whole atmosphere of the fair jolly. The lights were on all day, flashing and flickering as the roundabouts gyrated. Against the background roar of engines, there was the crack of rifle fire, the odd scream of pretended terror from the ghost ride or peal of raucous laughter from the hall of mirrors. The hurdy-gurdy music bounced off the tin roof and made her want to dance. With so many people around who were out to enjoy themselves, it was impossible not to feel the fun.

On warm days, the front of the building could be slid open, allowing the delicious scents of the fish-and-chip shop on one side and the doughnuts cooking on the other to drift in.

Compared with the laundry, selling tickets for the rides was a pleasant job, but Greta found working on the refreshment bar more interesting. Agnes Watts, the woman in charge, was in her forties and immensely fat. She wanted to mother everybody, especially Greta. She showed her how to cut ten slices of equal size from the blocks of solid ice cream and slide wafer biscuits each side of the slices. There was a drum of softer ice cream with a scoop for the cones – one scoop for the penny cone, two scoops for the twopenny.

Greta immediately felt a member of the staff when she put on the white overall and cap. There were also little packets of fancy biscuits, bars of chocolate, packets of potato crisps and bottles of pop to sell. The fair was usually busy and they were kept on the go, but when the number of customers fell off, Agnes would gossip to anyone willing to listen. She was good-humoured and had a loud voice, which attracted the other staff over for a chat when they were slack. To her friends, she introduced Greta as Mungo's girlfriend.

'He's picked out a real pretty one this time, hasn't he?' she'd smile. They'd look Greta up and down and agree.

The staff talked about Mungo all the time. They asked Greta about his house and his garden. She tried not to describe it too well because she was afraid Mungo wouldn't want them to know these things, but Agnes lapped up every detail. They talked about his car, his business, his divorce and his wife and son.

'Don't tell him we said that,' they'd urge, as another anecdote came out. 'He'll be cross and we don't want the sack. This is a good place to work. He pays top whack on the wages and it's fun here, isn't it?'

Greta got to know and like the other people working there. This afternoon, she'd been making up two twopenny cones when she heard Agnes greeting an elderly woman customer like a long-lost friend. She had unruly grey hair and one long grey whisker curling on her chin.

'He's taken on extra help?' She was smiling at Greta. 'He wouldn't do it for me, though I told him I needed it.'

'This is Greta.' Agnes dropped her voice. 'His new girlfriend.'

'His? My goodness! Can't he pick them?'

'Florrie used to work here,' Agnes told Greta.

'Until Mr Masters sacked me,' she said.

'Why did he do that?' Greta knew she shouldn't ask. Mungo would call this gossip.

'She was too friendly with Fanny for her own good,' Alf Parry guffawed. 'Talked to her too much when she worked here.'

'The boss didn't like me getting the lowdown.' Florrie laughed too. 'Didn't want any of us to know.'

'You'd better watch yourself,' Alf advised Greta.

She asked, 'What didn't he want you to know?'

Alf pulled a face. 'He knocked Fanny about for years, but I suppose you know that already?'

Greta felt the strength ebbing from her knees. 'Knocked Fanny about? How d'you mean?'

'Belted her, punched her, hurt her. She said he was violent.'

Greta shivered. She couldn't believe that. She'd found him tender and loving, and he'd gone out of his way to be generous and kind to her family. Very generous. No, he'd never belt anyone.

Alf said, 'You watch out, love. He's a hard man. You could be playing with fire.'

'I hope you know what you're letting yourself in for,' Florrie said. 'Here, Agnes, give us a packet of Smith's crisps.'

Greta couldn't get what she'd heard out of her mind. It seemed such a vindictive thing to say about Mungo.

That evening, over their dinner, she told him what she'd heard. She saw the telltale crimson flush run up his neck but he seemed more sorrowful than angry.

'That's defamatory,' he said sadly. 'Slander. I do wish they wouldn't upset you like this.'

Greta asked, 'It's Fanny's fault? Is she to blame for these things being said?'

He sighed heavily. 'I can't blame her. Fanny had a nervous breakdown. She's suffered from psychiatric illness for years. I've had to protect her, but it's been hard for us both.'

Greta got up from her seat to give him a hug and a kiss. She felt overwhelmed with sympathy for him. A sick wife like

167

that, needing constant support, would be a heavy burden for anyone.

Mungo stood in his office rattling the change in his trouser pockets as he looked down at his fair. He was pleased with the way his business was holding up in the present depression. Youngsters wanted to enjoy themselves and if they managed to earn a few pennies they were rushing to spend them on his amusements.

His New Brighton site was exceeding his wildest hopes, and Prestatyn was doing well too. It was the Southport fair that was giving him a problem. It was paying its way at the moment but there was no doubt he'd need to find another site to replace it within the next year.

At Prestatyn he had a long lease that gave him no worries, but at Southport the lease had only another eighteen months to run and he'd been told by the Council that it would not allow him to carry on his business there after that. Funfairs, it seemed, were not in keeping with the character of the town.

Mungo had received permission to open a funfair there during the Great War. It was attracting day-trippers from Liverpool, who tended to be rowdy and lowered the tone of the town.

Southport had pretensions. Merchants who made a fortune in Liverpool moved out and built themselves big houses in the more select town. Lord Street, its main shopping area, had smart and glossy shops. The inhabitants were, on the whole, the well-to-do retired, who did not seek their fun in fairs. It seemed now that some of the front at Southport would be redeveloped.

Mungo knew he'd have to find himself another site in time to move his attractions when his lease in Southport was up.

Louis thought they discussed every aspect of the business, but nowadays Mungo told him only what it was good for him to know. All the time the Southport fair remained open, Mungo wanted his staff – and that included Louis – to believe they had permanent jobs. If they thought otherwise, he'd find the best of them seeking work elsewhere and leaving before he was ready.

He thought he might eventually move Louis to the new site, or he might groom Rex Bradshaw to manage it. He'd see how things went.

Suitable sites for a funfair were few and far between and Mungo was anxious to find somewhere before he had to close the one at Southport down. First, it needed to be in a town that attracted holiday-makers, and the site needed to be in the middle of the town, preferably on the sea front and amongst other facilities for those bent on amusing themselves.

Mungo no longer enjoyed long drives in the Bentley on his own. Over the lunch table, he said to Greta, 'Would you like a trip out this afternoon?'

'Instead of work? I'd love it.'

'We'll go up to Blackpool,' he said. 'Have a look round the funfairs there and call in at Morecambe too.'

'Lovely.' Greta was thrilled. 'Phyllis had a holiday in Blackpool last summer. She said it was a wonderful place.'

When they got there, Mungo walked Greta up and down the promenade, looking inside every amusement arcade and round every funfair. Of course, Blackpool was the jewel in the crown. It drew workers from the mill towns in their thousands, but other people had established funfairs there already. After a lot of thought, he had to conclude that he was too late. The competition would be enormous.

He was anxious to find another site soon and a week later he suggested another trip to Greta.

'I need to check on my fair at Prestatyn. Why not come along with me for the ride? We could go on and take a look at Rhyl and possibly Llandudno too, if we have time.'

It wasn't Mungo's way to discuss his business affairs. He hadn't to Fanny and he didn't intend to involve Greta. He neither wanted nor needed another person's opinion.

At the Prestatyn fair, Mungo checked through the books and spent a good deal of time talking to Peter, his manager there, about improving the business. Carpenters were erecting a new shooting gallery in one corner. The rifles were already on order and Peter had drawn up orders for toys and ornaments to be given as prizes. Mungo was adding to them before he signed the orders.

It was a fine but sunless afternoon as he and Greta drove on to Llandudno. There was a strong breeze and it wasn't warm. At the sea front, Mungo pulled Greta's hand round his arm and walked her along. There weren't many people on the prom and even fewer on the sands.

'This town reminds me of Southport,' he frowned. 'A sedate place for the elderly. Not the best clientele for a funfair. Let's go back and look at Rhyl.'

Mungo could feel the different atmosphere in Rhyl as soon as they got out of the car. It was a brash place, with advertisements plastered everywhere touting concert parties and other amusements. It pleased him and he set off with Greta to inspect the sea front. There were more ice-cream sellers, more vans selling cups of tea and more litter than in Llandudno.

'It's just as chilly and overcast here but there are more people out and about,' Greta said. 'Even one or two swimming.'

'They're younger and the shops and arcades are busier. This is more the sort of town I'm looking for.' Mungo was enthusiastic.

The promenade was a long one and they'd gone some way before he saw the shabby buildings with several 'For Sale' signs plastered on them. Mungo slowed his step, feeling a prickle of excitement. The buildings were actually on the beach side of the promenade, which couldn't be better. He craned his neck. They seemed to rise straight up from a narrow strip of sand, which was lapped by a greyish sea.

Greta was still hanging on to his arm. 'You seem very interested in this place.' She was laughing up at him. 'Are you hoping to open another fair here?'

Mungo was startled that she'd guessed what he was doing. He'd started to pace out the length of the site but had lost count of his steps. Although he'd made up his mind to keep the closure of the Southport fair to himself, here he was betraying what he was doing to Greta. He kept his business affairs very much separate from his home life.

But he didn't think she'd understand fully anyway, so he smiled and said, 'When I see a "For Sale" sign on a building or a piece of land, I can't help weighing it up as a possible site.'

'If you did set up a fair here, it isn't very far from Prestatyn and you could check on both on the same afternoon,' Greta pointed out.

He was surprised again. That had been his first thought too. Greta was sharper than he'd realised. All the more reason to keep his own counsel on this.

They were nearing the edge of town when he made up his mind. He couldn't concentrate properly with Greta hanging on to him like this.

He said rather awkwardly, 'There's something I want to do,' and pushed a couple of pound notes in her pocket. 'You go shopping or get yourself a cup of tea or something. I'll meet you back at the car at half-past four.'

He headed into the town; he'd done his homework before setting out and had the address of an estate agent specialising in business premises. He didn't know the town so he took a taxi. The agent, a youngish man who never stopped giving out facts and figures about the town and the property, seemed keen to have a possible buyer and drove him in his own car to look round it.

Everything he saw and heard made Mungo more sure he'd found the site he was looking for. In the last century, there'd been a fish market here. Two moles had been built to make a small harbour where the fishing boats could tie up and unload their catch, but during the Great War they'd been damaged in a storm and the fishing boats had had to go elsewhere.

After the war, the town of Rhyl grew, attracting day-trippers and youngsters looking for fun. The site had been used as a terminus for charabancs for a time, but more space had been needed for that.

'These buildings are almost derelict,' Mungo said.

'They're mostly still watertight,' the agent assured him. 'They've been used to store boats over the last few years.'

The town stretched away on both sides of the site and, being on the sea front, it was prime property. The asking price was high but Mungo decided it was ideal for his purpose. When the Southport fair had to close, he could move all his attractions and open up here.

The buildings would need work, but the ground round them had been turned into hard standing for the charabancs and would do equally well for outdoor roundabouts. He imagined a much smarter building on this site, large enough not only to house all his equipment from Southport but to add more. Rhyl was the sort of seaside town that was crying out for a funfair.

Mungo was pleased the site was offered for sale. There'd been a time when he'd thought a lease equally good, with the advantage of not having to fork out capital, but after this problem in Southport he didn't trust leasehold property. This would be a sound investment.

He'd need to get a surveyor in and set the building work in hand as soon as the sale was complete. He was delighted with his find, but the less he said about it at this stage the better.

CHAPTER ELEVEN

GRETA THOUGHT it was wonderful to be taken to visit seaside resorts up and down the coast, when she was being paid to work. She'd hardly been out of Liverpool before, and it was a great treat to see other places.

While Mungo had been busy with his manager at Prestatyn, she'd walked round the amusements to compare that fair with the New Brighton one. Then she'd had a short stroll along the promenade. They'd got back in the car for the drive to Rhyl, and Greta expected to have Mungo's company for the rest of the afternoon.

It surprised her to be left on her own again in Rhyl, and upset her a little to think Mungo was doing something he didn't want her to know about. She watched him set off briskly through the streets behind the promenade while she dawdled, looking in the shops.

His business took him a little longer than he'd expected. While she waited for him, Greta bought ice creams for herself and Georgio, and sat beside him on the running board to eat hers, as she didn't feel she could risk dropping ice cream on the thick carpet or leather upholstery inside. For once, Georgio unbent sufficiently to talk to her about his ninety-year-old mother. They both lived in the flat over the garage. Mungo had told Greta that Georgio's mother had borne him out of wedlock at the age of twenty-seven, that neither had ever married and they were devoted to each other.

Georgio's hair was coarse and still almost black. It curled up over the edge of his uniform cap. His dark eyes could be cold and flint-like and he gave the impression of not being very bright. He did what Mungo ordered him to do; otherwise he stood outside the New Brighton fair and acted as doorman. If any of the youths became too unruly or started a fight, Georgio would be called in as security and would evict them.

Greta thought he was also there to protect Mungo, should his men at the fair turn nasty. There was an air of menace about the set of Georgio's heavy shoulders. He was not the sort of man anyone messed with.

When Mungo finally appeared, he was rubbing his hands with satisfaction and seemed in high spirits. Greta was full of curiosity about what he'd been doing.

'Did you manage to look inside those buildings?' she asked. 'Are you going to buy that site?'

'It depends,' he told her, 'on a lot of things.' She could see he didn't want to tell her. He changed the subject and on the journey home he didn't stop talking.

'The Prestatyn fair's going very well. I'm very pleased with Peter. He's trustworthy and has some good ideas – plenty of energy too, and he's always ready to try out something new.'

'He's been working for you for a long time?'

'Must be about fifteen years now, ever since he left school. He used to come in in the summer holidays before that.'

'He must like funfairs as much as you do.'

'Peter always knew what he wanted.' Mungo paused. 'A girl like you, working in a laundry and you say you didn't like the job – that surprised me. Didn't you know what you wanted?'

'I knew I didn't want that.'

'You should have thought about what you *did* want. There must have been something.'

Greta smiled. 'I used to go to the pictures with Phyllis and we'd fantasise about how marvellous it would be to work on a film set.'

'You wanted to be an actress?'

'We'd have loved that! Even to be a bit player. Work would have been fun then but we knew it was never-never land, just a dream.'

'I can't see why. Lots of girls do it. You could have.'

'I wouldn't know where to start.'

'There are drama schools to teach you.'

Greta shook her head. 'They cost money. I couldn't even think of that.'

'You were earning something.'

'Mostly it went to Mam, to help with food and rent.'

'Greta, you aren't selfish enough. You should have gone for what you wanted.'

She shook her head. 'That would have been chasing rainbows, but there were other jobs in the real world I'd have liked. To work in an expensive clothes shop, or in one of the big Liverpool department stores would have pleased me. I tried hard, went round asking, but no luck.'

'You like clothes?'

'Love them.'

'I must take you out and buy you some.'

Greta wondered what Mum would think of that. Now they were engaged, could she, Greta, accept presents like that from him?

She smiled. 'The laundry was advertising for girls and took me on straight away, but I went on applying for jobs, writing letters every weekend. I suppose we all accept our lot in time.'

'No,' he said. 'I've always gone on fighting for what I want.'

To Greta, there seemed to be no end to Mungo's generosity. A few days later, he said, 'We must get you fitted out with some new clothes.'

'For the wedding?'

'Yes, certainly for that but I meant for you to wear now. Something a little smarter.'

Greta was surprised because she'd been wearing her best clothes to work. She'd wanted to look her best for him and the fair wasn't like the laundry where she'd been handling dirty linen.

'With the right clothes you'd look like a film star. More fetching than Mary Pickford. I'd like you to wear clothes to enhance your figure,' he said.

'You mean these don't?'

'They don't make the most of it.'

'I don't have much of a figure.'

'You have the daintiest figure I've ever seen. Tiny, yet quite voluptuous. There are clothes that would do much more for you.'

One afternoon, instead of going back to the fair, he took her out to the biggest department store in Birkenhead. She found he had very definite ideas about what he wanted her to wear. His taste ran to dresses cut lower in the bodice than she'd have chosen for herself, and which clung to her. He liked her to wear high-heeled shoes.

'If you've got it, flaunt it,' he told her. He insisted on buying her a very expensive green silk dress, saying, 'It matches your eyes and makes you look even more gorgeous.'

He started taking her out in the evenings. He bought the most expensive seats in the Liverpool theatres, and they ate in the best hotels and restaurants.

'I want to show you off,' he said. 'You're so beautiful.'

If when they were out they passed a shop window full of women's clothes, he would stop and study them and tell her whether he thought they would suit her or not. Sometimes he took her back the next day to try a garment on. It surprised Greta even more to find him picking out silk underwear for her, all of the highest quality.

Within a short time she had many new outfits and drawers full of underwear; fashionable and expensive clothes she could never have afforded to buy herself. He wanted her to keep them at his house, rather than take them home. Greta thought it would be as well if she did so. Mam would not approve of him buying her knickers, especially not the new French knickers she now had.

However, she did occasionally wear her new things when

she went home. She was getting dressed one morning, when Mam had noticed her underwear.

'No elastic in the legs?' She'd been amazed.

'These are the very latest style,' Greta had said.

'Where did you buy those?'

'They came from Lewis's,' she'd replied.

'Things are dear there.' Mam had felt the silky material between her fingers and thumb. Greta had known she'd be horrified if she knew Mungo had chosen them for her and paid for them.

It was June and the weather was noticeably warmer. Greta had spent previous summers incarcerated in the laundry, where the heat had been stifling and sweaty. On some days, she'd found it almost unbearable. This summer was going to be very different.

She started each morning leaning over the rail of the ferry boat as it took her down to the Mersey estuary. Almost always there was a fresh breeze off the Irish Sea and she could watch the cavalcade of ships large and small from all over the world nosing their way up to the docks.

Greta disembarked on the New Brighton pier, which had a pavilion at the end where band concerts and pierrot shows were given several times daily. Holiday-trippers were already thronging the refreshment rooms and buying peppermint rock and ice cream from the shops.

By mid-morning, the donkeys were tethered in a straight line ready to give rides to children along the beach. There were miles of promenade and golden sands, and she could see the hills of Wales in the distance. The doors along the front of

Mungo's Pleasure Arcade were kept wide open and the breeze blew into the booth where Greta sold tickets for the rides. The atmosphere generated by the crowds it attracted was lovely.

Rex Bradshaw could still make her feel uncomfortable when they came face to face. He'd let her know he strongly disapproved of her engagement and of allowing Mungo to take her to his home for lunch. She knew it upset Rex to see them together, and was sorry they couldn't remain friends.

Greta was glad their hours of work were different and she didn't have to travel to and from work with him. She knew Rex was watching her – she'd looked up several times to find his gaze on her – and it embarrassed her. He helped out on the swingboats if he had no repair work to do, and they were directly opposite the ticket booth.

She avoided him whenever she could but everybody could see whether she was busy in the booth or waiting for more customers. When she saw Rex coming across to the ticket booth she wanted to curl up inside, dreading to hear him warn her again about being alone with Mungo when she knew she was already a wife to him in everything but name.

She told herself nobody but Mungo knew that. It wasn't something people talked about. Mam would be terribly shocked. Greta could hardly believe she'd been so daring herself, and she was still nervous that there might be consequences. Mungo told her it was impossible when he was taking great care to avoid a pregnancy by using French letters. She really loved him. She'd never felt like this about a man before. He had only to touch her arm to cause thrills to zigzag through her. She really looked forward to being alone with Mungo in the bedroom now.

To head Rex off she smiled and said, 'I don't understand where people get all this money to spend on having a good time. Not when we found it so hard to make ends meet and there's so many on the dole.'

'It's not the families on the dole that come here.'

'They can't, not when it pays only seventeen shillings a week for a man and another nine to keep his wife.'

'It's the youngsters that come,' Rex said, looking round. 'It's easier for school-leavers to get work as their wages are lower. I suppose if their fathers are in work too they'll have cash to spend on themselves.'

'There's always some who spend more freely than others.'

A girl was coming to buy tickets so Rex had to move away. Greta sighed with relief.

After lunch that day, Mungo suggested a visit to the Tower Funfair. Once there had been a tower in New Brighton that had been higher than the tower in Blackpool, but it had had no maintenance during the years of the Great War, and had now been demolished. There was still a ballroom and a theatre, and every summer a funfair opened in the tower grounds.

'I want to see if they have anything new this season,' he smiled. 'It provides competition. I'm sure it does well on sunny days and hot nights, but when it rains all their customers come running down to us.'

'Everything looks fresh and recently painted.' Greta thought it attractive. 'It's bigger than yours?'

'Yes, quite a bit bigger. I can't compete with these high roller coasters, but this one can only earn during the four summer months.'

Mungo's workers were already talking about their summer holidays. If they'd worked for him for a year, he allowed them to take a week off on full pay. They had to take turns to do this.

He said to Greta, 'Will you stand in for Dorothy when she takes her holiday? Do her afternoon and evening shift?'

'Yes, of course, I'll work whenever I'm needed.'

She could see Mungo watching her closely.

He added, 'When you do, it might be better if I gave you a bed for the night to save you going home late.'

Greta said sharply, 'Mam wouldn't want me to do that.' She knew her mother was already uneasy about the time she spent alone with Mungo.

He looked apologetic. 'I know, Greta, I'm sorry. But it could be very late. Ten is our official closing time, but it's often much later at the weekends. If the customers want to stay, I don't turn them out.'

'No.'

She'd heard Rex had been one of the first to leave the other night and he'd had to run to catch the last ferry. It had been midnight when he'd reached Pier Head.

'Explain it to your mam,' Mungo said. 'She won't want you out late on your own.'

'But I won't be on my own. Rex will be going home at the same time.'

'So he will.' Mungo was frowning. 'I'd love to have you stay all night with me and it seemed a good reason.'

Greta was tempted. It could seem a long journey home when she was tired.

'Think about it,' he urged. 'It's a busy time of the year,

and once the holidays start we all have to double up. I might have to sell tickets myself in the mornings. It'll ruin our little routine.'

'Mam would hate me to stay,' Greta told him. 'She'll see it as proof that I'm sleeping with you. She'll say my reputation is tarnished.'

'I know,' he sympathised. 'I feel very guilty about that. I wish I could marry you now.'

Rex Bradshaw threw back his bedclothes and began to dress twenty minutes earlier than usual. He was worried about Greta. He'd hoped she'd be his wife one day but here she was, engaged to Mungo.

He ached for Greta. He saw her every day and couldn't stop his eyes searching her out across the fair, but she no longer seemed interested in him. To be honest, she'd told him she wasn't even before she'd taken up with the boss, but Rex felt he had reason to be upset. If it weren't for Mungo, she'd have eventually turned to him, he was sure of it. They'd always shared everything and been the best of friends.

He loved Greta and couldn't bear the thought of her being married to Mungo, but even worse was the feeling that Mungo was playing with her. Rex was afraid she was going to be hurt.

He was very grateful to have a job; though he would enjoy it more if he was not so unhappy about his boss. He was beginning to dislike him, though Mungo had always been pleasant and generous to him. He tried not to feel jealous, though he felt a profound longing for the days before Mungo had come into their lives.

Gossip about Mungo was rife amongst his employees, especially since Greta started to wear his engagement ring. Nothing was said openly – they all valued their jobs too much to speak out – but Mungo's wife had worked alongside them for years and was more popular than her husband. They took her side, and disapproved of his picking such a young girl to take her place.

Nobody was expecting Mungo to marry Greta. He couldn't – he still had a wife, though she'd run away from him. They all knew he'd been knocking her about for years. They reckoned the time would come when Greta would want to run away from him too. They believed Mungo had compromised her and had ruined her reputation. It was easy for a rich man to turn a young girl's head. It wasn't right that he should ruin a girl's life for his own pleasure. He was exploiting Greta and they wanted to help her.

Rex sat on the edge of his bed for a moment, remembering when nine-year-old Greta had been left in his charge because both their mothers were at work. She'd walked miles with him to the recreation ground and they'd had a fine time on the swings until she'd fallen off and cut her elbow badly. She'd cried, and to comfort her he'd put his arms round her and got a goodly amount of her blood on his shirt. Then he'd walked her to the Southern Hospital where they'd put stitches in her arm. Ruth had praised him for taking care of her.

Rex glanced at his alarm clock: it was gone eleven o'clock and his mother was out working in the greengrocer's on Balfour Road. The house was cold and empty. He made himself a cup of tea and set about making some sandwiches to take to work. Mam had provided his favourite, a pot of bloater paste, for this.

He usually put off eating brunch until near to one o'clock – that way he didn't feel so hungry when he was at work – but today he meant to have a word with Ruth before he went, so he set about making his main meal. He fried a sausage and an egg and made some fried bread.

How he wished he could take care of Greta now. She'd never been in greater danger and he wanted to protect her from Mungo, but he could think of no way he could do that on his own. He'd tried to talk to her about going home with the boss at lunch time, but he'd just embarrassed them both. Rex thought perhaps her mother would have more influence. When he'd eaten and cleared up he crossed the road to talk to her.

Ruth was waiting for Kenny to come home from school. Rex had forgotten about Kenny and this was not a subject anybody would want to have a child listening to, so he wasted no time before starting.

'It's about Greta,' he said. 'I feel I've got to warn you, Mungo's taking advantage of her.'

He saw the colour fade from Ruth's face, leaving her looking ill.

'He likes to have her working for him – well, that's fair enough. The trouble is, he takes her home with him at two o'clock. They're often missing for hours. Everybody at the fair is talking about it. They're saying she's his mistress.'

He saw Ruth run her tongue round her lips to moisten them. 'Rubbish,' she said hotly. 'Greta would never do anything wrong.'

Rex understood. No mother wanted to think her daughter was free with those sort of favours.

'I'm afraid we all think it's happening. I'd feel so much happier if she wasn't working there.'

'But she is, Rex, and she says she loves the job.'

Rex left hurriedly when he saw Kenny come running up the back yard. He was kicking himself now for opening his mouth. He'd upset Ruth and he doubted if anything would change Greta's mind. For the first time she had a job she was enjoying and in this day and age, nobody walked out of a job like that. She'd be lucky to get another.

Ruth busied herself ladling out two bowls of soup. Most people didn't regularly have soup for their midday meal once the days grew warm, but it was the cheapest thing she could make to give Kenny a satisfying lunch.

Her head was in a whirl. Greta had told her last night that her hours of work were changing so she could cover Dorothy's holiday. Now Rex had shown his concern.

She'd said, 'Mungo has offered me a room in his house next week, so I don't need to come home late at night.'

Her face still had the innocent bloom of childhood, but Ruth had said sharply, 'I don't like you staying with him overnight. It isn't right. I think you should come home.'

'I want to stay, Mam.' She'd sounded stubborn and wouldn't meet her gaze.

Ruth had had a sinking feeling in her stomach. 'I think you should come home, Greta.'

'It will be far less tiring for me to stay there. I won't be alone in the house with him, Mam. There are two servants living in. I'll be perfectly all right.'

Ruth was afraid that what Rex had told her was true. It seemed to confirm that Greta was already his mistress. Mungo knew how to get his way with her and Ruth felt she could no longer influence what her daughter did. She was fearful for her.

She worried about it all afternoon. She'd meant to ask Greta outright if what she'd surmised was true, but when she came home in the evening she couldn't. Was it better to suspect something or to know it for certain?

She blamed Mungo. He knew exactly what he was doing and he knew how wrong it was. He should take care of Greta, not use her for his own ends. He was not a suitable person for Greta to be involved with.

Ruth blamed herself too. She should not have allowed it to happen. She should have been stronger; should have ordered Greta to come home. But what could she do now? Sex was something she'd never mentioned to her daughter. Her situation was so dangerous. What if . . . ?

All evening, Ruth felt the unspoken question between them like a barrier. When they went to bed, Ruth was unable to sleep but Greta had no difficulty.

The next morning over breakfast, Ruth asked, 'Will you come home on Sunday?'

'I haven't thought that far ahead,' Greta said. 'The fair opens so I might have to work. My day off has been Sunday but Dorothy has Mondays.'

'Then we won't see you till Monday?' Mam was chewing on her lip.

'I don't know. I'll have to talk to Mungo and let you know.'

More than anything else now, Ruth wanted see Greta safely married. She comforted herself with the thought that Mungo could give her a much better life than she'd had working in that laundry. That is, if he really meant to marry her; if he really did love her.

CHAPTER TWELVE

FANNY MASTERS dressed herself carefully in her cubicle at the Formby convalescent home. It was 10 July – she'd circled the date in her diary some time ago. Today she was going home. She looked much better, more normal, and she felt euphoric. As she powdered her nose and combed her hair she couldn't stop smiling into the mirror. This time she was cured and she wouldn't be coming back, not ever.

She went to the window to watch for Louis driving in, and laughed out loud to see his Austin Seven already parked outside. Seconds later he was coming upstairs to give her a heartening hug.

'I'm all ready.' She felt quite excited. He took her case while she went to say goodbye to the staff. They had been kind and had made her think positively.

It felt marvellous to walk out into the bright sunny day and get into Louis's car. This was real life. She was never going to buckle under the weight of it again.

Fanny sat in the narrow seat beside her son, twisting so she could watch him drive. She said, 'I've so looked forward to this moment. I feel I've been shut away for an age.'

Louis glanced at her. 'You're better now, that's what matters.' Clearly he didn't want to remind her it had been four long months.

'I'm cured this time, Louis. I'm not going to let Mungo get at me again. I blame him for my illness and for taking my father's money to buy the fair in his own name. He's done me down. I've had plenty of time to think about it all, and I've decided I'm going to get my own back.'

Louis said, 'That's fighting talk, Mam.'

'I'm going to get a job and I'm going to stand on my own feet.'

'No need to rush things. You can spend a few days getting used to being back home.'

As Louis turned into Delaney Street and drove slowly past the house that used to be theirs, Fanny told herself she'd been silly to make such a fuss about returning to live there. She could do it; she felt strong enough for anything now.

Louis pulled up further down the street. 'Pa won't know where you are now, but it's still Delaney Street. Ena's just a few doors down.'

'I've put you to a lot of trouble, Louis. I'm sorry.'

'It'll be worth it if you can settle here.'

'I will. I'm cured, I told you.'

Fanny went from room to room, taking it all in. 'I've been curious about this house. It looks almost the same. But not the grate.'

'Different coloured tiles round it, that's all.'

'And no Jess. That's going to be the hard part. I miss her still.'

'Once you get back to work, you'll have less time to think of Jess. Less time to look after her too.'

'I want her back, Louis. I won't be really happy until I get her back and until I've got even with Mungo.'

'Much better if you forget Pa and concentrate on settling down and getting back in your stride. Perhaps you'd like to start at the fair next week?'

Fanny smiled. 'You're encouraging me to do that?'

'You understand all there is to know about fairs. You'll soon find your feet again.'

'I'm sure I will.'

Fanny was delighted to be out and about. She spent a week walking round Southport, glorying in the busy shopping streets, the handsome public gardens and the sea shore. She visited Bobbins and Ena, and both told her she was looking well. She felt full of energy and took over the housekeeping from Louis. She also went to see Mr Danvers, her solicitor, and learned he was waiting to hear when her case would be heard.

The following week, Louis took her to the fair. She'd expected to go back on the books as Daisy Parker.

'We'll call you Betty Rowlands this time,' Louis said. That sobered Fanny up for a while. It must mean he was taking precautions so that if Mungo did discover her here, he wouldn't be able to tie up the whole story. But to be working again, even if it was only for four hours a day to start with, made her feel she was back in the swing of life. She felt a new woman.

'You really are cured this time, Mam,' Louis beamed at her. 'You're back on track in a very short time. You've achieved what you wanted.'

Fanny smiled. 'There's a few more things I'd like to do.'

'Such as what?'

'Money's still a worry, isn't it?' She'd used up a good deal of the cash she'd saved.

'We'll manage,' Louis told her.

Fanny knew she'd find it difficult unless Mungo was prepared to help her. She felt incensed by the way he'd treated her and was determined to get her own back on him. She meant to start by getting Jess back.

Over the first few weeks she was home, Louis was delighted with what his mother did. Everybody at the fair was pleased to see her back. She was helping him with the office work, had insisted on extending her hours and was coping well.

He was leaving more for her to do, well aware that she knew the routine. Hadn't she been his first teacher? She was cashing up at night and Louis thought the responsibility was giving her new confidence.

Today, Louis was updating the accounts, and comparing the figures in the cash-book to those of a month previously. His mother came in, her eyes shining and her cheeks glowing. She sat down at the small desk where she worked.

Louis said, 'I thought the fair was getting busier. It usually does in high summer but the takings don't reflect that. They're down a bit.'

'Oh!' Something in the way she was staring at him alerted Louis even before she told him.

'I've helped myself to a few pounds from time to time,' she admitted. 'I need to, Louis. Your father's going to cast me off without a penny piece. This might be my last chance to get anything.'

Louis was shocked, his heart pounding. He got up to make sure the office door was tightly shut. He needed a few minutes to pull himself together. Mam was fiddling the takings! He knew she'd often dipped her hand in the till but this time she'd taken quite a bit more. He sat down at his desk again and pulled the cash-book in front of him.

'He'll notice, Mam. If I can see it, it'll stick out like a waving flag to him. He'll go crazy.'

Fanny's face was set in hard, fierce lines. 'He's going to do me down – he always does. It's his way. You can tell him he put me in hospital for months on end but that I'm better now. Tell him I'm going to fight him. That I want a legal separation and an allowance to live on.'

'He won't listen. He'll be so furious, anything I say won't get through to him. I want you to put this money back.'

'No, Louis. He's never going to get the better of me again. I think we should go on syphoning off some of the takings while we can.'

Louis covered his face with his hands. 'No, Mam. You're making me nervous. Pa'll be like a rampaging bull when he finds out.'

'*If* he finds out . . .'

'To him, it'll be only too obvious.'

'Not if you went over to see him at home, took the books with you,' she said. 'Mungo owes me. He tricked me into marrying him. I think he always wanted my father's money more than he wanted me. He had a blinding obsession about getting on in the world, of becoming a rich man.'

'He's succeeded,' Louis said.

'Yes, and he didn't care who he hurt in the process.'

Louis could understand her deep feeling of loathing, after what Mungo had done, but he still had to protest. 'He didn't force you to marry him.'

'He courted me, did everything he could to persuade me. I was twenty-three, I believed him when he said he loved me.'

'Mam, he must have done.'

'Perhaps . . . The early years were happy. Looking back I can hardly believe they were. While my father was alive, Mungo was kind and considerate to him and loving towards me. I thought everything was going well. He was overjoyed when you were born.

'But once he'd put a wedding ring on my finger and was sure of me, he changed. He'd been moody from the beginning and aggressive enough to shout and storm to get his way with the others at Fhundi's, but Papa's death altered the whole dynamics of our family. Mungo wanted everything done his way and believed he knew better than anybody else how to earn more money from the roundabouts. I went along with him when I shouldn't have done.'

Louis had never heard Mam talk of her early life with Pa before. He was trying to understand how all this hate had come about.

'Until he started hitting you?'

'It was all verbal to start with.'

He frowned. 'I remember seeing him hit you. I was quite small at the time.'

Fanny sighed. 'We'd been married for about two years when he first laid into me. We'd had a row. It wasn't about anything important, it just blew up from nothing. Well, it was about the roundabouts my father had owned. Mungo wanted to sell them off and buy something newer and faster. I was reluctant to see them go.'

'Mam, I remember seeing him punch you, kick you, knock you downstairs.'

She shook her head in misery. 'Afterwards, Mungo would be overcome with guilt and plead for forgiveness. I was stupid enough to believe him when he promised it would never happen again. It did, many times. He blamed me for his outbursts. Told me I was making stupid mistakes. I felt such an incompetent fool to be always upsetting him.'

'I wanted to stop him but I couldn't.' It was a cry from Louis's heart.

'You tried, but you were too small. He just lifted you and your flailing fists out of his way. I should have left him and taken you away.'

'You did.'

'Yes, you were four years old then.'

'But you had no money and we had to come back.'

'I tried to find the Fhundi Funfair but failed, and working in a fair was all I knew. I had to come back to Mungo so we could eat and have a roof over our heads.

'He had the nerve to tell me he loved us both and wanted us back, that he was prepared to forgive me, but by then I knew he didn't. It was all lies, just a front. He might well have wanted you back, but he didn't love me. I was frightened of him, Louis, and frightened the violence would damage a growing boy like you. No child should grow up subjected to scenes of violence as you were.'

'I'm all right, Mam.'

'Yes, a miracle really that you still have both feet on the ground. You're a survivor – even though by the time you were eight Mungo was hitting you too, harder than any parent should. I could see you shrinking from him, showing Mungo that you were frightened of him too.

'After that, there was only one thing I could do. I started making plans to leave him, knowing then that when I did, I'd have to have money. I did what Mungo had done at Fhundi's Funfair. I started bleeding a little out of the takings and opened a bank account in my own name. I went on saving money over the years because I knew that if I didn't take it with me, I might get no more.'

'But you had to spend some.'

'Now I have, on the hospital and the convalescent home. I need more and there's only one way I know to get it. He put me back in hospital – why shouldn't he pay? Tell him I'm here working in his fair. Blame me – I insisted on it. He owes me, Louis. This time I'm going to make him pay.'

He saw a new determination on Mam's face and felt like pig in the middle between his fighting parents.

She said, 'Why has he suddenly stopped coming to check on this fair? He's been making a weekly visit for years.'

Louis felt exasperated. She was more concerned about what was making Pa change his habits than the figures in the cash-book. He said, 'I could lift the phone and ask him. Perhaps he isn't well.' That seemed infinitely preferable to going to see him as then Pa wouldn't be able to check anything.

She said, 'If you went over, you could bring Jess back. I'm bothered about her. By now, he's probably fed up with Jess and wishes he'd left her in the office.' Mam had said this half a dozen times. 'And he's no longer summoning you over to have dinner with him on Sundays, but I don't understand why. Something else is taking up his time.'

'It's because you're pushing for a legal separation.'

Mam retorted, 'You're not separating from him. That's not a reason to avoid you. You're his only son and you're managing his business. I want you to go over to see him. Take the books with you. He'll only glance at them there. Not like coming to the office to comb through everything. And I want Jess. Please ask him if you can bring her back.'

Louis said, 'Perhaps next week.' He dreaded the thought of showing Pa the books. 'What if he does notice?'

'He won't,' Mam said confidently, 'not if you keep pleading for Jess.'

'You don't have to face him,' Louis complained. 'You don't have to pretend to be on good terms with him. He could give me the sack.'

'Not if you blame me,' she said. 'He deserves to be cheated, doesn't he?'

Louis had to admit that Pa did.

The following afternoon, Mungo was ready to go back to work and running downstairs ahead of Greta when the postman sent a shower of letters through the front door.

'The post should be here before this time,' Mungo complained, picking them up. 'But since they've come, I might as well see if there's anything important.'

He took them to his study and sat down at his desk. Greta followed and stood leaning against the door post. With the flourish of a showman, he picked up a wicked-looking knife with an ornate brass handle and a blade of sharpest steel to slit open the first large envelope on three sides.

Out fell copies of correspondence between Fanny's solicitor and his own. It seemed Fanny had ignored his letter inviting her to return home. He started to read. She was petitioning for a judicial separation and a date in August had been set for their case to be heard in court.

He was suddenly conscious of Greta's eyes watching him and pulled up short. He couldn't let her know about this. A judicial separation from Fanny meant he'd never be able to marry her. It would also mean a change of plan that he'd have to handle carefully. It might even be better for him to avoid getting married again. He didn't like legal proceedings.

Hastily, he covered that letter with the rest of the post, reached again for his letter opener and began slitting envelopes open with savage intensity. Damn and blast Fanny.

Greta said, 'You make that knife look positively vicious.'

'It's a family heirloom.' He said the first thing that came into his head. 'My grandfather brought it back from India. A maharaja gave it to him for saving the life of his pet dog.'

Actually, Mungo had seen it in the window of a second-hand shop in Liverpool and paid half a crown for it. The shopkeeper had told him he'd taken it from a lascar seaman in part exchange for a clock he wanted to take home to his family. Mungo laughed with enjoyment at his story, and that he'd deflected her attention from Fanny's letter.

Greta was frowning at him. 'I thought you said you were

an orphan? How did you manage to obtain something from your grandfather?

'Oh!' He knew he ought to be more careful. 'Well, you see, this knife was among the few things taken into the home with me. And a note, of course. That's why I value it so much.'

At two o'clock the following afternoon, Dorothy came to relieve Greta in the ticket booth. She was a thin girl with a pale washed-out face, but today she was flushed with excitement.

'I'm counting the hours to my holiday. My mother's taking me to Blackpool for the whole week. She's paying half as my birthday present. I'll be nineteen while we're away.'

'You'll have a lovely time in Blackpool.'

'Roll on the weekend!'

That evening, Greta asked Mungo about working on Sunday.

'Yes, I'd like you to,' he said. 'The customers are different on Sundays, mostly parents bringing young children for a treat. They go home much earlier.'

'So I'll be going home on Sunday evening?'

Mungo pulled a face. 'I'd like you to stay always.'

Greta saw that as very daring. 'I don't know that I can do that.'

'Don't you want to?'

Greta said, 'You know I do.' She really enjoyed the luxury of Mungo's home. Having the maid to wait on her and the use of an indoor bathroom was utter bliss. 'It's Mam I'm worried about. She isn't ready to let me do that yet.'

'Does it make much difference now?'

'She thinks it does.'

'Invite her and Kenny to come over to the fair on the Sunday afternoon,' he suggested. 'We can take them home for supper, and then if you must, you could go home with them.'

Greta was thrilled at the thought of staying overnight with Mungo, but she felt guilty too. She'd told Mam about the separate room Mungo had set aside in his house for her to use. What she didn't tell her was that he came and joined her on the bed there every lunch time. It seemed a very daring thing for her to do, but as Mungo said, things had already gone so far that it was pointless to deny themselves the pleasure.

Once Greta started standing in for Dorothy, she realised how busy the fair was in the evenings and often until late at night. Both she and Mungo were working long hours and their routine had to be very different. She was tired when the fair closed for the night and Mungo was often exhausted; it was a treat to get into the Bentley with him and be driven to his home for the night.

Mungo liked to sleep late in the mornings; they got up slowly to make the most of their leisure time.

'It's lovely to have you here all the time,' he told her. 'I used to sit around in the mornings and do nothing.' Now, she persuaded him to go for a swim or take Jess for a long walk.

He ordered a substantial brunch to be served about midday before they went to work. Greta started selling tickets at two o'clock and was relieved for half an hour at five. If the weather was good Mungo would take her for a short walk along the prom to have a cup of tea and a cake in a café. On wet days, he made tea in his office and sent Georgio out to buy cakes. It was back to the ticket booth after that until ten o'clock or even later.

But Greta reckoned she enjoyed the week of Dorothy's holiday almost as much as Dorothy did. She was sorry to revert to her original working hours.

'I'm lost in that house without you,' Mungo told her.

Rex knew that now Dorothy was back from her holiday, Greta had reverted to her former routine and he'd be able to catch her at home first thing in the morning. He'd decided at last that he had to talk to her, tell her what was on his mind. He'd found it agonising all these weeks to see Mungo getting her to do what he wanted.

He waited until he saw Ruth go to work and then went over to tap on their front door. Greta opened it with a piece of toast in her hand. She was already fully dressed.

'Hello,' she said. 'I'm going to work for ten today, are you?'

'No. Can I come in for a moment? I want a quiet word.'

She opened the door wider. 'D'you want a cup of tea?'

'No, thanks.' He'd left one half drunk on the table at home. He wanted to take her into his arms and make her see sense.

'You're not going to tell me again they're talking about me at the fair because Mungo takes me to his house?'

'They're saying much more than that. About his divorce . . .'

'I know all about that.'

'I hear such awful things about him. Do you know he was cruel to his wife? I'm scared for you.'

'She was telling lies. She's made an enemy of Mungo.'

'They say he's a hard man. They're all a bit scared of him and daren't cross him. Their sympathy is with Fanny.'

'It's just tittle-tattle.'

Rex felt he was getting nowhere. 'Look, I know how things are with you and Mungo.'

All the men working in the fair said Mungo was after sex and getting it. Rex was afraid they were right. He would have liked to say now that he knew Greta was Mungo's mistress, but that was almost too hurtful for him to put into words. Anyway, he was afraid it would make her angry.

As it was, he saw her expression change. 'Just hear me out,' he begged. 'I love you. I always have and I can't bear to see this happening.' He took a deep breath, nervous now that she might refuse. 'Greta, we could run away together. Let me take care of you, forget Mungo Masters.'

He saw her mouth open in shock. 'No, Rex, no.' She was agitated.

He had to tell her what was on his mind. He went on, 'I know it's a risk but we could try and get jobs in London. They say it's easier there.'

'It isn't easy anywhere right now,' she said softly.

'But we'll be together. We've always been all right together, haven't we?'

'No,' Greta told him. 'No, Rex, I'm sorry, I don't want to run away with you. You don't understand. I love Mungo.'

Rex went home feeling he'd been kicked in the gut. Greta didn't want him, but he was afraid Mungo would treat her badly. He couldn't bear it if Greta was hurt.

*

Later that day, Greta went home with Mungo for lunch. It was hot and sunny and the table had been set outside on the terrace at the back, overlooking the garden. The two gardeners Mungo employed kept the grass neatly clipped and the flowers blooming in stunning drifts of colour. Jess had gone to sleep in a patch of shade beneath a beech tree.

Norah gave them Melton Mowbray pie with salad, followed by fruit and ice cream. To have ice cream served on a plate at home seemed to Greta to be the height of luxury.

When Norah brought out a tray of tea, she spoke softly to Mungo. Greta understood he had an unexpected visitor. She watched him jump to his feet and knew he was annoyed.

'What a time to come! Couldn't be more inconvenient. Finish your lunch, Greta, then go upstairs,' he said. 'I'll get rid of him as soon as I can.'

He went bounding into the house before she could ask who his visitor was. The dog came to life suddenly, jumped up and followed him. It seemed so peaceful on the terrace, the very opposite of Henshaw Street. Greta lingered, sipping her tea, enjoying the warmth of the sun on her face.

Mungo had very definite ideas about how he wanted things done, but as it seemed to benefit her and her family, she was more than happy to fall in with his wishes. She drained her cup and headed indoors through the french windows of the dining room. After the bright sunlight outside, she couldn't see much, but in the hall she could hear a strange voice that made her pause.

'Mam wants Jess back, she's missing her. She said she'd written to ask you for her but she's heard nothing. She's sent me to plead with you. Please can she have her back?'

Mungo spoke with angry emphasis. 'The dog stays here. I bought her and I'm keeping her.'

By this time, Greta realised the visitor must be Mungo's son, Louis. She was curious about him, especially as his father hardly mentioned him.

'But you gave Jess to Mam as a present.' There was determination in Louis's voice. 'She took Jess with her when she left.'

'You wouldn't tell me where she was, but I found the dog abandoned in the fair office.'

'You took Mam's dog because you couldn't get Mam back.'

'No, I only wanted to speak to her.'

Greta heard the increase in aggression. 'You took Jess from the office to spite her. You knew how fond she was of that dog.'

'It wasn't like that.'

'You never liked Jess. It's easy to see when Jess likes people and she never liked you. Please let me take her now.'

Mungo spat, 'I've told you, no. You should have learned by now that when I say no, I mean no.'

'Pa, why can't you be reasonable? It's like talking to a brick wall.'

'Where are you going?'

'Back to work.'

'Running away, are you? I haven't checked your ledgers yet.'

Greta had reached the bottom of the stairs and had started to climb, when Louis came careering out of Mungo's study and saw her. Jess was at his heels.

'Good God!'

Louis pulled up, with his mouth open. He was a younger edition of his father but more quietly dressed. He turned back to Mungo, his lip curling with contempt.

'You haven't moved another woman in already? What will Mam say?'

'It's none of her business.'

'You're still married to her, Dad.'

Greta's heart turned over. Louis was her own age, with every muscle taut and firm, but he was more slightly built and had none of Mungo's authority. Like his father's, his hair was dark and curly but the colour was richer, the texture more bouncy, and his cheeks had the glow of youth. He was looking Greta in the eye. She felt his cold appraisal.

'She's too young for you, just a girl. You ought to be ashamed of yourself, Pa.'

Mungo had followed him out, his face purple with rage. He took a firm hold of Jess's collar. 'Go, for God's sake, before you make me mad.'

Greta saw them side by side and realised for the first time how very much older than her Mungo must appear. Was she doing the right thing?

'No, wait a minute, don't go rushing off without the books. You can't run the fair without them. You said you'd come over to talk business but all you've done is argue.'

Louis followed his father back to his study and came out with several ledgers on his arm.

Greta hadn't moved. As he went past her he said in a low voice, 'Take my advice. Get out of here while you still can. If you've any sense, you'll run like hell.'

For her, the peace had been brutally shattered. She turned and ran upstairs. What she'd heard had scared her. She'd never seen Mungo in a state of fury like this before, and what Louis had said about the dog had the ring of truth about it. Mungo was not fond of Jess. Was he keeping her out of spite?

Greta threw herself across the bed in the room she'd been allotted. She didn't think Mungo was capable of that. He was gentle and kind, considerate of others, but if he had bought Jess as a present for his first wife, he should not have snatched her back.

Suddenly Greta was sitting up, deep in thought. Was that how Jess had come to be roaming the streets, hungry and bedraggled? On the night she'd found her, Jess had been lost and frightened. Mungo had said his driver had had an accident, but Greta had never seen any sign of damage to his car.

She threw herself across the bed again in a fever of indecision. Was she right to stay here and marry a man like this? She heard him coming upstairs and stiffened. The door opened.

'Greta, love.' His arms went round her and his voice was warm with sympathy now. 'I'm so sorry you heard all that. I know it must have upset you.'

'Yes,' she gulped. 'It has.'

'It's upset me too. I feel quite shaken inside.' He went on slowly and seriously, holding her close, 'Divorce is a terrible thing, Greta. Those you thought were your nearest and dearest turn against you to stab you in the back. Fanny's full of loathing and resentment, and scheming to get everything she can out of me, even the family dog.

'It's a very hurtful business. I've been fighting to put Fanny out of my mind for months, I have to if I'm to stay sane. Here I am, trying to rebuild my life with you, and you hear Louis ranting against me. You won't let him change things between us, will you?'

Greta was biting her lip. 'The dog . . .'

'Jess wasn't bought as a present for Fanny. I won't deny she was fond of her but the dog was bought as a family pet. Fanny thinks up these lies to tell her solicitor, to make me seem cruel. You haven't found me cruel, have you?'

Greta shook her head. She hadn't.

'Come on, Louis has ruined our rest time. I'm too het up. We might as well go back to work. Do you feel up to it?'

'Yes.' Greta went to wash her face and comb her hair. As they walked out to the car, she found herself examining its immaculate paintwork for any sign that damage might have been repaired. She could ask Georgio if he'd ever had an accident but she'd wait until Mungo was elsewhere. If he heard, he'd think she doubted his word.

They sat together on the back seat of his car, silent now, but Greta was still churning with indecision. Mam didn't trust Mungo; both she and Rex had tried to warn her about him. And now Louis had told her to run like hell while she still could.

All right, Mungo was quick-tempered and he made enemies, but he was working very hard and finding his divorce stressful. She didn't want to believe ill of Mungo – she couldn't. Towards her, he was always tender and loving. She loved him and must put doubts like this behind her.

CHAPTER THIRTEEN

M UNGO COULDN'T settle to his work when he
reached his desk at the fair. Damn Louis. He'd turned
up at the house when he'd least expected him and upset both
him and Greta.

That Louis had seen her in his house worried him.
Mungo was afraid he'd mention it to Fanny, who was out to
get all she could out of him. Would they realise that if Fanny
could prove he was committing adultery, she could change
her petition from judicial separation to divorce and be a kept
woman for the rest of her life?

Greta had changed things for him, and though he would
welcome a divorce now, it really went against the grain to let
Fanny get the better of him. He just wasn't prepared to allow
that.

Mungo felt he'd brought this on his own head. He knew
now he should have gone on visiting the Southport fair and
checking through the books every week or so, as Louis would
have expected. But as the fair would have to close next year,
there had seemed little point in going to any trouble over it.

He'd been spending his time with Greta and neglecting Louis.

He had mixed feelings for his son. He looked very much as he'd done himself at his age, but Louis had never had to work for what he wanted and he'd made no effort to improve the fair since he'd been in charge. When Louis had been young, Mungo had decided to make him a partner as soon as he was able to take the responsibility. He'd hoped they'd achieve great things together. Now Mungo saw him as a disappointment and knew nothing would come of it.

What had really upset Mungo was that, despite all he'd done for him, Louis had chosen to support his mother and turn his back on him. Louis ought to be grateful for all he'd been given.

He didn't trust Louis. Louis was too much under his mother's thumb. It was habit that had brought him over for his dinner on Sunday evenings until recently.

Mungo sighed. Having Greta in the house, though a comfort in many ways, was also fraught with danger. He hadn't wanted Greta and Louis to come face to face. He was afraid Louis would say too much about Fanny and frighten Greta off, and he'd wanted to keep Greta's existence a secret from his wife and son.

When Louis had turned up here earlier with the books, Mungo knew he should have kept his wits about him and not given them back to his son to take away. He'd glanced at the cash account for last month and noticed the amount of money coming in seemed lower than it had been this time last year. He should have followed it up, asked about it. Was business falling off, or was Louis extracting a little to line his mother's pocket, prior to the separation? Mungo understood the tricks for doing this all too well.

Although he'd more or less written off the Southport fair in his own mind, it didn't mean he was prepared to let Louis help himself to the takings. Also, Mungo understood that when he was worried about something, he must tackle the problem right away, or it would go on worrying him. He locked up his desk and went downstairs. Georgio was acting as doorman; he told him to bring the car round to the front.

Then he went in search of Greta. She was laughing with a customer whilst serving him with two cones and a wafer. Mungo didn't like to see her being friendly with every Tom, Dick and Harry, or wearing the white overall and cap, but that's how it had to be while she was serving ice cream.

'I have to go out,' he said, putting a proprietary hand on her arm. 'I'll be a few hours. You'll have to get your own tea and cake today. I'll be back well before closing time.'

Mungo was soon on his way to Southport. Another reason for his haste was he wanted to stop Louis mentioning to his mother that he'd seen Greta in his house.

As Georgio drove along Marine Drive, he decided to take a look round the fair before going to the office, to see if Louis had made any changes over the last few months. It was busy, the atmosphere was jolly and everything pleased him, until . . .

Mungo gasped in disbelief. Was that Fanny in charge of the ice cream? No doubt about it, it was!

With difficulty, he stopped himself charging over to demand what she was doing in his fair. Louis had a nerve, taking her on without saying a word. Mungo knew he'd made a mistake by not keeping a closer eye on what his son was doing.

Mungo went bounding upstairs to the office and slammed back the door. Louis looked up, his face registering surprise to see him again so soon.

'Hello, Pa.' Louis was at his desk, entering figures in one of the ledgers. He asked hopefully, 'You've changed your mind about the dog? You've brought her?'

'I have not,' Mungo growled. 'I said I was keeping her and I am. You've got your mother working here. Who gave you permission to do that?'

'You've seen her . . . ?'

'Of course I've bloody seen her.'

'Pa, if you won't give her an allowance she's got to work. What else does she know? She's more useful to me than anybody else.'

'Fanny is bent on cutting herself off from me. I don't want her on my premises.' Mungo couldn't help himself. He had to ask, 'Have you told her?'

Louis's face had the wary expression Mungo knew so well. 'I told her what you said about the dog.'

Mungo wanted to swear. Now he had to ask outright. 'Did you tell her about seeing a girl in my house?'

'Not yet. She was busy and I didn't want to upset her.'

Mungo should have felt relieved, but he was bothered now that Fanny could realise that this might give her the grounds she needed to sue for divorce and the right to demand maintenance. The thought of paying money to Fanny stuck in his craw and the last thing he wanted was for Greta to be named as co-respondent. He had to protect her from that.

He said, 'You're right, better if you don't mention it. Anyway, she's just a girl from the fair. I took her home for a spot of lunch to have somebody to talk to. It's lonely now you've both gone.'

He saw Louis's lips straighten. 'You and Mam are tearing me in two. I just want to have everything between you settled and be able to forget about it.'

It hadn't occurred to Mungo that Louis might care about that. 'How is your mother?'

'Better, more her usual self, but still missing Jess. She wants her back, couldn't you—'

'No!'

Louis sighed. 'And she's afraid you're going to do her down, that she'll not have enough to live on.'

'You can tell her she'll get her pound of flesh,' he said curtly. 'What I've come for is a proper look at the books.'

Because Louis had been working on them they were spread all over his desk, some of them open.

'Let me sit down.' Mungo nudged against Louis's chair, making him get to his feet. 'I opened the cash-book at home, and after you'd gone it occurred to me that the takings seemed to be falling off. Are they?'

He saw Louis close his eyes as though a wave of horror was sweeping through him. He'd half expected this. He was heading for the door.

'Where are you going?'

'Over to the fair.'

'Sit there for a minute.'

That took his son by surprise too. He looked guilty.

Ten minutes later, Mungo could see the takings were well

down from this time last year. The fiddling he'd done in his
youth stood him in good stead for picking up this sort of
thing. He knew all the tricks of the trade. He opened the safe
himself, took out the cash that was in it and began to count.
It wasn't lost on him that Louis was now too anxious to sit.
He was pacing up and down his office.

As Mungo expected, his suspicions were well founded. He
found more cash in the safe than should have been there,
according to the books.

'You're bloody thieving!' he screamed. Vitriol was
spurting through him like fire.

'No,' Louis said.

'No, it won't be you, it'll be your bloody mother.'

Another surge of outrage left Mungo panting. He wanted
to hurt Louis as much as this was hurting him.

'I trusted you,' he shouted. 'Why do you think I made you
manager here? Because you're my son, that's why. I trusted
you to look after my interests. You knew this was going on
and you let her do it.'

'Mam thinks she's helping herself to what's rightfully
hers.'

'You both thought you'd get away with it, didn't you? But
you won't when you're too damn lazy to hide what you steal.'

'You haven't been near in months. The safe seemed the
best place to keep money.'

'You stupid fool!'

They hadn't taken the first precaution when thieving –
always keep it hidden!

Mungo was counting the money, taking exactly the
amount Fanny had meant to steal.

'Tomorrow, pay this into the bank,' he ordered. 'And sack your mother. I don't want to see her on my premises ever again. And I'll sack you too if I find you doing anything you shouldn't. Understand that, do you?'

'Yes,' Louis said. 'About Mam, please let her—'

'No, explain it to her. I'm not going to employ her when she does this.'

There was something about Fanny that had always infuriated him. She was too easy to humiliate; it was too easy to believe she was stupid and worthless.

Mungo said, 'I'm taking your books, just to make sure there's nothing else you're hiding.'

'There isn't, Pa.'

'Then get me a pot of tea and something to eat from the tearoom and leave me in peace.'

Mungo felt calmer now he had the office to himself and could think. There was no point in worrying about the fair itself. It no longer mattered how Louis ran it; it would have to close.

He was angry because he'd caught Fanny stealing money from him and he didn't know how much she'd taken before he was on to her. Angry too because Louis had seen Greta in his house and if he told Fanny, she would be on to it in no time. He was guilty of adultery but he couldn't see how she could prove it. She might be suspicious but proof was another matter.

Ruth had been asking about his son for some time, Greta was very curious now, and if Louis were to meet Greta's family he'd realise exactly how serious Greta and his father's relationship was. Mungo rubbed his face in indecision. A divorce might not be a bad thing for him. In time, he'd be bound to lose Greta if he couldn't marry her. Her mother would get impatient. Also, he needed to get Fanny and Louis off his back. Perhaps he should reconsider his plans to go for a judicial separation.

Louis came back with a tray, which he slid on the desk beside him. Mungo felt in a better mood now.

'I'll have this and go,' he told him, tucking into the cheese on toast. 'I haven't had time to check your books. I'll take them with me and you can fetch them back on Sunday.'

He smiled up at his son. 'Come over and have dinner with the young lady from the fair. You'll like her.'

'I don't want to come to dinner.'

'Yes you do, Louis. You sound like a spoiled child.'

Mungo knew he had to accept that if he was going to give Fanny her divorce, he would have to grant her maintenance. It was a bitter pill to swallow but he'd have to if he wanted to keep Greta. They must all meet; it was what families did.

'Think it over – a nice family dinner. Come and act as a dutiful son should. No later than seven o'clock on Sunday and on your best behaviour. All right?' Mungo reached for the teapot. 'Don't say anything to your mother,' he added, knowing full well Louis would.

It was Sunday evening, when with sinking heart Louis got into his car to drive over to The Chase. Pa kept saying how he wished the road tunnel under the river was finished as it would cut the journey time. Louis didn't care how long the journey took. It was being seated opposite Pa that made him nervous.

He wished he'd refused to go to dinner, but it had been an order not an invitation, and he was afraid that if he didn't turn up, Pa would come to Southport looking for him again.

Louis had not sacked his mother, neither had he told her Pa had ordered it. She had to earn money. She was settled here and a sudden change could upset her. He counted himself lucky Pa hadn't looked in the books and found he'd employed Mam under a false name. If he had, he might have gone round scrutinising the faces of the other workers. It seemed a small miracle that Pa hadn't seen Frank Irwin working there at the same time.

The last person Louis wanted to see was Pa. He didn't want to discuss his mother and was afraid he might have to.

'Of course you must go,' Mam told him. 'Keep an eye out for Jess. If you can sneak her into your car when you're leaving, see you do.'

Louis didn't want to think about Jess. 'I'm worried about the money you took.'

'I'm sorry I caused that row, Louis, but your pa will have forgotten it by now. He flares up, makes a fuss and then puts it behind him. We must too.'

Nevertheless, Louis could feel his heart thumping as he put his key into the front door of The Chase and let himself in. He'd been brought up in this house; he ought to feel more at home here than he did. Norah was crossing the hall, as po-faced as ever. He heard voices from the drawing room.

He asked, 'My father and the young lady are here before me?'

'Yes, sir.'

Louis went in and was unable to get over his surprise. He

found that as well as the girl there were other guests. This had never happened before. Pa rarely invited guests to his home. But with other people present, Pa would not be finding fault with him. He'd be out to impress them.

'Ah, my son, Louis. I didn't hear the doorbell.' Mungo was on his feet and advancing with hand outstretched; patting Louis on the back and giving him a momentary hug to demonstrate warm family feelings.

'You've met Greta before. Come and say hello to her mother, Ruth, and young brother, Kenny.'

On his best behaviour, Louis greeted them as his father would have wished. The boy was down on the carpet, stroking his mother's dog. Was this why Pa wanted to keep her?

Pa had described Greta as 'just a girl from the fair I brought home to have somebody to talk to'. She was certainly more than that if he was inviting her mother round too.

This was the first time Louis was able to study Greta. She was wearing a low-cut red dress and with her long golden-blonde hair he thought she was the prettiest girl he'd ever seen.

She smiled at him and said, 'I've been looking forward to meeting you properly. You were in such a hurry last time. You're so like your father.'

Louis almost choked out, 'I hope not.' But it would have put Pa's back up and have made him seem churlish, because he did look a bit like him.

Was this girl his mother's replacement? That she could be, that she surely must be, made him quiver with indignation.

He mustn't tell Mam how flawlessly beautiful she was. How did a bad-tempered and violent old man like Pa get a girl like this? She was an absolute stunner. The sort he wanted for himself.

Louis was still looking for the perfect partner, a girlfriend who would truly love him and want to marry him. He needed a person of his own age to stand by him and stop his father and mother pulling him this way and that.

Greta was smiling at him, her whole face lighting up. 'Your father says you were keen to go to art school rather than work in the fair. Does that mean you wanted to paint?'

That set Louis off, but since he could see Pa watching him he was careful to say first that he was very happy to be running the Southport fair. He talked about all the jobs he might have enjoyed, designing prints for fabrics or posters to advertise different products.

He glanced anxiously at his father. Greta's face was like a magnet: he couldn't tear his eyes away, but he must. If he let Pa see he fancied his girl, it would be like throwing a stick of dynamite in the fire.

Sunday dinner with Pa had never passed so quickly, and for once Louis was reluctant to leave. It seemed Greta was going home with her family, so he told them he had to go through Liverpool and offered to drive them home. Going into the city would mean he'd have to cross the river on the luggage boat, but he deemed it well worth the trouble.

Unfortunately, Pa ushered Greta's mother into the front seat beside him but he was very conscious of Greta chatting to him from the back seat. It shocked him to find they lived in a slum, though they spoke nicely and didn't seem in any way rough. All the same, Pa must really be smitten to invite a family from that district to dinner.

As he drove on to Southport, he couldn't get Greta out of his mind.

His mother was already in bed when he got home, but she'd left her door ajar, and called to him as he came upstairs.

'Louis? Did you get Jess?' He could hear the eager note in her voice.

'Sorry, Mam, no.' He went in to lean on her bed rail.

In the dim light of his candle, he saw her face fall. 'Did you see Jess? Is she all right?'

'Yes, she looked fine. But there is some good news for you . . .'

'If I could drive,' she said in exasperated tones, 'I'd go at a time when I know Mungo would be out and just take the dog. I wouldn't let Norah stop me.' She looked up at him. 'Why don't you drive me over one day next week?'

'No, Mam. Pa'll go berserk if he finds the dog gone. Norah would tell him who took her. I don't want to have anything to do with that.'

'You could stay in the car; she needn't see you. I'll get the dog.'

'No, Mam, please don't. I'll have to face him the next time he comes to the office.'

Louis felt sorry for his mother but knew he was losing patience. 'Mam, Pa's got a new lady friend.'

'What?'

'I told you he'd taken a girl home from the fair. Well, he asked her mother and brother to dinner tonight. Pa wanted them to meet me – that's why I was invited. This changes everything, doesn't it? You can sue for divorce on the grounds of adultery and get your maintenance.'

His mother pulled her eiderdown closer and tucked her arms underneath. 'It's not that easy. Anyway, it doesn't sound as though he's committing adultery to me. He isn't trying to hide his new girlfriend from us. A mother with a family? Perhaps it's the mother Mungo's interested in? Perhaps she's already married too?'

'Mam, I told you, it's the girl, not the mother. They're engaged. She's wearing an engagement ring.'

Now it was his mother's turn to show impatience. 'Louis, he can't marry anyone. He's still married to me.'

'He's engaged to Greta.'

'She and her family may think so, but he could just be leading her on to get what he wants. Mungo seems happy to go ahead with a legal separation. The date's already set, for heaven's sake. If he wanted to get married again, he'd be pressing for a divorce. It stands to reason.'

Louis agreed that it did.

'I hope you're right,' she said. 'If he really wants to marry her, I'd get what I want. Mungo would be handing it to me on a plate. I don't think he intends to marry again.'

His mother was curious about the family and kept on asking questions.

It took Louis a long time to calm down after he'd gone to bed. He slept only fitfully, fantasising about Greta in the hours before dawn. She was in his arms and he loved her. She was whispering that she wanted a younger, more virile man; that she found him much more attractive than his father.

It irked Louis that Pa seemed to be able to get all he

wanted: a fine house, a car and servants to look after him; all the money he could spend, and he was earning it himself from a business he'd built up. To be able to attract a girl like Greta too must mean the gods favoured him. Louis felt very envious. He wished he'd inherited his father's abilities as well as his looks.

He got up the next morning feeling quite bouncy, despite his wakeful night. He could suddenly see a marvellous way to get even with his father. If he could attract his girlfriend away from him, he could make Pa jealous. If Pa was leading Greta on and had no intention of marrying her, Louis reckoned he'd be rescuing Greta from trouble. He shivered at the thought. Would he dare do that?

He was counting off the days, looking forward very much to seeing Greta again. At one time, he'd been summoned to eat all his Sunday dinners at The Chase, and now he hoped he could resume the same routine.

On Wednesday afternoon, there was a problem with the swingboats. Louis spent an hour helping their maintenance man and they'd just got them working again when he saw his father coming into the fair. It knocked him off balance to see Pa again so soon. It seemed he'd turned over a new leaf and meant to keep a closer watch on things.

It took Louis a moment to collect his wits. Mam was not yet working full time and had already left to do a bit of shopping on the way home, but he'd asked Frank to go up to the office to make a couple of phone calls for him. Fortunately, Pa had stopped to talk to Fred Chambers, which gave Louis the moment he needed to send a lad to warn Frank.

They went round the other attractions in the arcade and

then Pa led the way to the office. He got the books out and spread them across the desk while Louis organised tea and cake to be brought up from the café below.

Louis was not worried that he might find fault with the books this time. He watched him eat the cake with relish, expecting every moment to be told to come to The Chase for dinner again this week. When the invitation was slow to come he tried to prompt it.

'I had a good time last Sunday,' he said. 'Lovely food. The company was good too, thank you.'

His father was reaching for his hat. 'Yes, we had an excellent evening. I understand you saw the family home safely. They were grateful.'

Louis sank back on his chair, feeling raw with disappointment. No invitation! No orders to eat with Pa next Sunday. He couldn't believe he wasn't asked again. Full of frustration, he bit into the last cake on the plate. Pa had the upper hand, the power to do what he wanted. Louis was afraid he wasn't going to be allowed to see any more of Greta, and his mother, despite what she'd insisted on Sunday night, wasn't going to get her divorce.

Louis turned the problem over in his mind: how was he to see Greta again? Pa hadn't invited him, but neither had he said don't come.

He wondered if he dare just turn up. If Greta were there, Pa wouldn't throw him out. He'd be allowed to sit down and eat with them. Could he scrape up the courage to do that? Why not? He'd eaten at that table for as long as he could remember.

By Sunday afternoon, Louis knew he could. To have Greta's jade-green eyes smile up at him, he'd face anything. He drove over with his heart bouncing against his ribs, and was careful to time it so he arrived at the right moment.

Norah was not in the hall tonight. He took a steadying breath, marched straight to the drawing-room door and went in.

'Hello, Pa,' he said as brightly as he could.

The beautiful Greta was on her feet to welcome him. 'How nice to see you again, Louis,' she said, all smiles. Louis hadn't expected her mother and brother to be here again, but that made it all the harder for Pa to tell him he wasn't welcome.

'I wasn't sure whether you were coming or not, Louis,' he said. It sounded a little pointed but that was all. 'I'll get Norah to set another place at the table.'

Louis made up his mind to go every Sunday. He'd never felt so drawn to anybody as he did to Greta, yet all the time he knew Pa would never allow him to get close to her. Louis spent the evening with his hands in his pockets, afraid they'd reach out to touch her. He could barely control the urge to stroke her yellow hair, feel the softness of her white skin and take her in his arms.

He'd learned to hide his true feelings from Pa, now he'd have to learn to do the same with Greta.

CHAPTER FOURTEEN

WEDNESDAY STARTED like any other for Greta. It was after midday when Mungo came down to the ticket booth and knocked for her to unlock the door. She was busy with a customer but sensed Mungo's excitement as he squeezed in behind her.

'I've a bit of a problem. Dorothy's sick. She won't be coming to work.'

A lad came to the front of the booth asking for a shilling's worth of tickets. Greta sold them to him as she spoke. 'Dorothy complained of feeling queasy and having a pain in her side yesterday. Agnes said she was worse in the evening.'

'I've just had this note from her mother. She says she's in hospital and has had her appendix out this morning. She won't be back at work for some time.'

'Gracious! Poor Dorothy, that's awful.' Greta realised what this would mean for her. 'You'll want me to take over her shift again?'

Mungo agreed. 'Yes, if you would. It's a good reason for you to stay overnight, and you'll be doing it for longer this time. Long enough for your mother to get used to the idea.'

'She'll never get used to it. Not until I'm married.'

Greta saw Mungo pull a face. 'We are engaged, we'd be married if only it were possible,' he pleaded. 'I love having you at home with me.'

'I love staying, but I'll have to go home for at least one night each week.'

'Before your day off?'

'Yes, Mam will expect it and I need to pay over my wages.'

'If you're staying with me, you're no longer an expense to her. She won't expect you to hand over your money.'

'You don't understand,' Greta faltered. 'She doesn't earn enough to manage the rent, coal and food. She needs my contribution.'

'Oh! I hadn't thought of it like that. I've forgotten what it's like to be really poor. How would it be if I made her a regular allowance?'

'You don't have to, Mungo. She wouldn't expect it.'

'She's going to be my mother-in-law and I don't like to think of her being hard up. I could pay it directly into her bank account by standing order.'

Greta shook her head. 'Mungo, you really have forgotten. Mam doesn't have a bank account – neither do I. I mean, none of us do. If I didn't go home, I'd have to send her postal orders.'

She could see Mungo turning it over in his mind. 'I'm going to open a bank account for her. It's less trouble for me to pay her that way, and she'll be able to rely on it. Buying postal orders or handing over a few pounds ... well, you could forget or be late. She'd never know where she was, would she?'

Greta felt a rush of gratitude. Mungo was very kind. She knew Mam didn't trust him, and neither did Rex, but they were wrong. Nobody could be more thoughtful for them.

'You're very generous.'

'Look, why don't you write a little note to your mam, telling her about Dorothy and that I want you to stay here for the next few nights? You could give it to Rex to deliver. Why not ask them over to the fair on Sunday afternoon? You and I can finish about six o'clock and take them back for supper. Then if you really want to, you can go home with them.'

'Perhaps I will . . .'

She saw alarm in his eyes. 'I'd much rather you stayed with me. I don't want to lose you.'

'You won't. I couldn't possibly give you up now.' She smiled. 'I'll go home one night a week until Dorothy's back.'

'And when she is?'

'That could be a long way off.'

'Three weeks perhaps. Couldn't you tell your mother you want to be here with me? To live with me, I mean?'

Greta felt agonised. 'I don't know. No, she'd think I was terrible.'

'I'll fix that bank account for your mam tomorrow,' he promised.

'Thank you. I do appreciate what you're doing for me and Mam.'

'You're going to be my wife,' he said, 'and I want to get on well with my in-laws.'

Greta knew the next few days would be wonderful.

229

Mungo hardly let her out of his sight and told her many times how much he loved her. Going home with him every night to share his life, sleeping in the same bed, brought lovely nights of passion, and waking to find him still there beside her was marvellous. This was what being married to him would be like, but they'd never have to separate.

Sunday hung over her like a black cloud. She felt guilty that she'd let her mother down, forsaken her for Mungo. Mam wouldn't like her doing this.

Sunday turned out to be hot and sunny. New Brighton was thronged with visitors and the fair was busy. When Kenny and Mam arrived at the fair, they came to the ticket booth to say hello. When Mam's eyes bored into hers, Greta saw the questions there and felt uncomfortable.

Mungo joined them and took them off to his office, treating them like honoured guests. Kenny had countless turns on the attractions and, from the ticket booth, Greta saw Agnes Watts provide ice-cream cones for them.

At six o'clock Mungo arranged for Rex to take over the ticket booth, and in the car going to The Chase, Mam couldn't wait to talk about the allowance Mungo was to arrange for her. Kenny was bursting with his news.

'I'm to come over at opening time on the first Monday of my holidays.'

Mungo said, 'I've arranged for Kenny to help on the helter-skelter.'

'It's going to be a real holiday job,' Kenny said. 'I'll earn seven shillings and sixpence a week and Mungo will pay my ferry fares.'

Greta knew her mother was pleased and Kenny was

excited, but he was asking about Jess before he was out of the car.

'Come on,' Greta said, 'we'll go and get her.'

She led the way through the kitchen where Mabel had a cold roast chicken set out and was preparing a salad to go with it for their supper. Kenny had never been here before. Jess had been waiting in the hall on previous visits.

'What an enormous kitchen,' Kenny said, looking round. 'What's that room there?'

'It's a sitting room for Norah and Mabel.' Greta led the way out to the small yard. Jess shot out of her kennel, showing her teeth in something between a smile and a sneeze, and her tail was wagging like fury.

'An enormous kennel too,' Kenny laughed. Norah had followed them out to take in some towels from the washing line.

'It belonged to a big Alsatian we used to have here,' she said. 'A guard dog. Boris, he was called.'

Kenny unfastened Jess's chain.

Greta asked, 'What happened to Boris?'

'One day he bit Mr Masters and had to be put down.'

'Oh.' Kenny was wrinkling his nose with distaste. 'Put down? Poor thing.'

Greta said, 'At least Jess is safe from that fate. She's an old softie.'

'Snarls a bit at the boss sometimes,' Mabel said, coming to the back door. 'I've told her it's not the wisest thing to do.'

It was getting dusk when Mungo sent Norah to ask Georgio to bring the car to the door to drive them back to the ferry.

Greta had packed a few things in the smart overnight case Mungo had given her. When she went upstairs to fetch it, Mungo went with her.

'I wish you weren't going,' he said. 'I shall miss you tonight.' She turned to give him a goodbye kiss and he wrapped his arms round her in a hug and rained passionate kisses on her face.

'I'll come and see you off. I can pop to the fair afterwards and cash up.'

He carried her overnight bag along the pier and when the time came to board the ferry, he kissed Greta goodbye. She knew it was a lover's kiss and felt a little embarrassed. It was the first time he'd kissed her under her mother's gaze. They waved to him from the rail of the ferry as it pulled away.

'He's a kind and generous man,' Ruth said as they stared at his figure getting smaller in the distance. 'I'm afraid I misjudged him, didn't I?'

'Yes,' Greta said. 'I think you did.'

'Run like hell,' Louis had told her, but she'd put that, and what the people at the fair had told her about him, out of her mind. Greta felt she had to base her own opinion on how she saw Mungo.

Her mother went on, 'I feel guilty. There aren't many men who'd feel the need to make me a monthly allowance. Before you're married too. He said he didn't want me and Kenny to go short.'

Greta was thrilled with the way things were working out. Her life had taken a turn for the better. Her family were growing to love Mungo as much as she did.

From the back of her mind, unbidden, came the question

of whether Mungo had bought Mam's goodwill by making her the allowance and by promising a job for Kenny.

Louis was feeling more fraught. He would be in trouble with Pa if he discovered Mam was still working for him. She was coming to the fair with him every day, taking over more and more of the work and was coping well. She was more sociable with the neighbours too, and said she was enjoying keeping house. Louis shared the work with her both at home and at the fair, and was pleased with the way she was shaping up.

After the trouble she'd caused him by helping herself to the takings of the fair, she'd accepted that she must not do that again, but Louis knew Pa and his new lady friend were playing on her mind.

One day she said, with a puzzled, frown. 'He's the sort who'd want her living with him permanently; probably he'd want to remarry. But surely Mungo would be asking for a divorce if that was the case?'

They both half expected the post to bring a letter from Mr Danvers announcing the change, but it didn't come. It seemed Pa was happy to go ahead with the judicial separation.

Louis knew the scars Pa had inflicted on his mother were not gone. She was missing Jess and when she remembered how he'd taken the dog just to spite her, she'd boil over with anger.

Today, a bright morning in July, across her office desk, she'd said vehemently, 'I'll never be satisfied until I get my own back on Mungo. I'd like to see him dead. In fact, I could kill him with my bare hands. That would solve everything, wouldn't it?'

'Mam!'

Louis had heard young mothers in the fair shouting, 'I'll kill you,' to their disobedient children. 'Wait till I get my hands on you, I'll kill you.' He knew it was just a saying and they didn't mean it literally. But Mam had said it with a great deal of aggression. It sounded as though she did mean it.

It shocked Louis, though he could understand and feel sorry for her.

On the following Saturday morning, Fanny sat up in bed feeling refreshed and ready to act. She ached to have Jess back and was determined to get her if she possibly could.

At breakfast, she said to Louis, 'I'm going to fetch Jess myself. I'll take the day off and go today.'

'No, Mam! It'll only upset you again.'

Fanny said, 'I can't understand why I haven't done it before. Mungo's out all day – what is there to stop me?'

'No, please don't. I'll nag at him when I see him on Sunday.'

'Louis, you've tried and failed. Nothing you can say will stop me now. I've got to learn to stand on my own feet.'

Louis was doing his best to stop her but Fanny knew she needed to go now while she felt strong. She was determined to take back what was rightfully hers.

Every time she saw Jess's lead hanging on the hook behind the back door, she was reminded of what she'd lost. She lifted it down and put it in her handbag. To have Jess back would be a great comfort. She remembered how soothing it had been to stroke her silky coat and see her eyes look up with affection. She needed to get Jess back.

Fanny planned the trip carefully, looking up the time of the trains, deciding what she'd wear. She could walk from Meols station, go quietly round the back of the house to where Jess had her kennel and just take her. Nobody need know she'd been.

When she'd first gone to live at The Chase, she'd occasionally taken the train to Liverpool to go shopping. In the old days, Mungo would drop her off at the station on his way to work, or if he was going in late Georgio Higginbottom could run her there. On her return, she'd usually walked back, as taxis were not available at Meols, which was just a railway halt. Fanny knew what she planned was feasible.

It was not a difficult journey as there was a good service from Southport to the Wirral. All the same, as Fanny drew closer to her old home, she had to steel herself to go through with her plan. If she'd been intent on stealing the Crown Jewels it couldn't have been more difficult to summon up her nerve.

She kept telling herself she was cured and could do it but she could feel her throat constricting when the house came in sight. She took a deep breath. There was no need to be scared. Mungo would not be at home now.

There was a little yard behind the house where the washing was hung and where Mungo had decided the dog kennel must go. Fanny had chosen to wear her rubber-soled walking shoes so that Mabel and Norah would not hear her, but now she was near enough to be heard, she found herself creeping almost on tiptoe.

She was worried too that if she surprised Jess, the dog would bark and alert the women in the kitchen. She hoped to avoid that, but if she had to, she'd be able to outface Norah. She reached the yard gate, which was slatted. Through it she could see a line of washing flapping in the breeze. The kitchen door was shut. Fanny could feel herself breathing faster and her heart began to pound.

'Jess,' she hissed. The huge kennel seemed as solid as the house, and she couldn't see inside it from this angle.

'Jess,' she called a little louder, expecting to see a black and white head come round to find out who was calling her, but it didn't.

The bolt was on the gate. Fanny squeezed her hand through the slats to pull it off. Jess must be fast asleep and Fanny was afraid the noise of the bolt coming off would wake her and make her bark.

'Jess,' she called louder still. Then, with a growing ball of fear in her throat, she eased the bolt off. The gate creaked as it opened. Fanny froze for a moment.

'Jess?'

It took two or three steps to reach the kennel and see it was empty. It made her jolt back in surprise. She was awash with disappointment. It had never occurred to her that Jess wouldn't be here. Had she come all this way for nothing?

Where was the dog? Mungo had insisted on tethering her here. The chain he used was coiled neatly where she hadn't been able to see it from the gate. She collapsed against the kennel roof, struggling to get her breath and stem the rising tide of panic. Jess must be in the house. Did that mean Mungo was at home, that he hadn't gone to work?

She was backing out of the yard, meaning to look in the garage to see if the Bentley was there, but the kitchen door opened and Mabel, the cook, came out on to the step, squinting into the sun.

'Oh! Mrs Masters, you gave me a shock.'

Fanny could feel herself shaking with nerves. Mabel didn't say, what are you doing here? But Fanny sensed she almost let the words tumble out.

Mabel recovered. 'I'm afraid your husband isn't here. He's gone to work.'

Fanny was relieved she wouldn't have to face him. 'I'm looking for my dog,' she said as calmly as she could.

'Jess? Mr Masters sometimes takes her to the fair with him.'

'Why? He never used to.'

She could see Mabel struggling for words, not wanting to say too much. 'There's a family . . . The boy's keen on Jess. The boss will bring them all back this evening.'

'Oh!' That caught Fanny's interest. The family was coming here again? Louis had seen them here only last Sunday. That did sound as though Mungo was very interested in them.

'I'll come in, Mabel,' she said, knowing this was her chance to find out more about them. She'd always got on well with Mabel and felt she took her side rather than Mungo's. 'Perhaps you'd make me a cup of tea?'

'Of course,' she said, but looked somewhat surprised.

Fanny pulled out a chair at the kitchen table and sat

down. Facing her on a fancy cake stand was a large iced cake. Mabel hurried to tidy away the icing bag and other used kitchen equipment.

'That looks nice.' Fanny craned forward to read the ornate lettering in pink icing. 'Happy Birthday Ruth'.

'For tonight,' Mabel said. 'A special birthday dinner. As you know, Sunday is Mr Masters' usual night for entertaining.'

When Fanny saw her taking out a tray cloth and laying it on a tray, she said, 'I'll have it here with you.' She'd learn nothing sitting back in the drawing room on her own.

'Good, it's time Norah and I had our morning break. I'll make tea for us all.'

Mabel was bringing out the cake tins. Fanny sliced off a piece of cherry cake for herself. She'd forgotten how good Mabel's cakes were.

'Tell me about this family,' she said. From the moment she'd heard Mungo was asking women to the house, she hadn't been able to banish the possibility of adding adultery to her petition and thereby getting both a divorce and maintenance.

In all the time she'd lived with him, Mungo had rarely brought people home for meals. Peter from the Prestatyn funfair once in a while perhaps, but nobody else.

Norah came in with her mops and brushes, looking as sour as ever. All along, Mabel had seemed careful about what she said. Now suddenly she started talking about the weather.

Fanny finished her tea. 'I'm going to look round,' she said. 'There's a few oddments I forgot to take: my umbrella, for one. I might need that before I get back to the station.'

Norah got up to follow her. 'I can manage on my own, thank you, Norah,' Fanny told her with as much firmness as she could muster.

Fanny headed upstairs and found, thankfully, that she was alone. The servants were easier to cope with than anyone else. She made herself go to the bedroom she'd shared with Mungo. Everything here reminded her of him and the bad times he'd given her. It made her feel he was here behind her, watching what she was doing. The tea she'd drunk threatened to regurgitate into her mouth.

The room hadn't changed much. She'd left some books here but they'd gone. The silver clock Mungo had taken from her was on the dressing table. She slid it into her bag. It was rightfully hers, his birthday gift to her.

She hesitated. Would taking it make him search her out again? Was it worth that? She almost put it back, but no, she was cured. It was only natural to be nervous, but she must be strong and do it.

She opened the wardrobe. Fanny had taken all the clothes she wanted with her. Now the few she'd left behind were gone. Mungo had hung some new clothes of his own here. Good, it looked as though he didn't expect her to return, but neither was there any evidence he'd moved another woman in.

There were six bedrooms at The Chase. She started going round the others, leaving all the doors open so that Mungo might conclude she'd been through them all.

She paused inside the third bedroom. It seemed to have been used recently. On the dressing table was a silver powder bowl with her initials, F.M.M., engraved on the lid. She slid that too into the bag she carried. There was also a cut-glass scent bottle with an ornate pink bulb attached. She sprayed some on herself. It was lovely and no doubt expensive, just the sort of thing Mungo would buy for a lady friend.

On the spur of the moment, she went back to his bedroom and opened the little drawer where he used to keep his French letters. She had to stifle a giggle. Mungo had a fresh supply on hand, so yes, he was committing adultery. This was her proof positive. She felt victorious.

Mr Danvers had explained to her that she could get a judicial separation in August, when their case was heard, and seek a divorce later. She was hopeful now that she wouldn't have to wait. The sooner this was settled to her satisfaction the better she'd feel.

Returning here after her eyes had grown used to her own simple terraced house brought home to her just how wealthy Mungo was. All his furnishings were expensive and many were new.

Fanny returned to the other bedroom and looked in the wardrobe. Just as she'd expected, she found items of ladies' clothing hanging there. She took out a two-piece outfit in pale blue silk and, holding it against herself, she looked in the mirror. His new lady friend was as slim as a wand. No middle-aged mother of adult children would be able to wear these. It must be the daughter Mungo was interested in. The clothes were more glamorous than anything he'd ever bought for her. It made her feel old and ugly. Fanny didn't need the mirror to tell her she was stout and had run to seed.

She opened a drawer in the chest and found lovely silk underwear. Had Mungo bought all this too? The French knickers were far too small to fit her and everything was very dainty.

She was torn between wanting to slash at these smart clothes with the black anger she felt for a younger rival, yet wanting to exult that now a divorce and a more comfortable future were possible for her.

'I'm all right,' she told herself. She had to find out all she could about this woman before she left. She went back to the kitchen and pinned Norah to the sink. 'How old is this daughter?' she asked.

'I don't know. She's just a girl, doesn't look twenty.'

'What is her name? What does she do?'

'Greta, her name is, she works in the fair.'

If Mungo had taken the dog to the fair for her brother, it meant he would be there too. She could go and see them, but no, she couldn't risk coming face to face with him. She'd done all she could today.

Fanny walked briskly back to the station. She was disappointed not to have Jess padding along beside her, but she was quite sure now that her husband was an adulterer. That should give her a divorce and allow her to hit Mungo where it hurt him most – in his pocket.

Greta had asked Mungo to make Saturday a bit special for her mother because it was her birthday. She didn't want her to spend it cleaning the house as she spent every other day.

That afternoon, when Ruth and Kenny came to the fair, Mungo sent Greta out to take them and Jess for a long walk on the sands. Three of the bumper cars were out of service as well as the chairoplanes. Mungo didn't go with them, feeling he had more pressing things to do.

He was a bit late taking them home for the special birthday dinner. Mungo was looking forward to the baked ham he'd ordered Mabel to cook but he wasn't in a good mood because nothing had gone well today and he was afraid the takings would be down tonight when he returned to cash up. It had been a fine summer Saturday but even so, they'd had fewer visitors than usual. Mungo was afraid the depression was biting harder.

The dog followed them into the drawing room; Kenny sat on the carpet, stroking her. Mungo felt out of sorts and wished he could have Greta here on her own. He was finding Ruth's company a little tedious as her eyes seemed to follow every move he made.

He rang the bell for Norah and told her to get the meal on the table as soon as possible because he would have to return to the fair.

What he really wanted was to get this meal over. He was doing too much to get Ruth on his side and needed to think of some way to have Greta here permanently without her family.

'Can I give Jess her dinner?' Kenny asked.

'Right, Norah will have it ready. Chain her up by her kennel.'

Kenny scampered off and they were all sitting at the table within minutes. Both the ham and the birthday cake were delicious. Mabel was a good cook but Mungo had never taken to her. She'd been far too friendly with Fanny. Then Greta tried to prolong her mother and brother's stay by suggesting a walk along the coastal path afterwards. 'It's such a lovely evening,' she smiled at him. He couldn't refuse.

Later, when his guests were getting ready to go out Mungo headed towards his study to see if there were any letters in the afternoon post.

Norah met him in the hall. 'Can I have a word, sir?'

'What is it?'

'Mrs Masters came here this morning, sir.'

'What, Fanny? What did she want?'

'She wanted to take Jess.'

Mungo strode furiously out to the yard. Jess was half asleep. She lifted her head as the back door slammed behind him. What a good job he'd taken her to the fair this morning. He couldn't believe Fanny had found the nerve to come here. If she'd come once, she could come again. He wasn't having that. He'd keep the dog chained up so she couldn't take her.

Norah came out after him.

'I'm going to put a padlock on this gate,' he told her. 'In future, it's to be kept locked.'

'Mabel and me – we come and go this way, sir,' she said. 'And the tradesmen deliver.'

'Damn.'

'You'd need to leave us the key. Or we'd have to use the front door, sir.'

Mungo rushed to the garage and hammered on the door of Georgio's flat. He came to the door yawning, his boxer's face looked crumpled and sleepy.

'Tomorrow morning, I want you to go out early and buy me a dozen feet of heavy-duty chain and a strong padlock,' he ordered. 'Come with me and I'll show you what I want done with it.'

Mungo strode rapidly back to the yard. 'I want you to bolt it here to the fence near the kennel.'

He watched Georgio run his fingers along the light chain that was already tethering Jess.

'That isn't strong enough,' Mungo said. He could break that with a hammer and chisel, and it probably wouldn't defeat Fanny.

Georgio said, 'It was strong enough to tether that German shepherd dog you had. Jess would never be able to break free from it.'

Mungo barked, 'I want it changed to heavy-duty chain. All right?'

'Yes,' he said. 'But it's Sunday tomorrow. Everywhere will be closed.'

'Damn and blast. As soon as you can, then.'

Kenny came out and was about to unfasten the dog. He said, 'We'll be taking Jess on the walk, won't we?' She was wagging her tail with every appearance of delight. Mungo saw Greta and her mother behind him. Hell! Mungo remembered he'd agreed to go for a walk with them. Now he knew Fanny had been sneaking round, he didn't feel like it.

'Do you mind if we don't have that walk, after all?' he asked.

'I wanted to show Mam the coastal path,' Greta said. 'I'm sure she'll love it.'

He said stiffly, 'I'm sorry, Greta. Something's come up and I have to get straight back to the fair. Do you mind, Ruth?'

Disappointment made Kenny screw up his face until his

freckles stood out. Mungo patted his shoulder. 'We'll go for a walk next time you come. Come on, I'll drop you off at the ferry on the way.' He made sure the dog was still securely chained up.

Mungo sat beside Greta on the back seat and fumed. Damn and blast Fanny. What he hated was the thought of her poking round his bedroom. There was plenty of evidence that he had Greta here with him. Could he hope that she wouldn't have noticed? Anyway, if she came back for the dog, he'd make doubly sure she wouldn't take her.

CHAPTER FIFTEEN

FANNY RETURNED to Southport feeling tired but exultant. Such marvellous luck to have found out for sure that Mungo was an adulterer. He wouldn't want her to know; that she did made her feel she was getting the upper hand. It looked as though he had no intention of marrying the girl and that made her despise him more.

As she walked up Delaney Street, Fanny could see Ena standing at her front window. Ena waved to make sure she had her attention and seconds later opened her front door.

'Fancy a cup of tea? Have you got time to come in?'

'I'd love to.' Fanny needed a friend but knew better than to confide in Ena. Instead she chatted about the weather and the flowers that would thrive best in the plant pots they kept in their back yards. It relaxed her. Ena made Fanny feel more settled. After that, it was a rush to get supper ready for when Louis came home.

He asked, 'Did you get the dog?' She saw him look under the table.

'No.' Fanny told him why. 'But he is committing adultery,

I'm sure of it now. The girl keeps a lot of her things there.'

'Didn't I tell you? Go and see your solicitor on Monday.'

'I will. I'm pleased about that but sorry I didn't get Jess. Perhaps if I went again . . .'

'For heaven's sake, no,' Louis said. 'Norah's bound to tell Pa and he'll expect you to make another visit. I'll buy you another dog.'

'But it's Jess I want . . .'

'Mam, like the rest of us, you've got to accept you can't have everything you want. You might never be able to get Jess. But a different dog, a puppy, you'd like that?'

'I don't know. It wouldn't be the same.'

'Think about it, Mam.'

'A stray from the dog pound perhaps?' Fanny had sympathy for any animal in trouble and knew a dog would help her settle.

'I could take you to choose one.'

'It's not easy to give up hope of having Jess back.' But Fanny was buoyed up by the thought that divorce and maintenance might now be possible.

The following night Louis arrived at The Chase in time for Sunday dinner as usual.

'You're out of luck,' Pa told him as soon as he sat down with them in the drawing room. 'You won't get much to eat tonight.'

Louis could feel a cooler, less sociable atmosphere and knew Pa wasn't in a good mood.

Greta explained that her family had come here the night before, and tonight there was just the three of them and they'd be eating leftovers. It turned out to be cold roast ham and chips with salad and cake to follow. Louis enjoyed the meal more than usual.

On past Sundays, he'd sometimes wished Ruth and Kenny were not here too. Now he missed their company. He knew he mustn't let Pa see him paying too much attention to Greta. He found holding a conversation with his father hard going.

They'd barely finished eating when Pa said, 'We're having an early night tonight. I'm shattered. I locked the cash from the ticket booth and the refreshment counter in the safe before leaving. I've put Rex Bradshaw in charge – he'll close down tonight. I'll cash up in the morning.'

Louis recognised that as a signal he must leave. He was draining the last of his coffee when Greta said, 'Mungo, what about a little walk down to the coastal path? It's a lovely balmy evening.'

Mungo yawned. 'No, I want to go to bed.'

Louis's spirits soared. A walk with Greta, just the two them? That would be marvellous.

She said, 'We ought to take Jess for a run. She hasn't stretched her legs all day.'

Louis realised he hadn't seen Jess. When Kenny came, she was always with them.

'Yes,' Pa said to Greta, 'you'd better give the dog a little run.'

He was leading the way through the kitchen to the yard at the back.

'I do wish you wouldn't chain her up like this,' Greta said, frowning.

Louis followed them, knowing Pa meant him to see the heavy chains and padlock tethering Jess to her kennel so that he'd tell his mother. All evening, neither of them had said anything about Mam trying to snatch her back. Pa unlocked the padlock and, with a rattle, the chain dropped back on the concrete. Jess spun round with excitement.

Louis was suddenly conscious that Pa's intense gaze had settled on him. With all his heart, he longed to go for this walk with Greta, but knew he must not. Pa was watching him and his whole body told Louis he'd be very much against that. He'd get Pa's back up and his job would be on the line if he so much as suggested going with her.

'I'll be on my way home, then,' Louis said, and together they all went through the yard gate and round the front of the house to where he'd parked his car. Pa was waiting to make sure he went.

'Good night, and thanks for the dinner,' Louis said, getting in. Jess gambolled about and Greta waved.

He thought of parking his car a little way away and running back to catch Greta up, but he knew that was madness. He drove straight home.

His mother hadn't yet gone to bed. 'You're back early,' she said.

He told her Pa had taken drastic steps to stop her taking Jess; that he'd wrapped heavy chain round her body and locked her into it with a padlock.

'There's no way you're going to be able to get her now.'

On Monday, Fanny got in touch with Mr Danvers and went in to see him that afternoon. She told him she'd been to her husband's home to try to get her dog back, and described the concrete evidence she'd seen that he was committing adultery.

Mr Danvers stroked his chin thoughtfully. 'You want to change your petition from one of judicial separation to divorce on the grounds of adultery?'

'Yes, and persistent cruelty.'

'And it seems he's wilfully refused to maintain you?'

'Yes.'

'When your case is heard, you'll need proof of these allegations to put before the court. We have a statement from your doctor regarding the injuries for which he has treated you . . . yes, and let me see . . . hospital admissions on several occasions.'

He closed the file he was keeping on Fanny's case and looked at her over his steel-rimmed spectacles.

'Regarding his adultery, I can set out the facts you've given me, but to guarantee being granted a divorce you need someone else to support this evidence.'

Fanny could feel her confidence draining. She was afraid that wouldn't be possible.

'Your husband employs live-in servants?'

'Yes, two.'

'They will have seen another woman in the house? Staying the night?'

'Yes, they must have done.'

'One of them would be ideal.'

Fanny shook her head. 'That's difficult.' As Norah enjoyed Mungo's confidence, Mabel was the only person she could possibly ask. 'She'd lose her job if my husband found out.'

'He's bound to find out. If he goes to court he'd see her there. Her name would be in the transcripts.'

Fanny buried her face in her hands. Everything was so hard.

Mr Danvers said kindly, 'Ask her. You may have her sympathy.'

Fanny knew sympathy wouldn't be enough. 'She'll almost certainly refuse. It would guarantee her the sack and my husband could be violent towards her too.'

'You can only ask,' he said. 'Unless you can think of someone else? Those people running the fair, for instance?'

'He employs them too so the same thing applies.' Fanny thought of Louis, he was the one person she could rely on to help her. 'What about our son? He's twenty-three.'

'Would he do it? What is his relationship with his father? It could change it for ever.'

Fanny sighed. She mustn't ask him. 'He works for Mungo too and it's vital he keeps his job.'

'Perhaps an unrelated person would be better. Think about it. In any event, proof of adultery will be inferred from circumstances showing there was association with opportunity to commit it. I'll formally request that he pays alimony to you in the meantime. I'm afraid the amount will be limited to . . . let me see, yes, two pounds a week at present.'

'Anything would be a help,' Fanny said.

That evening Louis ate his evening meal and listened to his mother recounting at length what Mr Danvers had said to her.

He said, 'I don't think Mabel will be prepared to testify in court. I mean, to stand up in front of everybody, possibly Pa himself, and say she's seen evidence of his adultery . . . ?'

Fanny sighed. 'Neither do I, and I'm afraid to ask in case she says no. That would close the door.'

'Unless you ask her, the door will never open,' he pointed out.

Louis was sure Pa was taking Greta to bed, but the last thing he wanted to do was stand up in court and say so. But Mam was desperate to get a divorce and maintenance, and he wanted to help her.

He made himself ask, 'Do you want me to testify for you? I see Greta in the house when I go for Sunday dinner.'

It would label Greta as a fallen woman, and Louis was afraid it would also guarantee Pa would never speak to him again.

'Is seeing her there enough?' Fanny asked. 'You said you drive her and her family home afterwards.'

'Only because Monday, the next day, is her day off. I think she stays overnight in the week.' He couldn't let his mother be cheated by Pa yet again. 'I'll do it for you.'

'No,' she put her hand on his, 'I can't let you. You have to keep your job, Louis. You must stand back from this. I'll ask Mabel. She's in a better position to see what's going on in that house. And the Court is more likely to believe her.'

His mother never stopped asking questions about Greta. Louis told her that Greta was very young, and when he saw her with Pa, they looked more like father and daughter than an engaged couple. But Louis didn't want to say too much. Greta was in a dangerous position too, and he'd want to help her if she needed it. He felt in an impossible position, caught up in a fight between his parents.

Fanny brooded about Jess, she felt it was her fault the dog was being chained more heavily and was afraid her chance of getting her back had gone.

'Come on, Mam,' Louis said, as they ate their lunch in the teashop on the following Tuesday. 'Let's get you another dog.'

'You think I should give up hope of getting Jess back?'

'Yes.'

'Right, if it's to be a different dog or no dog, then yes, I would like one.'

Louis drove her to an RSPCA dogs' home in Liverpool. Fanny fancied another collie like Jess, but found most of the dogs there were indeterminate mongrels.

The kennel maid said, 'This one has some collie in him and he's under a year old. He's another cross, though, and with a much larger dog.'

The animal was nervous and cowered at the back of the concrete cell he was kennelled in. His eyes were sad and his tail drooped. Fanny thought he looked pathetic. That was what drew her to him. She recognised in him something of the same emotional distress she felt herself. She thought she could give him a good home and make him happier.

'What's his name?'

'He wasn't wearing a collar when he was brought in, so we don't know.'

'I'll call him Gyp,' she said.

She took him for a walk along the Southport front, afraid

to let him off the lead in case he ran away. He seemed timid and nervous, reminding Fanny of herself.

'It's going to take a long time for him to settle down and be a normal happy dog,' she said to Louis when they got back. 'I wonder if his last owner was cruel to him?'

Fanny was pleased to see Gyp responding reasonably well. She made it a habit to take him for a walk before she went to work and for him to spend a few hours each day in the office. The afternoons he usually spent in their back yard.

Asking Mabel to testify was very much on Fanny's mind. She kept talking to Louis about it whenever they were alone. She was torn between telephoning her and going to see her. She put it to Louis across his desk one morning.

'Phone,' Louis advised.

'It would be easier to persuade her, wouldn't it, if I went?'

Louis shook his head.

'And I could have another go at getting Jess back. If we had two dogs, well, they'd be company for each other.'

Louis didn't look too pleased about that. 'Phone,' he repeated. 'Pa knows you've been and will have given Norah orders not to let you near Jess. If you go, she'll probably be listening to every word you say to Mabel and she'll repeat it to Pa.'

Fanny knew he was worried she wouldn't be able to cope. She'd told him she hadn't found it easy to go in person last time. Perhaps he was right. She said, 'I'll phone her tomorrow.'

Louis looked up. 'If Mabel agrees and you get your divorce, Pa will have to pay you maintenance. Don't you see, you could afford to employ her if Pa gave her the sack? You could tell her.'

'I don't know . . .' Fanny hadn't thought that far ahead. 'I'm quite happy looking after the house myself. I don't need anyone, and at the moment we can't afford it. Anyway, she probably won't agree.'

She went to work with Louis the next morning, determined not to put it off any longer. When she'd allowed plenty of time for Mungo to leave for work she said to Louis, 'I want to ring Mabel now. Would you mind going somewhere else? I need to concentrate; I've got to get this right.'

'Of course. I want to see if Frank's managed to get those spare parts for the bumper cars, anyway. Make a note of what you want to say first, Mam.'

Fanny already had. She felt harassed and under pressure but knew she must try. When the door closed behind him she lifted the handset and asked the operator to put her through to The Chase. She listened to it ringing, hoping Mabel would answer.

Norah's voice said, 'Mr Masters' residence.'

'Can I speak to Mabel? It's Mrs Masters.' The handset banged down and the silence seemed long. Then a timid voice said. 'It's Mabel here, Mrs Masters.'

Fanny took a deep breath. 'I've got a favour to ask of you, Mabel. You know I saw ample evidence when I came to the house the other day that my husband has a new lady friend?' She went on to tell her what her solicitor had said about getting somebody to corroborate the facts and possibly give evidence in her divorce case.

'Evidence of Mr Masters' adultery?' Fanny could hear the horror in Mabel's voice. 'I couldn't. What would he say? I'm sorry, very sorry but . . .'

Fanny put the phone down, feeling cold with disappointment. She told herself it was what she'd expected and at least she'd tried, but she felt she was about to lose out yet again.

Greta had been standing in for Dorothy Wild for two full weeks, and had found staying with Mungo for six nights a week total bliss. But the unaccustomed late and wakeful nights of lovemaking were taking a toll on both of them.

The days were busier than ever. On Friday night it was eleven thirty when they got home, and a little later when Mungo led the way to the dining room to have their supper. Greta was sleepy and almost past wanting to eat, but Mungo expected a full dinner however late the hour and Norah stayed up to serve it.

In the car on the way home, he'd been cock-a-hoop because the takings had touched a new height. Now at the table, he seemed to sag and looked exhausted.

Norah brought the soup to the table and that was very tasty, but Greta could see Mungo didn't like the look of the pork chops that followed. He tried to cut into his, but gave an impatient snort and started stabbing at it with his fork.

'This meat's dried up,' he barked at Norah, who was bringing more plates to the sideboard. 'So are the vegetables. This is good food ruined.'

'I'm sorry, sir.'

Greta struggled with her chop. It was a little dry but

ordinarily she had a good appetite and, had she not been so tired, would have eaten it with gusto.

'It isn't fit to eat.' Mungo crashed his knife and fork down on his plate. 'Tell Mabel to come here.' Norah fled. Greta could see a crimson tide running up his neck and into his cheeks.

'It's not too bad,' she said mildly. 'The runner beans are nice.'

'They're cold,' he snapped.

There was a scuffle at the door and Mabel peered round it. She slid in nervously to stand with her back to the sideboard, a timid-looking woman not yet thirty. 'You wanted to see me, sir?'

'Call yourself a cook?' Mungo thundered. 'I can't eat this chop. It's overcooked.'

'I'm sorry—'

'It's no good being sorry. I pay you to cook my meals. I expect them to be edible.'

Her head jerked up – she wore an ugly cap covering every hair. 'It had to be kept waiting, sir. I'm sorry.'

'Don't keep saying you're sorry!'

Greta hadn't been hungry to start with, but now her appetite vanished. She was shocked at Mungo's anger and could see Mabel was struggling to stand up for herself.

'Your orders were to have your dinner ready at half-past ten and I cooked it for that time. It's now ten to twelve. Food can't be at its best if it's kept warm for ages. It does dry out.'

Greta was surprised at her daring and Mungo looked taken aback. 'Don't you speak to me like that,' he bellowed. 'I won't have it.'

'I'm sorry, sir, but it's the truth.'

Mungo flared up in an even wilder temper, his face puce. 'Get your bags packed and be gone from here tonight. Go on, get packing. I can't be doing with servants who answer back.'

'Mungo!' Greta was scared but felt she had to protest. 'It's the middle of the night. Mabel can't leave now.'

He stood up. 'I can't eat any more. I'm going to bed.'

'Tomorrow,' Greta insisted. 'That will be soon enough. We can talk to Mabel again then, can't we?'

'Have it your way,' he grunted at Greta. 'I'm too tired to fight you now. Come to bed.'

Mabel was cowering by the door. 'Good night,' Greta said as she followed him out. She dropped her voice. 'Don't worry.'

As soon as she was in the bedroom, Mungo shut the door. 'Don't ever do that again,' he said. 'Do not interfere.' Greta could see his temper was rising again. 'I control the servants, not you.' Mungo began throwing off his clothes.

'But when we're married,' Greta protested, 'then it will be my job, won't it? To see to domestic matters?'

He turned and stared through her. 'Mabel's a stupid woman,' he shouted. 'She can't do anything right. She'll have to go.'

He got into bed, tossed himself away from her and put out his bedside lamp, leaving Greta in the dark.

She was upset. Mungo had always been attentive and loving towards her, but now she sensed he was within a flicker of losing control of his temper completely. Instead, he had to ignore her.

She felt her way over to switch on the lamp on the other side of the bed. She'd never seen Mungo in a mood like this. She knew his employees at the fair thought him a difficult man and he certainly had a temper that could erupt like Vesuvius. But it was midnight and he'd been working all day so he must be tired. Everybody got cranky when they were tired.

Greta, exhausted too, told herself things would look different in the morning. When Mungo had calmed down she'd make him see how wrong he was to blame Mabel when they'd been so late coming to the table. Of course he had to hire and fire his own servants, and she shouldn't have pushed herself in between them. When they were married perhaps, but not yet. In time, she thought, she'd be able to change him, help him keep his temper.

Greta was woken at nine thirty the next morning, when Norah brought in their usual tray of tea. She pulled herself up the bed, watched Norah draw back the curtains and let in bright sunshine.

Mungo was lying inert beside her, until Norah announced in a flat voice, 'Mabel's gone. She left early this morning. What d'you want doing about your lunch?'

'I'll come down to see to it,' Greta said.

Mungo sat up, instantly wide awake. 'Good God! She's gone?' He was choking with fury. 'Stupid woman – she was no good anyway, but she might have had the courtesy to work out her notice.'

Greta thought that outrageous after what he'd said to poor Mabel last night.

'I paid her but she works a week in hand – I'm surprised she's gone without that.'

Greta asked, 'Has she been working here long?'

'Far too long. Years . . . I don't know. Today's Saturday. I'll ring the employment agency, but I don't suppose we'll get another cook until next week.'

Greta poured out two cups of tea. 'I can cook.'

'I don't want you to cook, I want you to do other things. And you've asked your mother and Kenny to come again tomorrow night. They'll expect a meal.'

'Mam's a good cook – she'll help.'

'I'm not having your mother in my kitchen.'

Greta could see his temper was threatening to boil over again.

'Please don't get angry, Mungo. It doesn't help. Let's get up and go for a walk. It's a lovely morning and it'll make us both feel better.'

Mungo was getting out of bed. 'If there's a problem, it has to be dealt with. Going for a walk won't help. I'll see what there is in the kitchen and Norah can do a bit of cooking. It won't hurt her.'

Greta wanted to tell him to calm down, but was afraid that would have the opposite effect.

'We'll have soup and then something cold tonight,' he grunted, still angry. 'She can do a simple roast on Sunday.'

It surprised her that he wanted to be in charge of domestic matters, and even more that he was capable of choosing a menu simple enough for Norah to manage. He didn't seem to want anyone else to interfere. She told herself this wasn't the end of the world, it would blow over, but his treatment of Mabel left her less sure about Mungo. Perhaps he wasn't as kind and caring as she'd thought.

*

On his next Sunday night visit to his father's house, Louis discovered, much to his surprise, that his father had a new cook.

'We're trying her out,' he said. 'She's not cooked a full meal for five before. I was lucky the agency could send her here straight away. I hope the food's all right.'

'I'm sure it'll be very nice,' Ruth told him.

'What's happened to Mabel?' Louis wanted to know. He'd thought Mabel well established and had heard Pa praise her cooking, especially her cakes. Had she got fed up with Pa and given in her notice, or was this something to do with Mam?

'I sacked her,' he said in his high-handed manner. 'She was letting her standards slip.'

Louis saw immediately that this might help Mam.

Before the meal was served, Greta sent Kenny to wash his hands in the cloakroom and took her mother upstairs. Louis wanted to ask where Mabel was now and how he could get in touch with her. But he didn't dare, and knew Pa would never tell him anyway.

He took the opportunity to tell him that Mam had a new dog. He wanted him to know he'd won yet another round, so he wouldn't be expecting Mam to come back. He wanted the row over Jess to die down. He knew Pa well enough to realise that when he was fighting about one thing, his temper was likely to boil over about something quite different. Mam needed peace.

Louis had an enjoyable evening, and this time when they were preparing to go home, he managed to get Greta in the front seat of his Austin Seven. He spent most of the drive home trying to steer the conversation round to Mabel, to find out if Greta knew where she'd gone, but with no success.

Greta chatted on, telling him how much she was enjoying the fair. He found she was working in the ticket booth and on the refreshment counter, just as his mother had.

When Louis got back to Southport the house was in darkness. He thought his mother must be asleep, but as he reached the landing she called out to him.

He went in to perch on her bed and tell her Mabel had been sacked and a new cook installed in her place.

'Why?'

'I don't know. Nobody wanted to talk about that.'

His mother sighed. 'I expect Mungo got himself worked up about something she'd done or left undone. Where has she gone? If only we knew that . . .'

'She could be anywhere. She could be working for someone else by now.'

'It's possible she'd be willing to testify against Pa now. He'll have caused a row.'

'I tried to ask Greta where she was but I don't think she knows. I don't think any of them know. Apparently she packed her bag and was gone the next morning.'

CHAPTER SIXTEEN

I T WAS a busy summer's day and the Southport fair was thronged with day-trippers from Liverpool. The music was blaring out and Fanny felt buoyed up by the jollity. She was in charge of the chairoplanes and was collecting tickets for the next ride and allotting customers their chairs.

She noticed the rather staid young woman looking at her because she seemed out of place in her brown straw hat and long-sleeved dress. With a jolt she realised it was Mabel; without her cook's uniform she hadn't immediately recognised her.

Bursting with hope, Fanny was galvanised into action. She asked the schoolboy helping her to set the roundabout spinning and went to talk to her.

'Mabel, what brings you here?'

Her face was screwing up with worry. 'I'll do it,' she said, 'if you still want me to. I'll testify against Mr Masters. It's only the truth, after all.'

Fanny felt her heart bounce. 'Thank you, thank you very much.' She threw her arms round her in a hug. 'I'd be very grateful if you would.'

'The girl's been practically living there – just goes home for one night each week. But her mother knows, she comes too. It isn't right, though, is it?'

'I'm so glad you changed your mind. What made you?' Fanny asked.

'He sacked me without a reference, told me to get out of the house at midnight. How could I do that when it's miles from anywhere? He expected me to walk away with my suitcases in the dark.' There was an angry flush to Mabel's cheeks. 'It'll make it hard for me to get another job.'

Fanny said. 'I can vouch for your cooking skills. Didn't I eat your meals for years?'

'He said I couldn't cook . . .'

'You're a good cook, Mabel.'

'The dinner was spoiled that night, that's why he sacked me, but they were over an hour late coming home. Stands to reason food won't be as good after that.' Mabel was breathing venom for Mungo.

Fanny put a hand on her arm. 'Come and have a cup of tea in the office. I can write a reference for you straight away.'

'Thank you, I did hope . . . most people would expect my references to come from the wife . . .'

'I'll just tell Frank I'm going, so he can keep an eye on the chairoplanes.'

It gave Fanny satisfaction to sit at what Mungo still considered to be his desk and write out the reference he'd refused. 'For how long did you work for us?'

'Seven and a half years.'

'That speaks for itself,' Fanny said. 'Mungo wouldn't have

put up with bad cooking for all that time.' She wrote about Mabel in glowing terms.

That done, Fanny sipped her cup of tea. 'About what you said you'd do for me – you're sure?'

'Is it wrong to want revenge? I want to pay him back for what he did to me. I gave him good service, though he's not an easy man to work for. He's domineering and bossy, and thinks he can do everything better than anybody else. Even cooking.'

'Don't I know?' Fanny sighed. 'I'll telephone Mr Danvers, my solicitor, and suggest I take you down to see him.'

It was arranged that she should and they walked down together. Mabel agreed to sign a statement saying Mungo had had Greta Arrowsmith in his house and in his bed for the last three weeks as well as on earlier occasions. Under Mr Danvers' guidance she quoted dates. She also said Norah had made their bed every morning and had done Miss Arrowsmith's washing. Mabel agreed to testify in court to that effect, should it be necessary.

'He can't hurt me any more.' Her smile was wan. 'Not now I've lost my job.'

'Where are you staying now?' Fanny asked.

'With an auntie in Liverpool. I want to go to stay with my sister in Carlisle and have a rest and a holiday, but I'll have to start looking for another job.'

'I'm looking for a new cook,' Mr Danvers said. 'My present one is retiring next month. It would be so convenient if you . . .'

Mabel took the reference Fanny had just written for her from her bag and pushed it in front of him.

Fanny said, 'She's an excellent cook – roasts and stews, makes cakes too. You won't be disappointed.'

He said, 'Could you spare the time now to come and see my wife? She decides, of course, but since you've been highly recommended there seems little point in looking elsewhere.'

For the first time, Fanny saw Mabel's worried frown disappear. Her rather plain face broke into a wide smile.

Friday morning brought Mungo another thick envelope from Mr Fox, his solicitor. He stared at it for a long moment, feeling queasy. Then he picked up the Indian knife and slit the envelope on three sides before lifting out the contents. The word 'divorce' leaped out at him from the letter.

Seconds later he hurled the papers across his study. Fanny had changed her petition from one of judicial separation to divorce, citing adultery as well as persistent cruelty and refusal to pay her alimony. He swore, afraid this was going to prove expensive.

Mr Fox wrote, 'You should start paying your wife two pounds a week as an interim amount of alimony with immediate effect.'

Mungo was furious. Fanny's list of complaints against him was growing and her ill will was all too evident. He was afraid the greater the grounds Fanny felt she had for divorce, the greater the amount of maintenance he'd have to pay her when the judgment was decided. He immediately telephoned for an appointment to see his solicitor. He was sure his wife meant to fleece him of every penny she could but consoled himself with the thought that it would mean he'd be free to marry Greta.

The letter he'd received this morning also gave him the date of 18 August when the case would come before the court. It was horribly close, and now Mungo could think of nothing else.

He wanted to be a free man again and have the whole thing behind him, but he was afraid details would be reported in the papers and Ruth would hear of it and it would cause more trouble for him.

He forced himself to think of Greta. What good was a fine house if he had no one here to share it with? He needed her here.

Mungo knew little about the processes of the law. The only occasion when he'd been summoned to court in the past had resulted in a stiff fine. It was with a sense of foreboding that he was counting off the days until the divorce case was heard.

Fanny had become bitter and revengeful, and he was fearful of what she might accuse him of doing and the friends she might find to support her allegations. He said nothing to Greta. The only person he could discuss the divorce with was his solicitor. He set out for Mr Fox's office straight after breakfast.

Mungo was furious with himself. He'd known he was risking this by taking Greta home with him and persuading her to stay the night. It was over a year since Fanny had deserted him, what was a man with normal feelings supposed to do?

He wanted to protect Greta from what might be printed in the newspapers. He blamed Louis. Somebody must have told Fanny about Greta. He felt powerless, he could do nothing to influence events and he hated that most of all. The law was going to exact its toll.

He was somewhat reassured to hear Mr Fox explain that since Mungo now wanted a divorce too, he'd recommend they did not defend the case. And the greater the grounds for divorce, the more likely it was to be granted. Furthermore, the grounds had no bearing whatsoever on the amount of maintenance he'd be required to pay.

Mr Fox looked at him over the top of his glasses and said, 'When a decree is granted, an order will be made by the court for permanent maintenance according to your means. It's usually set at one-third of the spouse's income.'

Mungo was shocked. He'd been happy to pay Fanny two pounds a week alimony as an interim amount, but one third? That put him in a turmoil about what it would cost to pay Fanny off.

'Yes. Alternatively, you can make one full and final payment and have a clean break. But your wife would have to agree to that and to the amount.'

'Can it be negotiated?'

'Yes.'

That sounded a better way of doing it. Mungo disliked the thought of paying over regular sums to Fanny. He had no way of working out what the total would amount to, and it would sour him to have a permanent reminder of her.

He felt so churned up, he couldn't go on to the fair. He went home, meaning to shut himself in his bedroom until he calmed down, but he couldn't settle on his bed. He went for a long coastal walk, although it was raining.

It came to him, as he strode out, how it could be done and at no great expense to him.

It seemed that a fitting way of getting his own back on Fanny would be to offer to make over the Southport funfair to her as a one-off maintenance payment. What could be more suitable when she and Louis were already running it?

Mungo was glad now that he'd never talked seriously about the business to Fanny, not even in the early days. He'd wanted it to be his business and not one he shared with her. He'd wanted to run it alone and always had.

He congratulated himself on keeping quiet that the Southport funfair would have to close down next year anyway. Few knew about that – he was almost certain Fanny and Louis did not. They'd jump at it, thinking they'd struck gold.

It would put Louis out of a job within the year, but Mungo had little sympathy for him remembering how, when Fanny had tried to fiddle the Southport books, Louis had sided with her.

Mungo regretted that he wouldn't be able to move the roundabouts and stalls to Rhyl as he'd intended, but he still had plenty of time to order more and could open with everything brand new.

Yes, that's what he'd do. He'd opt for a divorce and offer the fair as part of the settlement. He'd teach Fanny to steal from him.

Mungo felt calmer when he returned but Greta had come home by taxi in the meantime.

'Mungo, you're soaking wet. Where've you been to get like that?' She looked very surprised. 'A walk in this? And you didn't take Jess? She'd have loved it.'

Mungo wanted to kick himself. He'd drawn her attention to the fact that he was distraught. He spent the rest of the day trying to appear more relaxed than he was.

When the day came on which his case was to be heard, Mungo went to court, although Mr Fox had advised him not to. He felt he had to know what was going on. He flattered himself on being strong and resilient, but today he felt apprehensive.

He hadn't seen Fanny since he'd spotted her at the Southport fair. She'd looked thin and haggard then, a shadow of the handsome woman she'd once been. Her appearance in court surprised him. She'd put on a little weight, her hair showed she was going to a good hairdresser and she had colour in her cheeks. She looked healthy and in control of things.

On the charge of adultery he was shocked to see Mabel, his ex-cook, stand up to give evidence. In a strong voice she said he'd invited a young woman by the name of Miss Greta Arrowsmith to the house. He cringed with horror to hear Greta's name and was grateful neither she nor her mother was here to hear it. Mabel said firmly that she'd stayed overnight for six days at a time on several occasions and quoted the dates.

Mungo wanted to kick himself for giving Mabel the sack. Of course, like Fanny, she was out to get her revenge. He should have remembered she knew Fanny and foreseen how she might get back at him.

He blamed Fanny: she was doing her utmost to hurt him in every way she could. Her allegations about cruelty appalled him. She'd blown up all sorts of minor incidents and even accidents to support her story. With the help of hospital records and the testimony of her doctor, she got her divorce.

As Mr Fox had expected, judgment was given against him; Mungo was found to be the guilty partner, to have committed adultery and shown persistent cruelty to his wife over the last twenty years.

With a swimming head and rubbery knees, Mungo almost had to feel his way back to Georgio and the car. Yes, he was glad to be free of Fanny, but he was shaking with fury at all she'd said and done. He couldn't face the people at the fair and neither could he face going home. He couldn't trust himself to act as a normal man would. He wanted to scream that most of it was lies.

He ordered Georgio to take him to Prestatyn, because the journey there would give him longer to pull himself together. He closed his eyes and sank into the cushions of the back seat. The palms of his hands itched; he wanted to wrap them round Fanny's throat and squeeze the life out of her. He found he'd twisted his own hands so hard they were white and creased.

The nightmare wasn't yet over. He had his decree nisi, but he'd have to wait another six months to have his decree absolute and be free to marry again.

He was worried now about the publicity that might be given to this. He'd always had national and local weekly newspapers delivered to his home, but now he was careful to remove them so neither Greta nor his staff might read anything about his divorce. He knew there was a piece about it in one of the local papers, though he didn't read it; the headlines were enough. He hardly looked at any newspaper that week.

It bothered him that he had no control over what his staff at the fair might read. Many of them knew and liked Fanny. He couldn't help but see newspapers lying about in the fair, and had to tell himself he was imagining that some of his employees had developed an accusing attitude.

He was afraid they would gossip behind his back and even more afraid Greta would hear of it. She was isolated in the ticket booth during the mornings, but he'd seen staff stop for a chat when she wasn't busy. She helped the loud-mouthed Agnes Watts sell ice cream and lemonade in the afternoons and they seemed to be getting quite chummy. He saw that as the danger point, but there seemed little he could do but trust to luck.

After considerable haggling between solicitors, Mungo heard that Fanny would agree to accept as maintenance all his Southport businesses as going concerns: the funfair with its roundabouts and slot machines, the tearooms in the building next door, together with their fittings, fixtures and the leases on the premises. In addition, he had to agree to buy for her the freehold of the terraced house in which she was now living. He found it daunting that he was also forced to pay her legal costs.

Mungo didn't want to part with so much of what he'd so painstakingly built up. He was furious with Fanny for driving such a hard bargain. In his calmer moments, he realised that when the time came, the best thing for him to do was to grit his teeth and sign over to Fanny what had been agreed.

It pleased him to think of the shock she'd have when she found the fair would have to close. It served her right. Nobody would get the better of him.

Mungo told himself it was over, and all he had to do now was wait six more months and he could marry Greta. Then he would start a new and happy life. He had to put the divorce behind him, forget Fanny and Louis and keep his mind on the future.

Greta handed back the note Mungo had wanted her to read. It was from Dorothy Wild. Her recovery had taken far longer than originally expected but at last she was well enough to return to work the following week.

'I'd prefer you to carry on doing her job,' he said. 'It provides a good excuse for you to stay overnight and I like that, don't you?'

'What about Dorothy? She needs the job.'

'She's not very strong. She shouldn't be working until late at night.'

'You aren't thinking of giving her the sack?'

Mungo was pulling a face. 'I could swap your duties with hers. That would do it.'

Greta bit on her lips. 'I told Mam I'd be going back on earlies and live at home once Dorothy was back. I think I should.'

'All right, do that for the first few days. Then we'll say the late hours are proving too much for Dorothy and I'll swap your hours permanently.'

'Mungo! That's a bit underhand.'

'It's what you want, isn't it?'

Greta did.

'I'll fix it with your mam,' he told her. 'I'll have a word with her about it next time she comes over.'

The following Monday Greta went into the fair early and at two o'clock a pale and fragile-looking Dorothy returned to work. Greta had a busy afternoon on the refreshment bar with Agnes. Around five o'clock, the crowd in the fair began to thin as they drifted home for their tea.

'Lordy me, it's hot.' Agnes propped herself up against the counter. 'Make us a wafer each, Greta. We've earned it today.'

It was one of Mungo's rules that all staff must pay for everything taken from the refreshment bar. Greta knew Agnes didn't always pay, though she charged everybody else.

'Cutting ice cream up and handling all this chocolate and these fancy biscuits – I can smell them – makes my mouth water,' she explained to Greta. 'He can't expect us to put our hands in our pockets all the time. Shop girls never have to pay, do they? The owners know they can't stop them tasting the wares. Don't you tell him. He doesn't need to know everything.'

'I'm afraid Mungo wouldn't like it,' Greta said, cutting another two slices of ice cream. 'But I won't tell him this time.'

'There's a few things I reckon he doesn't tell you.' Agnes was feeling for her handbag, which she kept at the back of a cupboard. 'I bet he hasn't shown you this?'

She unfolded a newspaper cutting and pushed it close to the fridge as she accepted the wafer. Greta licked at hers before picking the cutting up to read.

CAROUSEL OF SECRETS

Wife of fairground owner granted a divorce on the grounds of adultery and persistent cruelty.

Greta gasped. Black horror was sweeping through her, but she couldn't stop reading. All the details were here, spelling it out for her.

'It's all right, love. The boss can't see what you're doing. This is the safest place in the fair,' Agnes laughed. 'We're right under his office, really tucked out of his sight.'

Greta read on, 'Miss Marguerite Mary Arrowsmith was cited as co-respondent.'

It even gave her address as Henshaw Street and her age. Greta couldn't get her breath. He'd done this to her? She remembered the day Mungo had come home soaking wet from a walk. Was it 18 August? It must have been around then. He'd known all about this and deliberately kept it from her.

Mungo hadn't mentioned his divorce for ages, certainly not that he'd received his decree nisi. Why not? She thought it momentous news that opened up the future for both of them. Could it be that he didn't want to marry her after all?

She turned the cutting over to see the date. Now she thought about it, she hadn't seen any newspapers at The Chase this week. She'd commented on it to Mungo and he'd said the newspaper boy must have forgotten to bring them. Had he deliberately removed them so she wouldn't see this? Had he deliberately lied when she'd asked about the papers?

'You all right, love?'

Greta was churning with shock, rage and reproach. Why

should Mungo do this to her? Suddenly she was aware of ice cream dripping down her overall.

'Yes.'

Clutching the cutting, she ran for the stairs. She was going to face Mungo with it. She almost bumped into Rex, who intercepted her, holding her up against the wall.

'Look at these.' He brought out a bundle of newspaper cuttings that he'd folded small enough to fit into his pocket.

'I've already seen them,' she said. 'Let me go.'

He held on to her; she could see he was upset.

'To be quoted as co-respondent, with your name in the paper – what's he thinking of to let that happen? He's ruined your reputation.'

'I don't like it either,' she snapped. 'But I expect it's Fanny's fault. Mungo says she's mentally ill, suffering from some psychiatric illness. She doesn't understand what she's doing.'

'Nonsense. That's not what the others in this fair say.'

'It's defamatory,' she said, waving his cuttings away. 'Slander.'

'No, it isn't. It's a report of what happened in a court of law. Mungo's got his divorce, but he's been found to be the guilty partner.'

'It's none of your business.'

'It is. How d'you think your mother will feel? I hate to see this happening to you.'

'Let go of me.' Greta shook him off and scrambled upstairs to Mungo's office. She was shaking with fury when she burst in on him.

Mungo was at his desk; he looked up from the papers he was working on. 'What's the matter?'

'This.' She slammed the cutting down on top of his papers. 'A report on your divorce. My name has been published in a newspaper. I'm publicly labelled as a loose woman for all to see. Why didn't you tell me? Why keep me in the dark?'

He was on his feet, wrapping his arms round her. 'How could I? I knew it would upset you.' He was trying to hug and kiss her.

That enraged Greta more and she wriggled out of his arms. 'Don't soft-soap me. I'm not having it. Why let me find out this way? Didn't it occur to you that I'd find this even more upsetting?'

'Who gave you this cutting?' She could see he was getting angry too.

'Agnes.'

'Oh, Agnes Watts! That's her finished. I'm not having her work for me after this.' He was about to charge down to the fair.

Greta caught at him. 'No, Mungo! You'll make things worse. Sit down and calm down. She's not the only one with cuttings to show me.' She didn't dare mention Rex's name now.

With a groan, he lowered himself on to his chair, propped his elbows on his desk and dropped his head on his hands. 'If only Agnes . . . I hoped you wouldn't find out.'

'You must have known I would! You have all these people working for you – how did you think you were going to stop them reading the newspapers? They know Fanny, they know she wanted a divorce. You must have realised their eyes would be drawn like magnets to any mention of your name.

Agnes was the first to tell me, but if she hadn't the others would have done.'

'I'm sorry.'

Greta shook her head angrily. 'What I find really hurtful is that you didn't tell me, didn't even mention your divorce. Didn't you think I'd want to know? You told me we'd be married once it came through.'

'This is just the decree nisi. It makes no difference to you and me.'

'It does,' she shrieked. 'It's progress towards it, isn't it?'

'Yes, but I've another six months to wait before I can remarry.'

'Mungo, I want you to share things with me, the bad things as well as the good. You treat me as though I'm a nobody; as though I won't understand or can't help. Don't you want my support? Now Agnes knows you tried to keep me in the dark, they all will.'

She saw his lips tighten. 'I can find somebody else to sell the ice cream.'

'Don't you dare. It's not her fault, it's yours. Your problem is you think you can handle everything and everybody. You're not in charge of the world, Mungo.'

Greta could hardly believe she was saying such things to him, but they needed saying. She was throwing off her overall and cap.

'I can't stand your godlike attitude. This is not the way a fiancé should act. I'm going home.'

'Please don't leave me like this. You will come back?'

'Wouldn't it be better if I didn't?'

She went tearing downstairs. She had to get away from

him. The whole thing was a mistake. Better the laundry and poverty. At least there, she'd been treated like a human being who could think for herself.

She'd go home and stay home. Once out on the pavement, she could see a ferry waiting to cast off. She broke into a run, heading for the pier. Mungo was following. She quickened her pace.

'Greta, wait for me. We've got to talk this over.'

She was running along the pier. Through the planks she could see the sand had given way to swirling water. They were about to lift the gangway on the ferry but saw her running and waited.

'Don't go, Greta. Don't leave me,' Mungo called.

She ran straight on. 'Thank you,' she puffed to the man working the gangway. He was still waiting, expecting Mungo to board the vessel. As she climbed the stairs to the top deck she heard it rattle up and saw the boat was casting off.

She could see Mungo still standing on the pier, looking bereft. She'd expected him to follow her on too. The two feet of water between the boat and the pier was rapidly widening.

Greta moved to the opposite side of the boat where she couldn't see him and stood staring down into the muddy waters of the Mersey. She knew already it had been a mistake to run away from him. She was sorry she had. She told herself Mungo had had a lot of worry, with Fanny and the divorce. He'd hidden the newspapers to protect her; he'd meant well. In her mind's eye she saw him again at his desk with his head in his hands. He'd been full of regrets. She couldn't end everything like this. He was right, they had to talk it through. Greta was sure that once they were married and settled, he'd be a calmer person and quite different. She'd be able to change him.

If Mam saw any of those cuttings she'd tell her straight that she was ruined. Her reputation was publicly soiled. She'd say the only thing Greta could do was to marry Mungo, that she'd already made her choice. It was too late to leave him. If she backed off now, not only would her own job be gone, but Mungo would have good reason not to carry on paying Mam the allowance as he'd promised, and Rex might get the sack. There was Kenny to think about too. He didn't want to go back to school for a last term; he was counting the days until he could have a full-time job at the fair. Not only would she upset her own life but also the lives of those she loved and who were closest to her.

By the time the ferry was tying up at Pier Head she'd made up her mind. She ran up to the booking office and bought a return ticket, then came back to the boat. There was so much about Mungo that was drawing her back to him.

When she returned to his office she found him at his desk, sunk in misery, just as she'd imagined he would be.

CHAPTER SEVENTEEN

MUNGO HEARD the light steps on the stairs and thought it sounded like Greta coming up. Wishful thinking, he was telling himself when the door opened and she was standing in front of him.

His spirits soared and he jumped up. 'You've come back? To stay?'

She looked deflated and miserable. 'I was a fool to go. I'm sorry.'

'I'm so glad.' He was round his desk and wrapping his arms about her. 'I thought I'd lost you. I was kicking myself. I should have talked to you, explained everything, shouldn't I?'

Greta nodded. 'I lost my temper . . . I wasn't thinking straight.'

'Neither was I. What I should have explained was that Fanny walked out on me.'

'You did,' Greta said. 'You told me that.'

'I want to tell you everything. I must. Sit down.' He backed her to a chair and sat down himself. Frowning heavily, he tried to collect his thoughts.

'I spent fifteen months trying to persuade Fanny to return. In other words, she deserted me. According to the law, that made her the guilty partner and she wouldn't be able to claim the alimony she wanted from me.

'Fanny consulted a solicitor, who told her that if she petitioned for divorce on the grounds of cruelty and adultery, and won her case, it would make me the guilty partner and she'd be entitled to maintenance. I didn't contest it because by then I'd met you, and that changed everything.'

'You wanted the divorce?'

'Oh, yes, I have to have a divorce, don't I?' Mungo sighed. 'I've been worried stiff. Fanny made out I was a serial adulterer, but it's the last thing I am. Once there was her and now there's you, and that's it. Honest. It was all trumped up to give her grounds to claim maintenance from me.

'You remember Mabel, our old cook? She gave evidence that she'd seen you staying the night at my house. She was out for revenge because I sacked her. That's what did for me.

'I'm ashamed and embarrassed I didn't handle things better. If only I hadn't sacked her!'

'You should have explained to me what was happening.'

His dark eyes pleaded with her. 'I know. I failed there too. Am I forgiven?'

'Of course,' Greta sighed. 'Let's forget it. I'd better go back to work, though it's nearly time for me to finish. I ought to show Agnes I've taken your divorce in my stride.' She put on her cap. 'Did you say anything to her?'

'No, you were right: I'd only have made things worse. You tell her that everything Fanny claims is not the truth.' Mungo watched her take a clean overall from the cupboard, feeling in a lather of relief that she'd returned. Fanny would no doubt be pleased if she knew the divorce had almost caused a rift between them.

'No, wait a minute, don't go yet. I'll have my decree absolute by the eighteenth of February. We could be married any time after that.'

Coming so soon after their first tiff, it took Greta's breath away. She'd expected to feel heady with joy when Mungo wanted to arrange their wedding date, but now . . . ?

'Well,' he was smiling, 'what d'you say to that? It's what we intended, isn't it?'

It make Greta feel churlish so she gave him a hug. 'I'm thrilled, Let me get the calendar.' She was turning to the one on the wall but he'd already decided.

'Monday the twenty-first of March. We're less busy at the beginning of the week. We could have a few days' honeymoon then.'

'Lovely.' Greta was laughing with the joy of it. 'We really can set the date? That's wonderful.'

Greta forgave him everything. She'd been right to trust Mungo and believe him when he said he loved her and wanted to marry her.

'Come on,' he said. 'We'll walk along to the Grand Hotel and have a drink to celebrate before you catch the ferry home.'

Greta was throwing off her cap and overall again. To have a glass of champagne in the lounge at the Grand Hotel was a marvellous way to mark the event. She admired the way Mungo could put their differences behind him and concentrate on what was good. She must do the same.

Over high tea later that evening, she felt on top of the world as she said to Mam and Kenny, 'Mungo's divorce has been settled. He wants us to be married as soon as it becomes absolute; he's suggesting the twenty-first of March.'

Her mother gave a little cry of delight and leaped round the table to kiss her. Greta could see pleasure and relief on her face in equal measure.

'At last! I'm so pleased.'

Kenny smiled up at her over his plate of hotpot. 'Does that mean I'll see more of Jess?'

'Yes, you'll see more of Mungo as well.'

'Will that make you rich?'

'Yes,' Mam said. 'Our Greta will be a rich man's wife. You'll live in a different world. No more penny-pinching for you. I'm delighted for you.'

By the following week Mungo had switched Greta's duties with Dorothy's.

'Mungo's very thoughtful for his staff,' Greta had said to her mother. 'He's worried that working late is too much for Dorothy just yet.'

It meant Greta was staying at Mungo's house again and that it was becoming a regular fixture for Mam and Kenny to come over to the fair on Sunday afternoons, and for Mungo to take them home for supper afterwards. Louis usually came too, and Greta enjoyed it as the most sociable night of the week.

One Sunday evening Ruth asked rather nervously if they were making plans for their wedding. Greta had expected Mungo to want a quiet ceremony in a register office. After all, it was his second marriage and the first had just ended in a painful divorce.

'I'm giving it a lot of thought,' Mungo said. 'A register office, of course, followed by a formal church blessing, simple and tasteful. It's the first time for Greta and I want to make a bit of a splash. I'm going to get a firm of caterers to come in and hold the reception here in the house. I don't want a huge crowd here, perhaps twenty or twenty-five. I've decided to put on a few refreshments down at the fair for my employees and keep this end more select.'

Her mother beamed round the table. 'Greta will make a beautiful bride.'

Mungo agreed. 'I can't wait to see her in her wedding dress.'

Greta knew Mam was pleased to hear his wedding plans. It would seem to her to bring it nearer.

'A white wedding?' Mam asked.

'Yes,' Mungo said firmly. 'A white wedding.'

Mam raised her eyebrows and looked uncomfortable, which made Greta feel uncomfortable too. Clearly Mam thought that it would be more fitting if Greta did not wear a white dress to signify virginity. But she said, 'I'll come with you, Greta, to choose the style. Isn't that what mothers are expected to do?'

'We've already ordered the dress,' Mungo said shortly.

'I'm going for a fitting tomorrow,' Greta added quickly to get over the embarrassment. 'We went to a shop in Bold Street.'

She could see her mother was disappointed but thought she would have been intimidated by the elegant shop and haughty assistants. Mam would not have picked out such an ornate and expensive dress for her. In fact, Greta would have preferred something simpler.

Ruth asked, 'What are you going to do about bridesmaids?'

'Will I need bridesmaids?' Greta faltered. 'If it's to be a blessing in a church?'

'Of course you do,' Mungo said irritably. 'We want to do this with style.'

'Then I'll ask Phyllis Wood.'

'Just one?' Mam ventured.

When Mungo had started discussing arrangements for their wedding with Greta, he'd suggested she have two or three bridesmaids, but when she'd mentioned her other friends, Mary Geraghty and Lily Bates, he'd said girls from the laundry would be no better than girls from the fair.

She'd protested, 'Phyllis is a nice girl.'

'Let's stick with her then,' he'd said crossly. A few minutes later he'd said, 'I'm sorry, Greta. You must think I'm a real bear. You have as many bridesmaids as you want.'

Greta decided she'd be very happy with just one. Phyllis had been her special friend.

He'd said by way of excuse, 'Things didn't go right at work today, but I mustn't let myself get upset.'

'What went wrong?'

She wanted him to confide his worries in her but he'd shaken his head and said, 'Better if I forget the whole thing.'

Now Mam straightened up in her seat. 'If you want more attendants, what about having Kenny as a pageboy?'

'No,' Kenny objected, 'I'm not going to be dressed up in

white satin. I'm too old for that. No, I don't want to be a pageboy.'

Greta said, 'Mam, we need to draw up a list of guests you want to invite.'

'Not too many,' Mungo cautioned.

'That won't be our problem,' Greta told him, getting out pen and paper.

'We have to ask cousin Edward and his wife,' Ruth said, 'and Greta's two maiden aunts. Then there's Esther and Rex.'

Greta decided she was going to invite her friends Mary and Lily whether Mungo approved of them or not. She added their names to the list, together with that of Phyllis's fiancé. They could think of no one else.

'I was an only child,' Ruth said, 'and my mother was an only, too. We never did have many relatives.'

In the past, Greta had always gone home with Mam and Kenny to spend her day off there, but now Mungo began to find reasons why she should stay with him. He told her the fair was continuing to be very busy and he needed every available hand. Mam no longer seemed to expect Greta would go back with her.

Greta had written to Phyllis asking her to be her bridesmaid.

'I'd love to,' she'd written back. 'You must be thrilled to be marrying a man like Mungo, and to know you'll never have to work in a laundry again.'

Today, Greta had arranged to meet her in Liverpool so they could choose her bridesmaid dress.

'You pay for it,' Mungo had told her. 'You don't need to

spend the earth on it. You'll stand out all the more if her dress is nothing special.'

Greta decided it would be special. She wanted Phyllis to have the most flattering dress they could find. She would take her to Lewis's. Phyllis was waiting for her in the doorway on the corner of Ranelagh Street, her face shining with excitement.

'You are lucky, Greta! Mary and Lily send their love. All the girls at the laundry are drooling with envy. You must be having a marvellous time.'

Greta gave her a joyful hug. It was lovely to see her friend again. 'I miss you.'

'But not the laundry?'

'No, not that.'

In the bridal department there was a lovely selection of gowns for bridesmaids.

'What colour do you want me to have?' Phyllis asked.

'You choose,' Greta said. 'As you're to be the only one it doesn't really matter.'

'Not pink then – it makes me look sallow. That blue dress is lovely and so is the lavender one.'

'Try them on. I like that pale green one too.'

'Eau-de-Nil,' corrected the assistant. 'A very popular shade.'

They both decided the pale green suited her best. They picked out a headdress of green leaves and white flowers and a pair of satin shoes to tone in. It gave Greta great pleasure to see how thrilled Phyllis was with her outfit and to hear her praise Mungo's generosity.

She took her to a teashop for a cup of tea, and they had

the sort of heart-to-heart chat they used to have at work. Phyllis related all the latest gossip from the laundry and wanted to hear about Mungo and his funfair. Once Greta would have told her friend of the misgivings she'd had about him; now she kept them back. All the same, talking to Phyllis reassured her that she was definitely doing the right thing.

In the run-up to the wedding, Ruth was on edge, half expecting some hitch at the last moment and that the whole thing would be called off. She couldn't get the dread out of her mind that Mungo had led Greta on to have sex with her and that he had no intention of marrying her. But the days continued to pass without the wedding plans being changed and Greta seemed happy.

To start with, Ruth had been against her daughter marrying Mungo. She couldn't see him as a suitable husband. But now Greta was living with him, he'd spoiled her for anyone else and the sooner Greta had a wedding ring on her finger the better. Ruth was reassured when her daughter came home one Saturday and showed her a bulging wallet.

'Mungo says I'm to take you and Kenny out to buy you new outfits for the wedding.'

'He doesn't have to do this,' Ruth said. 'I've saved enough from the allowance he makes.'

'Come on,' Greta said. 'Get your mac, Kenny – it's raining. Let's go into town.'

'Which shop would be best?' Ruth wanted to know. 'Blacklers?'

'No. Let's go to Bunnies for your outfit.'

'Things are expensive there.'

'That's why Mungo wants me to take you. You're to have the best – Kenny too. Do they do boys' outfitting as well?'

'I think so.'

'We'll fix him up first.'

Ruth had hardly ever been in the shop before; she'd certainly never bought much there. The prices asked for boys' clothes horrified her. Mostly she made Kenny's things herself. There was a dressmaker a few doors down the street who made his coats and blazers.

She let Greta choose the new suit and everything Kenny would need on the day: shoes and a shirt and tie. He was particularly taken with a red velvet waistcoat he saw, so she bought him that too.

The choice of hat caused the most trouble. He wanted a trilby, but they thought him too young. He wouldn't have a boy's cap. Ruth lost patience and decided there wasn't much wrong with the one he already had – he could wear that or go without. She put him on a bus with his parcels and sent him home so she could concentrate on her own outfit.

Greta swept her up to the ladies' fashion department and helped her pick out several outfits that might suit her. Ruth tried them on and chose a costume of tan-coloured wool and a very fashionable hat of the same colour, small and swathed with net. She was delighted with it, but running out of energy. Greta brought some cream blouses to the changing room for her to try on and find the one that looked best with her costume. Then she insisted she have a fox fur to set the outfit off.

'Greta, I shouldn't. We've already been very extravagant.'

'You've always fancied a fox fur.'

'But I never expected to have one.'

'Well, now you can. Mungo would want you to have it.'

Ruth felt she'd misjudged him. All those weeks of suspecting his motives, but at last she could believe he really did mean to marry Greta. She was really looking forward to the wedding now.

Mungo was being unbelievably generous to the whole family. Ruth was pleased at what she thought of as Greta's good fortune. Penny-pinching was behind her for good. She felt more prosperous herself. She'd bought new curtains and new lino for her living room, and there was no shortage of food in the house these days. She had coal in the yard and had bought Kenny new boots for the winter.

Best of all, Ruth had given notice to her customers that she'd no longer do their weekly wash. She no longer needed the money it earned. With her two cleaning jobs and Mungo's allowance she could manage.

The following week she went with Esther to choose her outfit. She bought it from Blacklers, but Esther said it was the smartest outfit she'd had since her own wedding.

Winter was not a busy time of the year for the fair, and Mungo was looking forward to a quiet Christmas too.

'Let's spend it on our own,' he said to Greta at breakfast one morning. 'Just the two of us. We need a rest.'

'Surely not at Christmas? Let's have Mam and Kenny over on Christmas Day instead of on the Sunday,' Greta said. 'Please.'

'I'd rather have you to myself.'

'Mam will expect to have her family together at Christmas. If we don't ask them, she'll invite us there. She'd be upset if we refused.'

Mungo sighed. 'If we must.'

'I think we must. We might as well ask Louis too,' Greta said. 'Have a real family Christmas while we're at it.'

'Louis won't come,' Mungo predicted. 'He'll want to stay with his mother. She'll have no one else.'

Mungo decided the fair would remain closed on Christmas Eve and Christmas Day, but would re-open on Boxing Day afternoon.

'People will be looking for amusement again by then,' he said, 'and it is school holidays. I'll tell Elsie we'll be five for Christmas dinner, if that's what you want.'

Mungo liked to indulge Greta. He liked to see her excited about buying little presents for her family. He organised a large tree, an outsize turkey and bought a gold watch, a Rolex Princess, for her.

On Christmas morning he could see she was thrilled when she opened her present. 'It's lovely, Mungo. Thank you.'

'Let's see it on.' He fastened the moire silk band round her slender wrist and was pleased with its elegance. Picking up the cheap chromium-plated watch she'd taken off, he said, 'You can throw this old thing away.'

She shook her head sadly. 'I can't do that. It was a Christmas present from Mam, no doubt the best she could afford.'

'Sorry, love.'

'It's quite a good timekeeper and big and plain. I'll ask Kenny if he'd like it.'

He'd noticed two gift-wrapped presents for him under the Christmas tree. He knew one was a tie before he opened it.

'What do I get for a man who already has everything?' she asked. 'I hope you like it.'

Mungo mostly wore bow ties to tone in with his fancy waistcoats. This was a standard necktie. 'I'll wear it when it gets too hot for my waistcoats,' he told her, forgetting that he liked to wear open-necked shirts to show off his gold jewellery in the summer.

'It's silk,' she added.

'It's very nice,' he told her, though he thought it a little plain. 'What else have you given me?' He opened the other parcel to find an Edgar Wallace thriller. Now that was to his taste. 'Right up my street,' he enthused.

'It's his latest.'

He sent Georgio over to collect Ruth and Kenny because Greta was worried about how much public transport would be running. They arrived with little gifts for everybody. Kenny had even bought a ball for Jess. She had to be brought in to receive it, but didn't seem much taken with it.

Now they were here Mungo was glad they'd been invited. Greta's family were quite excited and chatted happily. Mungo hadn't expected Louis to come at all, but he did. He brought some expensive perfume for Greta, and a diary and a fancy calendar for Mungo. He hadn't forgotten Ruth and Kenny either, but he seemed to lack the yuletide spirit.

They sat down to their Christmas dinner at two o'clock and the turkey was delicious. Louis continued to look serious and preoccupied. Mungo was afraid Fanny had found out the Southport fair was about to be closed and Louis was waiting to have a word about it.

While they were eating the Christmas pudding Mungo had to ask if everything was all right in Southport.

'Did you hear we had a fire?' Louis asked.

'At the fair?' Greta was aghast.

'Not quite, but close enough to have us worried. I believe it started in the museum of games and toys behind us. It's a wooden building and went up like a box of tinder, then it spread to the bandstand and that pavilion on the end.'

'When was this?'

'The night before last, in the early hours of Christmas Eve. The wind was blowing off the sea and that saved us – that and the road. It's only narrow but it acted as a firebreak.'

'Too close for comfort,' Mungo agreed. He turned to Ruth and Greta. 'Our building is of wood too, so we wouldn't have stood much chance if it had caught fire. Is there much damage to that end of the front?'

'Yes,' Louis said. 'It's all gone, just a blackened mess now. There were a couple of brick walls in the museum but they had to demolish what was left of them.'

'Gracious!'

'To make it safe,' Louis added.

It irked Mungo to hear Greta's family providing so much sympathy for him.

Louis went on, 'The sound of fire engines woke Mam up. She could see the glow in the sky and knew it must be near our arcade. She wanted to see what was happening and woke me up. It was a terrible shock to find how close the fire was. We watched from the promenade above. You should have seen the sparks it was throwing up. We were afraid we were going to lose the whole lot. Everyone was praying for rain. It was total chaos and the police wouldn't let anyone any nearer.'

Mungo said, 'You've had a chance to check the fair now – is there any damage?'

'No, thank goodness, but the stink of fire and smoke hangs over everything.'

Ruth said, 'That should soon go. I mean, there on the front, with the wind straight off the Irish Sea. It's blowing half a gale today.'

'Yes. Yesterday the fire was still smouldering. A fire engine stood by all day and the whole front was cordoned off. I'm glad we decided to close the fair on Christmas Eve. It couldn't have opened anyway.'

'We usually do,' Mungo said. 'Everybody's thinking of other things by then.'

'All those businesses lost,' Louis said. 'I feel sick every time I think of it. Mam says she does too. It could so easily have been us.'

'We had fire insurance,' Mungo said coldly. Then seeing Ruth look at him in surprise, he added, 'That would cover the cost of doing it up.'

'But think of the income that would be lost until it was rebuilt and able to operate again.'

Mungo mused about the fair closing down. Here was Louis moaning about how worried he and his mother were about the fire, but they wouldn't have cared one jot if Fanny hadn't wrangled to get it from him. He hoped she wouldn't find out it would have to close until their divorce became absolute and it was safely signed over to her.

Kenny said, 'I've left school now. It's official, I've brought my school leaving report to show you.'

'After dinner, Kenny,' Ruth told him. 'We're both very grateful you're going to give him a job, Mungo.'

'When can I start?'

'The fair's reopening tomorrow,' Mungo told him. 'But if your mother wants you at home on Boxing Day you can start the following morning. Ten o'clock.'

'Thank you, I'll come tomorrow,' Kenny beamed at him.

Mungo liked to see enthusiasm. 'You'll be useful during the school holidays,' he told him. 'We're likely to be busy for the next week or so. As you worked for us in the summer, you'll be able to run one of the smaller roundabouts.'

On his first day, Greta watched him from her ticket booth. She knew he felt very important to be in charge of a roundabout, even if it was the one for toddlers. He looked as though he was really enjoying his new job. He told her the lads in his class at school had been very envious.

CHAPTER EIGHTEEN

LOUIS BEGAN to see Gyp as one of the family, and taking him for walks had become part of Mam's daily routine. They were both growing fond of him. He knew his mother felt triumphant to have her decree nisi and also to have Mungo agree to such generous maintenance until the decree absolute came through. He was paying her the interim allowance regularly and it was making a big difference to her.

'Once I get the fair it'll guarantee your job too.' Mam was exultant. 'We no longer need worry that he'll take against you and give you the sack.'

Pa's visits to the Southport fair had stopped as soon as it had been offered as part of the divorce settlement. No longer did he come to find fault with everything Louis did. It was a huge relief. He and Mam were much more relaxed and the business had done well over recent months. He would make one last payment into his father's business account for January, split that for February and after the decree absolute, the profit would be Mam's.

She was beginning to worry that Pa was deliberately holding things up by not producing the lease for the fair, but Mr Danvers told her not to worry, he'd insist on her having interest on the money due to her if he was late handing it over.

Louis and his mother discussed endlessly what improvements they could make to the fair and whether they could improve the profitability, but his father had been a good manager and it was not easy.

'There's this burned site right next to us,' Mam said. 'I've been wondering if we could do something with that.'

Louis said, 'I was talking to the man who had the museum of games and toys. He told me he's going to take his insurance money and retire. He's lost his exhibits, there's no way he can go on.'

He saw his mother shudder. 'How awful. If that happened to us, it would break my heart.'

'We could try to take over his lease and expand the fair,' Louis suggested. 'There's the other two sites as well.'

'I've been thinking about that too,' Mam beamed at him. 'I'll be earning money from the fair once it's mine. I'd have cash to spare.'

'Could you afford to take on another lease?'

'Yes. We need to think this through first, very carefully, but yes I could.'

'Of course we'd have to look into every detail.' Louis was pleased to find her so optimistic about the future, and he too felt excited at the prospect of expansion.

Fanny said, 'We'll show Mungo we can run this business as well as he can.'

As usual when she thought of Pa, her face clouded. Louis knew she was still bitter about what he'd done to her.

'We have to stop him, Louis. Mungo doesn't care who he hurts as long as he gets his own way. He's got a violent nature and he takes against anyone who tries to stand up to him. You're his son, and right now, he's not sure whether he loves you or hates you, but he certainly hates me. He's doing his best to destroy me. If he succeeds, he'll turn on you. You must be careful.'

'Once your divorce comes through, you'll be free of him.'

'I'll not be free of him until he's dead. He'll resent me more because he's had to give me the Southport fair.'

He could see she was frightened and it made Louis feel guilty. He'd sworn he'd fight his mother's battles for her but he'd done nothing.

'I feel it here.' Fanny had her hand on her heart. 'It's only a matter of time before he does something else to hurt us. Sooner or later he'll lose his temper, turn on whoever is near. Look what he did to Frank Irwin, and you couldn't have a nicer man.'

That sent cold shivers down Louis's spine. Mam was safe now but Greta was not. To think of her alone with Pa at night, as his mother had been, worried him. Sometimes he couldn't sleep for thinking about what Pa could be doing to her.

He believed sooner or later his father would turn on Greta, that he'd punch her and twist her into an armlock as he had Mam. The thought of Greta's beauty spoiled with black eyes, swellings and grazes, if not broken bones such as his mother had suffered, made him feel sick. As the need to protect those he loved grew stronger, so did the urge to get even with his father.

He wanted Pa off the scene for good. He wished he'd die, but he was strong and healthy and had the vigour and drive of a man half his age. Louis ached with love for Greta; he wanted her for himself. To kill Pa seemed the only answer. That would solve the problem, both for Mam and Greta. It wasn't as if Pa didn't deserve it.

Louis didn't doubt his mother's strong feelings, but he couldn't see her carrying out any plan of revenge. She'd be scared and get cold feet. Louis was afraid that if he wanted Pa dead, he would have to do it himself.

It would have to be the perfect murder. Louis spent hours letting his mind drift over the possibilities. He could poison Pa with some rat poison he already had. Pa had bought it a couple of years ago, which meant Pa's signature would be in the chemist's register. He'd wanted to get rid of some rats that had made homes for themselves under one of the roundabouts. The youngsters were always bringing in food – chips and crisps and cakes – and dropping enough to feed them.

But if Louis put rat poison in the food at The Chase, who was to say Greta would not eat it too? Or Norah? He had to be sure it was something only Pa would eat. Even then, his death could be thought unnatural and be investigated by the police and suspicion might fall on Greta. Louis didn't want to be forced to own up and be hanged for it.

He thought of staging an accident. The problem was, how to ensure his father was killed but no one else? Pa never drove, and any car accident would involve Georgio. Louis didn't care much for him but he couldn't involve him in something like that. Also, the Bentley was a strong, safe car. He gave up on that idea.

An accident at the fair itself? Louis had read about occasional accidents at fairs when people had been killed. Anything like that made him shudder and hope such a thing would never happen at his fair. He had everything regularly checked over to make sure it wouldn't, and Pa very rarely rode on the roundabouts these days, which seemed to be essentially a pastime for youth.

Louis thought of arranging for a chairoplane to come loose but would it throw Pa far enough to guarantee he'd be killed? To have him end up in hospital with a broken leg just wasn't good enough to free Greta and it would bring Pa's wrath crashing down on his own head.

Bumper cars wouldn't do more than jolt him. They were built to bump without causing injury. Louis knew what he needed was a big dipper, something different, really high and exciting. Then possibly Pa could be enticed to try it. That was out of the question on their present site.

Louis turned over in bed, pummelling his pillow. If Main could get a lease on the burned site behind them, they'd be able to set up an open-air funfair. It could easily be run from the office above the teashop.

He could certainly erect a big dipper there and invite Pa to have a go on it. Perhaps he could tamper with the safety gate and make sure it wouldn't lock properly; give Pa a bounce while he was at the highest point and jerk him out. Was there some way of doing that? It could be said Pa hadn't fastened himself in properly. Louis felt excitement surge through him. He was wide awake now. He thought he might have hit on a feasible plan at last.

He'd keep his ideas to himself and his mouth firmly shut about this. Mam couldn't stand worry of any sort, and to involve her in this could crack her up again. But she'd be pleased with the result.

Pa would applaud the idea of installing a big dipper. It would give them a big fair both outdoors and in – the best of both worlds. But Pa wouldn't be visiting any more to see what was going on. He might not even like to see Mam expanding the place. Pa was like that: if he hadn't thought of it himself, he'd think it no good.

Louis knew he'd have to appear the dutiful and affectionate son over the next few months until he got this organised. He must get closer to Pa, be more friendly with him. Perhaps then, curiosity might bring him here, just to see what they were doing.

When he did get him here, it would be a good idea to relax Pa a bit first. He liked the cheese on toast they made in the teashop. Louis could take some up to the office and have a bottle of whisky handy. Pa would probably have a glass if it was offered. There were a lot of 'ifs', but for the perfect murder there would have to be. He'd stage the murder before the fair was open to the public and advertise stringent safety checks afterwards.

Louis went to The Chase again on New Year's Eve. Greta's mother and brother were there again. At the dinner table, Louis told his father about his ideas for the burned-out site next to the Southport fair.

'What d'you think, Pa? It's a good idea to expand while we can, isn't it?'

'Well . . .'

Louis thought he saw Pa grimace, but the expression was gone in an instant. He was forgetting for the moment that Pa was shortly due to hand the fair over to his mother. Of course, he wouldn't like her expanding, and it wouldn't just be sour grapes. It would increase the competition to attract Liverpool's youth. If they wanted to visit a fair, they could go north to Southport or south to New Brighton.

'Depends whether you can get the site or not,' Pa was telling him in measured tones.

'We're going to try,' Louis said. 'Don't you think it's a good idea, to have an open-air fair too?' He felt his heart beating faster as he dared say it. 'I could get a big dipper.'

'Yes, but don't count your chickens. Others may want that site. You've got to have the lease on it first.'

Louis vowed to himself that he'd make sure Mam didn't waste any time putting in her application. He was going to do his best to see they got that lease. Then he'd stage an accident for Pa. He wasn't going to get away with what he'd done.

At midnight, Greta kissed him and wished him a Happy New Year. It was all Louis could do to stop himself taking her into his arms and hugging her. He caught her scent and it was the perfume he'd given her for Christmas. He felt almost as though she'd agreed to forsake his father and take up with him. He felt elated and hoped 1932 was going to be the year when everything went his way.

*

A week later, Mungo saw Greta yawn as she was finishing her dinner.

'You need an early night,' he told her. 'I've got work I need to do before I go back to cash up. Don't wait up for me.'

She said, 'Then I'll have a bath and read in bed for a while.'

Mungo kissed her and almost changed his mind. 'I'll try not to be too late.'

He went to his study. He liked coming here in the evenings to mull over the affairs of his business. When he'd been alone in the house, he used to do this almost every night. Before sitting down, he helped himself to a generous whisky from the bottle he kept in a cupboard here.

There was a letter waiting for him on his desk that must have come in the afternoon post. He took up his Indian knife and slit three sides of the envelope with a slash of the blade.

It was from his solicitor, telling him that in order to transfer the ownership of the Southport fair to Fanny, he would need all the documents relating to it. It asked Mungo to send the lease for the site and buildings, together with any documents relating to the side shows and roundabouts such as bills of purchase, warranties and insurances.

Mungo was not pleased. He hadn't foreseen this difficulty and he should have done. He would have to disclose the true length of the lease.

He'd never trusted his important documents to anyone else's safekeeping; he needed to control them himself. He'd had his safe bolted through the cupboard floor and into the foundations of the house. He kept the cupboard locked, so nobody knew he had a safe in the house. Servants could be incredibly nosy about their employer's affairs and he'd also wanted to keep his papers away from Fanny.

He rolled his desk chair over to the cupboard and unlocked it. With the Southport documents spread out on his desk he studied the lease for a few moments before locking it back in the safe.

He'd told Mr Fox it was a long lease, that he couldn't remember whether it was for 99 years or 999 years. He knew very well that he'd taken the tail end of a lease originally granted to someone else and it now had less than a year to run. The fact that the fair would have to close very soon, substantially reduced its value.

But he'd forgotten the role of solicitors. They were there to scrutinise the documents and point out any shortcomings. Now he was very much afraid he would have to give Fanny more to make up the value that had been put on the fair.

Fortunately, old Fox knew nothing about it. Mungo decided he wouldn't send the lease to him for another few weeks. He'd say he'd mislaid it and promise to search for it. The longer he could stall, the better, and the longer it would take them to pin him down and make him pay more.

He wanted to make Fanny suffer. Any uncertainty like this would get to her. If he worked on her for a few months she'd settle for less just to be sure she'd have something. He was not going to pay through the nose to be rid of her if he could help it.

By Sunday, Louis was aching to see Greta again. He had fantasies about her: Greta putting up her face for him to kiss her, Greta holding him tightly, he making love to her. But no fantasy equalled seeing her in the flesh.

Pa never did invite him these days but last Sunday Greta had said, 'See you next week,' and the cook always prepared enough dinner to feed him too.

He had to see Pa regularly to keep on normal friendly terms. He needed to ask his advice, make a point of discussing his plans for the fair and the big dipper he intended to install there, otherwise he'd never get Pa to come and see it and be able to act on his plan to stage an accident.

Louis had decided he would not disclose his plans to kill Pa to anyone. His chance of escaping detection would be better if no one else knew. And he couldn't possibly tell Mam. If she became ill again, he couldn't trust her not to tell others. On top of that, he was afraid that something as shocking as murder would push her over the edge again. No, he couldn't afford to breathe a word of his plan to his mother.

Louis and his mother couldn't stop talking about expanding the fair into the burned-out site. She said, 'It's probably what Mungo would do if he still owned it.'

'I talked to him about it,' Louis told her. 'He thinks other people will want those sites.'

'The bowling club will want to rebuild their pavilion. I'm not sure about the bandstand now there's a newer one in Victoria Park. It would still be worth doing, wouldn't it, if we could only get the museum site?'

Louis could see his mother thinking it over. 'If we're going to buy more attractions, I'll need to go to the bank and see about a loan, but first . . . I think we'd better approach the Council and ask if we can take on those leases. It'll mean a change of use from museum to funfair, so we'll have to get their approval for that.'

Louis rang up to make an appointment with the town planning officer and was asked to put the topic to be discussed and the reasons for it in writing. That took several more days and when he called in person to make the appointment, it was another full week before they could be seen. Louis fumed at the delays.

On a wet Wednesday afternoon, he took his mother to the council offices. 'I hope,' he said, while they were kept waiting well beyond the appointed time, 'this will be a mere formality.'

Fanny shuffled on the hard bench. 'Probably there'll be another week's delay while they discuss it.'

At last a clerk led them along a corridor and knocked on a door to announce their arrival to Mr Jordan, the town planning officer. He was a rather august gentleman who rose to greet them from behind a large desk. After shaking hands with them both, he settled back in his seat and shuffled papers across his desk.

He cleared his throat. 'I'm sorry to tell you, Mrs Masters, that we cannot reconsider the matter of the funfair.'

'Reconsider?' Fanny looked bewildered. 'We haven't asked for this before. The fire on the sea front just before Christmas destroyed the toy and games museum, and we're asking if we can lease that site and expand our funfair.'

'Yes, yes, the site adjacent to it.'

'We aren't thinking of rebuilding on the site,' Louis explained. 'We want to place roundabouts and other amusements on the open ground.'

Mr Jordan was on his feet, unrolling a plan of the area across a nearby table. 'You want to move the amusements from your covered building to this area?'

'No,' Fanny said, 'I want to expand my business, run both sites together.'

'But our letter of the . . . let me see. We wrote to you explaining that in our view a funfair was not in keeping with the character of the town, and therefore permission for it to carry on would not be extended beyond the end of the present lease. That expires in November this year.'

Louis's mouth went suddenly dry, he was taken aback. His mother was sucking on her lips but she recovered first.

'This November! You say you've written to us about this?'

'Yes, here it is.' He took a letter from his file. 'It's dated the third of May last year.' He pushed it in front of them. The typewritten words danced before Louis's eyes.

He heard his mother's sharp intake of breath. It was addressed to his father, of course. Pa had known about this! They hadn't realised there was such a short lease on the premises. He was trying to do her down again.

'We thought perhaps a formal flower garden on the site.' Mr Jordan removed his glasses to wipe them. 'Perhaps a new bandstand. We feel the town needs something to enhance the sea front.'

'So what is to happen to my business?' Fanny asked. Louis heard the panic in her voice but she looked dignified and in control of herself. He couldn't believe it. All their plans, all their hopes for the future – they'd never had a chance of materialising.

Mr Jordan spread his hands wide in a gesture of defeat.

'We've had complaints about the funfair; the noise late at night, the litter dropped in the street. You do understand?'

'It seems we'll need to find new premises,' Louis said, getting to his feet. He felt he had to get away from this suave gentleman before he thumped his desk in a fit of rage equal to any of his father's.

Pa had known all this when he was negotiating Mam's maintenance. He was cheating her. Louis didn't want her to be upset, but how could she not be? As he hurried her out into the rain, he could see her eyes shining with unshed tears.

'Mungo must really loathe me,' she said, biting her lip.

'Mam, you haven't signed that you'll accept the fair as your divorce settlement, not yet. Mr Danvers said he was waiting for Pa to send all the documents.'

'He's been holding them back. I thought it was all taking a long time. Mungo doesn't want us or Mr Danvers to see the lease. He was hoping it would go through without us noticing.'

'We're in time,' Louis comforted.

'That fair is not worth what we thought it was. Unless we can find alternative premises, it's worth only the second-hand value of the amusements.' Louis could feel his mother quivering with indignation. 'I could kill Mungo for this,' she grated between her teeth.

Louis said, 'Your solicitor will sort it out. Let's go and have a word with him now, if we can. I'll phone him from the fair.'

Mr Danvers could see them within the hour. When they reached his office, he had Fanny's file open on the desk in front of him.

After hearing them out, he said, 'Let me see, where was I

with this? Yes, I was waiting for your husband's solicitor to send me the lease. I understood it had a substantial number of years to run.'

'So did I,' Fanny said.

'I couldn't finalise any agreement until I received all the documents. I'll telephone and ask him to send them forthwith.'

'I'd seen that as a mere formality,' Fanny sighed. 'I was already thinking of the fair as mine. My husband never comes near any more.'

'If the lease expires this November we will negotiate additional maintenance on your behalf,' Mr Danvers told her. 'That would be quite within your rights.'

As they walked back to the fair, Fanny said bitterly, 'Your father's done it again. He's trying to do me down. It makes me furious, the way he's playing with me. He can't be straight about anything.'

'At least you have your divorce,' Louis reminded her.

'It's not enough. I want my settlement too. I want us to be able to get on with our lives. I want to forget him.'

Fanny found forgetting Mungo was the last thing she could do. She was fuming about what he'd done and couldn't get his latest ruse out of her mind. She'd thought it ideal that she would own the fair and that she and Louis could manage it together. On top of all the other things Mungo was guilty of, Fanny saw this betrayal as the last straw.

'I could kill him,' she said. She went to bed that night seething inside, bubbling away like a hot spring about what she'd suffered at his hands. She woke up in the middle of the night boiling over with hurt. It wasn't the first time she'd imagined herself taking revenge on him. She'd seen herself collecting up his chunky gold jewellery and flushing it down the lavatory. She'd buy some scarlet paint and write slanderous messages on his car. She'd pour sand into the mechanics of his roundabouts and bring them all to a standstill. Just to think of these things had made her feel better, but she'd never dared do any of them. She'd let Mungo drive her out of her mind. She'd endured months in hospital because of him, but now she'd recovered she was going to get even with him. Nothing she could do was too bad for Mungo.

Louis was incensed too. His plans to buy a big dipper and kill Pa would have to be abandoned if they didn't have a fair. In a way, it was a relief. He could admit to himself now that his plans had been a comforting fantasy. He hadn't known whether it would be possible to carry them out. Even if it had been, he didn't know whether he'd be able to find the courage to do it.

Mam couldn't talk of anything but Mungo's duplicity. Every time they sat down to a meal at home she had something to say about it.

'I'll kill him,' she kept saying. 'Nothing's too bad for Mungo. I'll kill him.'

Louis buttered another slice of bread and went on eating. He'd heard her say this before when she was angry.

'You don't mean it.'

'Yes I do. The way I feel, I'd like to torture him first. Dying is too good for him. He's got away with too much already.'

Louis realised that perhaps she did mean it. Literally mean it. Since the meeting they'd had with Mr Jordan when Mam had learned that Mungo had deliberately misled her about the Southport lease, she'd been stronger and more vengeful.

'This is the last straw,' she said. 'I'm going to kill him.'

'Mam,' he replied, 'do nothing.' He tried to sound forceful. 'I don't want you to hang for him; he's never worth that. Don't you do anything.'

'It's becoming an obsession with me,' Fanny said, pouring herself more tea. 'He's still doing his best to hurt me.'

'He's done you a lot of harm.' Louis was trying to stay calm and sympathetic. 'But that's in the past, you've got away from him now.'

'An eye for an eye, a tooth for a tooth. I want to get even.'

'But if you murdered him,' Louis explained, attempting to humour her and remain logical, 'it would be more than an eye for an eye. You're still alive and well, aren't you?'

'He deserves it. Nothing is too bad for him, he deserves to die. Besides, if I don't, he'll go on to pulverise someone else in the same way.'

It frightened Louis to hear her talking of these things. 'Mam, you won't say anything like this to Ena or to Bobbins or anyone at the fair?'

'Of course not,' she said. 'I can say it to you, Louis – you understand. You know how things really are. I hate him. He deserves to die and I'm going to do it.'

Louis knew he had to dissuade her. He found it hard to believe she'd try, but she'd more than likely get herself in trouble if she did.

'Mam,' he said, 'I know that to dream up trouble for Pa, to imagine him suffering in a dozen different and violent ways, is comforting. It's a way of keeping up one's own confidence.' He'd done it himself, had been doing it for years. 'But there's a huge difference between imagining you're killing Pa and actually making it happen.'

'I know,' she said, 'but I'm going to do it.' There was a new determination about his mother that bothered him. Her face was twisting with hate. 'I'd like to stick that fancy letter opener he has into his neck, cut his jugular vein and see him bleed to death.'

Louis shook his head. 'Sounds violent, not like you at all. Not like me, either. Even I couldn't do that. Come on, let's get ready for work. We can't sit here all morning.'

Fanny got up and started to clear the table. Louis helped. It was what they did every morning – so ordinary, so normal. Mam looked so normal too, so well, and yet here she was telling him how she was going to kill Pa. This was fantasy too but he didn't know whether she was aware of that.

Mam was humming to herself as she washed up. Louis picked up a tea towel to dry the dishes and only narrowly missed dropping a cup. He couldn't let things stand as they were; he wanted to stop her thinking of these things.

'Pa's physical strength is so much greater than yours,' he said. 'It's no good thinking of knifing him. He'd snatch it and turn it on you.'

He saw his mother shudder. 'Do you remember coming home one day and finding me grappling with him on the stairs?'

Louis did.

'I was terrified. I thought he meant to throw me down.'

'I came home in the nick of time.'

'Yes, I was hanging on to the banisters like a limpet.'

Louis said, 'There you are then. He's too strong for you. You can't fight him.'

She turned to meet his gaze. He could see rock-fast tenacity in her eyes as she said, 'Poison is said to be the best bet for women who want to commit murder.'

'Mam!' Clearly she'd been giving this more thought than he'd realised. 'But what do you know about poisons?'

'Nothing.' That was more comforting.

She tipped the water out of the washing-up bowl, 'But I can learn. I called in to the library yesterday and found a book on poisons.'

Mam would find it too hard, he didn't think she'd ever manage it. He must forget it and hope she would too.

'I also took out a couple of Agatha Christie books.'

'You'll enjoy them, she's good.'

'I read in an article recently that she'd been trained as a pharmacist and gets all the details about poisons exactly right.'

'You're not hoping to pick up tips from her?' Louis laughed. He felt a little hysterical. 'I doubt if you'll find her books much help.'

He told himself he was worrying about nothing. Mam wouldn't get herself into trouble by reading Agatha Christie. Anyway, she wouldn't dare poison Pa. No, Mam would do no more than talk about it, dwell on it and dream up new and evermore fanciful ways to harm him. She wasn't likely to *do* anything.

*

Louis was still going to his father's house for Sunday dinner every week, but he was finding it harder to hide his true feelings from him. He disliked him intensely but he kept going because he wanted to see Greta.

Louis had worked out which subjects must never be mentioned in Pa's hearing, and the list was growing. It had never been politic to talk about his mother or anything that concerned her. Pa was no longer interested in the Southport fair, and Louis had no intention of mentioning the lease, though he and Mam talked about it all the time. It was a huge worry but it was part of Mam's divorce settlement, and to mention it to Pa would almost guarantee he'd fly into a rage. Louis was leaving his parents to argue it out through their solicitors.

It was Greta who innocently brought it up this week. The conversation was beginning to flag and they were talking of the mild sunny weather, so unusual at this time of the year and how good it was for the fair.

'I hardly saw any of it,' Louis lamented. 'No time to get out in it.'

'Mungo and I had a lovely day at the seaside on Friday. He went to see his fair at Prestatyn again and took me with him. Then we went for another look at his new site at Rhyl.'

Louis was astounded. It was the first he'd heard of Pa having a new site. He didn't miss Pa's flinch and knew this was a subject he wanted to avoid.

Louis couldn't stop himself saying, 'You've found a new site at Rhyl?'

'You know me,' his father said, shrugging it off, 'always

trying to expand my empire. A business can't stand still. If you don't work to expand it will lose profitability.'

Even as Pa started on generalities like that Louis guessed. 'You meant to move the Southport fair there when the lease expired?'

He knew he shouldn't have said that as soon as the words were out of his mouth. His father's face contorted with rage.

'I'm going to open another fair at Rhyl. As I've been forced to give one away to your mother I need to replace it. With a fair at Prestatyn already, Rhyl is ideal because I can visit both on the same day.'

By now, Greta understood this wasn't a safe topic. She was usually as wary of his explosions of rage as Louis was himself. 'North Wales is such a beautiful place,' she said.

'The mountains certainly are.' Louis was relieved to find they were on safer ground, but his suspicions remained.

Pa must have been looking for another site for some time. Louis was sure his intention must have been to move the attractions there from Southport when the lease expired. He wondered how big the new site was, and what it was like. If Pa thought it was good, it would be. Perhaps Mam could ask for this site at Rhyl? Suitable places for their purpose were few and far between.

Pa was sullen for the rest of the evening. Louis left early, wanting to tell his mother this latest snippet of news, which could make a big difference for her.

Mam was making herself a cup of cocoa when he reached home, and was very surprised when he told her.

'Another site at Rhyl?' she said, her face working with anger. She came to the same conclusion Louis had. 'Mungo knew the Southport fair would have to move. He's been making these arrangements for months – must have been. Isn't he despicable, trying to cheat me like this? Oh, I'm going to pay him back. Mark my words, I will.'

CHAPTER NINETEEN

M UNGO WAS about to leave for work the next morning when he saw Norah answer the phone in the hall. 'It's Mr Fox, sir,' she said. 'He'd like a word.'

His solicitor was the last person Mungo wanted to talk to. Greta was with him. He was tempted to hustle her out of the front door and tell Norah to say he'd already gone. But he knew that might alert Greta to the problem and Fox would be able to catch up with him at the fair. Besides, he believed in facing his problems and doing something about them as soon as possible.

'Sorry, Greta,' he said. 'Won't be a minute.'

As he turned to go to his study he saw her sit down in the hall to wait. Norah had left the phone off the hook. It was lying on the hall table beside her and Mungo was afraid she might lift it and listen in. He didn't want her to know what he was doing.

He closed his study door, picked up the instrument on his desk and said, 'Good morning, Mr Fox.'

'Good morning. It's about the lease for the Southport fair.'

It was what Mungo had expected. He felt his spirits plummet. He heard the crackle as the handset in the hall was replaced.

'Hello, hello?'

'I'm still here, Mr Fox.' Mungo felt he'd be able to give his full attention to the speaker now.

'Mr Danvers, acting for your wife, is asking for the lease; says it's a matter of some urgency now. Your wife seems to think it has only a short time to run.'

That gave Mungo another jolt. So it was Fanny who'd rumbled him.

'Yes, it has,' he agreed, changing direction instantly. 'I found it yesterday – you know I've been searching every-where for it? It was caught up with some other documents in my safe.' The lies rolled off his tongue smoothly. 'I've posted it to you already.'

'I'm glad it's turned up. What is the expiry date?'

'I was very surprised to find it's November this year.'

'Oh dear, that confirms . . . You realise this puts a very different value on the place? Your wife seems to believe she was misled. It means she's bound to ask for additional maintenance.'

'Yes.' Mungo was not pleased. All he'd done was make more trouble for himself and he hated the thought of paying Fanny yet more money.

'We'll have to reopen negotiations. Do you have some-thing else you want to offer in place of the Southport . . . ?'

'No,' he barked. 'Get Fanny to put a figure on what she wants and then we'll beat her down.'

'All right. I'll ask Danvers what she wants. Will you give the matter some thought? I'll be in touch.'

Mungo put the phone down and swore. Then he opened his safe and took out the lease. He'd have to put it in the post this morning. He could do it from the office. Give it some thought, indeed!

If Fanny knew about the site he'd bought in Rhyl she'd demand that. Greta had mentioned it in front of Louis, and Mungo tried to remember what exactly had been said. He was afraid Louis had grasped that they could move the Southport fair there and make it viable.

Mungo was making his own plans for the Rhyl site and didn't want to part with it. He decided to offer money instead. It would be in his own interests to drag this out and keep Fanny hanging on.

How to best Fanny filled Mungo's thoughts for the rest of the day and made him feel on edge. He was glad when it was time to go home. He hoped to be able to relax, but when they arrived, a nervous Norah met him in the hall.

She said, 'Elsie saw somebody in the trees at the bottom of the garden. He seemed to be hanging about . . .'

'A prowler?' Mungo asked.

Greta said, 'I saw some people take a short cut through here to the coastal path once.'

'The dog's barked a lot this afternoon, as though there's been someone near,' Norah went on. 'Elsie first noticed a man down there at about three o'clock, and I definitely saw him again when it was getting dark. And I don't think he was alone.'

'Might it have been lovers wanting a secluded spot, d'you think?' Greta suggested.

'They have no right,' Mungo growled indignantly. 'That's trespassing. I'll ring the police and report it.'

'Elsie did that, sir. They said they'd keep an eye on the place.'

Mungo was full of suspicion. 'Could it be Fanny you saw? Did she come back for the dog?'

'I don't think so. She wouldn't hang around at the bottom of the garden. She'd have come to the door, wouldn't she?'

'It'll be her,' Mungo said irritably. He felt tense with foreboding. She wanted that dog and was doing her best to take her.

'Is Jess still here?' Greta asked Norah.

'Yes, we brought her in because she was barking such a lot.'

'Good.'

That put Mungo in a worse mood for the rest of the evening. 'I'll bet you anything it was Fanny,' he grumbled. 'She's determined to steal my dog.' He was equally determined to stop her. Fanny could come again at any time, but locking Jess on to the heavy chain would stop her being taken.

'Louis said she had another dog now,' Greta reminded him, 'and she'd given up the idea of having Jess.'

But Mungo would not be pacified.

Louis had encouraged his mother to see her solicitor again. He suggested she ask for the Rhyl site as an addition to her divorce settlement, so that she could move the Southport fair there. It seemed the only thing that would make having it worthwhile.

Pa was keeping them waiting for his reply and in the meantime they couldn't stop talking about the things they could do if they did get it. Louis knew his mother was as curious about the site as he was. They longed to know more: where it was exactly, how large it was and would the attractions be indoors or out? Or both?

Louis still went to see his father every Sunday but he couldn't bring himself to ask about the site. He didn't think Pa would tell him if he did. He'd be told it was none of his business.

Things between them had cooled alarmingly since Mam had found out about the Southport lease. Louis felt he had his work cut out to make Pa speak to him at all. Tonight, the only subject he wanted to talk about was his forthcoming wedding and that stuck in Louis's throat. He hated to think of Greta marrying his father, though her eyes shone with anticipation as she talked about the arrangements they were making. He was beginning to think about giving up his Sunday night visits altogether. He was finding them both tantalising and frustrating. It was only the hope that Mam might get the Rhyl site and he could think again about a big dipper that would keep him going.

They'd finished eating and moved to the drawing room when Norah called Pa to the phone and Louis was left alone with Greta. This was a chance he hadn't expected to get.

As she handed him a cup of coffee, he said, 'I understand Pa's bought a new site at Rhyl. Is it on the sea front?'

'Yes. Sugar?' She was holding out the bowl to him.

He helped himself to two lumps. 'It's not already a funfair? Some other business was run there?'

'I believe it was once a fish market. A long time ago, that is.'

'But more recently?'

'I don't know, Louis.' She seemed reluctant to talk about it. 'I've only seen it from the outside.'

Louis believed her: that's exactly how Pa would treat everybody; not allow them to know too much.

Pa came back and helped himself to coffee while Louis wondered if he had enough information to find the place.

The following week he suggested to his mother that they take the afternoon off to go to Rhyl to see if they could find the site. Louis drove along the seafront and spotted it almost immediately. The agent had pasted a poster, now peeling and faded, on the main gate, proclaiming the property was sold.

The gates were wide open and a lorry was driving in, loaded with bricks. Louis took his mother by the arm and followed it. A workman told them the buildings were being given a new and smarter façade, and the inside refurbished, and that the place would reopen as a funfair.

They peered inside the buildings and Mam began to allot the space to the roundabouts at present in Southport.

'Indoors and out,' Louis crowed. He could erect a big dipper here if Mam should be lucky enough to get the site. They saw all there was to see and spent more time walking round the outside, both on the promenade and on the beach below.

'I'm very impressed,' Mam said, clinging excitedly to his arm.

'Pa might refuse to part with it,' Louis said. 'He could do a lot with this site. Don't raise your hopes too high.'

*

Ruth was looking forward to Greta's wedding and counting the days. Her maiden aunts arrived in Henshaw Street the night before. Ruth had to give up her bed to them. She'd intended to sleep on a few cushions downstairs but Kenny insisted he'd do that and she must have his bed. Nevertheless, Ruth didn't sleep well. She was too excited.

The twenty-first of March turned out to be a blustery spring day with pale sunshine. The wedding was to take place at eleven in the morning. Mungo had arranged for a large car to come to Henshaw Street at nine thirty to collect Greta's family and the Bradshaws, because it took quite a time to cross the river on the luggage boat. To Ruth it seemed a rush to get breakfast for her guests and get herself ready.

Greta had told her and Kenny to come to the house, so Ruth asked to be dropped there; the car took the others straight on to the register office. The maid brought them coffee and Ruth went upstairs to see Greta.

She was ready in all her finery and looked so beautiful it took her breath away. Ruth had seen her dress before. It was a froth of white lace. A circle of white flowers kept her veil in place. Ruth kissed her daughter's cheek.

'Phyllis came early, Mam, and we got changed together.'

'Doesn't she look lovely, Mrs Walsh?'

'You both do.' Phyllis was a picture too in her eau-de-Nil gown.

There was a tap on the door. It was Mungo. 'Are you ready, love?'

Ruth had to say, 'Mungo, you aren't supposed to see the bride in her wedding dress until the ceremony.'

'Those are just old traditions,' he scoffed. 'Our wedding's going to be different. I helped choose the dress and I don't want to miss any of the fun. Doesn't Greta make a magnificent bride?'

She did. There was a real sparkle about her. Ruth thought it was happiness and was so grateful that things had turned out so well.

'Come down to the hall,' Mungo said. 'It's almost time I left for the register office. I think we should all have one glass of champagne to settle our nerves before we go.'

He introduced his best man: 'Peter, the manager of my fair at Prestatyn.' They both looked very elegant in morning dress. 'You can see I don't have any relatives either.'

To Ruth it seemed only moments before she was back in the car with champagne bubbles still on her face.

Afterwards she could hardly remember the civil ceremony in the register office. The place was plain and rather anonymous. It was the church blessing that thrilled her. Secretly she regarded that as the 'proper' wedding, and, indeed, Mungo had gone to a great deal of trouble to ensure it was as full and formal a service as possible.

The organ was playing softly and the church was almost full, which surprised Ruth. She'd been told it was to be a quiet blessing. It was Kenny who whispered that the fair wasn't opening until two o'clock today, so the staff could come. A buffet lunch was being provided at the fair, so they could celebrate too.

The organ thundered out as Greta and Mungo came slowly up the aisle to stand together before the priest. The notes reverberated round the church, then died to silence.

Ruth was blinking hard, tears were clouding her sight as the newlyweds were blessed. Altogether, Ruth could not have imagined a more splendid wedding for her daughter.

The wedding party returned to Mungo's house. Twenty-two in all sat down in the dining room to a splendid wedding breakfast. Ruth was brimming with relief and contentment. What she'd most wanted had taken place. Mungo had made her daughter an honest woman and it was easy to see he was very happy. He couldn't take his eyes off his bride.

With the meal over, he stood up to make a speech.

'Greta has made me very proud . . .' he said, together with a lot more, praising of her beauty and all she'd done to help him with his business.

'I couldn't have expected more from any girl,' he went on. 'It was love at first sight.' Ruth thought it sounded romantic. Then he said, 'But now she's my wife, she's all mine. I'll be able to mould her to my ways.'

That bothered Ruth. She thought it struck the wrong note.

Louis, hearing his father say those words, thought how typical it was of him. Pa thought he owned people, mind, heart and soul, and they were his to twist to his bidding. He fought to control everything and everybody.

Louis couldn't look at his father without feeling his anger burn up again. Pa was trying to cheat his mother even now. Here he was, masquerading as a loving bridegroom, when what he really wanted was to have that same power over Greta. He wanted to bend her, force her to his will.

Louis took another sip of champagne and let his gaze

settle on Greta again. She looked radiantly beautiful in her wedding finery. She fascinated him; he couldn't look at her without feeling a stirring of devotion. He was more than a little in love with her himself. It had been painful watching her marry Pa; he could no longer hope she'd change her mind and turn to him. Pa won every round. He always had.

Louis had been invited to the wedding but thought it was because it might look odd to Greta's family if he were not. For the same reason, he'd been allowed to join them at Sunday dinner. He half expected Pa to cut him out of his new life now he'd got Greta where he wanted her. Louis didn't want to be cut out; he couldn't bear it if he were never to see her again.

He wondered if Pa treated Greta in the way he treated everybody else. He didn't think he could change. Would Pa thrust his fists into Greta's pretty face? Louis's fists clenched at the thought. He didn't think Pa had hit her yet. She held her head up in a way his mother never had; she hadn't had the self-confidence knocked out of her and she looked at Pa with love in her eyes. No, Greta had never felt a cane about her shoulders or had her head held in an armlock as Mam had. It looked as though Pa really did love her. He hoped, for Greta's sake, that he always would.

Louis accepted another glass of champagne. The bride and groom stood up and were about to cut the three-tier cake.

'Louis!' Mungo hissed sharply.

Louis fumbled for the camera his father had pushed into his hands to record these moments. He knew he'd never be forgiven if he didn't get good pictures.

Resentment was rising in his throat, acid and corrosive. Pa had claimed Greta as his own. They looked more like father and daughter than man and wife, though nobody would dare tell him so. That he'd found another wife so quickly soured Louis's mood still further, but especially when his new wife was Greta. He wished he could do something to help her. He was afraid she was going to need help in the years ahead.

To Greta, the day seemed unreal. Mungo had told her early in the morning how very much he loved her. She knew he was a bridegroom to be proud of. Mam fussed round her and was so happy that it was all taking place at last, and Phyllis was bubbling with joy and thrilled with everything she saw.

'You are so lucky,' she breathed.

Greta felt she knew what to expect because she'd been living with him; married life would be better but not so very different. All the same, she was excited and perhaps a wee bit apprehensive, but happy too. She'd never received so much attention; every eye seemed to be on her. Mungo had not told her where he'd arranged for them to honeymoon. It was to be a surprise.

Mam and Phyllis helped her change into her new blue wool going-away costume. She had a warm travel coat of blue and fawn checks to wear over it, for which she was grateful because the day was turning cold. Georgio drove them to Woodside to catch the London train.

As Mungo bought chocolates and magazines for the journey, she said, 'It's to be a London honeymoon, then?' She could think of no better place at this time of the year and was looking forward to the restaurants and theatres.

'No,' he smiled, 'We're going to Paris. By air.'

'Really?' Greta knew nobody who had done that. She wanted to jump for joy. 'Don't I need a passport?'

'I need a passport,' he said. 'You're my wife. I had you put on mine.'

'How marvellous.'

'I wanted to do something different, something extraordinary.'

'Such a treat . . .' Greta felt sparks of excitement running through her. Mungo, too, was clearly enjoying himself.

In London they just had time to snatch a light meal. Mungo insisted on having champagne to drink with it. Nothing less would do. They flew from Croydon Aerodrome to Le Bourget. Greta couldn't stop looking round at her fellow travellers, they all seemed so rich. Looking down on the clouds through the window of the plane was another thrill. The evening sun was shining up here though it was very grey beneath. She thought how fortunate she was to have seen such a sight. Surely very few had.

They arrived at their Paris hotel in the early hours of the next morning. Greta had the impression of a very grand building, and their room was enormous. Mungo said he was pleased with it but they were both very tired. He immediately rang room service to order another bottle of champagne.

'One last glass to round off a long and exciting day,' he said, rubbing his hands. 'It'll help us sleep.'

Greta yawned. She felt spent and wine had been served on the plane coming over. 'I won't need any help to sleep,' she told him. 'I've had enough champagne. I'd rather have a cup of tea.'

'Tea?' Greta knew she should have been warned by the storm clouds she saw gathering on his brow. 'Come on now, we can't celebrate with tea.'

'I think I'm past celebrating, Mungo. I'm dead on my feet.'

At that moment there was a knock at the door and a waiter wheeled in a small trolley, set with glasses. The bottle of champagne was standing in a silver bucket. 'Open it,' Mungo ordered.

The waiter did so with a flourish. The cork popped loudly. Greta had her case open, looking for the special nightdress Mungo had chosen for her. He held out a brimming glass to her. She took it and put it on the bedside table.

'Drink it,' he bellowed as soon as the door closed behind the waiter. 'We're doing this in style. It's our honeymoon.'

Greta really didn't want it. She hesitated.

'Bloody hell,' he swore. 'I can't celebrate on my own. Come on, show some appreciation. Let's have a bit of fun.'

She was shocked. 'Mungo, please . . .'

'Drink it.'

She hadn't the strength to argue. Nearly in tears, she drank it but she could feel his anger pulsating as he sat in an armchair opposite, grimly downing his own drink.

For Greta, it was an ordeal, not a celebration, and she found it hard to understand. How could he say he loved her and then behave like this? She'd seen his temper flare up at other people but this was the first time he'd raged at her.

It had been a fairy-tale wedding day until now, but his temper burst the bubble and sent her to bed on her wedding night feeling she'd failed him. He'd wanted to celebrate and she had not.

Greta felt all churned up when they got into bed. She couldn't sleep, but Mungo seemed to have no difficulty. It was late the next morning when he took her into his arms and started kissing her.

'I'm sorry about last night,' he said. 'We were too tired, I shouldn't have insisted on champagne.'

Greta wasn't properly awake now but recognised he wanted to make love, and she was wary of upsetting him again. She pretended more passion than she felt and kept her eyes away from the still half-full bottle of champagne standing on Mungo's night table, uncorked and flat.

As it was long past the time breakfast would be served in the dining room, Mungo rang room service for tea and rolls. They were bathed and dressed by the time the food came. He complained about the quality of the tea but he pored over his maps eagerly and seemed keen to get out and explore the city.

He'd brought guide books with him and had already worked out where he wanted to go and what he wanted to see. Greta fell in with his wishes and was enthralled by the sights and sounds of Paris. She loved Montmartre, the Madeleine and the Arc de Triomphe. After a splendid dinner he took her to the Folies Bergères that night.

Greta thought Mungo had enjoyed it all as much as she had. He'd been in a buoyant mood all day. She pushed his bout of temper the night before to the back of her mind and forgot about it.

They were even later getting up on Wednesday morning. Mungo had planned to visit the Eiffel Tower, but it was lunch time before they were ready to go out and he decided they should find a restaurant and eat first. They enjoyed a three-course meal with wine.

'I feel sleepy,' he said, stretching himself in his chair. 'We'll go back to our hotel room for an hour's rest first.'

Greta was full of energy, and bursting to see as much of Paris as she could.

'Oh, come on, Mungo,' she said persuasively. 'Don't let's waste time by going back to bed in the middle of the afternoon. If you don't feel like walking to the other side of the river we could take a taxi. Climbing the Eiffel Tower will wake you up.'

Too late, she saw his face contort with anger. 'I'm tired, I want a rest,' he spat out. 'I won't be able to enjoy anything until we've had that.' He set off at a brisk walk back towards their hotel and left her to follow in his wake.

The doorman held open the hotel door for both of them, though Greta was ten yards behind him. She caught him up as he waited for the lift.

'Don't ruin our honeymoon like this,' he grated.

Greta believed he was the one causing the present rift but couldn't say so. It would make matters worse. She'd thought she knew Mungo, but she'd never seen him like this before.

She told herself he was a lot older than she was and didn't have her energy. He was tired and he got grumpy when he was tired. She must be more careful; keep his needs in mind if she was to avoid more of this. They visited the Eiffel Tower at dusk that evening. Mungo said he didn't care for it and refused to go to the top.

They flew back to Croydon on Thursday morning and were back home that evening.

'Down to earth again,' Mungo joked to Georgio when he met their train.

To Greta, it wouldn't be coming down to earth at all. She loved the luxury of his home and didn't think marriage would change her life a great deal. Mungo had said he wanted her to continue working in the ticket booth during the mornings and helping out, mostly at the refreshment bar in the afternoons and evenings. But she did expect to take over the running of the house. It was what all wives did.

On their return home, Norah and Elsie were in the hall to greet them.

Elsie was an asset in the household, and Greta liked her and felt at ease with her. She was a stout motherly woman of fifty, who looked to Greta for instructions.

'I didn't know whether you'd want supper tonight,' Elsie said to her. 'I thought you might have eaten.' It was nearly ten o'clock.

'We haven't,' Mungo retorted.

'I have some leek and potato soup ready and I could make omelettes with salad to follow. Or cheese and tomato on toast.'

'Omelettes, I think,' Greta told her. She knew Mungo complained of indigestion after having cheese at night, and he was busy directing Georgio to take their bags upstairs.

Mungo was none too polite when Norah brought the omelettes to the table.

'Is this the best Elsie can do?' he demanded. 'I thought I ordered liver and bacon for tonight. Did the weekly order not come?'

'Yes, sir, it did.'

The next morning, when Norah brought in their morning tea, Mungo said, 'I'm hungry. Tell Elsie to make us egg and bacon for breakfast, with fried bread. We'll be down in half an hour.'

While she ate her breakfast, Greta thought about her household duties. She said, 'What would you like for lunch? I shall visit Elsie in the kitchen after breakfast each morning.'

'Don't you worry your pretty head. I'm used to looking after all that,' Mungo told her, 'and I'd prefer to carry on.'

'I thought a wife—'

'No, I don't need any help running my house.' Norah was bringing in another pot of tea. 'Tell Elsie to come here,' he ordered.

It surprised Greta, although she had noticed he wanted to organise everything. But surely not the shopping and the cooking? She didn't think he'd want to be bothered with that sort of thing when he had a wife to do it for him.

She was thrilled to be his wife though she was afraid it might prove more difficult than being his fiancée. A wife seemed to attract his anger in a way a fiancée never had. Was it because he was more sure of her now?

That thought made her shiver. It frightened her to see his rage blow up and made her wary of him and more vigilant about his moods. The trouble was, his anger cut into the love and goodwill she felt for him. Though in his better moods he told her he loved her, there were times when he really didn't show it.

CHAPTER TWENTY

Rex Bradshaw had been put in charge of the waltzer. This was a roundabout with wrap-round bench-type seats to hold three or four passengers. He was busy lowering the metal bars that came down across their laps to fasten them securely to their seats.

His schoolboy helper was collecting the tickets and threading them onto a wire so they couldn't be used again.

The seats not only circled round the central column but each one could be made to spin on its own axis at the same time. The direction of the spin changed continually and the movements could be violent and abrupt. It provided a thrilling and popular ride.

Business had been brisk all morning. It was getting on for midday when Rex noticed Mungo bringing Greta round the fair. He flinched when he saw Mungo's arm was round her waist in a proprietary fashion. Rex thought Mungo was showing off, proclaiming to all of them that he'd married the prettiest girl in town. For Rex, their wedding day had been the worst day of his life. It had put Greta beyond his reach for ever.

He couldn't bear to look at them, but at the same time couldn't drag his eyes away.

He was bringing Greta to the waltzer. Rex could see her shaking her head and saying no, but seconds later he heard her laugh behind him and they were getting on. Keeping his face as blank as he could, Rex fastened them on to the imitation red leather bench. He could feel his cheeks burning with jealousy. Mungo had the ability to take whatever he wanted; he had an arm round Greta's shoulders by this time. Mungo knew how to worm his way into anybody's good books.

Rex was torn in two. On one hand he hated him for what he was doing to Greta, but he was also grateful because Mungo had given him this job. Rex turned on the music and started the roundabout. It made several slow turns round the central column to start with, then as it gathered speed he lowered the lever that set the benches spinning on their axes.

He stood back against the solid central column with his eyes half closed to shut out Greta's flying blonde hair and scarlet dress as she came spinning past him.

Above the blaring hurdy-gurdy music, he could hear the girls screaming. They always did; little screams of pleasure and enjoyment to show they were half nervous, half appreciative of the thrills. Greta was hanging on to Mungo, who was laughing out loud, full of bonhomie. Rex recognised her little squeal of pleasure above the many.

The next time they came past he glimpsed her face, her mouth open in a wide smile. She looked alert and lifted high on fun. The atmosphere was one of enjoyment and jollity.

Suddenly, Rex heard a scream that was very different, a scream of pure panic. From the corner of his eye he saw what looked like a bundle of rags fly out of one of the seats, but he knew it was a falling child. Despite the merry beat of the music, the atmosphere changed instantly to one of cold shock. A crowd was gathering where the child had fallen. His parents were on the waltzer, screaming and trying to stand up.

Horrified, Rex switched off the roundabout and rushed to release them. The mother was dragging another child after her and screaming that her son had been killed. Other customers were struggling to escape from their seats too.

The recorded hurdy-gurdy music finished with a flourish. In the dead silence that followed, the sister of the casualty, a little girl of about five, opened her mouth in a piercing wail of distress.

'Get me out,' Mungo was thundering, his face crimson with rage. Rex ignored the others and went to him next. Greta was out and pushing through the crowd towards the casualty.

The child who'd fallen was white-faced and still. He had a cut on one arm. Greta tried to stanch the bleeding with a clean towel from the refreshment bar. The child was limp and he moaned as his father picked him up.

Mungo immediately took over. 'Stay where you are, ladies and gentlemen,' his voice boomed. 'Sit tight. We'll soon have the ride going again. Sorry to interrupt the service.'

One or two people shouted to Rex, wanting to be released.

'Ignore them,' Mungo ordered. 'Turn that damn music on again.' Mungo soon had the ride gyrating again.

'A double turn for everybody,' Mungo was shouting. He added more quietly to Rex. 'Give them five minutes extra.'

Greta had come back, saying the child ought to go to hospital straight away.

'Take him to hospital? No, not in my car. Send Georgio to get a taxi and put them in that.' He took a pound note from his wallet and pushed it at her.

He said to Rex, 'It's not our fault. The parents should have kept hold of their child. You'd think they'd take more care of their own offspring, wouldn't you?'

The accident was glossed over as soon as possible so the customers would forget it. Strident jollity belted out more loudly than ever but the staff couldn't forget.

'He's more interested in keeping the fair going than helping the poor bugger that got hurt,' Agnes whispered to Rex. She'd come over from the refreshment counter. 'It's a three-year-old boy.'

'The waltzer isn't for toddlers.' Mungo was still sounding off about it. 'Look, I put up notices to make it clear.' He took the child's father by the arm to point it out and imply it was his fault: '"No children allowed on unless accompanied by a responsible adult." It's up to you parents to look after your children.'

The father could say nothing. He shook his head and looked shocked and upset.

'The mother had the little girl to look after,' one of the hands muttered. She was swinging on her mother's hand and still wailing at the top of her voice.

'Shut that kid up, for God's sake,' Mungo grated through his teeth. 'She's screaming like a stuck pig, a right pain in the neck.'

Greta was bringing her an ice-cream cone. Rex thought the child was going to knock it out of her hand with her flailing fists, but she saw it and calmed down. One lick, another little gulp of distress and silence at last.

'Get that family out of here,' Mungo ordered Rex. 'They're turning customers off.'

When Rex asked them, the crowd parted so the family could move to the door. The taxi was drawing up outside, Greta ushered them into it and told the driver to take them to the nearest hospital. She paid the fare and received a handful of change back.

'Thank you,' the father said. 'Thank you for your help.'

Greta returned the change to Mungo. Rex could see him shaking with fury, his cheeks crimson and his eyes bulging.

'Strewth! Have you got rid of them? Thank God for that. Accidents like that can ruin my business. Greta, you were great. You did everything right.'

She said, 'I hope the little boy isn't badly hurt.'

'So do I,' Rex said.

Mungo turned to him. 'Stop that damn ride now and get those people off. They're not paying for that so there's no point in leaving them on for the rest of the day.' His mouth was contorted and ugly.

Rex hastened to do so. Greta was running round helping him and the boy unfasten the bars to free the customers. Mungo started up the music again and turned up the volume. The crowd seemed to evaporate. For once, the buoyant fairground mood was gone.

'I wish it hadn't happened while I was in charge of the ride,' Rex said to him. He wasn't happy about that.

'It wouldn't have happened at all,' Mungo bellowed to make himself heard above the music, 'if only you'd followed my orders and not allowed children on it.'

Rex was affronted. He pointed to the printed notice fixed to the central column. 'No *unaccompanied* children,' he protested, 'that's what it says. That child was with his parents.'

Mungo ripped off the notice with one swift movement. 'No children on it, not ever again. Don't forget.'

Rex was indignant. 'I was following what I thought were your orders.'

'No children at all, not even if they are accompanied,' Mungo bellowed at him before stamping off to his office, still muttering under his breath. 'I'm not liable for that sort of an accident.'

Rex was appalled at Mungo's attitude. That would show Greta the sort of man he was. He had absolutely no thought for anyone but himself.

Rex saw Greta staring after Mungo. Then after a moment, she ran to catch him up.

Greta could feel fear pulsing through her as she closed Mungo's office door behind her. She had to do this without showing the effort it was costing her. He turned on her with a wrathful torrent.

'I hope that blood on the floor has been cleared up. There

must be no sign of what happened. I don't want to be reported to the Council, I don't want them say my rides are dangerous. You know they have the power to close me down? Would you believe parents could be so careless of their own children?'

She said stiffly, 'They didn't do it on purpose.'

'An accident like that can cut into the takings. Ruin my business.'

Greta took a deep breath and said, 'You upset Rex.'

'I'm upset myself.'

'You said you were going to train him as a manager.'

'I have thought of it,' Mungo admitted.

'Then you shouldn't upset him in the way you did. If you put him in charge of a fair, he'll be looking after your interests when you aren't there to do it. You need his loyalty.'

'Damn Rex.'

'You implied that accident was his fault. You lost your temper again. I thought we had a pact: we were both going to control our tempers in future?'

Mungo grunted. 'When I'm angry, I can't bottle it up. It makes me feel better if I let it blast out.'

'It might make you feel better, Mungo,' Greta said with a touch of sharpness, 'but it makes everybody else feel worse. If you fly at people like that, it cuts into them. You scare people off.'

'Do I?' Mungo was looking at her as though he'd not seen the truth of that before.

Greta put her arms round him. 'Come on, Mungo. You know Rex didn't deserve that. The accident wasn't his fault. Why don't you apologise?'

'Apologise to Rex?' The idea seemed to outrage him further.

'You know you have a problem with your temper. You did promise you'd try and improve.'

A few moments later, Mungo stood up. 'You're right, of course. You're good for me, Greta. Ask Rex to come up and I'll make my peace with him.'

Greta smiled. 'Good. You say it makes you feel better if you let fly at people, but I don't think it does. You feel bad too. You'd feel much better if you stayed calm.'

As she went downstairs, Greta told herself it was possible to reason with Mungo. She must not be afraid of doing so.

Rex looked scared when she told him Mungo wanted him in his office. 'He's not going to sack you,' she assured him. Then she had to stay and help run the waltzer in his absence.

Rex looked happier when he came back. 'Mungo apologised.' He sounded amazed. 'He said I was doing everything right. The bars were correctly in place in accordance with the safety rules. He said the father should have kept hold of the child and he'd have been all right. Fortunately, he was thrown clear or he could have been badly hurt.' There were a lot of moving bars beneath the seats.

'If he'd been caught up in the machinery . . .' Greta shuddered at the thought.

'He said it wasn't my fault and I needn't feel guilty, but in future no child under twelve must be allowed on the waltzer. He's going to have new posters printed with that on.'

'I know he upset you—'

Rex stopped her. 'All I want is to do a good job. I want to go on working for Mungo.'

Greta phoned the hospital later that afternoon to try to find out what had happened to the child. In the heat of the moment she hadn't asked his full name and knew only that he was called Dennis. A member of the hospital staff told her they had no record of a child with that name being admitted to any of the wards, but it seemed a three-year-old boy had attended for emergency treatment with a cut on his arm that had needed stitches. He'd been X-rayed but no fracture was found and he'd been sent home.

Greta went to tell Rex, 'The child wasn't badly hurt after all.'

'That's a comfort,' he said.

Greta thought Mungo's bad temper would lift when she told him the child had not been seriously hurt in his fall from the waltzer. But he snapped, 'Anybody could see he wasn't. I don't know why you have to waste time and money phoning round about him.'

'It's put my mind at rest,' she said, but she couldn't relax when Mungo was still so full of rancour.

Greta was back working on the refreshment counter when Milly, the girl who helped in Mungo's fish-and-chip shop, went up to his office to tell him she wanted to leave soon because she was having a baby. Greta got the backlash of that when they went home for their dinner later on.

'Always the way,' he complained. 'Get a girl trained up and doing a good job, and she'll want to leave.'

All evening, he ranted on about Milly wanting to leave and how inconvenient it was for him. Greta rather fancied having a baby herself now she was married but she kept quiet. She didn't know how to jolly him out of his cantankerous mood.

As usual, he had dinner with her and returned to the fair to cash up when it closed. She went to bed early, glad to end a difficult day.

She woke up the next morning to find Mungo's arms round her and his lips against hers. She was glad to find he wanted to make love. She welcomed it, assuming he'd put the events of the day before behind him. Later, because she thought he was relaxed, she told him what was in her mind, that she would quite like to have a baby too.

Mungo sat up in bed. 'No,' he said firmly. 'No.'

'Oh!' Greta was disappointed. 'I thought marriage was for the making of babies. It says so in the marriage service. For the procreation—'

'No. Not for us.'

Greta could feel her heart hammering. She knew this wasn't the best time to talk about babies and she should have discussed having a family with Mungo before now. Mam talked of her and Kenny as her reasons for living, as the whole point of it. Greta had seen herself with a family of her own one day.

'Mungo! Why? I mean, if not straight away, then next year?'

'Never.' She could see irritation on his face again. 'I don't want any more children. You give them everything and they spit in your face. That's all the thanks you get.'

Greta was shocked. Had Louis spat in his father's face? She didn't think so. 'Louis's grown up now, surely a new wife and a new family . . . ?'

'No, Greta. I don't want children in my life.'

'What about what I want?' she demanded. She knew now that Mungo was a difficult man to live with and the fact that she'd got her own way once, didn't mean she always would.

'I'm sorry, you can have anything else you want, but not babies.'

'It's early days yet, perhaps you'll change your mind?'

'I won't. A baby in the house upsets everything, Greta. There's no peace any more.'

'I wish I'd known,' she said wistfully.

'I want you to be here for me, not feeding babies and changing napkins.'

Greta thought this was one subject on which she wasn't likely to talk Mungo round. Not yet, anyway. Well, she wasn't in any hurry, it was Milly's baby that had put it in her mind. She wished she'd never mentioned it. She'd thought Mungo was in a better temper today but she'd made him almost as tetchy as he'd been yesterday.

Greta took a quick bath and started to dress, taking a clean blue sweater from her drawer and pulling it over her head.

She felt Mungo's gaze on her. He said, 'Don't wear that old jumper.' He opened her wardrobe, where all the new clothes he'd bought her were hanging.

'Let's see . . .' He flicked the hangers along the rail and brought out a blouse. It was low cut and tight fitting, in a soft shade of lavender. 'You look so much nicer in this.'

'For work?'

'Why not?'

'I don't want to spoil it.'

'No point in having nice clothes if you're going to leave them hanging in the cupboard.' He picked out a skirt of royal-purple wool, slightly flared and of the new longer length. Then a pair of high-heeled court shoes to go with it.

'Much more elegant,' he said, waving away the sturdy flat-heeled shoes she used to wear to the laundry.

Greta could feel his temper simmering just below the surface, and didn't want him to explode with rage at her. 'I'm not too sure about the high heels for work,' she said, willing to meet him halfway. 'All right this morning, I suppose, as I'll be sitting down selling tickets. I'll need a cardigan too.'

'No, you'll spoil the effect.'

'I'll freeze there. It's still cold and everybody else comes in wearing their coats.'

He picked out a black lacy stole and put it round her shoulders. 'That's it,' he said.

Greta knew it was an eye-catching outfit, and felt like a film star as they drove into New Brighton to the fair. All the same, she felt very much on edge.

At two o'clock, when Dorothy came to relieve her, she said, 'I love your blouse. I wish I could have some decent clothes. When you're tired of that, Greta, think of me.'

Rex was just coming in to work. 'Wow!' he exclaimed when he saw her. 'You are smart. Going somewhere special now?'

She shook her head.

'You're all dressed up. You look a real stunner.'

'Thank you.' She tried to smile. She knew his eyes followed her as she went up the stairs leading to Mungo's office.

When she was returning to the fair after having had lunch at home, she changed into her old flat shoes. 'More practical,' she told Mungo. 'I'll be on my feet selling ice cream for the rest of the day, won't I?' Her overall hid her fine clothes.

That same evening, when they came home to have dinner, Greta went up to their bedroom to take off her smart outfit, wanting to wear something more comfortable when she played with Jess and lounged around.

She went to her chest of drawers to look for her blue jumper and couldn't find it. She looked in her wardrobe for it and also for her old skirt and couldn't find either. She started again checking through the hangers one by one. With a pang, she realised none of the clothes she'd brought from home were here any longer, not even the blue coat she used to keep for best.

Mungo had not come upstairs. Greta raced down to find him in the sitting room, having a glass of beer and reading the evening paper.

'What have you done with my clothes?' she asked.

He looked up without smiling. 'Thrown them out.'

'What?' She couldn't believe her ears. 'That's going too far, Mungo.'

'They do nothing for you, love.'

Greta had saved up hard-earned cash for those clothes. She was indignant. 'I want them. What have you done with them?'

'I told Norah to get rid of them.'

Greta let out a gasp of outrage. 'Mungo, you had no business to do that.'

She hadn't brought the clothes she used to wear to the laundry, only the things she thought of as her best. 'They're far too good to throw out.'

'Norah won't have thrown them out,' he said easily. 'She'll wear them herself.'

'She can't, Mungo. She's bigger than I am.' Norah was quite heavily built. 'I want them.'

Greta was rushing towards the kitchen when Mungo leaped to his feet to swing her round. His manner was menacing.

'Don't be so stupid.' He was barring the passageway. 'You aren't going to ask for them back?'

'Yes, of course I am. They're my things.'

'No, you will not. I've given you plenty of clothes that suit you better.'

She twisted out of his grasp and ran back upstairs to the bedroom, wanting to escape. She couldn't stop herself looking for her favourite pink cardigan and dragged open a drawer. That had gone too.

Mungo came slowly into the room and closed the door behind him. He was frowning and seemed a threatening presence but that wasn't going to stop her now.

At the laundry, the girls had begged her to speak up for them. It was Greta who'd gone to the boss to negotiate for them all. The other girls told her they wouldn't dare. Perhaps it had made her overconfident of her own powers.

She'd warned herself several times to be careful not to upset Mungo and push him into a rage, but there was a limit to what she was prepared to take lying down.

She said scathingly, 'You've overstepped the mark this time. I decide what clothes I'm going to wear.'

CAROUSEL OF SECRETS

'Don't be a bloody fool.' He came nearer. She could see his fists clenching and thought he was going to punch her. 'You're my wife. You'll wear what I want you to wear.'

She was sweating. She had to stand up for herself. It was now or never. Greta held up her hand like a policeman holding up traffic.

'Don't you be the fool, Mungo. Those high heels and fancy clothes are for going out – restaurants, theatres and that. I can't wear them to work. It's agony standing in those shoes for hours on end. And what's the point of wearing fancy clothes to sell ice cream if I'm to cover them with an overall? Nobody can see them. That blouse is too tight.'

'No, it's not. It shows your dainty shape.'

'The dainty shape is still under an overall. I say it's too tight. I might as well wear my own clothes and be comfortable. I feel more at ease in them. All right?'

To Greta's relief he was backing off. 'All right,' he agreed.

She said as firmly as she could, 'I'm going down to tell Norah I want my clothes back so you'd better come with me.' She was afraid Norah would think she was going against Mungo's orders. She went downstairs on legs that were so stiff they felt as though they didn't belong to her.

Elsie was stirring a pan on the stove.

'Where is Norah?' Greta asked in a voice she hardly recognised as her own.

'In the ironing room,' Elsie replied. It was a small room off the kitchen. Norah came to the door with Greta's favourite pink cardigan held against her own body.

'I'm afraid Mungo misunderstood me,' Greta said. 'I want

353

my clothes. Please return them to my bedroom. All of them, especially that cardigan.'

Mungo was behind her, his face held stiff, without expression. Norah's shocked eyes went to him for guidance.

Mungo asked Elsie, 'Is dinner ready?'

'Yes, sir.'

'Then we'll eat straight away,' he said. 'You can take Greta's clothes back upstairs after that, Norah.'

Greta headed towards the dining room, feeling tears of utter relief scalding her eyes.

Mungo put his arms round her. 'I'm sorry, love. So sorry. I wouldn't upset you for the world. You know I only did it because I want you to look beautiful.'

Norah came in and put the soup tureen on the table in front of Greta. She could see the ladle shaking as she filled two plates with pea soup. Some splattered on the white tablecloth but she didn't care. She didn't care about anything else; she'd been able to stop Mungo having his own way.

'Clothes are so personal,' she choked. 'I have to be able to choose what I wear.'

He looked at her for a moment. 'Don't you like the things I bought for you?'

'Yes, I love them. I wouldn't have let you buy them if I didn't. But they're for evenings out, high days and holidays.'

He nodded. 'Please forgive me,' he said.

Greta did. She couldn't be angry with Mungo for long. He didn't go back to cash up that night. They ended up making love again, more passionately than ever.

CHAPTER TWENTY-ONE

T HE NEXT morning was fine and spring-like. Now it was April, the weather was becoming milder. Greta was wide awake and soon out of bed. She hoped Mungo would be less irritable today.

'Let's take Jess for a walk before breakfast,' she suggested. 'It sets us both up for the day.'

'All right.'

She'd noticed before that ill humour always made Mungo slow to get up. She had a head start this morning, which didn't bode well. Mungo was still in the bath when she went down to get Jess from her kennel. She was shocked when she saw the heavy chain was in use again. It wasn't fastened to her collar, but twisted twice round her neck and body. Greta could see it was locked on to the dog and causing her discomfort. Jess looked very sorry for herself. Greta rushed back to the kitchen.

'Norah, why is Jess chained up like this again? Who did it?'

'Mr Masters, madam.'

'Where's the key?'

'He hasn't given it to us. You'll have to ask him.'

Greta had noticed that before they were married Mungo had bought this much stronger chain for Jess and, for a few days, when she'd suggested taking her for a walk, he'd leaped to his feet and gone to fetch her. Once she'd seen this chain she'd spoken her mind and told him it was far too heavy to use on Jess. He'd stopped, but now here was Jess with heavy chain wrapped round her again.

She raced upstairs. Mungo was still in the bathroom, shaving with his cut-throat razor. Greta was so angry she could hardly get the words out.

'Jess can hardly move under the weight of that chain. Why are you using the heavy one again?'

'She's dangerous.'

'Of course she isn't.' Greta's voice was scornful. 'She's a very even-tempered dog. She wouldn't hurt anybody.'

Mungo scraped the blade carefully down his cheek, pulling a face as he did so. 'She bit the postman.'

This was the first Greta had heard of this. 'When?' she demanded.

'The morning you went to the dentist.'

Greta had had toothache, and it turned out she needed a filling. Mungo had made an appointment for her with his own dentist at nine o'clock one morning last week, and Georgio had run her there.

'Jess is cowed by it,' she said. 'Poor thing, how do I take it off her?'

He told her the key was in his dressing-gown pocket and she went down to release the dog. There was a white bench

outside on the terrace at the back where she sat down to wait
for Mungo. Jess came and put her chin on Greta's knee and
licked at her hand. She fondled her ears. 'Poor old Jess,
what's he doing to you?'

She was uneasy about Mungo's story and found it hard to
believe what he was telling her about the dog.

Mungo came but was in a very tetchy mood. Greta strode
out along the high-water mark. The tide was out and Jess
bounded ahead only to rush back to her. She seemed
overjoyed at being free of her chain.

When they went back to the house for breakfast, Greta felt
she had to persuade Mungo to free Jess, however much it
upset him. She said, as she cut her bacon, 'It's cruel to keep
her chained up all day. No dog should be treated like that.'

He was determined. 'I don't want to leave her here free.'

'She never is free, Mungo. She can't get out of that yard.
Norah and Elsie used to take her for a walk but now they
can't.'

He said sharply, 'We've taken her for a walk. She doesn't
need another.'

Greta felt forced to keep on at him. 'Can I take her to work?
She can stay in the ticket booth with me. It'll make a change
for us both.' Greta thought he was going to refuse. He was in
a really black mood. 'Please,' she wheedled.

'All right then.'

She smiled with relief. Mungo gave a bleak little
answering smile.

Once in the ticket booth, Jess squeezed in under the tiny
desk. Greta slid off her shoe and with her stockinged foot
fondled Jess's soft silky hair. She couldn't understand what

had made Mungo think the dog was dangerous. Jess drowsed through the morning hours.

They didn't go home at lunch time. The schools had broken up for Easter, it was a fine day and the fair was busier than usual. Mungo sent Georgio to fetch fish and chips for himself and Greta, and they ate them in his office. Jess immediately took a great interest in Greta's lunch and she fed her a few chips.

It made Mungo grunt, 'You spoil that dog. You're making far too much fuss of her.'

'You're cruel to her,' Greta retorted. 'That new chain is strong enough to tether a raging bull. It must feel a dreadful weight round her neck.'

It was a long time since Greta had felt so out of sympathy with him. Mungo didn't finish his chips. Without offering them to Jess, he screwed up his papers and threw them in his waste-paper basket. Jess got up and went to the basket, sniffing at the papers.

'No you don't.' Mungo aimed a bad-tempered kick at the dog, snatched the basket up and set it on his desk. 'You get quite enough food at home.'

Jess growled but backed off. Greta was shocked. She felt fear shaft through her. Mungo was in a very ugly mood.

'I'm thirsty,' he said, slamming back the cupboard door where he kept bottles of pop and a few tumblers. He swore when he found the bottle that held his favourite dandelion and burdock was nearly empty.

Greta could hear steps running up. The office door was ajar and she caught a glimpse of Kenny before his head came round it.

'Please, Mungo,' he squeaked – his voice was just breaking – 'can I take Jess out on the sands for a run in my dinner hour?'

Mungo turned to him coldly. 'I want a drink. Go down to the refreshment counter and bring me another bottle of dandelion and burdock first.'

'Right.'

'Here, take this empty bottle with you.' Kenny collected it and stampeded back down the stairs.

Greta stood up to put her chip papers in the basket too. She sensed Mungo's anger was building, but she couldn't stop herself.

'No animal deserves to be kicked like that.'

He turned and she saw his face twisting with aggression.

'How I look after the dog is none of your business,' he grated out. 'It's my responsibility to make sure she doesn't bite anybody else. I decide what happens here, not you.'

'I don't believe she's ever bitten anyone,' Greta told him hotly. She knew now he came out with little stories to add drama but doubted there was any truth in them. 'I hate to see you being cruel to her.'

Greta saw Mungo's fist come shooting out to punch her viciously in the stomach, but shock paralysed her. She gasped, doubling up in pain.

He'd hit her! She couldn't believe it! He'd intended to hurt her! She could see he did. His face was ugly and contorting with anger. He pushed it to within four inches of her own.

'Shut up about the dog,' he spat out. 'I'm sick of hearing you go on about it.'

Greta could see he was livid and itching to give her more. She had to stand up to him. Squaring her shoulders, she said, 'Don't you dare touch me again. I think it's despicable to punch a girl like that.'

'You're my wife and I can do what I like to you.'

Greta fell back against the window, terrified, watching his knuckles clenching and knowing he was about to ram his fist into her again.

'No . . .'

Without warning, a bundle of black-and-white fur flew at him and sharp canine teeth latched on to his wrist.

Mungo let out a scream of agony and knocked the dog away from him. 'What the bloody hell . . . ! I told you that dog was dangerous.'

Seconds later, still bellowing with rage, he was kicking out with both his feet. He had Jess pinned down and she was yelping and whimpering.

'No!' Greta screamed, and threw herself between Mungo and the dog. His fist caught her under the chin and sent her staggering back again.

The next moment Greta saw him felled to the floor in the way a large tree is felled by a logger. Behind him, his face white with shock, Kenny was using both his hands to grip a large bottle of dandelion and burdock by its neck.

After the crash of Mungo's fall, he lay still and silent, face down. Kenny dropped the bottle; unbroken, it rolled across the floor.

'Oh God! Have I killed him?' Kenny was panic-stricken.

Greta could hardly breathe. Her heart was pounding. It had all happened so quickly, and seeing Mungo stretched out on the floor so still, her first thought was that he *had* killed him.

'He was hitting you,' Kenny screamed in terror. 'Kicking Jess. I had to stop him.'

Greta wrapped her arms round her young brother, hugging him tight.

'He isn't moving! What are we going to do?' he sobbed. 'They'll hang me.'

'No,' Greta sobbed, 'I won't let them. It wasn't your fault.' She could feel him shaking with terror.

Kenny was only fourteen. For as long as she could remember, Mam had been saying, 'Look after Kenny.' As a child, she'd seen him safely in to school and brought him home again, taken him across busy roads and made sure he was all right. She had to protect him from Mungo's wrath and any criminal charges, whatever it took.

He wept, 'I had to stop him or he'd have killed you. I didn't know he was like this.'

'Neither did I.' Greta hugged Kenny tighter and let agonised tears roll down her face. Up here, the roar of the fair's engines and the hurdy-gurdy music was softened but still insistent.

Nearer at hand she heard a groan and saw Mungo move. 'He's not dead,' she hissed, putting Kenny from her. She was relieved the worst hadn't happened but was scared stiff. His temper had been uncontrollable before; he'd surely be wild after this.

'Mungo?'

He groaned again, pulled his arm out from under his body and collapsed back face down.

Anne Baker

'D'you think he'll be all right?' Greta asked. She could feel herself coming out in a cold sweat.

'He's bleeding. I've gashed the back of his head,' Kenny whispered. 'He'll give me the sack.'

'He won't know you gave him that whack,' Greta said with more assurance than she felt.

'He'll say it was assault, or grievous something.'

'Bodily harm?'

'Yes. I could be sent to prison for that, couldn't I?'

'You were protecting me.'

'And Jess. Mungo could still die, couldn't he?'

'Calm down,' Greta said. 'I'll say Jess bit him and he slipped and banged his head on the floor.'

'I'm in awful trouble, aren't I?'

'No. Nobody need know you were here.'

'Agnes knows. She gave me the bottle of pop for him.'

'You brought it up and he said you could take Jess for a run along the shore. You didn't see anything out of the ordinary.' Greta picked up the bottle and put it in the cupboard. 'Where is Jess?'

'She's hiding under that cupboard.' Kenny got down on all fours to drag her out. It was only eight inches off the floor. 'Poor thing, she's petrified.'

'Aren't we all?' Greta said, fixing the lead on her collar. 'Go on, take her for a walk and try to pull yourself together. Did you bring your lunch with you?'

'Yes, Mam made me sandwiches.'

'Eat them and have a good run. When you feel better, bring Jess back and shut her in the office for the afternoon. See you get back to work on time.'

'Did Jess bite him?'

'Yes, that's what infuriated him. Remember, you mustn't say a word about this. Not to Rex or Mam, not to anyone. Say nothing about Mungo hitting me and Jess – it would only worry them. Forget it happened; put it out of your mind.'

'I can't do that.' Kenny's eyes were wet.

Mungo groaned again and tried to roll over on to his back but failed.

'Go on,' Greta hissed. 'I'll deal with him.'

'How?'

'Go, for heaven's sake. I'll have to give you a few minutes' start.'

'Come on, Jess.'

Seconds later his feet were echoing on the stairs. Greta went over to Mungo. What on earth was she going to do?

'Mungo?'

He was conscious now, mumbling something.

'Are you all right, Mungo?'

He needed help. The gash on the back of his head looked nasty. She'd been thinking of getting him home, but now she wondered whether he had better go to hospital. She was fluttery with panic, her stomach hurt and she felt sick. She couldn't think properly.

She had to have help. Greta ran down to the fair. Georgio was on the door, dressed in his gold-braided uniform.

'Georgio,' she said, 'Mungo's had an accident. I want you to help me take him to hospital.'

His mouth fell open. 'Gracious! What sort of an accident?'

Greta's whole aim now was to protect her little brother. If it wasn't for her he'd have been miles away.

'Jess bit Mungo – he was teasing her with chips. He offered her some, let her sniff them but wouldn't give them to her. Then he slipped on some he'd dropped.' Greta rarely told lies but felt she had to now. She hoped that sounded feasible. 'Will you bring the car round to the front and then come up to the office? I think he'll need a hand getting downstairs.'

She raced back up, took the chip wrappings from the waste-paper basket, tipped a few chips on the floor and squashed them into the wooden boards. She turned to see how Mungo was. He'd rolled over on to his back and was staring up at the ceiling. Even so, he seemed more with it. She was able to help him to his feet and put him in the chair behind his desk. He was shaky and looked dazed.

'How d'you feel, Mungo?'

'It hurts.' He stared numbly at his wrist. Jess had punctured a series of holes in his flesh.

'So does my belly where you punched me.'

That brought his dark eyes up to meet hers. He was remembering.

'Jess bit me,' he accused. 'She is dangerous. I'll have her put down.'

'You were punching me,' Greta told him. 'Jess was trying to protect me. She's a lovely, loyal dog. Don't blame her for what happened.'

'Something hit me.' His fingers felt the back of his head.

'You slipped on a chip and banged your head on the floor,' she told him.

Georgio came in and gasped when he saw the state Mungo was in. Blood had dripped from his head on to the back of his shirt. It took both of them to get him downstairs and into the car. Even with Georgio's help Greta found it a struggle.

At the hospital, Mungo was taken to a bed to lie down. He was able to talk now but seemed a little confused. Greta thought either he didn't know what had happened or he was pretending not to know that he'd lashed out at her and kicked the dog.

They treated his dog bite, dressed the cut on the back of his head and seemed to accept her version of the accident. The nurse asked Greta questions she found difficult to answer. She was determined that Kenny would not suffer because of this and, anyway, she was ashamed to tell anyone that her husband of a few weeks had used his fists against her with deliberate intent to hurt. She'd meant to be a good wife to him, she'd done her best, but clearly she'd not met his expectations.

Eventually, a doctor came to speak to Greta. He asked her if Mungo had any underlying medical conditions.

She shook her head. 'No, I don't think so. No, he's always very healthy, except that he has indigestion sometimes.'

'When he eats rich food?'

'Yes, his doctor's given him bismuth for that.'

'Well, we want to keep him in overnight because he lost consciousness. We'll need to keep an eye on him over the next few hours, but he'll probably be able to go home tomorrow morning.'

Greta was relieved. She felt she needed time to think.

Before leaving she went to see him to say goodbye. Mungo was very changed.

'I'm sorry, I'm sorry,' he said. His mind was clearer now. 'I shouldn't have hit you, I know. Come and sit here on this chair. I do love you.' He was kissing her just as though nothing had happened. He stroked her hair tenderly. 'It was a misunderstanding. Please, please forgive me. Will you?'

She blurted out, 'Mungo, I believed you to be a gentle and loving person. I'm sore and stiff where you punched me.'

'I know. I'm stricken with guilt. I didn't mean to hurt you.'

He wrapped his arms round her and kissed her again. His eyes were shiny with earnest tears. Greta kissed him, but with reservation. If he really loved her, would he suddenly hit out at her like that? He'd meant to hurt her, she was in no doubt about that.

'I'll make it up to you, I promise.' He put his legs out of bed. 'Things will seem more normal once we're home.'

'Didn't they tell you they want you to stay in overnight?'

'Yes, but I'll be more comfortable at home. I'll tell them you can look after me. I'll be fine, I know I will.'

Greta lost patience. This was the old Mungo who knew better than anybody else.

'The doctors think otherwise, Mungo. Better if you stay here where they can look after you.'

'You know I can't stay. I'll need to cash up at the fair and lock up.'

'I'll get Alf to do that . . .'

'Don't let him near the money.'

'Mungo, relax. You need to rest and you have to stay here. I'll come back for you tomorrow morning.'

*

When she went out to the car park, Georgio was dozing behind the wheel of the Bentley. He pulled himself upright as soon as she put her hand on the door.

'Take me back to the fair, please,' she said. 'I want to collect Jess, but then I want to go home.'

'Yes, madam,' he said. 'What about Mr Masters?'

'He's to stay in hospital overnight but it's just a precaution. They think he'll be all right.'

They'd covered the best part of a mile when she asked, 'Georgio, have you ever had an accident in this car?'

'No, I take care not to. The boss would give me the sack. He thinks the world of his car.'

'Not ever? Not a long time ago when Jess got lost?'

'No, never.'

Greta settled back into the soft leather cushions, knowing Mungo had lied to her. She was realising now how wrong she'd been about him. That burst of fury that made him hit out at her had showed him in his true colours. She was not going to stay and be punched and kicked for twenty years as his first wife had.

But she felt trapped like a fly in a spider's web. Why had she believed Mungo when everyone was telling her what he was really like?

Mam had had her doubts about him, but she hadn't listened to her. Rex had done his best to persuade her to run away with him. He'd told her Mungo was a dangerous man, but she had believed neither him nor Agnes Watts when they'd claimed he'd abused Fanny.

Instead, she'd chosen to believe Mungo loved her, that he

was an honest and generous man. It hurt to find how wrong she'd been. She couldn't forget how he'd kicked out at Jess and threatened to have her put down.

This changed everything for her. But what was she going to do about it?

Run home to Mam? Mam would welcome her back, she was sure. Greta knew she'd have to find another job, even go back to the laundry if she could find nothing better.

But she wouldn't be the only one to suffer. Mungo would stop paying the allowances to Mam, and Kenny and Rex would probably lose their jobs. Mungo had known what he was doing when he'd set up all these strings to tie her to him. They'd bought him her love and Mam's goodwill, but only for a short time. It shocked Greta when she thought what she'd got into and what she'd led Kenny into.

When she was getting ready for bed that night, she inspected her abdomen. It hurt when she bent over and when she touched it. She could see livid red, weals which she thought would look more like bruises by tomorrow.

She didn't want to go home to Mam. She felt enough of a failure without running home for shelter. Besides, a marriage shouldn't be abandoned so lightly. She'd stay, but she'd have to lay down her terms to Mungo.

She didn't sleep well and was glad to have the bed to herself. The next morning she went to the fair first to make sure everything was functioning there. When she rang the hospital to ask if she could take Mungo home, the answer was yes. The doctor had done his morning rounds and decided he could be discharged.

Yesterday, she'd been told to take his clothes home. Now

she returned and handed a small suitcase of clean clothes to the nurse. Mungo appeared before her neatly dressed in what seemed moments.

'Where've you been?' he demanded. 'You've kept me waiting. The doctor said I could go home over an hour ago. I rang Norah to get her to send Georgio, but she said he'd taken you out.'

'To the fair,' Greta said. 'To make sure all was well there.'

His mood was no longer one of apology and contrition, but he said gruffly, 'I was afraid you'd left me.'

'No, I've decided to stay, but only on certain conditions.'

He looked severe. Georgio was holding open the door of the Bentley for him and asking him if he felt better.

'Take us to the fair,' Mungo said abruptly, and once in the car he closed off the sliding partition between the driver and the passengers so that Georgio would not be able to hear what they said. He was tight-lipped as he asked, 'And what are these conditions?'

'If you ever hit me again, I'll go.'

'I won't, I promise. I love you, Greta. You know I do.'

'It's understood then, you don't lay so much as a finger on me. Not ever. Neither do you swear at me or be nasty in any other way.'

'I promise, I'll do my best.'

'You must keep your temper and never fly off the handle like that again.'

'I'm sorry, I know I am short-tempered at times.'

'Mungo, I lost my temper with you when you didn't tell me I was being named as co-respondent in your divorce.'

'That was Fanny—'

'You didn't tell me. You let me find out from Agnes Watts. There's to be nothing more like that either. I want to know what's going on from you. We'll make a pact. We'll both try harder not to lose our tempers in future. We'll make more effort to stay calm.'

'It was the dog—'

'Yes, now that's another thing.' Greta very much regretted taking Jess to work. 'You told me Georgio had an accident and when you got out to see the damage, Jess shot off out of the car. Georgio never has had an accident, has he? Anyway, you don't take Jess for rides in the car.'

'On that occasion, she was in Liverpool in the car with me. I got out without thinking of the dog, and she shot out before Georgio could shut the door again. That's the truth.'

Mungo's face was like thunder. Greta couldn't face any more argument about that.

She said, 'The dog seems to make you angry.' She was sure Jess was Fanny's dog, though Mungo denied it and she didn't dare suggest he return Jess to her. Instead she said, 'I want you to give her to Kenny. He'd love to have her. I know he'd take her out for a walk, both before coming to work and after. The dog would be company for Mam too. She'd take her out when she went shopping and so would Rex's mam. It would be better for Jess and less worry for you.'

Mungo seemed lost in thought.

'Will you do that?' she asked. 'Give Jess to Kenny?'

'Is that one of your conditions?'

'Yes, it is.'

'All right. What about the kennel? Will he want to have that?'

'No, there wouldn't be room in our yard. Jess will sleep in the wash house.'

'Any other conditions?' Greta thought she heard a hint of sarcasm.

'You keep reminding me that I'm your wife. I want to be treated as a normal wife. Not as a doll for you to dress or a punch bag for you to work off your fury.'

For the first time, she thought he looked ashamed. 'What happened to me, Greta? I went berserk, didn't I?'

The car was pulling up outside the fair.

'I want things to be like they were when you first brought me here,' she said wistfully.

'They will be.'

'We had some good times then.'

'We'll have them again,' he said. 'I promise.'

CHAPTER TWENTY-TWO

Louis was eating breakfast when he heard the postman come. His mother went to pick up the letter, opened it, and he could see her lips straightening as she read. It must be bad news.

'From Mr Danvers.' She tossed the typed page towards him. 'I can't have the Rhyl site. Mungo's refused to give it to me.' She slumped back on her chair and covered her face with her hands. 'He's offering cash instead.'

Louis felt a stab of disappointment but he felt guilty too. He should never have taken Mam to see the site. That was when she'd set her mind on it.

He said, 'We'd still be all right if we could find another site.'

'To find one as good as that at Rhyl? Well nigh impossible, isn't it?'

'You don't have to accept the Southport fair,' he pointed out. 'You could ask for all money.' But he knew Mam wanted to have a fair. They both needed to work, and funfairs were what they knew best.

'Mungo's playing with me like a cat plays with a mouse,' she said tonelessly. 'He doesn't mean us to have a decent life without him.'

Louis felt beaten. After looking forward to having a fair of their own, their hopes were dashed. He prodded listlessly at his breakfast sausages. When he looked up, his mother had pushed her plate away from her and was sucking on her lip.

He said gently, 'It seems you'll have to choose . . .'

She gave him a half-smile, and said, 'I feel stronger than I have for years.'

'You are, Mam,' he told her. He had to reassure her. Mam wasn't good at taking setbacks. He didn't want this to make her ill again.

She said, 'This settles it. I'm taking no more whip from Mungo. I'll kill him.'

Louis met her gaze. Her eyes were burning with aggression. She was deadly serious. He was afraid this time she really meant it.

'I'm going to pay him back for what he's done to me. He's not going to get away with this. I'm going to kill him.'

Louis was alarmed. 'No, Mum! Don't do that. You leave Pa to me.'

'I'm going to get him. Nothing will stop me.'

But when his mother didn't mention it again for several days, Louis hoped she'd forgotten about revenge. They continued with their usual routine. She went home an hour or so before he did every afternoon to get their evening meal on the table.

Tonight when he reached home Louis found she'd made a stew. They sat up to the table. He was hungry and the meal was hot and savoury. Mam was mashing her potatoes into the gravy when she said, 'I've decided to poison Mungo.'

That pulled Louis up with a jolt.

She went on, 'Arsenic poisoning is a very painful death. Cyanide—'

'Mam, you'd have to sign the poisons book at the chemist if you wanted to buy anything like that.' He had to put her off. 'Then if Pa were found suddenly dead and poison was suspected . . . well, these days they can find out which poison killed him and how much was in his body.'

'That's not going to stop me.'

'You could hang for it, Mam. Don't do it. We'll be all right. We just need time to find a site of our own.'

'I can't think of anything but finishing him off. I go to bed thinking about it and wake up with it still on my mind.'

'Mam, please . . . I'm afraid you'll make yourself ill again, even end up in court or worse still, prison. Give up these wild ideas.'

'I can't. It'll do me no harm to work out the details in my head.'

He was appalled. 'Of how to commit murder?'

'Yes. Did you know there are lots of accidental poisonings? People die of it quite often. In the paper yesterday there was a coroner's report: a three-year-old boy in Liverpool self-administered cyanide that his father had bought to kill the rats in the cellar. How awful that father must feel.'

Louis's appetite was gone. 'I doubt you'll get Pa to self-administer poison.'

'Well, I've been thinking about it. It might be possible.'

'How?'

'I could put it in his drink. He's got decanters of sherry and port. You know he likes to set the scene, as though he's living the high life.'

Louis's knife and fork clattered down on his plate. 'Don't do that! He used to pour you a glass of sherry before Sunday dinner, didn't he?'

'At one time.'

'That way, he could poison his new wife!'

'I don't see that as such a bad thing.'

Louis was appalled. 'I do.' Of course he could understand her dislike of a younger, prettier woman who'd replaced her, but he had to stop her doing anything that might harm Greta.

'Mam,' he said hotly, 'you can't go round putting other people in danger. You don't want to poison the whole household. For God's sake, promise you won't do that.'

'You're right, of course,' Fanny sighed. 'All right, I promise.'

'Anyway, you never go to the house now.'

'I did last year, when I hoped to get Jess.'

'So you did, I'd forgotten.'

'I could go again.'

Louis took a deep breath and changed tack. 'And how will you get the poison? Don't forget chemists have a poisons register.'

'Oh, I wouldn't sign anything.' Her face shone with fervour. 'I wouldn't need to buy it. There's lots of poisonous plants. I'm aiming to commit the perfect murder and get away with it.'

'Pigs might fly, Mam.' He couldn't understand where she

found this new confidence. 'What plant is poisonous enough to stop Pa in his tracks?'

'Did you know there's cyanide in peach stones? Peach kernels actually. If Pa crunched them up like nuts . . .'

'He doesn't like nuts. Anyway, I bet they'd be bitter and he'd spit them out.'

'Yes, that's another problem. I'm still reading up about poisons. I'll come across one that'll suit Mungo sooner or later.'

Louis shuddered. He didn't think so. 'Poison can stay in the body, Mam. Have you read about that yet? Even if you got away with it at the time, the evidence would always be there. Pa could be exhumed years later, if any suspicions arose. It would always be hanging over you.'

'I'm bearing that in mind.'

That left Louis feeling distinctly uneasy.

A month later, Louis came home late one Friday night after cashing up at the fair and was surprised to find his mother still in the living room. Night had fallen, it was very dark in the house, but she hadn't lit the gas.

'I've been thinking,' she said. 'I'd like to take a day off tomorrow.'

'Of course.' Louis felt his way to the kitchen to find the candles they used upstairs. He lit hers too and set it beside her. 'You want to go shopping?' He was tired and heading up to bed.

'No, I've decided on the foxglove plant. You've heard that it's poisonous?'

Louis pulled up sharply. Because Mam hadn't mentioned

poisoning Pa for some time, he'd been hoping it had gone from her mind.

He said, 'The foxglove plant is used in medicines. Isn't it supposed to be good for the heart?'

'It makes the heart beat with greater force, that's why it's useful to patients with heart failure. But in large doses it upsets the heart rhythm, sends it out of control. It can kill. I think foxglove tea is the best poison to use on Mungo.'

Louis swallowed hard. Foxgloves grew wild and they were in season now. 'Calling it "tea" makes it sound ordinary and safe.'

'It isn't. I could just as easily make sweet laurel water, or get deadly nightshade or belladonna or aconite. Aconite is a very efficient poison. Nowadays chemists reduce them to measured doses in pills and potions but poisons still grow all round us.'

'Mam, please don't do this.' Louis was placing the salt, pepper, mustard and sugar bowl in a straight line along the living-room table. His scalp crawled. Surely Mam wouldn't be capable of such a thing? All the same, he was horribly fascinated. 'Would it be a painful death, foxglove tea?'

'I don't know. It will alter his heartbeat, make it race and go out of control. I hope he'll be afraid and know he's going to die. I believe arsenic gives a very painful death and strychnine produces fits. I'd have chosen them except they're harder to get. They stay in the body too, and scientists can diagnose their presence years later.'

'There, didn't I tell you?'

She smiled at him. 'I understand foxglove tea goes from

the body within six weeks and leaves no trace. You see, I take note of what you say.'

'I say, don't do it,' he rounded on her. 'Will you take note of that?'

'No, I've made up my mind. I'm going to do it.'

Louis's mouth was dry. 'Mam! Will foxglove tea kill him straight away?'

'I'm not sure.'

'You don't know enough about it.'

'I think the time it takes depends on whether he's just eaten his dinner and also on what he's eaten. I've read that fat will help to delay the effect but unless he gets effective treatment, a lethal dose will eventually kill him. I want to take the day off tomorrow, so I can pick the foxgloves and make the potion.'

'Mam, no. I don't want you to.'

'I hate him and I'm scared of him and I can think of no better way.'

Louis knew he mustn't let her do it. 'I want you to come to work as usual. We won't be able to manage without you on a summer Saturday.'

'I won't stop now. Mungo deserves to be killed.'

Louis feared for his mother. She terrified him when she was like this; he was afraid she'd get caught.

Unaccountably, she seemed happy, her mood was buoyant, she was humming under her breath. It made him fear for her mind. Perhaps she'd just take a day off work and go out and buy herself a new dress. No harm in that.

But what if she made the foxglove tea? He couldn't see her doing it. It would mean poison here in their house.

Surely that would be dangerous to have around? He said, 'I hope you'll never fall out with me.'

She laughed like a carefree young girl. 'I never will – you know that, Louis. I'll take good care that none of it gets into our food.'

Nevertheless, he insisted on taking her to the fair with him the next morning.

Fanny went to work with Louis the next day because he insisted. He hovered close, barely letting her out of his sight all day. But it didn't matter, she could wait until Monday. She knew she was telling him too much, that she was making him nervous. In future, she'd keep her plans to herself.

It wasn't difficult to leave the fair without Louis, she did it almost daily to buy food and necessities. On Monday morning, she went out, taking her shopping bag. As well as buying half a pound of minced beef and some carrots, she went into Woolworths and bought a cheap aluminium stewpan in the largest size, a big spoon and a pair of rubber gloves. She took them home and hid them under her bed.

Fanny felt frustrated because she could find no clear recipes for preparing foxglove tea. She needed advice on how strong she needed to make it and how large a dose would be needed to kill a man. Neither had she found any information about how easy it would be for Mungo to detect the taste. She'd decided to put it in his whisky. That, she thought, should cover any odd flavour more effectively than anything else.

She couldn't afford to delay too long because the foxgloves were in flower now and she needed to pick the leaves before they died back. She planned to get them on the following Sunday, and had collected together at the fair the things she'd need to take with her.

Louis was going over to have dinner at The Chase and left before five because he needed to go home to change first. As soon as he'd gone, Fanny asked Frank Irwin if he'd cash up and lock up for her tonight.

It was a pleasant summer evening and she was in high spirits. Tonight, she'd take the first step towards her goal. She caught the Liverpool train, but travelled only a few stops down the line. There was a lot of uncultivated heath land along the coastline behind the sandhills and she'd seen foxgloves growing wild in a small dell a short walk from the station.

When she got there she was pleased to find them still growing in profusion, with lots of pink thimble-shaped blooms on each stem. It was the leaves she wanted. She put on her rubber gloves and picked handful after handful, pressing them down hard in the large brown-paper carrier bags she'd brought with her. One had the name of a man's outfitters printed on it; the other, one of the expensive shops in Lord Street where she'd bought a coat. They both fastened so the contents couldn't be seen. She thought them ideal for her purpose.

Once back home, she stuffed as many leaves as she could into her new stewpan, covered them with cold water and brought them to the boil. Then she let them simmer for half an hour.

The liquid was green and smelled quite pleasant when she drained it off. When she'd squeezed all the fluid she could from the leaves she put them down the toilet and started again with fresh leaves. She did four panfuls in all and then put the green liquid together and began to reduce it by turning up the gas and boiling it fast without the lid.

She aimed to reduce it to a few ounces but it grew thicker; it had turned brown and looked rather repulsive. When it had cooled a little, she bottled it in a well-washed brown sauce bottle and screwed the cap on hard.

Finally she scoured out the stewpan but there were thick brown stains inside she couldn't get off. Afraid some residue might be sticking to the sides, she bashed the pan against the yard wall to dent it, then filled it with ashes from her grate before dumping it in her dustbin. She didn't want anybody to use it for cooking food.

Then she crumpled the carrier bags she'd used, pushed them into her empty grate and set them alight. She sat and watched the blaze, knowing she was now ready to take the next step.

Fanny meant to put the poison in Mungo's whisky on the following Sunday. Nobody at The Chase must see her. She'd given a lot of thought as to the best time for her to enter the house. Her first idea had been to go there while Mungo and Greta were at work, but then Norah was usually about the house. Fanny came to the conclusion that a Sunday evening might be better.

Mungo had a big dinner then with Louis, his new wife, and possibly her relatives. They would all be in the dining room or the drawing room, and Norah and the cook would be kept busy well away from his study.

Throughout the week, she said nothing to Louis of her intention but she thought carefully about what she'd need to do. On Sunday morning she slid the bottle filled with poison into her handbag and walked to work with Louis, wearing her soft-soled shoes and a light pale grey coat and hat.

She'd decided she'd go by train and walk from Meols station as she had before. It would have been easier to get a lift over to the Wirral with Louis, but she didn't want him to know what she planned. He was very much against her doing anything and she didn't want to be persuaded out of it. She'd never settle until she knew Mungo was dead.

At lunch time, she felt buoyed up, alert and ready for anything, but as the afternoon drew on she could feel herself growing jumpy. Was she going to be able to manage this? True, she'd already made the journey once, but the intention to steal a dog is very different from putting poison in place to kill a man. She was glad she'd said nothing to Louis. She could, if her nerve failed her, just come home again. Nobody would be any the wiser. But at the same time, if things went wrong and Mungo caught her, Louis would be there to provide support and bring her home.

She had to wait for Louis to go. As soon as he'd driven off she asked Frank Irwin if he'd cash up and lock up the fair again tonight. When it was time for her to go, Fanny set off to the station, excitement running through her like an electric current.

On the train she opened her handbag and checked the poison. The bottle still had the HP Sauce label on it but it looked nothing like the real thing. The contents were the wrong shade of brown – more khaki – and they looked anything but tasty. She'd made the poison as strong as possible but was a little worried now that it might not kill Mungo.

She wouldn't know how much whisky he had left in the bottle until she saw it. It could be almost full or almost empty or anything in between, and then Mungo would dilute it again with soda water. She'd read everything about poisons and foxglove tea she could find in the library and the second-hand bookshops of Southport and Liverpool. She'd found another only yesterday but still didn't know exactly how much was needed to kill a man.

She stared resolutely out of the train window and tried not to think about what she was going to do. All the same, she was nervous. Anybody would be. It didn't mean she was going to lose control and end up back in hospital.

It was a lovely summer evening with some of the daytime heat remaining. There were a lot of people about near Meols station, but fewer as she strolled along the coastal path. The tide was out and the seabirds were calling; the walk seemed longer than it had before. Her heart began to pound when she looked up and saw the house with Louis's car parked on the drive.

Trying not to appear furtive, Fanny took the path to the house and went closer. The two french windows of the drawing room were open on to the terrace. The room was empty. It seemed she'd timed it right: they must be in the dining room now.

She paused to pull on the pair of cotton gloves she'd brought with her. She'd read that finger printing was now generally used by police to identify criminals. She meant this to be as near perfect a murder as she could make it.

It was an advantage to know the layout of the house and she still had the full set of keys she'd used when she'd lived here. There was a side door to the garage, she crept up to it and opened it silently. There was room for three cars in here but only the Bentley was parked inside, that meant Georgio Higginbottom and his mother would be at home. The stairs to his flat went up one wall. Yes, Fanny could hear somebody moving about above her.

As she passed the car, she put her hand on the bonnet. It was cold, that meant they'd been home for some time. She crept towards the door that led directly into the house and as she'd expected, it was locked. She slid in her key and turned it as gently as she could. It clicked, making her hold her breath but all remained quiet. She let herself into the passageway that led into the hall. She was about to creep forward when Norah, carrying a tray, shot past and into the dining room without seeing her in the shadows.

Fanny listened, she could hear the scrape of cutlery against plates. Then Mungo said something. He had the sort of voice that boomed round a room and commanded attention. He was talking someone down. There was a good smell of roast lamb. Her stomach rumbled; she'd eaten nothing since lunch time.

She peeped into the hall to make sure there was nobody there, then glided silently into Mungo's study. Her heart was thumping like a drum, her cheeks were burning and she could hardly get her breath. Nothing had changed since she'd lived here. She opened the cupboard where he kept his whisky. He'd had a mirror fitted into the back of it. In it, her face looked drawn and frightened.

A tray was set with a cut-glass whisky tumbler, a soda syphon and a bottle of Scotch. It was just under half full. Good.

She was about to unscrew the top of her poison bottle when she heard rapid footsteps crossing the hall towards her. She knew without being told they belonged to Mungo.

In a state of panic, she closed the cupboard and backed away. She'd be caught here within seconds if she didn't hide, but where? Why hadn't she given this some thought earlier? Desperately she looked round and noticed the curtains. They were were of floor-length heavy green velvet and hadn't been drawn. She stepped behind one, pulling it round her, squeezing herself back into the corner of the wall.

She'd left the door to the hall ajar; now it flew open and Mungo went straight to his desk. She knew he hadn't seen her but surely this curtain must bulge more than its partner? Would he notice? The sight of him in the same room and so close made the strength drain from her legs.

Fanny was quaking and she felt sick. Mungo was so close she could hear him breathing. It was hard to believe he wouldn't know she was here. She felt very exposed and on the brink of disaster.

She flattened herself back against the cold glass, and tried to guess what Mungo was doing from the noises she heard. She must make no sound but couldn't resist a peep. His gold cigarette case was open and empty on his desk. Georgio bought his cigarettes in cartons of two hundred so he wouldn't run out, and he kept them in a drawer of his desk. He was wielding his savage knife on the Cellophane wrapping of a pack of twenty and refilling his gold case.

Surely he must hear her heart? It was hammering in her ears and she was in a lather of sweat.

If he found her, and the bottle of poison she'd brought, it would tell him why she'd come and what she meant to do. Could she be charged with attempted murder? Terror jagged through her, she rested her head back against the wall and closed her eyes.

No, she told herself, keep your wits about you. Don't lose control, don't give up.

She heard the soft flop as Mungo threw the packet into the waste-paper basket, then he strode out, pulling the door to after him so that it clicked shut. She felt the draught and knew he'd gone. She staggered to his chair on legs that felt as if they were made of rubber, feeling such utter relief that she'd got away with it. She had to sit for a moment until the room stopped swinging round.

But she still had to escape from this room and every instinct was telling her to run. She took in a quivering breath. First she must do what she'd planned. She slid her poison bottle from her bag, unscrewed the top and tipped a good part of it into the whisky bottle. Her hand shook and she spilled a few drops. She mopped them up with her hankie and, panic-stricken again, wondered what to do with it.

Calm down, she told herself, ramming it back in her pocket. Calm down. You've done it. You'll be all right. She closed the cupboard and made sure everything looked as it had before.

Fanny had to steel herself to open the door so she could peep round it to make sure the coast was clear. Across the hall, she glimpsed Norah in the drawing room, collecting up used glasses. She waited until she was out of sight, then crept off in the opposite direction towards the garage. Her head was aching with tension and she felt ill, but once back in the garden, the evening breeze felt cool against her cheek.

She'd done it! Fanny was chortling with triumph as she hurried back to the station. Nobody had seen her; she'd succeeded. She caught the train into Liverpool and an onward connection to Southport and tried to relax. Every muscle in her body ached. Back home she washed out the HP Sauce bottle several times, before throwing it in her dustbin.

She lit a small fire in the grate and burned her handkerchief and her cotton gloves, then she scrubbed her hands. She made herself a sandwich and a cup of tea. When the fire had heated the water she got into a hot bath and afterwards went straight to bed, feeling totally spent.

She knew Mungo usually worked in his office in the evenings and had one glass of whisky as a nightcap, but not always on Sundays when he had more to drink before his dinner.

There was nothing more she needed to do. She could let herself imagine Mungo's end. If and when it came, she would have achieved what she'd set out to do and could start thinking of the future. It was not exactly an eye for an eye but Fanny knew her revenge was feverish; it demanded that Mungo should suffer even more than she had.

She settled down to sleep, knowing she'd have to wait to find out what happened next. She told herself she must be patient.

CHAPTER TWENTY-THREE

EARLIER THAT evening, going to The Chase, Louis drove out of his way to go past the cemetery. There was always a woman selling flowers there on Sundays. Flowers were the ideal gift to take to a stepmother when going to her house for a meal, the only gift he could give Greta that would not upset his father.

He chose a bunch of white carnations and then, as there didn't seem to be many of them, bought a second bunch of the same and asked to have them wrapped up together. He laid them on the back seat and their scent filled his car, making it impossible to get Greta out of his mind.

Louis had keys to the house but these days he was afraid he'd get his father's back up if he went striding in as though he still lived there, so he rang the bell when he arrived. Pa was crossing the hall and opened the door to him.

He didn't look pleased to see him. 'Good lord, you here again?'

'You invited me for Sunday dinner, Pa,' Louis said with as much confidence as he could muster.

'I don't think I did, but since you're here, you'd better come in.' Louis steeled himself not to take offence. 'Never let it be said I've refused to feed my son.'

Greta was laughing up at him. 'How nice to see you again. I'm glad you've come and really your father is too. He's just pretending.'

Louis put the carnations in her arms. 'How absolutely gorgeous, thank you. I'll put them in water.'

Mungo was scowling when Louis followed him into the drawing room.

'Business has been good this week,' Louis said without thinking. Business had long been almost the only thing he could discuss with Pa.

'Lot of breakdowns in Prestatyn,' Pa said, and went on to complain about them. Louis remembered the problem of the lease and dried up. Greta brought in the vase of flowers. There was time for only one drink before Norah announced that dinner was ready and they moved to the dining room. His father sat at the head of the table. Pa would never have agreed to sit anywhere else. Greta sat opposite him. Louis feasted his eyes on her.

As he ate the excellent roast lamb, Louis found it hard to find a topic they could all be easy with. There were so many that were out of the question. The weather was soon exhausted, and Pa wanted to keep his own business affairs private. Anything Greta said about the fair he dismissed as gossip.

Pa began talking about improving his garden, growing a wider variety of flowers. 'Wild flowers are being specially bred for gardens these days,' he said. 'They're much bigger and look quite exotic. I might try some.'

'Daisies,' Greta suggested.

'We've always had big daisies,' Pa scoffed. 'I saw some lovely honeysuckle and magnificent iris the other day.'

Louis could think only of foxgloves and became guilt-ridden and tongue-tied.

When they'd finished eating, his father jumped up and went off in the direction of the kitchen. Greta smiled at him and said, 'Shall we go and have our coffee?'

Norah always took the coffee tray into the drawing room so she could clear the dining table and reset it for breakfast.

Louis nodded. He'd never seen Greta look so pretty. She had a light tan and was wearing a cream-coloured dress. There was a glow about her. He followed her to the drawing room and watched her close the french windows. 'It's cooling now, but hasn't it been a lovely day?'

Her voice was like music to his ears. It was a delight to be alone with her. He could still smell the white carnations he'd brought – the hearth was full of them. He leaned against the mantelpiece and watched her pour the coffee. She was dainty and her movements quick and exact.

She was handing him one of the small coffee cups of fragile china.

'I don't need to ask now if you like cream,' she said, smiling up at him. 'I'm getting to know your likes and dislikes.'

Louis couldn't help it – his hand went out to touch her golden hair. 'Greta, I—'

Mungo's voice thundered from the doorway, 'Louis, what are you doing?'

Louis jumped, spilling his coffee, and only just managed to hold on to the cup.

'Look what you're doing, you clumsy fool. Norah,' he bellowed, 'fetch a cloth.'

Louis saw Greta's cheeks go pale. He was frightened and knew she was too. He could feel his father's rage boiling up ready to spill over like his coffee and scald them both. He knew what Pa had seen and was afraid in that one unguarded moment, he'd ruined everything.

Mungo felt anger zip through him more fiercely than ever before. He was struggling to get his breath. He was being cuckolded by his own son! He'd seen love on Louis's face as he'd looked at Greta. With his own eyes, he'd seen him stroke her hair. He wasn't having this!

Norah came to mop at the carpet. Mungo closed his eyes and counted to ten just as Greta had counselled, but this was going to be a force-ten storm and nothing could hold it back. He was shaking all over.

Mungo had wondered why Louis had changed his mind about coming over to have Sunday dinner with him. These days there was no keeping him away, when once he'd made excuses not to come and shown reluctance when Mungo had insisted.

Louis had clung to his mother, making it plain he was taking her side. Yet as the rift between him and Fanny grew, Louis was making an effort to placate him, chat him up and show friendliness.

Mungo had had his suspicions. He'd reasoned that Louis wanted a share of his money. Now he and Greta were married, Louis would expect him to leave some to her, but did he still hope to have a share? Once he'd thought that through, Mungo had been to see Mr Bishop, his usual solicitor, and made a new will naming Greta as his sole heir. He was not prepared to make life easy for Louis, not when he'd shown such support for Fanny.

As Norah left the room Mungo's rage bubbled up. He wanted to humiliate Greta, show her he could still control her. They knew they'd betrayed themselves; Greta's green eyes were full of guilt. He lashed out at her, catching her shoulder and sending her spinning backwards to flop on to a chair.

'Mungo!' It was almost a scream.

Louis came at him with the speed of an aeroplane accelerating down the runway. His fist hit him on the chin and made him lurch backwards.

'Don't you dare hit Greta,' he ground out.

Mungo didn't waste his breath replying. He put all his strength into punching Louis. He was trying to take Greta from him. His own son – where was his loyalty? Mungo thought he could handle both of them. Greta was as light as thistledown and Louis was much more slightly built than he was. But Louis was fitter and years younger, and could land as good as he got.

'Stop this! Stop this now!' Greta was trying to pull them apart. 'Where's the sense in it? Stop before you hurt each other. Louis, stop it.'

Mungo managed to land one more punch in Louis's abdomen after Greta had brought him to a stop. Good, he'd winded him. Louis was staggering back, clutching his belly, and his face had gone white with pain, but even so, Mungo felt his aura of power burst. His control over Louis had gone. Mungo had never quite had him in his grasp since Louis had put his fists up at him at the age of thirteen.

'Get out,' Mungo growled. 'Get out of here and don't come back. I never want to see you again.'

Louis was hesitating.

Greta said, 'I'll be all right. Mungo won't hit me again. That's right, isn't it?'

Mungo was breathing heavily. 'That's right,' he agreed, grinding his teeth. 'You get out, Louis. Don't come bothering us again. We don't want to see you.'

Louis groaned. He didn't want to leave her, not now they'd stirred Pa up like this.

'Off you go,' Greta said, her eyes pleading with him to hurry. 'We won't be able to calm down until you've gone.'

Greta heard the front door slam behind Louis. Mungo was staring at her and she knew he was a long way from calming down.

'You're in love with him,' he accused, spitting out the words.

'With Louis? Whatever gave you that idea?'

'He was making sheep's eyes at you as I came in. I saw it. He's in love with you.'

Greta was in no doubt about what had upset him. 'No, you're wrong, Mungo.'

'You're in love. You're cuckolding me, making a fool of me.'

'No, such a thing's never crossed my mind. Honestly, you're wrong. Louis's never said anything to me, never done anything to make me suppose . . . I don't love him anyway. It's all in your mind.'

She could see he was a little calmer. He said, 'Then nothing need change between you and me?'

How could he say such a thing? Everything had changed, but Greta knew she had to placate him. How could she feel love for a man who had such odd ideas? Who went at his own son like a raging bull? A man who hit out at her? Fear had taken over from the love she'd once felt.

She made herself smile; she had to. 'You forgot to count to ten again, Mungo.'

He met her gaze. 'I'm sorry.'

She broke out in a lather of sweat as relief flooded through her. He'd apologised, he'd be all right now. He always was. 'Shall we have an early night?'

'You go up. I'll have my nightcap and be up in a little while.'

She followed him to the door of his study and watched him pour a generous measure of whisky into the glass and follow it with the minimum squirt of soda water. He hadn't drunk much this evening so far and she thought it might help settle his anger.

'Louis is never to come inside this house again. I mean it. Nor into my fair. I'm disowning him. And you're never to speak to him again, do you understand?'

'I won't, Mungo. I assure you there's never been anything between us – that's the truth. He was your family and I tried to be friendly, that's all. You do believe me?'

'I'd like to.'

Greta climbed the stairs slowly. How had she not seen

how frightened everybody was of Mungo before she married him? Now it seemed so plain, so obvious.

Her shoulder hurt where he'd punched her and the back of her leg where she'd caught it against the chair. She'd been lucky to fall into that. It was lucky that Louis had stood up to his father. He was the only one who ever had.

These days she was always on her guard not to say or do anything to upset Mungo, yet she kept doing it. Mungo had been in a bad mood all evening, but to accuse her and Louis of being in love, of having an affair, was just plain silly.

Louis felt he had no choice but to leave. He went reluctantly, concerned for Greta's safety. He'd seen Pa hit out at her. What was to stop him doing it again?

The fight with Pa had left Louis shaking with shock. Despite all his intentions to stay on good terms, he'd been told never to show his face in his house again.

Louis reached his car, opened the door but couldn't bring himself to get in. He should never have left Greta alone with Pa. He should have said, 'Come with me, I'll take you to your mam.' But what could he do now?

He could ask Georgio Higginbottom to listen out for trouble. Pa always shouted at the top of his voice. Georgio was here on the spot and could protect Greta.

Louis strode round to the garage and went upstairs to knock on the door of Georgio's flat. It took Georgio some time to come and when he did he was wearing striped flannelette pyjamas. He was angry when Louis told him what he wanted.

'They'll be going to bed now – you can't expect me to go

charging into their bedroom? He's my boss! Anyway, I can't hear anything from here. The girl will have to look out for herself.'

Back at his car, Louis slumped on to the seat and debated whether he should stay where he was and watch the house. The kitchen windows were open; he could hear the murmur of voices and the clatter of crockery. Elsie's laugh wafted out. The lights were on all over the house, even in Pa's study. The upstairs landing window suddenly lit up. Louis knew he'd have to move his car, or Pa might see him still here. He drove it round the side of the garage and parked it in heavy shade.

He got out and, walking on the grass, went round the back where he knew the main bedroom to be. Yes, the lights were on there and in Pa's bathroom. He hated to think of Greta up there with him, but it must mean Pa had quietened down and all was well.

Louis shivered and went back round the front. After a while, the lights were switched off in the drawing room, the hall and the kitchen. He might as well go home now all seemed normal. He went back to his car but decided he'd hang on for ten more minutes and then go round the back again. He wanted to make sure the lights had gone off in their bedroom first.

It was so quiet Louis could hear the waves breaking on the distant beach. There was more cloud now, covering the moon. An owl hooted. Louis could feel himself relaxing.

Greta ran a hot bath and soaked her sore shoulder. The expensive bath oils were nice but didn't soothe her. Nothing could soothe away the nagging anxiety she felt. Fear was like a cancer: it ate into love and destroyed it.

She listened at the bedroom door. All was quiet downstairs. She wondered whether Mungo was still smouldering or whether he'd really calmed down. It was the eternal question these days. She was always waiting for his temper to blow up again and dreading to have him lash out at her. His complaints were becoming ridiculous. To accuse her of having an affair with Louis! Nothing was further from her mind. It didn't make any sense when Mungo said he loved her.

Louis knew Mungo was hitting out at her, just as he'd hit and abused his mother. Greta swore to herself that she'd never let herself get like Fanny. She had to stand up to Mungo. To let him see she was frightened brought out the bully in him and made him hurt her more.

Now she'd had her bath Greta would have liked to get into bed, curl up and go to sleep, but that could upset Mungo too. He hated to be ignored, especially if he wanted to make love. Her appetite for that had been killed off by her fear, but should Mungo want it, it was impossible to say no to him.

She knew she'd made a big mistake in marrying him. The luxury of her surroundings in no way made up for the way Mungo treated her. He used his anger to coerce her to do his bidding. He was controlling her so that she no longer had a free will. She was a marionette and he was pulling the strings.

She felt trapped. She had no way out and her only answer was to try to manage Mungo's temper, but she was failing there. Mungo's aggression turned her against him.

Greta slid her feet into her angora-trimmed satin slippers

and pulled a matching négligé over her blue satin nightdress. She'd go down and find out what he was doing. Mungo was taking a long time to come up to bed.

He was in his study where she'd left him, sprawled in his big leather armchair with his eyes closed. She thought at first he'd dozed off.

'Mungo? Don't go to sleep here. Come up to bed, it's getting late.'

He groaned. 'I don't feel well.'

'What's the matter?'

'My heart's pumping away twenty to the dozen and my head's swimming. I feel quite light-headed.'

'You'll be better in bed,' Greta said firmly. She was not displeased that he didn't feel well because it meant he'd lie down and let her go to sleep. 'Come on, let's get you upstairs.'

As he didn't move she went to help him. Suddenly he was twitching and hardly seemed in control of his limbs.

'How much whisky have you had?'

'One, just the one. Couldn't get up to pour another.' He was swaying on his feet and it was with difficulty she got him upstairs. She took him to the bathroom.

'I feel sick,' he said, bending over the wash basin, but he wasn't. She could see his face was wet with sweat. She got him to lie fully clothed on the bed. She'd never seen Mungo like this before and thought he must have had several glasses of whisky. She unlaced his shoes and took them off, then covered him with the eiderdown.

She got into her side of the bed and put out the light, expecting him to fall asleep and be his normal self in the morning, but Mungo started groaning and rolling round the bed.

'Such pain,' he gasped. 'It's terrible.'

'Where's your pain?'

'My chest! My stomach!'

He'd complained of indigestion from time to time before. She asked, 'Would you like a dose of your bismuth?'

Greta got up to get it for him, together with some water, and gave him a drink. She got back into bed, hoping he'd sleep now.

She'd no sooner got the light off again than he vomited on to his bedside rug. Greta ran down to the kitchen to get something to wipe it up and a bowl he could use if he felt sick again. She took off his tie and undid all the buttons on his shirt. She got back into bed but felt miles away from sleep.

Mungo grew more agitated and shouted that his head was leaving his body. For the first time she wondered if he was ill rather than drunk.

'My heart's jumping and fluttering and bouncing back and forth.'

It was only when he said he couldn't get his breath and it felt as though there were iron bands round his chest that she realised he really was ill.

Greta put the light back on. She saw that he'd soiled the front of his shirt and she tried to take it off. He fought her off, screaming in pain.

'Shall I get the doctor?' she asked.

Mungo swore and doubled in agony. Worried now, she pulled on her négligé, ran downstairs to the telephone and asked the operator to put her through to Dr Evans's number.

It was the doctor's wife who answered. She said, 'I'm afraid my husband won't be able to come right away. He's just been called out to another patient. If I can reach him by phone I'll let him know.'

'But he will come as soon as he can?'

'Yes, he will come.'

As she ran back upstairs, Greta could hear Mungo screaming with pain. He was throwing himself wildly round the bed; she knew now that he must be very ill and was scared because she didn't know what to do for the best.

Elsie came tiptoeing in. 'What's the matter? Is Mr Masters ill? We could hear on the other side of the house.'

Greta was glad to share her anxiety with anyone by then. Norah appeared too. She said to Elsie, 'It wouldn't be the lamb you cooked?'

Greta brushed that aside. 'I feel all right, and I had a second helping.'

'What can we do to help?'

Greta wished she knew. 'Could you make some tea?'

When it came she couldn't get Mungo to drink any of it. She drank some herself. 'I wish the doctor would come. It's been nearly half an hour. I'm going to ring him again.'

'I'm afraid the patient he went to doesn't have a telephone in the house,' his wife told her.

This time Greta gave as graphic an account as she could of Mungo's suffering. She knew she sounded desperate. 'Shall I send for the ambulance to take him to hospital?'

'I think I can hear my husband . . . yes, he's home. I'll send him straight round to you. He'll not be long.' She put down the receiver and Greta had to be satisfied with that.

She sat beside Mungo and tried to hold his hand, thinking it might give him comfort, but he couldn't bear to be touched. He screamed again in pain.

'My stomach! Strewth, it hurts. Medicine, get me more medicine.'

Greta felt his bismuth was unlikely to help. He needed something stronger.

'My medicine,' he bellowed. 'Get me more medicine.'

She poured out another dose, raised his head and held the glass to his lips. He swallowed it back, though some stayed white round his mouth. Moments later, he was sick all down himself and all over the eiderdown. Norah helped Greta clean him up.

From then on his movements became less vigorous. Greta was really worried now. Mungo went on moaning and groaning softly. She tried to soothe him with words.

'I've sent for Dr Evans. He's on his way now. He won't be long.' Mungo no longer seemed to understand, or perhaps he could no longer hear her. She was afraid he was losing consciousness.

She'd never seen anyone deteriorate so quickly. Only a few hours earlier, he'd been ready to fight both her and Louis; now she feared for his life.

Was he dying? She'd never seen anyone die. She was terrified at the thought.

CHAPTER TWENTY-FOUR

LOUIS DIDN'T know what woke him but now light was blazing from almost every window of the house. He stretched his legs, feeling stiff and heavy with sleep. Mam had bought him a new watch with luminous figures, but even so, he was so drowsy, it was a struggle to make out the time. Ten past two?

He shot out of his car and ran round the front to ring the doorbell. Something must have happened. He found his key ring and fumbled to find the one that fitted this lock. By the time he had it open, Greta was hurtling down the stairs towards him in a blind panic.

'What's happened?' He caught her in his arms, meaning to give her a comforting hug.

'Louis! Thank goodness you're here.' For a second her head rested on his shoulder, then she pushed him away. 'I've been so worried, I thought you were the doctor. It's your father.' She was towing him towards the stairs.

He asked, 'Pa's been taken ill?'

She nodded. 'I wish the doctor would come.' He could see

Greta was in a fever of anxiety. 'The second time I rang, his wife said he wouldn't be long. Mungo's so ill.'

She took him to their bedroom. Norah, looking unfamiliar with her grey hair covered with a pink sleeping net and wearing a heavy dressing gown, was removing a tea tray.

'Such a shock to see Mr Masters like this,' she murmured.

Pa was stretched out on their bed. Louis went to his side. His eyes were open and so was his mouth. He seemed to be grimacing with pain and fear.

'Pa,' Louis said. 'How are you?'

He gave no sign he'd heard. He was breathing very slowly with long pauses between each breath.

Louis gasped, 'Such a change in him since I left.' He felt for his hand. 'He's cold!'

'But he's sweating,' Greta said. 'There's beads of sweat on his face.'

The doorbell rang again. 'That must be the doctor now. Thank goodness!' Greta rushed out to the stairs again.

Louis heard Norah call, 'I'll get it.'

A few moments later she was bringing the doctor up. Louis and Greta greeted him on the landing.

'Dr Evans, I'm so glad you've come,' Greta said. 'My husband was taken ill suddenly. He seems very poorly. I've been so worried.'

'I'm sorry I've taken so long to get here. It's been a busy night.' He said to Louis, 'I didn't realise you still lived here.'

'I don't. I live in Southport now. I just came for my Sunday dinner.' Louis knew the doctor well. He'd seen him through his childhood illnesses.

Greta led him into the bedroom where he took one look

at Pa. 'Oh!' He seemed shocked. 'How long has your husband been like this?'

'Since bedtime,' Greta said.

Louis felt guilty. He'd punched Pa as hard as he could. Had he caused this to happen? He said, 'Pa and I had an almighty row this evening. He was livid, stamping and screaming at me. It came to fists. He told me to get out and never come back.'

Greta seemed close to tears. 'He was all right after that. He calmed down.'

The doctor was examining Pa. 'Did he bang his head?' he asked.

'No,' Louis said. 'I punched him but he didn't fall. I think I got the worst of it. Greta broke us up.'

She gave a little sob. 'He was fine all evening, ate a good dinner but the row upset him.'

'You all ate the same?'

'Yes, roast lamb with thyme and parsley stuffing and cherry pie to follow.'

'He had nothing else to eat or drink?'

'Coffee – we all had coffee. After the row, he calmed down and had his usual nightcap.'

'And that is?'

'Whisky and soda. Then we came up to bed.'

The doctor was trying to listen to Mungo's heart. Mungo's face was grey and his lips purple.

Greta said, 'Mungo didn't feel well. He complained that his heart was racing and pumping. I didn't think it was anything much and if he lay down quietly he'd feel better soon.'

'Was he in pain?'

'Yes, great pain. He was crying out in agony. That's when I telephoned for you.'

'I'm sorry not to have been here sooner,' the doctor sighed. 'His heart . . .'

'Nothing would ease his pain. It lasted for hours and got so he couldn't breathe.'

Mungo let out a fainter fluttering sigh. Louis waited, heart in mouth, for him to take another breath, but it didn't come.

'Is he . . . ?'

'Yes, I'm afraid he's gone, Mrs Masters.'

'Gone? He's died?' Greta's eyes were glazed over. 'Just like that?'

'A heart attack, I'm sure. He came to see me quite recently. Last week, I think.'

'He didn't tell me he had heart trouble,' Greta said. 'He said it was indigestion.'

Louis added, 'Yes, he'd been taking bismuth for some time. Years . . .'

'I did tell him last week I thought it might be his heart that was troubling him. He was ambitious and drove himself very hard.'

'He always has,' Louis agreed. 'Always did all the work. I don't think he could delegate.'

'I feel sure he's had a sudden heart attack,' Dr Evans said, looking sympathetically from him to Greta. 'I'm very sorry. It's difficult to accept when it happens as quickly as this.'

Greta said, 'He always seemed so well. I find it hard to believe . . .'

Louis could see tears on her lashes now.

'Think of it this way,' Dr Evans said. 'For the patient, to die suddenly can be kinder than lingering on in great pain. But for his loved ones it can be very hard. We must think of you now, Mrs Masters. Would you like something to help you sleep?'

'No,' she said, shaking her head numbly. 'I'll be all right.'

'Better if you're not alone at a time like this,' the doctor advised. 'Can you get somebody to stay with you?'

Louis said, 'Shall I take you home to your mother? That's the best thing for you now.'

'Yes, I'd be glad if you would. I don't want to stay here.'

'Come as you are,' he told her. 'Just put a coat on over that to keep you warm.' Greta was pulling a beige coat from her wardrobe. 'While you throw a few things into an overnight bag, I'll go down and find Norah. I'll have to tell her what's happened.'

The doctor was taking his leave. Louis saw him out at the same time.

'My deepest sympathy,' he said. 'You can collect the death certificate from my surgery tomorrow.'

Louis found Elsie and Norah in the kitchen. 'My father's dead,' he told them. 'A heart attack.' He felt more than a little shocked himself.

All the colour left Norah's cheeks, leaving them grey and drawn. 'Oh, my God!'

'Leave everything and go to bed,' he said. 'There's no need to get up early tomorrow. I'm taking Greta home to her mother straight away. I'll come back sometime tomorrow to make arrangements for the funeral,' he yawned, 'when I've had some sleep.'

Norah asked, 'What's going to happen to us?'

'I don't know. I don't think that will be up to me.'

He was driving down the drive ten minutes after the doctor left.

'I feel shattered,' Greta said, sinking into the small seat beside him. 'Wrung out.'

'So do I.'

'But you can still drive. I'm past doing anything.'

'I've got to,' Louis said. 'Mam will be worried stiff as it is. She'll have expected me home before eleven o'clock.'

He peered across his headlamps. There were few other lights to be seen. It was a long drive home. He had to go via the bridge at Widnes because the luggage boat and the ferries didn't run during the night hours.

He thought Greta was dozing, but she suddenly pulled herself up in the seat. 'What made you come back at two o'clock?'

'I didn't go away. I meant to keep watch outside but I fell asleep. I was worried about you.'

She sighed. 'That was kind. Very thoughtful.'

'I saw what Pa did to you. I saw my mother bruised and bleeding and sobbing. I was afraid to leave you alone with him, though you told me to go.'

'I was terrified all the same.'

'Were you? You didn't look it. You were very brave.'

'I knew I mustn't look frightened, that if I once let him see . . . it would tell him he had the power to do anything he liked to me.'

'You knew that? It's how I've survived for so long. It made me keep my fists in my pockets too, until tonight. I've never dared hit him before.'

'I think that upset him, that you turned on him.'

'It made him furious.'

'It wasn't that,' Greta sighed with exhaustion. 'He had some mad ideas. He thought you and I were in love and cuckolding him. That's what made him hit me.'

Louis knew his voice sounded thick with the emotion he felt. 'I let my guard down and my feelings show. He read them correctly. I think I fell in love with you the first time I saw you.'

'Louis!'

Louis felt his heart sink. 'Didn't you notice? That's why I kept coming over for dinner on Sundays – to see you.'

Greta shook her head. 'I was never able to see beyond Mungo. I was always on the alert, wary of something I might do or say to set him off. I thought he wanted to maintain contact with you so I tried to be friendly, that's all.'

'Oh!' That wasn't what Louis had hoped to hear. His hopes plummeted further. He drove in silence for a few miles. Then he thought he might as well know exactly where he stood.

'Greta, I'd do anything for you.' He was about to tell her he wanted to marry her but one glance told him she'd closed her eyes again. It was too soon; he'd be rushing her. There'd be plenty of time for that later.

It had been a dreadful night and Louis felt spent. He wished he could feel normal sadness at his father's death but he couldn't. He saw it as something of a miracle. Pa dead of a heart attack when he'd been prepared to kill him! Mam would be full of relief and he wouldn't have to worry about her getting into trouble.

Best of all, Greta was free and could marry again now. She was too tired to tell him how she felt, even if she knew. Everything would be better in a few days' time.

Louis drove slowly up Henshaw Street, not quite sure now of the right house. There was no light showing anywhere.

'Here,' Greta said. He left the headlights on so she could see and got out with her. She had the key in her hand and he took it and slid it into the lock. It turned but the door wouldn't open.

'Mam's got the bolt on,' Greta said. 'I should have remembered that she always does at night.' She rang the doorbell and hammered on the knocker, but there was no sign of life from within. 'She must be fast asleep.'

Louis found some small pebbles and threw them up at the bedroom window. They made so much noise that Esther Bradshaw opened her window on the opposite side of the street.

'Is that you, Greta? What brings you home at this hour?'

'We've had a terrible night,' Louis called. 'I've brought Greta home.'

'What's happened? I can hear Rex awake. He says he's coming down.'

Jess was barking in the back yard. 'We've woken half the street,' Louis said.

At last a glimmer of light showed through the curtains upstairs and came down to the front door. Ruth opened it, holding a candle aloft.

'Greta!' She threw an arm round her shoulders and drew her inside. 'What's happened? Are you all right?'

By now, Rex and Esther had joined them. They all went inside. Louis closed the front door and Rex began striking matches to light the gas mantle.

'It's Mungo,' Greta said. 'He had a heart attack and died.' She burst into tears on her mother's shoulder.

'There, love.' Ruth patted her daughter's back. 'Such a terrible shock.'

Louis watched with a heavy heart. Greta hadn't lost control of her tears on his shoulder. He'd been afraid from what she'd said in the car that she didn't love him and this seemed to confirm it.

She was drying her eyes but he could see she was still feeling shaky as she recounted how it had happened. When a sleep-sodden Kenny came down to join them, everybody was trying to fill him in.

Esther put on the kettle and was soon pressing a cup of tea into Louis's hands. He gulped it down. Never had he felt more in need of tea.

The small room was full to overflowing. 'Will you tell the people at the fair?' Greta asked Rex.

'Yes, of course. They'll all be shocked. Mungo was striding round larger than life yesterday afternoon. They'll want to know who'll be their new boss.'

Louis saw Greta blink in thought.

'Who will Mungo have willed it to?' Ruth asked.

'You?' Greta turned her green eyes on Louis.

He shook his head. 'I'd fallen out of favour before last night. More likely you.'

Greta shook her head too. 'I don't think he wanted me to have it. He kept the running of his business very much in his own hands. If I asked about keeping the books or anything like that, he'd put me off. I was curious, wanting to share some of the work and a bit resentful that I was confined to selling tickets and ice cream. I was a bit envious of you, Rex, when he said he was grooming you for management.'

'He only groomed me to do the jobs he didn't want to do,' Rex said.

Louis yawned. 'Just like Pa, typical. Either he's left it to you, Greta, or to the local dogs' home.'

Jess was still barking in the yard so Kenny went to let her in. She bounded across the room, wagging her tail, pushing her cold nose into each person's hand in turn. Each patted her head absent-mindedly. When she came to him, Louis thought her tail throbbed more vigorously, that she remembered him and all the walks he'd taken her on.

'I don't think Mungo liked dogs all that much,' Kenny said.

'That wouldn't stop Pa,' Louis smiled. 'Not if he wanted to spite me.'

'Or me?' Greta asked.

'I'd guess he's made you his heir, but I'll find out for sure. I'll ring Mr Bishop later on today and let you know.'

Rex sighed. 'We should expect Mungo to leave the world suddenly, in an unexpected drama. That's the way he lived. That's the way he'd have wanted it.'

'There's the funeral arrangements,' Louis said to Greta. 'Shall I see to them or do you want to do that?'

'I don't know what I want,' she said, 'unless it's to lie down and go to sleep.'

'I'll put them in hand tomorrow.'

'Today,' Ruth corrected.

Louis eyed the clock on her mantelpiece. It was four thirty. 'Yes, I'd better get home. My mother will be wondering what's become of me. She's probably worried stiff.'

'I'm dead on my feet,' Greta said. 'I can't sell tickets this morning.'

'Of course not,' Rex agreed. 'Not after that. Kenny can stand in for you. That's if . . . shouldn't we keep the fair closed? As a mark of respect?'

'No,' Louis said. 'Pa would expect it to open. He'd say it was bad business to close. What d'you think, Greta?'

She pushed her fair hair off her face. She looked as though she was past caring. 'We could close it on the day he's buried. Then everybody could go to his funeral. He'd like that better.'

Louis was glad to reach Delaney Street. He parked his car and turned his key in the front door as gently as he could. Mam would be asleep at this time of the morning. He was on the stairs when he heard her call out querulously.

'Louis? Is that you?'

'Yes, Mam.' He went into her bedroom.

'Where've you been until now?' He knew she was cross with him.

'Pa's dead.' He felt no need to protect her from the shock. She'd craved his death and never stopped talking about how it could be achieved. 'A heart attack.'

She shot bolt upright in bed. Her mouth dropped open. 'Already dead?'

'What d'you mean, "already"?'

'He's really dead? I've succeeded then?' Louis could see she was delighted. Suddenly, the soles of his feet were tingling. He listened dumbfounded as she told him she'd been out to The Chase last evening and had put foxglove tea in his father's whisky. It took him a few moments to take in what she was saying, and even then he found it hard to believe.

'You didn't think I ever would, did you? You'd written me off as all talk and no action.' Fanny started to laugh. 'But I've done it. I've got even with Mungo.'

Louis said. 'Did you really go to The Chase?'

'He who laughs last, laughs loudest. He'll never hurt me or you or anyone else again. In fact,' she couldn't stop chuckling, 'this time, I've got one up on him. A heart attack! Is that what they think it was? Couldn't be better, could it?'

'Mam . . .' Louis was hanging on to her bed rail.

'He had it coming, didn't he?' she chortled.

Perhaps there was a God up there who'd felt Pa's life needed to end.

His mother's eyes were shining with satisfaction. She was exultant, on top of the world. 'A bit more than an eye for an eye, after all,' she laughed. 'He deserved what he got.'

Louis felt doubts crowding in on him. Had Mam really done all she was saying she had? It was a long journey to The Chase by public transport. Perhaps she'd imagined all this stuff about foxgloves? What *had* Pa died of?

Dr Evans's diagnosis was that it had been a heart attack and he was a good doctor. He had an excellent reputation and he'd been sufficiently sure not to think a post mortem was necessary.

But that had been in the dark hours of what must have been a busy night for him. He hadn't yet provided the death certificate – what if he should have second thoughts and order an autopsy? Louis felt his scalp crawl with horror. If he didn't do that, he must feel very sure of his diagnosis.

Louis was undecided. Should he believe what Mam was telling him? Could he rely on it being true? Most of the time Mam was perfectly all right – in fact, she seemed better than she had for a long time – but Pa had turned her mind and she'd been treated for mental illness. Louis didn't know what to believe.

'Mam, this whisky of Pa's that you poisoned – how much was left?'

'There was just about half a bottle.'

He was filled with dread. 'So there'd be enough left to kill someone else?'

She wasn't laughing now. 'Yes. For months I've been reading everything I can get my hands on about foxglove tea,' she indicated the great tomes at her bedside, 'but it was only when I got home last night that I found what I was looking for. I had made my potion as strong as I could, and I think three drops of it would probably be enough to kill a man.'

'How much did you put in his whisky?'

'Three or four ounces.'

'What?' Louis felt his mouth go dry. Greta was no longer there, thank goodness, but . . . 'Norah might drink some, or Elsie.'

'They've no business to help themselves to Mungo's whisky.'

'Mam!' Louis shivered. 'They might need a little drink, you know – for medicinal purposes. They've had a shock too. They're worried about whether they'll still have jobs . . .' If what Mam said was true, there must be enough poison in that bottle to kill half Meols. 'I'm going back. I've got to get rid of it.'

'Leave it till daylight.'

'No.'

'I'll come with you.' Fanny threw back her bedclothes.

'No, Mam, you stay here.' To have Mam's company when he returned to The Chase was the last thing he wanted. 'I'll see to it.'

'The whisky bottle's in the cupboard in his study. You know where he keeps it?'

Louis pulled himself upright. He was wide awake now, he felt really shocked. For everybody's sake including Mam's, he had to get rid of all that whisky as soon as possible. He knew he wouldn't rest until he had.

'I'll register his death while I'm over there, Mam,' he told her. That's if he could get the death certificate. 'And I'll find an undertaker.' Surely if there was any doubt they wouldn't let him bury Pa. 'You open up the fair this morning. I don't know when I'll be back.'

At least the ferries would be running again by the time he drove back to Liverpool.

As he drove his car up the drive of The Chase he hoped the staff would be still in bed. He pulled up by the front door. Good, there was no sign of activity inside. Louis let himself in quietly and went straight to his father's study.

The cut-glass tumbler his father had used was still on his

desk containing dregs. He sniffed at it; it seemed innocent enough. If it smelled of anything, he'd have said it was whisky.

Louis knew where to find the bottle. It was on the tray inside the cupboard. He unscrewed the top and sniffed at that too. It smelled overpoweringly of whisky. He held the bottle up to the light. Perhaps the contents did look a little cloudy? He wasn't sure whether Mam had added something or not. Or even that what she'd added was as deadly as she'd supposed. Was it all in her mind?

He was going to tip it out, if only to rid himself of this worry. It would also get rid of the evidence that it had been tampered with so even if there was doubt and an investigation, the proof that Mam had touched it would be gone.

He took the bottle and glass upstairs to the bathroom he'd used in his youth and emptied the contents into the lavatory, flushing it twice. Then he washed the tumbler out with the scented lavender soap on the wash basin and rinsed both glass and bottle several times.

He went down through the kitchen and took the bottle out to the dustbin. In the store cupboard, he found an unopened bottle of whisky of the same brand. Opening it, he poured a little in the tumbler, tipped a small slug of it down the sink and ran plenty of cold water after it. Then he took the bottle and the glass to Pa's study and went back upstairs to scrub his hands with the same lavender soap. It was best forgotten now. He'd say nothing about this to anybody.

Relieved that he'd done what he'd set out to, he eyed the bed that had once been his. It was no longer made up. He pushed the folded blankets aside and lay down, pulling the eiderdown over him.

He expected to be asleep in moments but sleep wouldn't come. The events of the night filled his mind. After half an hour he could hear sounds in the house and got up again. He'd have to explain his presence here, because he'd told them he was leaving. Elsie was down in the kitchen dressed in her print dress and apron.

'I came back,' he said. 'There's so many things I need to do this morning.'

She didn't seem surprised. 'What a to-do last night. It must have been awful for you.' She asked, 'What can I get you for breakfast?'

Louis was hungry. 'Egg and bacon, please. I hope you were able to get back to sleep when we left?'

'Your poor father, gone like that. You never know the minute, do you?'

'Perhaps it's better to go like that.'

'Only in his forties, though. He was still a young man and had so much to live for, not long remarried. The poor girl took it hard, didn't she? I feel very sorry for her.'

Louis felt tired and low in spirits. He knew there were a lot of things he must do this morning, but wasn't sure exactly what, or how to go about them. He had very little energy. Having made sure there was no chance of anyone else at The Chase being poisoned, he telephoned his father's solicitor to let him know he'd died suddenly.

'Died! Good gracious! I'm so sorry. Please accept my condolences.'

'I take it he left a will?' Louis was afraid he was being too brisk but he felt the need to get on.

'Er . . . yes. Yes indeed.'

'Could I ask . . . ? I don't expect to be his sole heir any more, but did he leave me anything?'

There was a longish pause. Louis waited impatiently, hoping against hope.

'I'm afraid not. He came to see me recently to make a new will following his remarriage.'

'I take it he's left everything to his wife?'

'Yes,' Mr Bishop said. 'The will was written in favour of your stepmother. Is she there with you? I'd better have a word.'

'No, my father's death was a shock to her. She was very upset. I took her home to her own family.'

'Quite so. Ask her to come and see me when she feels better, will you?'

Louis put the phone down with the bitter taste of disappointment in his mouth. Despite what he'd said to Greta and her family, he had hoped for a legacy. He could remember, as a lad, Pa waving his arms round the New Brighton fair and telling him it would all be his one day. Of course, he'd displeased Pa and blotted his copybook recently, but he'd still hoped for a little. But if he couldn't have Pa's business, he was glad it was going to Greta and that in future she'd want for nothing.

He needed to go down to Dr Evans's surgery to get the death certificate. He'd feel a lot better when he had that in his hand and knew no trouble could blow up from that direction.

He felt nervous as he drove into New Brighton, but it turned out to be easier than he'd expected. He walked into the surgery and asked the doctor's wife, who acted as receptionist, for it. She handed him a sealed envelope.

'Please accept our sympathy,' she said.

Louis felt it must be her set phrase when handing out death certificates. She must know their family history, because his mother had received treatment there.

Once back in his car, Louis relaxed. He thought he was lucky Pa had consulted the doctor only a week ago and he felt confident of the cause of death. Louis was curious about what he'd written and opened the envelope. The cause of death was given as 'Coronary Occlusion'. He felt none the wiser but drove straight to the registrar to register his death and felt better when that was over.

He had to find an undertaker next, but which one? He knew nothing about undertakers. He went back to The Chase and looked in the phone book. Pa would want a big show.

He consulted the telephone operator. 'The premier funeral director in New Brighton? Hold on, sir.'

Moments later he was connected to their office, and made an appointment to see a Mr Cartwright at midday. The meeting took longer than Louis had expected. He booked his services but was so tired he found it difficult to make decisions.

Not having been to bed all the previous night, by two o'clock he was almost too tired to put one foot in front of the other and decided he could do no more. He was exhausted; he'd have to go to bed. He asked Norah to make up the bed in the bedroom he thought of as his own, while Elsie warmed some soup for him, but first, he rang Rex at the New Brighton fair and then his mother at the Southport fair.

'No point in driving all the way back here if you have more things to see to tomorrow,' she told him.

When Louis got into bed, sleep still wouldn't come. His life had been turned upside down. He and his mother had a lot to be thankful for, but they were not going to get all they'd hoped for.

CHAPTER TWENTY-FIVE

A S SHE closed her mother's front door behind Louis and the Bradshaws, Greta felt it had been a traumatic night. That Mungo was dead seemed unbelievable. It was now five o'clock in the morning. Greta felt so tired she could hardly pull herself upstairs. She climbed into the bed she'd shared with her mother before she was married.

'I might as well have another couple of hours with you,' Mam said, and got in too.

Greta pulled the bedclothes over them both and moulded her body round her mother's, seeking comfort, but sleep evaded them both. Too much had happened for them to be able to relax.

'I can't believe you're a widow too,' Mam whispered, 'and after such a short marriage.'

'It seems it's to be my lot, as well as yours.'

'Widowhood is a most dreadful state. A few months of wine and roses and then grief and misery and a terrible longing for what you've lost.'

Greta was too tired to explain that while it might look as though she'd had the wine and roses, she didn't think she'd long for what she'd lost.

'At least you've no children to bring up on your own. Perhaps you won't have to face a life of bitter financial hardship either. It may be different for you.'

Greta could feel herself drifting off to sleep. When she woke up she had the bed to herself and the room seemed full of afternoon light. She pulled herself up on her elbows to see Mam's alarm clock. It was four o'clock and she could hear Mam moving about downstairs. She pulled on her négligé and then her old dressing gown, which was still swinging on its hook on the door. Mam's house wasn't as warm as Mungo's had been.

'You're feeling better?' Mam asked her when she went downstairs.

'Yes,' she yawned, but in truth she felt sleep-sodden.

'I'll warm up some soup for you.'

'Just tea, please, Mam.'

'Right. I've got some cod – we'll have that later.'

Greta curled up in an armchair in the living room and half listened to Mam's new wireless, and half dozed. Her mother came to sit down too.

'What if Mungo has left everything to you?' she speculated.

'We don't know . . .'

'He'll certainly have left you something. I read somewhere that if you marry you have to make a new will because the old one automatically becomes null and void. You'll be a rich widow.'

Greta yawned again. She felt too tired to even think of that.

Ruth had just started to prepare the evening meal when Kenny came home with eyes shining like stars.

'It's you, Greta,' he said. 'Mungo's made you his sole heir. Louis rang Rex at the fair and he sent me home right away to tell you. Mr Bishop, the solicitor, says, will you come to his office when you feel up to it?'

'Good gracious me!' Ruth sat down with a little bump. 'Our Greta will definitely be a rich widow.'

Kenny was almost throbbing with excitement. 'Does that mean we'll all be rich?'

Greta shook her head in amazement. 'Surely he won't have left me his business? How am I going to cope with that?'

'I'll help,' Kenny offered.

'We all will,' Ruth added.

Greta yawned again. It was almost too much to take in. 'I still feel as though I could sleep for a week.'

That didn't stop Kenny and Mam mulling the news over and over.

That evening, Greta was back in bed by eight o'clock and asleep within minutes. The first thing she knew next morning was Kenny's head coming round the door.

'Mam's cooking egg and bacon for breakfast. She says do you want some too? I'll bring it up on a tray, if you like.'

Greta turned over. 'Thanks, Kenny, that would be lovely. What time is it?'

'Ten to eight.'

She lay back on her pillows and listened to the familiar sounds from below. Adding up the number of hours she'd been asleep, she couldn't believe she still felt so lethargic and unwilling to move. She felt secure and safe here with her family.

When Kenny brought her breakfast tray up she said, 'Did you tell me I was Mungo's sole heir last night?'

'Yes,' he said. 'Surely you remember that?'

'I wasn't sure whether I'd dreamed it or not.'

'You didn't.' Kenny wrinkled his nose in anticipation. 'Hooray, we're going to be rich. How rich was Mungo?'

'I don't know, he never did tell me.'

Later that morning, when Louis had done all he could, he set off back to Southport, but decided to detour to Henshaw Street to see how Greta was. It was almost twelve when he knocked on the door.

Ruth opened it. 'Come in, Louis,' she said.

He'd hoped to find Greta alone but it was not to be. Jess was on the hearth rug, and she jumped up and came to him, wagging her tail. Greta came hurriedly downstairs.

'I'm just getting up,' she said. 'I feel so lazy.'

Louis said, 'I came to tell you what I've done about the funeral. The undertakers have taken Pa to their chapel of rest in New Brighton. They want to know what sort of coffin you want and what day you want to have him buried?'

Greta turned solemn eyes on him. 'I hardly know whether I'm coming or going yet. You decide these things, Louis. He was your father.'

'All right. Would Thursday suit you for the funeral?'

'The sooner the better. I feel none of us will be able to rest until that's over.'

'Good, Thursday then. They can't do it any sooner. They suggest two o'clock at the church. I'd like to close his fair for the day as a show of respect. It's usual under the circumstances and I thought we could ask all the fair employees to The Chase for refreshments afterwards.'

Greta looked troubled. 'Mungo didn't do that for our wedding.'

'No,' Louis agreed, 'but we ought to give him a good send-off. You know how he liked a bit of a show.' Pa would have hated having his fairground staff in his house, which was why Louis wanted to invite them. It was his small revenge for the insults he'd suffered.

'I'll leave it to you,' Greta said. 'I'm sure you know best.'

'Then I'll get caterers in and get them to provide the usual sort of ham tea with plenty of cakes. Sherry and beer too? Are you in agreement with that?'

'Yes.'

'We really don't know what's required,' Ruth said. 'I'm sorry, we seem to be pushing all the work on you.'

'No, I'm only too glad to help,' Louis said quickly. 'Greta, you know my father made you his sole heir?'

Her troubled eyes met his. She seemed bewildered. 'Kenny said so. You are sure?'

'Positive. I telephoned Mr Bishop yesterday. It seems Pa made a new will shortly after you were married.'

'You mean . . . he's left me his business? All of it?' Greta stammered. 'The fairs?'

'Yes, everything. The house too.'

'Good gracious me!' Ruth seemed amazed. 'This will change Greta's life all over again.'

'It will, but for the better, yes?'

Greta didn't seem overjoyed. 'What about you?' she asked. 'What's he left you?'

Louis shrugged. 'Nothing.' He'd been hoping to marry Greta and see some of it that way – still was, though his hopes were fading for that too.

Her eyes were full of sympathy. 'There's no justice in that. Mungo should have left you something.'

'You'll have to run the fairs,' he said, hoping she'd ask him to help.

'Rex is there. He'll do all he can.' She smiled wanly. 'And there's Kenny.'

Louis was afraid she wanted no more to do with him. When he was leaving, he felt a terrible urge to take her in his arms. Instead, he said, 'See you on Thursday, then. Ring if there's anything else I can do in the meantime.'

Greta saw her mother's house as a sanctuary, a safe place. Mungo's death seemed a catastrophe, as though suddenly everything was out of control. She felt full of guilt that she hadn't been able to save Mungo's life.

She was walking about in a haze with no energy. She knew she ought to feel grief for Mungo but instead felt relief that she was no longer answerable to him. That brought more guilt.

She was in a turmoil, dazed and shocked and bewildered, and couldn't see how she'd ever manage to run the business. The responsibility felt like a ton weight on her shoulders. There were a lot of people depending on her to run it efficiently. It had been a full-time job for Mungo – how was she going to manage?

What had Mungo always said? 'If you have worries, face them immediately. It's the only way. Otherwise they'll plague you, pull you down and stop you concentrating on other things.'

Greta felt she'd been in limbo since the awful night when Mungo had died.

'I've got to pull myself together,' she said to her mother after she'd seen Louis out. 'I'm going back to The Chase so I can get on with things. I can't leave everything to him.'

She put her coat on. 'I'll walk down to the phone box and ring Norah. I'm going to ask her to send Georgio to collect me.'

'Take Jess. She likes a little walk.'

The dog was already at her heels. 'She knows I'm going out,' Greta said, attaching her lead.

To get out in the familiar street made everything seem more normal. She told Norah she was returning and when she asked about meals, told her she'd be there for her dinner that evening. Then she rang the solicitor and made an appointment to see him at three that afternoon.

When she returned home, her mother dished up two bowls of soup and put them on the table. 'D'you want me to come with you?' she asked.

'Being back here with you has been lovely,' Greta said slowly, 'but now I need time to think. Everything's changed. I'll have to get used to not having Mungo. He made all the decisions, but from now on it'll be up to me. Right now, I need to be by myself.'

A few hours later, she was sitting in front of Mr Bishop's

desk. He wore rimless glasses and was bald, with a domed head coming through a thin circle of pale hair.

'My deepest sympathy,' he said as he shook her hand. 'Such a shock for you.'

Greta tried to find the right responses. She hardly knew what she felt, but it wasn't grief. She'd felt held tight in a trap, with Mungo as a cruel keeper and now suddenly she was free. She'd been shocked at the way Mungo had punched her and fought with Louis, and most of all by the manner of his death. To find she'd inherited all Mungo's wealth was almost more than she could comprehend.

Mr Bishop was opening documents on his desk. 'Mr Masters recently made a new will leaving everything to you except for two small bequests.'

Greta swallowed. It was true then.

'There's one of two hundred pounds to Mr George Higginbottom and one of fifty pounds to Miss Norah Bell, providing they're still in his employment.'

'They are,' Greta confirmed.

'He's left everything else to . . .' he read from the will in front of him, '. . . my wife, Marguerite Mary, née Arrowsmith.'

After a moment's pause, she asked, 'What about Louis, his son?'

'No, nothing.'

Greta shook her head in disbelief. 'That's hardly fair.' Mungo had so much that he could have left them both well provided for.

'Now, as to what Mr Masters owned,' Mr Bishop continued, 'there's the freehold of his house, The Chase, together with the contents. The freehold of the buildings comprising the New Brighton fair, and the lease on the fair at Prestatyn and the amusements therein. Also, the freehold of a new site he meant to develop at Rhyl, together with all his monies and other investments.'

Greta felt stunned. 'He had other investments? What would they be worth?'

Mr Bishop smiled. 'That I can't tell you. He's appointed his bank as executors. You will need to tell them he's now deceased and ask them to apply for probate on your behalf. His assets will have to be valued and, as they include his businesses, they'll need his accounts for the last few years.

'You'll have to look for any evidence of stocks and shares in his home. He'll probably have had a stockbroker. If you can find his name and address you must get in touch with him and ask him to value his holdings for probate.'

Greta went back to the Bentley with her head in a whirl. Georgio leaped out to open the door for her as she approached. She saw the question in his eyes.

'Mungo has left you two hundred pounds,' she told him, and for almost the first time, she saw him smile. 'Mr Bishop told me it will take some months for his will to be proved and you won't receive the money until it is.'

'But I'll know it's coming. It'll come in handy for my retirement.'

'You're thinking of retiring? I didn't realise.'

'Yes,' he said awkwardly. 'I should have retired last year. Now the boss has gone I think I will. I'm going to miss him.'

Greta knew there'd been an understanding between him and Mungo. If anybody grieved for him it would be Georgio.

He drove her to The Chase. She knew she wasn't going to find this easy. She let herself in and went straight up to the bedroom where Mungo had died so recently. She had to force herself to look at the side of the bed where it had happened. The time she'd spent with Mungo had not all been bad. Norah had spring-cleaned the room and made the bed up with fresh bedding.

There was nothing here that had belonged to Mungo – no slippers, nothing. She told herself it was silly to be squeamish. It was the best bedroom in the house and she should continue to use it.

She looked in his adjoining dressing room. All his belongings had been moved in here: his watch, his keys, his wallet and small change were in a bowl on his tallboy. Even some of his clothes, his dressing gown and slippers. Greta shut the door firmly on them. She didn't feel up to sorting through Mungo's belongings yet.

She went down to the kitchen. Elsie was stirring something on the stove. Norah looked woebegone. She asked, 'What's going to happen to us now?'

'For you, nothing much need change,' Greta said, trying to soothe her. 'It appears I'm to inherit the house.'

She would have to live here. If she was to manage the fair, she couldn't afford to spend the time travelling backwards and forwards to her mother's house.

Norah's eyes glittered. 'Georgio says he's been left a legacy of two hundred pounds.'

Greta nodded. It hadn't taken him long to get in here and tell her that. 'Yes, Mungo didn't forget you either. There's a legacy of fifty pounds for you.'

An angry tide of crimson flooded Norah's neck and ran up her cheeks. 'He was more generous to Georgio?' she asked bitterly.

Greta was afraid she'd been hoping for more. She said, 'There's nothing for you, I'm afraid, Elsie.'

'Elsie's got plenty of years ahead of her to work,' Norah said sharply. 'Not like me. Anyway, she's only been here five minutes.'

Greta couldn't deal with Norah's anger just yet. She went hurriedly to the vast drawing room to ponder on what she would do with the rest of her life.

She ate her dinner in solitary style at the dining-room table and decided she didn't want to live here by herself. She'd be lonely in this big house. She took her cup of coffee to Mungo's study and sat down at his desk. She could almost feel his presence here. It was the first time she'd been in this room alone. She'd need a room to work in, so she'd have to get used to it or change it in some way.

Greta had to run upstairs to get Mungo's keys before she could open anything. She unlocked his cupboards first. She wouldn't need a drinks cupboard in her study so she'd start by changing that. She took the tray with the bottle of whisky, a soda syphon and some glasses to the dining-room sideboard.

Unlocking the other cupboards, she was surprised to find a hidden safe. She hadn't known of its existence. Mungo had played his cards very close to his chest. The key to that was on his watch chain, and when she opened the safe, Greta was even more surprised to find several rolls of paper money done up in elastic bands. Five-pound notes as well as one pound, and also a cardboard box full of gold sovereigns.

There were bank books too. It seemed he had accounts with several banks. She sat back and studied them. How angry Mungo would be if he could see her doing this! Sums were being paid in as dividends, so he must have big investments. There was a large manila foolscap envelope full of documents. She examined several before she understood these were Mungo's share certificates and were his investments. He'd looked after his money as carefully as he did his businesses.

At last she had his stockbroker's name, Giles Ronkswood. She telephoned him and told him of Mungo's death and that she was his wife and sole heir. He asked her to come to his office in Liverpool to see him. Greta made an appointment for the following week and he promised to have ready a full list of Mungo's investments and their value for probate.

Greta added up as much as she could of Mungo's assets on the back of an old envelope and thought it a prodigious amount. He'd been a very rich man. She could sell his business. On what Mungo had left, she and her family could live for the rest of their lives without ever doing another stroke of work. But no, there was Kenny to think of. He was interested in the fair; he'd enjoy running it. Even for herself, Greta decided, it would be more fun to carry on working than to sit back and do nothing.

She wandered round The Chase, going from room to room. It exuded an air of prosperity. It had been painted and papered recently, the furnishings were expensive and in new condition, the decanters in the drawing room were replenished with sherry and port as soon as they became empty. She could certainly afford to live here if she wished to do so, but it would be so lonely. It was taking Greta a long time to grasp how much her circumstances had changed, and in many ways she'd prefer to stay with Mum and Kenny. In fact she needed them now more than ever.

As Fanny timed the boiled eggs for breakfast, she felt a new zest sweep through her. It was another bright summer's day, more the weather for a fête than a funeral. Louis looked sombre in his dark suit and black tie.

He said, 'I don't want you to come, Mam. There's no need. Nobody will expect you to.'

'But I want to. I'd like to wear my red dress and dance on his grave.'

'For heaven's sake, Mam! You mustn't draw attention to yourself. Why don't you go to the shops or potter about here? It'll be enough if I go.'

She was indignant. 'I wouldn't miss this for anything. You don't understand. It's a victory celebration for me. I've succeeded in—'

'Don't say that! Or anything like it. You mustn't arouse any suspicion.'

'All right, but I'm coming with you.'

Fanny dressed in a light frock of black and white floral silk and wore a smart black hat. It was more the outfit of a successful businesswoman than widow's weeds denoting grief, but Louis agreed that she looked suitably dressed.

Fanny thought of it as an exciting day out. They had to wait for the luggage boat and Louis was afraid they might be late.

'Greta told me to come to the house and join the funeral procession,' he told her.

The Chase had never looked better. Its stucco was brilliant white in the sunshine. The hearse was already at the door, bearing the flower-covered coffin, and the cortège was lining up behind.

Fanny had been keen to see the woman who had taken her place in Mungo's affections. Louis had said she was pretty, but he hadn't conveyed any picture of her. Now, seeing her on the front steps for the first time, her youth and beauty took Fanny's breath away. Like herself, she was wearing less than total mourning. She had on a white linen suit with a black edging, and even had white shoes and gloves. She wore a froth of black net on a tiny hat and looked like the girl bride she was.

She'd seen Louis arrive and came over to speak to him.

'This is Greta,' he told his mother.

'Georgio's going to drive the first car with the family. Do you want to come with us?' she asked. 'There's room.'

'No, thanks. I've brought my mother. We'll follow behind in my car.'

'Hello,' Greta said awkwardly, offering Fanny her hand. 'I can't call you Mrs Masters. I mean . . .'

'You must call me Fanny.'

Fanny watched her get into the Bentley with her family and thought her far too nice a girl for Mungo. Louis had hired another car for Mungo's managers and foremen. The men who worked in his fairs were waiting at the church, unfamiliar in their Sunday suits and dark ties.

As the coffin was wheeled in on its bier, Fanny thought of

Mungo inert inside where he could never hurt anyone again. She was studying the congregation.

'Not a friend in sight,' she whispered to Louis. 'He didn't have any, not one. There's only his family and the people he employs.'

The atmosphere in church was very different to that of other funerals. To Fanny it seemed more one of thanksgiving than grief. She had been dreaming of this moment for months. When at last Mungo's coffin was lowered into the earth, she was pleased to use the fancy spade to throw a few grains of soil on top. She couldn't see a tear in anyone's eyes.

That's it, Mungo, she thought. The end for you.

Back at The Chase, Norah and the new cook handed round glasses of sherry and beer. It felt strange to be escorted by Louis into what had been her own home. To Fanny it was a glimpse of her old life that she was thankful to have escaped. Everything in this house reminded her of Mungo. He'd had it built to his design and chosen everything in it. That he was no longer here because of her efforts seemed a triumph.

Louis introduced her formally to Greta's family. 'This is Ruth, her mother, and Kenny, her younger brother.'

They looked solemn and far from happy. Clearly they didn't appreciate what she'd saved Greta from.

Greta said, 'Louis, I'm embarrassed about Mungo's will. It seems very unfair to me. I'm sure if I were you, I'd resent it.'

She added to Fanny, 'He should have left something for his only son, and you too, of course. Would you like to have the house? After all, it was your home for many years.'

Fanny felt beguiled by the girl. 'No,' she told her. 'The Chase is full of bad memories for me. I don't want to live here again. You keep it. You'll want to marry again one day. It would make a good family home.'

'No,' Greta said. 'I don't think I'll marry again.'

Although Fanny had wanted to escape from Mungo, as the deposed wife she'd resented the girl as traditionally she was supposed to, but now she'd met her she was fully on Greta's side.

What a monster Mungo had been to take such a young girl. Fanny was even more disgusted with him. She'd saved this child – younger even than Louis – from being abused as she had been. She'd done the right thing. Fanny was able to congratulate herself over again on that.

Louis had ordered a generous amount of drink and the buzz of chatter grew louder as time went on. The caterers had set up trestle tables under the trees where sunlight and shadow dappled the white cloth. They all sat down to eat together: the family with the strong and brawny men of the fair. Today there was no rough talk. They were all on their best behaviour. A traditional meal of ham and pickles and rich fruit cake was served, with cups of tea for those who wanted them.

When they'd finished eating, Georgio stood up to say how shocked they all were at Mungo's sudden death and how much they were all going to miss him. Fanny doubted that, Mungo had bullied them and most didn't like him. She thought their sympathy was mainly for her and for Greta.

*

As they all listened to Georgio's speech, Louis's gaze came to rest on his mother, who was sitting opposite him. In the few days since Pa's death she'd become a different person – happier and more sociable. She'd told him she was sure she'd never suffer from that terrible black depression again.

He didn't think she could have caused Pa's death, but even if she had, he was certain she'd never try to harm anyone else. There was nobody else she'd ever wanted to harm.

When Georgio sat down, Louis was surprised to see Greta get to her feet to speak. She stood erect with her head well back, squaring her shoulders as she waited for silence.

'Thank you, Georgio,' she said, looking confident and very much in control. 'I'm sure we all agree with what you say. I'm sure, too, that some of you are worried about what is going to happen to the fairs and to your jobs now.

'I want you all to know that Mungo has left his business to me. It's my intention to keep the fairs open and I assure you that I will do my best to keep all your jobs safe. I'm hoping the fairs will continue to thrive, but I don't know much about how they should be run. You've all worked in funfairs for much longer than I have and know more than I do. So I'm asking for your help and support over the coming weeks because I've got to make a success of this.'

A storm of clapping, cat calls and whistles broke out. Several men tried to say they'd give all the help they could, but were drowned by the noise. They gave her three cheers. The occasion was seeming less and less like a funeral.

'Thank you,' Greta said when the noise died down. 'Would you please pass the beer round again and I hope to see you all back on the job tomorrow.'

She pushed her chair neatly up to the table and came towards Louis to catch at his sleeve. 'I want to have a word. Let's go to the study.'

Louis felt his heart lurch. She wanted him! Did she love him after all? This was his chance to ask her. His spirits soared. He'd made up his mind to wait a few weeks, even months, until she'd had time to push Pa to the back of her mind, but her calm self-confidence amazed him. She looked as though she'd recovered already. There was no point in putting it off. He was eager to have it settled.

'You were marvellous,' he told her as they walked to the house. 'You said all the right things.'

Once inside, he looked round Pa's study. Already she'd changed the position of the desk. She noticed him doing it.

'I can see the garden now when I sit here,' she explained, 'and I've got rid of some of Mungo's bits and pieces.' She opened a drawer in the desk. 'They're here – can I give them to you?'

Louis glimpsed the savage knife Pa had used as a letter opener. 'No,' he shuddered. 'No. I don't want them.'

'There's his watch and gold cigarette case . . .'

'No, thanks.'

'What about your mother, would she . . . ?'

'No. We don't want mementoes.'

'I'll offer them to Georgio then.' She smiled. 'Louis, I've spoken to Mungo's solicitor about the will. He says I can make over part of his estate to you.'

'You don't have to do that,' Louis told her.

'I want to. Mungo left more than enough for both of us.'

'I was hoping . . .' Louis paused; would it be better to wait?

'Yes?'

He rushed on, 'I was hoping you and I would team up.'

'In the business?' Her eyes fastened on his eagerly. 'You'd like a share in that?'

It was obvious he wasn't making himself clear. 'I love you, Greta. That's what I'm trying to say. You're free of Pa. If you'd marry me, we'd share Pa's business, wouldn't we? You wouldn't need to make anything over officially.'

Greta said nothing. She was staring out at the garden. Louis knew from that moment she didn't love him. He'd been hoping for the impossible over all these months.

But he couldn't accept it. 'I'd be very honoured if you'd marry me.' It was a phrase he'd worked out in readiness when he'd been reasonably sure she would.

Greta looked troubled. 'I couldn't get married again, Louis. I'm sorry. It's the last thing I want to do. I felt I'd given away my freedom. Mungo dictated everything.'

'I'd be a very different sort of husband. I want to make you happy. I think we could be, once you've had time to put all this behind you.'

'No, I just couldn't contemplate . . .'

'You will in time. You don't want to spend your life on your own, do you?'

He could see her thinking about it. 'Louis, I value your friendship. I hope we can remain friends, but I don't love you. You wouldn't be happy with a wife who didn't love you. You wouldn't want that.'

After months of fantasising about Greta, that was a bitter

pill to swallow. 'I understand you need time. I'd be prepared to wait.'

'No, Louis.'

'You're saying there's no hope for me?'

She nodded. 'That's what I'm saying.'

He'd not handled this properly. 'I should have waited, kept my mouth shut, given you more time. I rushed you. I was so relieved that Pa . . .'

Her eyes were watching him. 'How did you feel about your father? I thought at first you loved and respected him.'

'He's terrified me ever since I was a child. That leaves no room for love or loyalty or affection . . .'

He saw her shudder. 'That's exactly how it was with me. For a long time he kept his vicious side hidden, but once I began to feel fear . . . It hasn't really sunk in yet.'

'But you did your best to save him – when he took ill.'

'I think that's second nature to us all. To die is so final. At the time, I did try to keep him alive. I was overcome with horror at his pain. He seemed to crumble before my eyes. I wanted him to have a chance.'

Louis mused that there was no chance for him, not where Greta was concerned. He said, 'If he was having a heart attack there was nothing you could have done. Pa wouldn't have wanted to live as an invalid, anyway. For him, it wouldn't have been life if he couldn't run his fairs and storm about bossing you and me.'

CHAPTER TWENTY-SIX

GRETA KNEW she'd disappointed Louis by turning down his offer of marriage, and she was sorry. She liked him and knew he'd suffered at Mungo's hands for much longer than she had, but she meant to stay in control of her own life from now on. Marriage didn't suit her.

In late afternoon, when the last funeral guest had departed, Greta took her mother on a tour of The Chase. She'd already seen most of the main rooms, but Mungo had not wanted people to see the more private part of his house.

'It's a magnificent place,' Mam told her. 'You're very lucky to have been left this.'

'It has its drawbacks.'

'I can't see any. It all looks lovely.'

'I offered to give it to Fanny. She wouldn't have it.'

Mam looked shocked. 'Why not?'

'Bad memories. She was very unhappy here.'

'But you?'

'I see Mungo everywhere. It seems vast when I'm alone.'

They were in her own bedroom and Ruth was admiring

the vast wardrobes. Greta paused in front of the window. It opened on to a small balcony with a wrought-iron balustrade. 'Mam, would you and Kenny come and share it with me?'

It was her mother's turn to pause. 'D'you mean that?'

'Of course.' It would put some heart into this large house. 'It would be nearer for Kenny to go to work.'

She saw her mother's face light up. 'That would be lovely, utterly marvellous. I'm thrilled to think of leaving Henshaw Street for good. Except that . . .'

'What?'

'I'd miss Esther. We've supported each other for years, through thick and thin, feast and famine.'

'Well, she could come too. There's the flat over the garage. It'll be empty next month, and it's as big if not bigger than the Henshaw Street houses. I could offer to rent that to her and Rex.'

'Oh, Greta! She'd love to come with us and I'm sure Rex would too.'

'Rex could come to work in the Bentley with me and Kenny. It would be much more convenient than the ferry.'

'And you'd be able to talk things over at home. He'll want to help all he can.'

Greta said, 'I hope so. I'm going to need all the help I can get. Mungo taught me nothing but how to sell ice cream and tickets for the rides. What about you, Mam? You'll have to give up your charring jobs if you came here. How about working in the fair?'

Her mother was enthusiastic. 'I'd like to – love to – you know I would.'

'Esther too, if she will.'

'She'll want to. It sounds exciting. A new life for us all.'

'A better life for us all,' Greta smiled.

That settled, they went downstairs and told Kenny. 'Hooray,' he shouted. 'Can I go up and choose my bedroom?'

'Yes,' Greta said. 'I want Mam to have the main guest room. It's the big one at the front with a gold-coloured eiderdown, and you'll see which one is mine. There's another four bedrooms – you choose which of those you want.'

Greta could hear him slamming doors up above. Then he came running down, his face wreathed in smiles. 'I want the other one at the front with a bay window. For me and Jess.'

'For you, yes, but not Jess,' Greta said firmly. 'She's always slept in the kennel in the yard and I want her to stay there.'

'You want to share my bedroom, don't you, Jess?' Kenny wheedled, with his arms round the dog.

'No point in asking her,' Greta said. 'Mam wouldn't let her sleep in your room at home and I won't here. Jess can come into the house in the day but not at night. I'll ask Norah to make the beds up and dust the rooms out and you can sleep here tonight.'

Greta felt better now she had her family with her and had made some decisions, but that night she didn't sleep too well. She was worried now about the business she'd inherited. She realised she had no idea how to run it. Today was Thursday and on Saturday the staff would expect to be paid. She didn't even know how to do that, and was afraid nobody else would either, because Mungo had done everything himself.

*

Greta got her family up early the next morning to eat breakfast at the dining-room table. Then Georgio took her and Kenny to the fair, dropping Mam off at the pier to catch the ferry home.

'I'm going to pop in to see my landlord on the way to give notice. Then I'll have to go to the chemist's shop to clean the upstairs rooms. I'm going to give them notice too. This afternoon I'll start packing.'

'Mam's excited,' Kenny said. 'So am I.' He was to stay with Greta until his next day off, then go home to pack his things.

She was pleased to find Rex had already arrived at the fair.

'I thought I'd better come early,' he said. 'There'll be a lot to sort out.'

'Come up to the office,' she invited. He followed her to stand at the window looking down at the attractions below. The doors had only just opened, the staff were chatting to each other, the roundabouts still. The hurdy-gurdy music started up.

'I've never felt very comfortable when I've come up here before,' Rex said.

'You'd better get used to it because I want you up here. I need to pick your brains.'

'There's precious little there to pick.'

Greta sat down at Mungo's desk and covered her face with her hands. 'What am I going to do?' she asked. 'I don't know how to run this business.'

'I'll do my best to help and so will everybody else. You know that.'

'I feel so unprepared. I happily sold tickets and ice creams instead of asking Mungo how he organised things.'

'He wouldn't have told you,' Rex pointed out. 'I could have asked him too, but he'd have thought I was getting too big for my boots.'

Greta said, 'Mungo explained more to you than he did to me. He was training you to be a manager.'

'I think he was training me to take the donkey-work off his shoulders.'

'Even that would be a great help,' Greta smiled. 'Can you show me how to make up the wages? Everybody will expect to be paid on Saturday.'

Rex shook his head. 'One of my jobs is to add up the hours each person's worked from the time sheets. We work a week in hand. I gave the figures to Mungo, he did the rest. I don't think he wanted me to know how much he paid people. I know he sent Georgio to the bank and then doled the money out himself.'

'Not Georgio in future,' Greta decided. 'I'll do that. What about the fair at Prestatyn?'

'I think the manager worked everything out and Mungo sent him a cheque.'

'I'll telephone and ask him,' she said, unlocking the desk to get out Mungo's ledgers.

The line to Prestatyn crackled and Peter's voice was faint.

'I work out what each of us is due,' he told her. 'I've already put the list in the post so you should get it today. Then Mr Masters made up the wage envelopes and either brought them himself or sent Georgio with them.'

'I'll do the same,' she told him.

When she recounted that to Rex, he said, 'I'll help you with that.'

'There must be a record here somewhere of hourly rates and what each person is paid,' Greta said. 'If we can find that, we'll be all right.'

'In the safe,' Rex suggested. 'He'd want to keep that from prying eyes.'

Like the safe at home, this one was hidden in a cupboard. When Greta got it open, the first thing she saw were drawstring bags full of coins, each labelled with a date.

'The daily takings,' she said. 'I thought Mungo banked them, put them in the night safe or something.'

Rex said, 'There's the record books.'

'You're right,' she crowed. 'We'll be OK now, but we're in for a busy time.'

'Mungo made up all the wage envelopes himself?'

'Yes, now I think about it, he used to lock the office door on Friday afternoons. He must have done it then.'

'Better if we get on with it now.'

'There's a whole box of new wage envelopes in that cupboard.'

'He'll have made up the wages from the takings, that's why he hasn't banked them. He'd need change, wouldn't he?'

'I bet Georgio was sent to the bank to get pound notes in exchange for coppers, not to draw more out.'

It was work that needed concentration but Greta thought she and Rex worked well together. It was almost two o'clock

when they finished and had rechecked everything. By then
the fair was bustling with activity.

'Let's lock these away and go and have fish and chips,'
Greta said. 'I'm shattered.'

Greta felt very much at ease with Rex. It was only when he
was sitting very close to her at the small table in the chip shop
that she told him Kenny and her mother were coming to live
with her at The Chase and that Mam was going to ask Esther
if she'd like to move into the flat over the garage when it
became empty.

'What about me?' Rex asked.

'Won't you want to come with your mother?'

'Well, yes . . .'

Greta smiled. 'We expected it to be a joint decision.'

'Yes, Mam will be voting to come, I'm sure. She'll want to
stay close to her friends.'

'And you?'

'I want to stay close to you.' He grinned at her. 'It's quite
a long journey on the ferry and I have to be careful not to
miss the last boat when we work late.'

When they'd finished eating they went for a walk along
the prom.

'To clear our heads ready for the afternoon stint,' Greta
said.

It was another lovely summer's day. The tide was coming
in and the waves were crashing on the golden sand. Rex took
her arm.

'I was afraid I was going to lose touch with you,' he told
her. 'You'd be the owner in your fine house and working in

the office, while I'd be just another employee coming in from Henshaw Street. And that wouldn't be the same once you and Ruth left.'

'I'll still need my friends,' Greta assured him, 'and so will Mam.'

She heard Rex sigh with satisfaction. 'I was worried about you. D'you know, I lived through purgatory thinking of you alone with him in his house and at his mercy. The men at the fair said you could handle him, but I didn't see how.'

'I could,' Greta said. 'Well, I had to think I could. I was teaching him to control his temper.'

Rex laughed. 'I have to hand it to you. We all saw him fly into a rage for virtually nothing and were scared it would be our turn to catch it next. We were all wary of setting him off. That night when Louis brought you home and you said he'd had a heart attack, I was awash with relief. I think everybody at the fair was when I told them.'

'I was too,' Greta admitted. She could admit it to Rex, if not to others. 'I'd come round to thinking it had been a big mistake to marry Mungo.'

'I always knew it was. Didn't I tell you you'd be better off with me?'

'Several times,' she said. Greta could see where this was leading. 'Don't say any more. I'm not ready for it yet.'

Rex went blithely on. 'That's another reason I'm glad Mungo's off the scene. He's left the field open . . .'

'No, Rex.'

'I want you to marry me. Will you . . . ?'

Greta shook her head. 'No, it's put me right off marriage. I don't want to marry anyone.'

Rex had straightened up to his full six feet, his step quickened. 'That's what you said last time I asked you, but it didn't stop you marrying Mungo.'

'I know, you're right, but I thought he loved me.'

'Greta, I love you, I always have. I've waited for you and I'll wait longer if that's what you want. We've always been a pair. We go together like fish and chips – don't you feel that?'

'I don't know. I want you to stay close. I feel I can trust you, but just now I couldn't marry anyone.'

Later that afternoon, Greta found she had another problem. Agnes Watts came up to the office to say she was running out of dandelion and burdock and would need more of all flavours of pop by the beginning of next week. 'Can you order more?'

'Where does it come from? Did Mungo get it from a wholesaler?'

Agnes didn't know. Greta started another search through the books, wanting to know if Mungo had put in a regular order or whether he just got more when they were running low. She couldn't find what she was looking for and decided she'd have to ring Louis up at Southport. She felt reluctant to ask favours of Louis when she'd already turned down his marriage proposal and offer of assistance.

'Please help me, Louis,' she said. 'I'm stuck on the ordering. We're running out of pop and I don't know where to buy more. There's such a lot of things I need to know and don't.'

'Shall I come over and give you a quick run through the main routine?' He sounded willing and cheerful, and didn't seem to be harbouring a grudge.

'I'd be very grateful if you would. Will you be able to come today?'

'Yes. We're well up with the work here.'

She told him of her plans to move her family and friends to live with her at The Chase.

'I'll come now. It'll take me over an hour – more if I have to wait for a luggage boat.'

Greta wanted Rex to be with her so they could both learn from Louis's instruction.

'I don't know whether I can be spared from running the chairoplanes,' Rex said. 'We're very busy.'

'They'll have to manage without you for an hour,' she told him.

She had the books spread out on the desk when Louis arrived. Rex had been watching for him and came running up a few moments later.

'It's very kind of you, Louis,' Greta said, 'to bale me out like this.'

'I was brought up to run these systems, so it's easy for me. But you're likely to run into problems over basic routine stuff. Pa liked to control everything himself.'

'Don't I know it,' Greta said.

Louis showed them the order forms and ran through a whole list of other things that needed to be ordered regularly.

'When I drove over, it gave me time to think,' he said. 'I know just the person to help you,'

He told Greta and Rex how his father had sacked Frank Irwin on the spur of the moment and how he himself had taken Frank on temporarily for the summer. 'He's working well below the level at which he could, and he's looking for something better.

'I won't let him go now, of course, but there's Mam and me running Southport and it doesn't look as though it has much of a future anyway. If you were to offer him the job of managing this fair, and make it permanent, Frank would jump at it. You need somebody like him.'

'I certainly do,' Greta said. 'Rex and I are groping round and don't know where to turn next. We haven't got the experience. Mungo worked hard. I really can't see how the fair can thrive without someone who knows what they're doing.'

'Frank's your man,' Louis said. 'He'll teach you and Rex all you need to know. He taught me.'

'I'd be glad to have someone to hold my hand.'

Louis was frowning. 'You wouldn't sack him when you feel you can manage without him? I'd hate him to go through that again.'

'Of course not,' Greta said. 'I promise I won't do that. Perhaps a month's trial to make sure we can get on together . . . ?'

'He'll be happy with that. I'll bring him over tomorrow morning,' Louis said. 'But he hasn't a car, and he won't be able to get home to Southport every night by public transport. Could you find him some lodgings until he can find a house to rent and bring his family over?'

Greta thought for a moment. 'I've still got empty bedrooms at The Chase. I could put him up for a few weeks until he gets organised. He can travel to the fair with us in the Bentley. That would probably be easier all round.'

'What a good idea,' Louis grinned. 'Pa would turn over in his grave if he knew. I think you'll get on well with Frank. I always have.'

When Greta met him the next morning, she thought he looked shabby and diffident. Louis had told her he had four children and she knew what poverty could do to a man.

'I worked here at one time,' he told her, 'while Mr Masters taught me how he wanted things done. So it shouldn't be difficult for me to keep things ticking over.'

Greta took to him and was relieved to have someone always on hand to guide her. She went out and bought two more desks to put in the office, so that all three of them would have their own space to work.

The days that followed were busy for Greta. Every spare moment she had she spent looking through Mungo's files and marvelling at the ramifications of his business. At the end of the working day she went home and turned her attention to the files he kept locked up in his cupboards there. Her curiosity led her towards those containing correspondence about his divorce.

Greta was shocked. The story Mungo had led her to believe was very different to reality. For the first time she realised how he'd been trying to cheat Fanny out of what the law had laid down she was entitled to.

Mungo had been very canny. He'd taken nobody into his confidence, not even Greta herself. He'd kept very quiet about all sorts of things – that the Southport lease was not being renewed, for instance. Greta thought he'd treated Fanny very shabbily and wanted to make amends from his estate. That he'd cut Louis out with nothing was even worse.

She took the train to Liverpool to keep her appointment with Mr Ronkswood, Mungo's stockbroker. He had a pretty secretary who treated her like royalty, and when she was shown into his office he apologised for keeping her waiting all of three minutes.

Greta hadn't known there was such a thing as stockbroking. Mr Ronkswood had to explain to her what he did. He had ready a list of Mungo's investments, which extended into several pages, and had worked out their value for probate.

She couldn't believe her eyes when she turned to the total. Quite apart from the property Mungo had left, his investments made him a millionaire. She couldn't understand why he'd gone to so much trouble to cut Fanny and Louis off without any money, when he had so much.

She went home and rang Louis up at the Southport fair. 'I want you to bring your mother over on Sunday evening to have a meal with us,' she said.

'That's kind of you.'

'You often used to come to Sunday dinner – I think we should go on doing that.'

'Thank you.' She thought he sounded pleased. 'About seven then?'

'No, I'd like you to come earlier. Mam likes her dinner about six – it's what we're used to. I'd like to talk to you and your mother. Can you come around four and have a cup of tea first?'

'Yes . . .' He sounded mystified. 'I'll see you about four then.'

Louis arrived carrying a bunch of large white chrysanthemums. Greta thought his mother was looking very well. Kenny had brought Jess into the drawing room and the dog made a great fuss of her. It was plain to see Mungo had been lying when he'd told her Jess had been his dog, not Fanny's.

Ruth brought in the tea tray and they were soon chatting happily about Jess. The dog put herself close to Fanny, who stroked her head continually as she talked about her own dog, Gyp.

When they'd finished their tea, Greta said, 'I'd like you to come to the study. I've something I'd like to show you.'

Fanny seemed reluctant to get to her feet. 'You too, Fanny, if you would,' Greta said. 'It concerns you too.' She took a file from a drawer in the desk and handed copies of the same documents to each of them.

'Mungo's estate has been valued for probate,' she said, sitting down herself. 'As you can see, he's left a prodigious amount.'

Louis whistled through his teeth. Fanny was blinking in shock.

Greta said, 'I want you both to have some of it. I've spoken to Mr Bishop about it. He says there's no problem. I can transfer part of it to you. We need to decide who takes what.

'I've read through his files. I know he offered you the Southport fair without telling you the lease was running out. What you need is the site Mungo bought recently at Rhyl. Would you consider moving everything there?'

'Greta, you're an angel,' Louis breathed. 'It's what we want to do. Southport's useless without another site.'

'I'd be thrilled if you would.' Fanny was blinking back tears of gratitude. 'My solicitor asked Mungo for it, but he refused.'

Greta shook her head. 'That's Mungo, all over.'

'He could have set up another good fair there,' Louis said. 'That's why he didn't want to part with it.'

'Mr Danvers thought it might be more difficult now it's passed to your ownership,' said Fanny.

'Not difficult at all,' Greta assured her. 'I've decided I like this house after all and I've moved Mam and Kenny in to keep me company. I'd also like to keep the New Brighton fair.'

Fanny said, 'You're entitled to keep any part of it you want. With capital like you'll have, you need never lift another finger. You don't have to work the fair. You could have a life of ease.'

'In our family we're all workers,' she said. 'We wouldn't know what to do with ourselves if we had no work to do. Kenny loves the fair so I want to keep it. One day he'll be running it for us.'

'Would you like him to come to me for training?' Louis asked. 'It helps to see how other fairs function.'

'Yes, what a good idea.'

'Not just yet, though. I need to get the place at Rhyl set up and working.'

Greta smiled. 'Kenny will be better here with us until he finds his feet, say, when he's seventeen or so.'

'Right.'

'Do you want the fair at Prestatyn too? It would be easier to run from Rhyl than from here.'

'That's very generous of you. Are you sure?'

'If you have the fair at Rhyl, Fanny, Louis will want something of his own. Prestatyn would suit him well, I think.'

He was frowning. 'I feel a bit guilty taking what Pa's given to you.'

Greta laughed. 'That's really how I feel. Guilty at taking what would have been yours if I hadn't married him. Look, everything's been valued. I think we should split it down the middle, go halves.'

'Half? You're thinking of giving us half?' Fanny looked as though she couldn't believe her ears.

'Yes, I want to do what's right. I must be fair to you both.'

'That's more than fair, Greta,' Louis said. 'I didn't expect anything.'

'An only child should be able to anticipate something from his father's fortune,' she told him. 'He left enough for us all.'

'I don't know how to thank you,' he said.

'It's awfully good of you,' Fanny added. 'I've always had to fight for what I got.'

'If Mungo taught me anything, it's that I mustn't do what he did,' Greta said. 'It made everyone hate him.'

On the way to work the next day, Georgio told Greta he'd like to leave straight away. His mother came from Seahouses, on the Northumberland coast, and had wanted to return to her roots for a long time. Although her parents had cut her off when she was expecting Georgio, her cousins had kept in touch with her. They still had family there.

Greta knew Georgio had been Mungo's henchman. He'd worked for him for twenty years, but now he could see big changes were coming and probably felt he couldn't stomach them.

That suited her very well, as she'd planned that Esther should have his flat. She talked about it to Rex when she reached the fair.

'I'll have to find another driver,' she said. 'One who'll live out.'

'I'd like to learn to drive,' he said. 'If I'm going to live over the garage, it's only right I should get to drive the car. I'd always be on hand to drive you anywhere you want to go.'

'What a good idea,' Greta said. 'I want to learn to drive too, but the Bentley looks dauntingly large. I might get myself a smaller car later on.'

She asked Georgio if he would teach Rex to drive and persuaded him to stay on two extra weeks until he was proficient. She was surprised how quickly Rex mastered it.

'I feel like a millionaire when I drive this car,' Rex said.

'It makes you look like a chauffeur,' Greta laughed. 'It's got this glass screen so you can be shut off from those of us riding in state in the back.'

'You need a big car like this to bus everyone back and forth to the fair. The family at The Chase is going to grow in the next few weeks.'

'Yes, I'm pleased with that. Mam will be here in two more days.'

Her mother had sold off some of her furniture and household goods to the neighbours in Henshaw Street. The pieces she didn't want to part with were going to come to The Chase and would be fitted in somewhere. Esther was packing too, but as the flat was unfurnished she'd need to bring all her bits and pieces with her. Rex said their mothers were as excited as a pair of schoolgirls at the prospect.

Because Rex was learning to drive, he and Georgio were going over to Liverpool and Southport quite a lot, and Frank was given a lift home. Ruth was carried backwards and forwards, and many of her possessions brought to The Chase. They brought Esther over to see the flat and have a meal with them one Sunday. She was thrilled to find it had an indoor bathroom.

By the following month everything was slotting into place. Mam and Kenny moved in, Georgio and his mother departed, and Greta arranged for the flat to be redecorated. Rex was confident enough to drive the Bentley and Frank Irwin fitted in easily, both at home, and at work where he took all the anxiety off her shoulders.

'Will you be happy with us?' Greta asked him over breakfast one morning.

'Very happy. Everybody's made me feel very welcome,' he said.

'Good. You can see there's a real job for you here.'

'Yes. Agnes Watts has helped me find a house to rent in New Brighton. I'm very pleased with it. There's a school nearby and it's within walking distance of the fair. Good views too, out across the Irish Sea. I'll move the family down on my next day off.'

'It hasn't taken you long to get fixed up.'

Frank smiled. 'Not that I haven't been more than comfortable here in Mr Masters' house,' he said. 'I've enjoyed it more, knowing it was his, but I've missed my family. Thank you for being so generous, feeding me and everything else.'

He was looking much better. He'd put on a little weight and had more colour in his face.

'I'll always be grateful to you and Louis for sorting me out,' he added.

CHAPTER TWENTY-SEVEN

10 August 1935

TODAY, GRETA was to be married again and she felt
fluttery with excitement. There was none of the
apprehension and worry mixed with it that she'd felt when
she'd married Mungo. At one time, she'd thought she'd stay
single for life.

She smiled to herself as she thought about Rex. He'd
never asked for any favours or pestered her to marry him.
He'd told her recently that he'd had to accept her refusal. It
had taken her years of seeing him every day to realise he'd
been right when he'd said they were a pair. For a long time
they had been growing closer and she noticed she'd been
giving him little hugs of satisfaction and pecking little kisses
on his cheek when things went especially well.

Rex had taught her to drive and the day she'd passed the
new driving test she'd given him a grateful peck on his cheek.
She'd felt his arms tighten round her and his lips come down
on hers in a real kiss, and she suddenly realised she was
falling in love with him. Six weeks later, when he took her to
the garage to collect the scarlet Morgan 4/4 sports car she'd

ordered, Greta knew she was deeply in love. She'd sworn she'd never get married again but now she changed her mind. She knew Rex through and through. She knew she could trust him. She knew he'd never stopped loving her and that they'd be very happy together.

That was four months ago. Today Rex had polished her car up. Later on, they'd be driving into Wales for a few days' honeymoon. She'd booked the first night at an hotel in Harlech, but afterwards they meant to meander around as the whim took them. This time, there'd been no secret about where they were going.

Greta had been to the hairdresser this morning and her blonde hair was shiny and sleek. For her wedding outfit, she'd chosen a blue chiffon dress with a blue straw hat covered in a froth of blue net, but now she clicked her tongue with impatience. Her hat didn't feel as secure as it should.

Alice, the pert young maid, who had taken Norah's place, was unpacking Rex's clothes in the dressing room that would be his. 'You need a hat pin,' she told her. 'Have you got one?'

'No.'

'Your mam has. I'll go and ask her.'

She was back with it within minutes. 'Your mam says you should have asked her to help you dress today.'

Greta had told everybody she didn't need any help to dress – she'd been dressing herself for years and would prefer to do it on her wedding day. She pulled her hat straight and pinned it at exactly the angle that flattered her most. It felt better.

She could hear Rex at her bedroom door. 'Is it safe to come in?' He elbowed the door open because his arms were full of boxes with his hats, scarves and books balanced on top. 'I hope it's all right?'

'Course it is,' she smiled.

He dropped his boxes at Alice's feet. 'That's the last of my clobber.' He was moving from the flat over the garage to be with her, and Ruth was moving in with Esther.

'So you newly marrieds can have the house to yourselves,' Mam had said.

'Are you ready?' Greta asked him. 'It must be nearly time for you to set off.'

'Yes.' He was studying her. 'You look beautiful, but then you always do. Today, you look absolutely radiant.' He went to kiss her cheek. 'A gorgeous bride.'

'Mr Bradshaw,' Alice said, 'you shouldn't be here. You shouldn't see the bride until she gets to church.'

'It doesn't matter,' Greta smiled. 'I told Rex I wanted less fuss and formality this time round.'

There was to be no showy pretension. They were ordinary folk and she didn't want to put on airs and graces. She watched Rex pause in front of the mirror to straighten his tie. He looked smart and handsome in his new grey suit.

He smiled at her. 'I feel very fortunate to be marrying you.'

'I feel the same,' Greta said, knowing her second marriage would be very different. 'Go on then, get off to the church so we can tie the knot.'

'Family and friends are still collecting down in the sitting room. Can't you hear them?'

Greta had decided she couldn't go on calling it the

drawing room. More than anything else, that reminded her of Mungo.

Rex said, 'If you're ready, you'd better come down and help me shoo them out.'

Out on the staircase, the buzz of conversation was loud. Greta went down to find Mam and Fanny helping Elsie collect the used coffee cups.

Rex's voice rose above the chatter. 'Time to be off, everybody. You've got to be in your places before the bride reaches the church.' They began to drift outside to the cars.

Her mother came to kiss Greta goodbye. 'I'm quite sure you're doing the right thing this time,' she said. 'I've always thought Rex would make a good husband. Shall I ask Elsie to bring you a cup of coffee?'

'Please, Mam.'

'Come on, Frank, we'd better be off too,' Rex said. Frank Irwin was to be his best man. Working together on a daily basis, they'd become good friends. Frank had settled into his job and said he was enjoying life again. Greta knew she could rely on him.

'Come on, everybody.' Rex raised his voice again. 'We can't keep Greta waiting today.' He turned to her. 'You won't be late, will you, love?'

'You know I'm all ready. I'll just have a quiet five minutes with this cup of coffee.'

'See you,' he whispered, and kissed the end of her nose.

Greta sank on to an armchair and closed her eyes. She wanted to hold on to the feeling of happiness. The ceremony in the church was timed for eleven o'clock and all their employees had been invited. Afterwards they would come here for the wedding breakfast. She'd organised caterers to provide it, but was a bit concerned it would remind everybody of the last time they'd been here.

'Mungo's funeral wasn't a sad occasion,' Rex had assured her. 'They all enjoyed themselves; they told me they had afterwards.'

Nevertheless, Greta wanted to make it as different as possible. She booked a different firm of caterers. They'd wanted to serve ham, but she insisted on cold roast beef and pork. But they would have to have trestle tables outside. It was the only way they could seat such a large number.

'What about putting up a marquee on the lawn?' Rex had suggested. 'That would make it seem different, and we wouldn't have to worry if it turned out to be a wet day.'

'A good idea.' Greta could see the marquee now from where she was sitting. As it happened, it was a lovely sunny summer's day with no sign of rain.

The third anniversary of Mungo's death had recently passed without anybody in the fair mentioning it. Greta couldn't forget him completely. She'd felt in an emotional turmoil during the first year. She'd thrown all her energy into the New Brighton fair and involved Rex, Mam, Kenny and Esther in the running of it. She felt the family business had kept them together and tightened the links between them. She was over Mungo now and hoped the rest of his family felt the same.

'Isn't it time we went?' She hadn't noticed Kenny coming in. He was sitting on the other side of the room with Jess beside him. Mam had decided that, at seventeen, he was old enough to stand in for the father Greta had never known and give her away. 'Rex said I was to be sure you got there on time.'

'Let's go then.'

'I'll just put Jess out in the yard.'

Greta was heading out towards the limousine waiting at the front door.

'Your bouquet,' Kenny reminded her. There was a posy of white roses and gypsophila on the hall table. She'd wanted something small and simple. He put it in her hands.

'What am I going to do without you, Kenny?'

He grinned at her. 'You're going to miss me.'

Kenny had his suitcase packed. Fanny was going to take him home to lodge with her in Rhyl while he gained experience in a different fair.

'I'm glad she's letting me take Jess. When I suggested it, she seemed quite pleased. She said, "I know I'll like her. I just hope she's going to get on with my Gyp." '

When they arrived at the church it seemed full of people and a little crowd had gathered outside.

'I'm going to disappoint them,' Greta said. 'They're waiting to see a bride in full regalia.'

'You're not a disappointment to Rex,' Kenny told her, 'or to the rest of us.'

To Greta, it seemed unreal. She was very aware of her groom making his responses, standing rock solid and reliable beside her. She felt she knew him through and through. He was good-humoured, charming and could be full of fun. As they paused on the church steps on the way out to have their photographs taken, he held her hand tucked into his and almost hidden between them.

They left in the first car with Ruth, so they could receive their guests at the entrance to the marquee. Greta found herself almost squinting against the strong sun as the first carload of guests arrived.

Alice was standing by, waiting to offer them a glass of champagne. Greta associated champagne with her wedding to Mungo and thought it was overrated.

'We've got to have some,' her mother had said. 'You don't want the ladies from the fair to think you're mean.'

Elsie was here too, offering a variety of other drinks, and Greta knew that after they'd eaten, tea would be a very popular choice.

Louis was one of the first to arrive, bringing not only Fanny but also his fiancée, Moira, a pretty redhead.

He kissed Greta.

'Congratulations,' he said, shaking hands with Rex. 'I suppose you do know I once proposed to your bride but she turned me down?'

'Yes, she turned me down three or four times before she said yes. I had to keep on at her.'

Louis laughed. 'She's been a very good friend to me since. I wish you both every happiness.'

Her old friends from the laundry came next. Phyllis was with her husband, Paul.

'It seems only a few weeks since I was at your wedding,' Greta told her, 'and I'm thrilled to hear you're already expecting.'

'None of us work at the laundry any more,' Mary Geraghty reminded her. 'I've got a job at Woolworths and, of course, Lily is married and has a son.'

'Yes, he's lovely,' added Lily. 'My mother's looking after him today so that Cecil and I can relax.' She patted her husband's arm and he grinned down at her.

At last all their guests were inside and Greta took a glass of champagne. At the first sip the bubbles burst upwards on to her face. There was something very attractive about champagne after all.

Greta was hungry and the food was delicious. While she ate, she looked round the table at all her friends.

Frank Irwin and his wife were both looking quite plump and the picture of health. Greta knew she owed her peace of mind to Frank. She could rely on him to run the fair better than she could do it herself. The business had had three prosperous years under his guidance.

She asked the Irwins to Sunday dinner at The Chase almost every week and they planned for the fair's future round the table. Greta knew she'd learned a lot from Frank and so had Rex. They were both more experienced now, and if they could find another suitable site, they would like to try to expand.

Louis caught her eye. He'd helped his mother close down the Southport arcade and move the attractions to Rhyl. It had been an immediate success and was soon earning more than Southport ever had. Fanny was in her element. She'd sold her house in Southport and bought another in Rhyl.

She'd told Greta that, in her opinion, the town planners at Southport had made a mistake in closing the fair. Every seaside town needed to appeal to all strata of society if it was to get the maximum number of summer visitors. The prosperity of the town depended on that. Recently, Fanny had heard they'd changed their minds, and that another funfair might open there in the future.

Louis had taken over the management of the fair at Prestatyn, but had found it difficult to get on with the manager. Peter had been another of Mungo's henchmen and he didn't like the changes. His parents had a boarding house in Llandudno, and when his father died unexpectedly a year later, his mother needed help to run it and he'd given his notice. Louis was now looking for a house in Prestatyn for himself and intended to marry Moira this autumn.

Greta hadn't expected friendship from Fanny. The relationship between the first wife and the second had seemed dauntingly difficult, but she felt she had it. She thought Fanny an unusual woman, who got on amazingly well with Mam and Esther too.

Greta had been pleased to find Mam and Esther had settled down to work in the fair so quickly. Between them, they'd completely taken over the job of selling tickets for the rides and they took it in turns to help Agnes Watts on the refreshment stall. They both said they loved working there.

Agnes was here, plumper than ever. Dorothy Wild was here too, but she no longer worked for them. She was married last year and now had a baby to look after.

To Greta, it was beginning to feel like one big family. A happy family, all friendly and supportive of each other.

Louis rapped on the table for attention.

'Raise your glasses,' he said. 'Let's drink to the bride and groom.'

Greta saw Rex fumbling for his notes. The speeches were about to begin.

'This is making me nervous,' he whispered to her. 'I haven't written a good speech, I don't know what to say. Would it be all right if I just told them I love you very much and though I've waited for years for this day, it's been well worth it?'